TALES
OF A
DEADLY
DEVOTION

Also by Jennifer Delaney

Tales of a Monstrous Heart

TALES
OF A
DEADLY
DEVOTION

JENNIFER
DELANEY

First published in Great Britain in 2025 by Gollancz
an imprint of The Orion Publishing Group Ltd
Carmelite House, 50 Victoria Embankment
London EC4Y 0DZ

An Hachette UK Company

The authorised representative in the EEA is Hachette Ireland,
8 Castlecourt Centre, Dublin 15, D15 XTP3, Ireland
(email: info@hbgi.ie)

1 3 5 7 9 10 8 6 4 2

A CIP catalogue record for this book is
available from the British Library.

ISBN (Hardback) 978 1 3996 1607 2
ISBN (Export Trade Paperback) 978 1 3996 1608 9
ISBN (Ebook) 978 1 3996 1610 2
ISBN (Audio) 978 1 3996 1611 9

Typeset by Born Group
Printed and bound in Great Britain by Clays Ltd, Elcograf S.p.A.

MIX
Paper | Supporting
responsible forestry
FSC
www.fsc.org FSC® C104740

www.gollancz.co.uk

For all the Almas. The girls who were forced to grow claws when all they wanted was to be understood.

Chapter One
Kat

JENNIFER DELANEY

TALES OF A DEADLY DEVOTION

Chapter Two

Alma

I'll keep you safe. Always.

I'd told many lies, but that one haunted me most of all, the guilt gnawing ruthlessly at my bones, right down to the marrow.

I'd told her she could do anything.

I'd lied.

Lying, sinful bitch.

How viciously those words hissed through my mind now, making me flinch as my aching fingers dug into my temples, clawed nails biting into my flesh. Yet the pain was no match for the agony tearing at my chest. Terror like iron bars closing around me as I watched the late afternoon sun slip across Kat's prone form, deathly still amongst the dark covers of Blackthorn's bed. The blue tinge to her chapped lips, parted so the barest rattle of breath could escape. Too weak. Too slow.

He's here. She'd screamed those words, nails digging deep into my forearms until I smelt blood. Her skin burning, the ruthlessness of her flame scorching my wrists with its wildness. She'd screamed my name. Then Emrys's in desperation, as she thrashed and sobbed helplessly.

Magic had a price, I knew that, but I'd never been prepared to witness her pay it. Not like this. Reliving every horror alone, as she begged for her death. As galmoth venom ran through her blood. Torturing her into madness.

Please. That word had crawled up her throat the most. The one I hated more than any other.

Maybe this was my final punishment, for all I'd done. For all the secrets and lies. To lose her.

My only friend. The only love I'd known.

Another tremor moved through my fingers. The sharp sting of scales forming as I balled my hands into fists, rubbing raw knuckles against the coarse fabric of my skirts.

She hadn't moved in days. Not even when useless healing incantations were cast or as I ran damp cotton across her dry lips.

I'll keep you safe. The lie bowed me forward over my knees, a muffled sob threatening to leave my lips, but I swallowed it down, refusing to break. To accept the closeness of her death.

'Alma?' The soft voice lurched me around to see William standing at the foot of the bed. The fire behind him had been freshly stoked, drenching his worried face in warm light, making his obsidian horns appear tipped with gold.

'William. I didn't hear you come in.' I wiped at my cheeks, ignoring the rough texture at my jaw.

'It's all right.' He smiled, a smudge of dirt on his cheek. The potent smell of soil, mint tea and fresh bread greeted my oversensitive nose at his presence. 'You should get something to eat and some fresh air.'

'I—' I shook my head, the mere motion making my neck hurt. 'I had something earlier.'

My tired eyes fell back to Kat, hoping she'd react to our voices, but there was nothing.

'Alma,' William coaxed gently, his hand coming to rest on my shoulder. I tried not to flinch at the contact. An old habit as my eyes lifted to meet his. 'That was yesterday.'

A horrid sinking dread made bile burn the back of my throat. Eyes darting to the window, to another darkening grey sky, bruised with an oncoming storm.

I hadn't noticed.

I'd lost another day and I hadn't noticed.

'I'll stay with her,' William offered quickly, sensing my distress as he held up the book from beneath his arm like a small trophy. Golden script I couldn't understand glinted in the firelight. 'I thought she'd like the history of Greyland herbs.'

His warm grin didn't touch the sadness haunting his eyes. He'd been reading to her. Ancient plants and herbs. Healing tonics and root remedies. I didn't understand at first, but then I watched the relief it gave him. Hope I couldn't find for myself.

That she was still here. That she was listening.

I nodded reluctantly, ignoring the fear that clung to the paleness of his skin as he bit his lip and avoided my gaze. It was an unease I'd seen before, one that chased away my grief and replaced it with sharp annoyance.

'They're fighting again, aren't they?' I demanded, gaining my answer from the boy's small flinch.

Bastards.

'Alma—' He tried to call after me but I was already moving. Crossing the room and pulling at the cuffs of my dress in irritation. Ignoring the dark spots that danced in my vision, how my exhausted limbs protested with sharp shooting aches, like bony fingers prodding my muscles. Allowing anger to chase all other emotions away. As I'd always done.

The claws at my fingertips burnt as they lengthened, and I stepped into the darkness of the hallway, moving for the stairs. My steps only faltered as I caught sight of myself in a speckled mirror, almost hidden behind bunches of dried herbs.

A simple, tired girl with strange eyes looked back. Dull, dark curls sitting limply against wan cheeks, sharp green eyes filled with sorrow and deep bruise-like shadows beneath.

'You always were self-destructive, Emrys, but this is taking it to another level!'

The voice echoed off the tiled floor in the hallway below, making my hand tighten on the banister before I moved down the stairs, ignoring the mocking glint in Lady Blackthorn's eyes as I passed her portrait.

'Of all the creatures you had to be entangled with – a *Kysillian*? I don't think there is a being on this earth the darkness wants to kill more viciously!'

'That's enough, Gideon,' came the terse tones of Blackthorn. The depths of the anger pressed into those words made a coldness streak down my spine. The lamps in the hall dimmed as if afraid of being noticed.

Then came the sharp, unamused and clearly deranged laugh from Gideon Swift, the rumoured Blackthorn bastard. The greatest healer of our time, and a dead man, if the Council records were correct.

What surprised me most about Gideon Swift wasn't that he was alive. It also wasn't that he was drunk or reeking of poppy smoke when Emrys dragged him rain-soaked through the portal days ago, forcing a cleansing tonic down his throat until he choked and vomited all over the entryway, much to poor William's horror.

No, it was just how he looked absolutely nothing like Blackthorn – golden unkempt hair that fell onto his brow. A handsome, serious face. An intimidating nature to his height but not holding any of Blackthorn's brawn.

The opposite side of a mysterious coin to the dark imposing form of Emrys.

No, Gideon Swift was the exact image of the portrait over the stairs behind me. The look of a witch.

Be wary of the witch. The children's rhyme came to mock me as I moved to the study doorway, curling my fingers around the weathered wood frame. The study had stayed in place right by the stairs since Emrys had brought Kat back.

It was a nightmare I couldn't unsee. The smoky copper scent of Kat's blood – the drip as it hit the carpet. The wrongness of Blackthorn's own scent. Different from before.

Then I'd seen that darkness curl beneath his skin. The pitch-black of his eyes that set off every instinct in me.

Verr.

My claws throbbed sharply with the memory. How easily they'd buried into his flesh. How my fangs had pierced my tongue with my scream. The taste of my own forsaken blood filling my mouth as I'd lunged for Emrys' throat. For what he'd done to her.

Alma, stop!

The high-pitched scream of William. The stickiness of Blackthorn's blood between my fingers as I went for my kill. Ruthlessly.

The bastard hadn't even tried to stop me. As if he saw it a fitting punishment.

Alma!

William's cries haunted me most of all. The desperation as he'd pressed himself into the space between us.

Emrys had reached for him to pull him away, but William had spread his arms wide. The boy's pale cheeks chapped with his tears, wide eyes begging.

Then in a blink I wasn't looking at William. I was looking at the small form of Kat. How she'd stood over me once. In nothing but her thin nightgown. How she'd taken the most brutal blows for it.

I'll keep you safe.

I shuddered at the memory. Forcing myself back to the present. To the feel of the smooth wood of the study doorway beneath my palm.

The room beyond was the same disaster it had always been. Too many books and papers. No sense of any order. The only thing that had changed were the occupants.

Thean Page sat in the shadowed corner close to Kat's desk, the voyav's usual cruel, mocking smile absent as they nursed a glass of wine with little interest. Despite being in female form, they wore ill-fitting men's clothes, as if they hadn't noticed they'd shifted. The richness of the dark wine staining their full bottom lip.

A thick air of apprehension lingered around the voyav like pipe smoke. Another game they were playing and one I wouldn't be fooled by. Nor the fact that they seemed to have become some kind of personal footman to Blackthorn, hunting down herbs, tonics and black-market remedies at his command. Night and day.

As if they cared. Cared about the madness that had consumed this house with grief.

The dark circles beneath their strange amber eyes were the only evidence of the burden of their tasks and the barely healed scabs over their knuckles from whatever resistance they'd endured.

'The venom has entered her blood, Emrys.' Gideon Swift slammed his palm down onto the desk, tension stiffening his back, as he ignored the items that toppled to the carpet. 'She's beyond my skill!'

'Everything is these days.' There was a harshness to Emrys's words that matched his curled fists. His features were sharper in the dim fire's light, his clothes crumpled, sleeves ink-stained and torn at the cuffs.

Unease crawled down my spine, making me glance at the voyav. Seeing how they watched the lord warily. Preparing for a building storm that would give no warning when it broke. Vicious and uncontrollable.

Then I noted the shadows creeping beneath Blackthorn's skin at the base of his collar. How the same darkness danced between his fingers, the fire lying flat in the hearth like a scared beast in his presence.

Exactly how he'd been when he'd brought Kat back. A madness in his eyes, pitch-black with something else.

Verr.

I hadn't believed it. Couldn't. Despite the restlessness of the wild magic in my bones. Not until Kat's wounds were healed and the venom swiftly took its course through her. When his mere touch had caused her to scream out in agony. Her magic sensing the ancient threat in him in those first hours as she'd viciously clawed at her own skin.

It had broken something in me to hold her down, to hopelessly try to comfort her. But it had broken something in Emrys too. I couldn't ignore that.

He'd recoiled from her side. Hadn't been near her since. Becoming nothing but some strange wounded shadow chasing the madness of theories, trying to find any hope.

I'd learnt long ago that hope was for fools. For little girls who devoured stories and were allowed to dream. Not for creatures like me.

'Blood loss, galmoth venom, iron burns and magic sickness,' Gideon continued, his words breathless with disbelief as his gloved hand raked through his dishevelled golden hair. 'The cures for that venom are dead. Just as the creature that caused it should be!'

Each word of that truth struck like a blow. Each moment of the agonising last few days flashing through my mind. Only my own grief couldn't compete with the sudden coldness in the room, how Thean lurched urgently to their feet, wine forgotten.

Shadows crept from every corner, long and lethal across the study's floor like claws. Blackthorn's anger made the room creak with unease, books on the table slamming shut of their own accord. Those warning bells from the back shelves of the library began to ring as if they trembled too.

'Stop it!' I snapped, feeling the sharpness of fangs against my lip and the tightness of claws at my nailbeds as I charged into the room. 'This bickering isn't helping her!'

Days. They'd been fighting for *days*.

The darkness eased, the fire returning to the barest glow as Emrys pushed away from the cluttered desk he'd loomed over, unable to look at me as he turned to the fireplace. I understood why.

I was another reminder of that night. Another reminder of *her*.

Gideon straightened, cool eyes assessing as embarrassment flushed his high cheekbones and his lips pressed into a thin annoyed line at my interruption. He assessed me with haunted, pale blue eyes. Eyes that appeared to have seen this world before and knew all the answers.

'You're wasting time.' I moved closer to the desk, to where their failed remedies lay scattered with little care. Empty vials and bright powders stained the healing pages. 'You said we were trying the clawfox venom next.'

'There are no clawfox samples left. Not even the remaining black markets are peddling them.' Gideon's words were clipped with caution. His cold gaze pinned on his brother as if anticipating an attack.

'Then we try the basilisk herb William harvested.' I threw out my hand in frustration in the direction of the door.

'She's not strong enough to survive another fever.' The healer's voice was terse with impatience.

I shook my head. 'There has to be—'

'*Miss Darcy.*' His tone was stern with authority, making my back rigid. Reminding me too vividly of all the masters that had come before. 'The best we can do is keep her comfortable and—'

'*Comfortable?*' Emrys turned from the fire, the word sharper than a blade as it cut through the air.

That one word crushed the air from my chest more brutally than any man's fist ever had, than any keeper or master I'd encountered, making it impossible to suck any more into my lungs with the tightness of my throat.

There was no comfort for her. Not when her screams still echoed in my ears.

Fear clawed at my ribs, deep painful lacerations that fuelled the vicious anger inside me.

No.

'She'd find a way.' I pressed the words through my lips. Feeling the sharpness of scales slip across my cheek before they slid away again, buried back within my blood. The beast inside coiling to strike, to find a way out of my meagre, mortal flesh.

'There isn't a way.' Gideon's voice softened, regret lightening his features as his eyes drifted to Emrys's rigid form.

'There wasn't one out of Daunton either.' The words escaped before I could think. My secrets protruding too easily from the shallow grave I'd buried them in. My voice didn't sound like my own. Too cold and distant.

It was the first time I'd said that word, almost making my lips tremble, but I tipped my chin, letting the feral rage in my chest consume everything else. All my sadness. All my fear feeding the monster that lurked beneath.

'No way out of the beatings, the bitterness of the cold or the unmarked graves they'd make us dig deep in those woods.'

I refused to waver, leering forward until one talon was pointed at the healer's throat.

'Kat found one.'

A muscle moved in Gideon's jaw but his stern expression remained.

'She found it for *me*,' I spat, my clawed finger resting the barest inch from his pulse point. 'So if you think I'm letting you stop, you're very much mistaken.'

All the things she'd done for me. How she'd saved me over and over and I had nothing to give. No brilliance. No intelligence. Nothing.

'You're not finished.' Fury made my spine sharpen and I heard the popping of stitches in my dress with the threat of a change, anger boiling in my blood. I didn't know all the stories. Knew nothing. Everything to save her was impossible and I wasn't smart enough to understand any of it.

I wasn't a mage. I had no hope of ever being one. All I had were beasts beneath my skin.

'We've been through every record. The samples we need haven't existed for a decade, long before the uprising.' Gideon's voice was tight but those regretful, blue eyes pooled with sorrow. 'That's the problem with basing magic upon monstrous things.'

'There could be more samples in the—' Thean began but their voice faded from my ears. A smell turned my focus to the desk beyond the healer. Bitter, earthy but distant. Almost faded. Familiar enough to pick at a memory in the back of my mind like a loose thread as I stared at the books and papers scattered on the desk.

I focused on the desk – the vials of scales, feather clippings and the beasts that each page depicted, following the scent, moving closer until I could touch them. Smears of dark paint for shadow creatures, thick scales and golden stripes for eternal beasts.

They were hunted and they were killed for what they were worth.

Kat had told me that. Why most creatures were nothing but stories. How mortals longed for the magic in their blood, in their scales and fur. Buried in their very bone marrow.

The rattle of a chain, a feverish burn to my scaled skin and the sour smell of rotting straw. The darkness and the reek of damp. Memories I begged myself in the dark of night never to see again, only now I let them have me. Let their foulness tear at my heart.

What profit you'll bring. The clammy touch of stubby fingers against my cheek. The inspecting glances. A vile caress and a spat curse.

I didn't listen to the nightmare of those voices. No, I listened to my magic as it rippled over my skin with unease, lingering in the tips of my fingers and brushing my palm. Like a hand trying to guide me the rest of the way.

I moved closer to the source of that scent, the bickering voices of Thean and Gideon nothing but a distant mumble as I looked at the grey dirt in the vial on the table, barely glinting with the texture of the scale that remained. I turned it over to see the dark specks that endured, how they crumbled with the barest of motions.

Dead things are worth the most. Why is that, little rat? The Keeper had asked in the silky sweet voice he always used before the beatings. Before the performance.

'They're beyond value,' I whispered to myself now, as my fingers curled around the vial. As I felt the curse buried in my blood sense it, hungry to change.

Only the dust in the jar wasn't enough. It had regressed too far but that distant smell made a memory pierce through the pain of all the others.

Small fingers dragging over vials. The dusty rot of it clinging to the back of my throat, the sharpness of tobacco smoke in the shadows of forgotten places.

The promise of magic concealed within the vials. My skin almost burning with the urge to be cut, for blood to come free and release another monster from within.

'What is this?' I demanded, holding the glass vial out, silencing the room.

Gideon's mouth was open from whatever insult he was about to throw back at Thean. He swallowed it, sharp eyes confused as they met my own.

'The useless remains of what's supposed to be a scale from the shadow drake. The closest thing we could find to the ravhorn.' His answer was hesitant. 'One of the suggested cures for shadow sickness.'

Ravhorn. I'd heard of that. Heard of it in one of Kat's boring fucking lessons when I had better things to do. A dark remedy. Poison from the shadows of the world.

Liar. That voice hissed in my memory. No, I'd heard of that dark beast long before Kat had fed me the story.

I rolled my wrist, feeling the tightness of the scarring there, the shift from scales to fur.

If you know it you can become it. How the Keeper had repeated that most of all. Beat it into my very bones. Whispered like a gentle caress, pressed the words against my tear-stained cheek with his dry, tobacco-stained lips as fragments of creatures were forced against my bloody palm.

I was consumed by the memories I begged to forget. The scratch of the scales. The patches of fur still attached to bloody skin, the bitterness of the venom, the endless dusty pages that made my nose burn. The drag of my finger over the dry paper, feeling the creases and the skin it had been made from.

What crumbs of those creatures could remain? What little was left for my magic to feast on? The dry dusty stench of his collection.

Pathetic, useless beast.

No. I'd allowed myself to be useless. Hidden so carefully, like a rat in its nest.

'That could bring her back?' I demanded, taking another step towards Gideon, feeling the cold bite of Blackthorn's magic, the deadly focus of it suddenly solely on me from where he remained in the shadows.

'If the writings are accurate,' Gideon offered, sending a cautious glance in his brother's direction.

A chill shot down my spine in warning. The beastly instincts in me too close to the surface. Like my ear twitching with the barest whisper of a new sound. I turned towards the study doorway just as William appeared. Deathly pale with that book clutched to his chest like a shield.

'Gideon.' He swallowed, eyes shimmering with tears. 'H-her tremors have started again.'

'Fuck,' Gideon cursed, turning to his desk and rooting through his things. That cold demeanour slipping away as the sharp determination of a healer took over. 'We're almost out of Longwood herb.' He ran a hand through his golden hair before he remembered William.

He reached for the boy and spoke softly to him in comfort as William blinked tears from his eyes, fingers trembling where they held the book.

I should have gone to him, should have gone back to her, but something rooted me in place. The sharp bite of my magic against my palm where I held that vial. Telling me what I already knew. There were no answers in that bedroom. They lay here. Right before me.

'I can look in the east fields,' Thean offered without hesitation, all the voyav's cruelness slipping away, their expression open and cautious as they looked at William, pale and lost.

'No,' I commanded, turning to Emrys, that poison still curled in my fist. I crossed the room to stand before him. Refusing to focus on the red marks my claws had made on his already scarred face and throat. The blooming bruises there, and how he hadn't properly healed them.

Almost as if he hadn't felt it. Or simply because he wished for the punishment of that pain. A horrid broken coldness lingering in the darkness of his eyes.

I swallowed down my shame. 'Kat made that doorway take her to those woods. To Paxton fields. Can it go anywhere?'

Pain cut into the sternness of his face.

'Within reason,' he answered carefully, his focus moving to William. Then to the hallway behind him as if he could move for it at any moment. To her. How the shadow of that darkness still rippled beneath his skin.

'I know where there could be samples.' I held the vial under his chin, something about my desperation making him look back to me. 'Like this.'

'The underground traders don't have—' he began but I was already shaking my head, dark curls falling around my face.

'Not the traders.' I grimaced, an agitation taking hold of my body with the urge to move. To hunt. 'The docklands of the west. The bone markets.'

Something in the room shifted at my words, the strange warm presence of Thean Page at my back, but I wouldn't look at them. *Couldn't.* Not to see the suspicion in their eyes. A rebel would know that place, but not the secrets I'd buried there. Beneath the ash and bone fragments.

Gideon frowned. 'How would you know the bone markets? They—'.

'A merchant worked out of the water cellars there. He dealt in dead matter. In things others couldn't find. My—' I wouldn't say keeper. Wouldn't give him the power of being remembered.

'The town was levelled.' Emrys's words were guarded, but not with the tone of a challenge – with a sense of protection against a hope I was offering. One even I was too afraid to cling to. 'They say a dark storm took it. A Verr summoning at the end of the war.'

'They're there. I saw them. Protected deep beneath the earth. They have to be there.'

It was a long shot but it was all I had. A memory of that horrid place. I saw Gideon's eyes move to his brother, doubt creasing his brow. I couldn't blame him. It sounded impossible even to my own ears.

'I need to try,' I pleaded. Hating the weakness of it. A madness, perhaps, but it was all I had. This one memory. This one chance.

Gideon's lips parted as if to argue but Emrys spoke.

'Then we'll try.' Firm, unwavering, as a light softened the darkness of his eyes. An olive branch between us. Between the secrets and lies.

Then he was moving across the room so he could lay a comforting hand on William's shoulder.

'Watch over her for me.' Emrys's command was gentle, but hoarse with pain. William blinked away his tears as a new resolve came over him with that order, his shoulders straighter, a soldier given new purpose.

'Thean,' Emrys instructed, sharp and lethal as he came back past me, striding deeper into the study, through those shelves the house moved without command.

Chapter Three

Alma

A dark wind pulled in from the east. Some say it was formed of nothing but putrid smoke, only no flames followed. Instead of thunder, there was nothing but distant screams contained in the storm winds, a storm so heavy and vicious it trapped the souls it killed. There was no relief when it broke, for its rains were nothing but blood, turning the canal waters red.

Whatever monster visited the bone markets was made of nothing but death, and all it left after its feast . . . was ash.

Council report from the eastern fields

I ran my palms down my creased skirts, trying to stop the sweat gathering against my skin. The rough nature of my hands snagged on the cotton. It didn't matter how many times I changed forms, I couldn't erase the callouses from my fingers. Couldn't erase the past.

This mortal skin is just another disguise. One of many. Just another form to hide within, making me wonder if I was real at all, or just a ghost encased in flesh. A beast with no name.

A sharp shiver moved down my spine, the restless bite of my scales pulling me from my own pity as my eyes focused on the old Portium door before me, how the paint had begun to crack and peel at the edges. Something else that shouldn't exist. A forbidden, dangerous thing.

Just like you.

'You've chosen madness then?' came Thean's words over my shoulder, followed by their sharp scent. Rich cologne, brandy and a telling tang of blood.

Against my better judgement, I turned. A wild urge streaked through me in response to their small, teasing smile as the shadows cut across the striking feminine face they'd chosen and those amber eyes gleaming with devious intent.

'I didn't see you as one for loyalty,' I challenged. Rebels didn't do things for free. They also didn't risk the wrath of their master for a Kysillian of all creatures. Not one beyond their master's bounds.

'I made a promise. Surely you of all beings understand that, darling?' The voyav shrugged, picking at a stray thread on their sleeve. 'Besides, your dear friend still owes me a favour.'

Thankfully, Thean's latest taunt was interrupted as Emrys moved towards us through the dark, narrow shelves. A glowing crystal rested in his gloved palm, the white light reflecting in the pitch-black of his eyes.

'You're certain?' He asked, an unforgiving shadow before me.

'I can't forget it.' That was the only certainty I could give. 'The trader didn't trust anyone. He blindfolded his clients but I could smell the way. Then I was brought there. They wanted to steal what he had, but they ran out of time.'

My voice was distant, detached from that version of myself I'd once been. Scuttling and weak. Refusing to remember that my Keeper never had a chance, not when he'd been foolish enough to loosen my leash.

Whatever Blackthorn saw in my expression seemed to be sufficient as he held out the iridescent crystal to me. A portal stone. 'Take this.'

'I can change.' I'd been a bird before and despite the fact the flight might hurt over such a far distance, I could get myself to safe territory, maybe even find my way back here.

'This will bring you back here.' He pressed the cold stone against my palm, clearly it wasn't up for argument.

'Do we all get one of those?' Thean raised a dark brow as they ran fingers through their loose auburn hair with mild boredom. 'Considering I'm being *coerced* into this madness?'

Emrys ignored them, turning to the portal door to rearrange another crystal in the compartment. Kat had explained to me how it all worked but I didn't dare allow myself to remember.

Everything about her hurt too much. Like picking at a scab. So, I watched Emrys's movements numbly as he let the door click and whirr before the knob turned on its own and the darkness of night greeted us. Stale cold air nipped at my cheeks and stole away the warmth of the house.

'Charming,' Thean sighed, their breath brushing upon the back of my neck, making scales ripple in the wake of that ghostly touch. Curious, perhaps.

I should have sent my elbow into their ribs at their sudden closeness, but fear had frozen me in place.

Welcome back, little rat, a ghost seemed to taunt in my mind.

Blackthorn crossed the Portium threshold, from polished wood floor to damp cobblestones into a cold grey night mist, forcing me to follow until we all stood in the shadows of the abandoned warehouses that filled the south side of the markets. Or what had survived the dark storm.

The crumbled remains of the old buildings pierced the shadowy night, as did the creak of the chains that still swung from the wooden loading cranes. The musty smell of the dank canal water filled my lungs as I noticed the rot from the abandoned wharf had shattered the wooden barrels lining the walkways. Ropes curled like waiting snakes turned green with time as weeds clung to the cracks in the stone.

This was what remained of the bone markets.

The reek of brine, stagnant water and bitter dead magic carried on the ruthless winter breeze. The horror of it all sent a shiver down my spine. I was unable to stop myself remembering how it had been before. I could hear the ghostly whistle of the barge workers through the mist. The cackling laughter of the night traders and calls of the street girls who had nothing left of value but their bodies. The sweet tang of sugar buns that would make my starved mouth water.

'The rebels never wanted to cleanse this place?' I whispered, turning to see that Thean was not considering the derelict streets beyond but looking down at me almost expectantly.

'The creatures here resisted rebellion law.' Their answer was careful, those amber eyes tracing every inch of my expression, seeking something unspoken from me. 'This is justice in her eyes.'

Her.

The Countess.

The name sent a wave of nausea through me, even though Thean hadn't spoken it aloud. How rarely it was said. As though speaking of her too often could summon her to your door. Just like all dark things in this world.

The leader of the rebellion. A blood witch hiding in her lair in the midlands.

Some said she was ancient, others young and vicious, only her cruelty was a commonality in the tales.

A murky memory threatened to surface. Small rodent eyes peering through cracks in stained floorboards, hearing a sharp cruel laugh as soft lamplight played through strands of inky hair.

Show me what you have. A dark purred command. The scent of marrow and iron. A memory I recoiled from as a shiver dragged down my spine like an unwanted caress.

I shook it away. There was enough horror before me without wallowing in the haunting agony of my past. The bone markets had been slums, taverns and brothels, but there were beings here who had no choice. Lost and poor. Left in the shadows of the world. Those the rebellion saw as having little value. Lesser fey and impoverished mortals.

A screech cut through the misty night.

Emrys's arm forced me deeper into the safety of the shadows. The wildness in my blood sent a piercing pain into my temples, alerting me to a threat. My nails shifted into claws just as a grey silhouette cut through the fog barely feet away.

Its hunched, spiked back and long thin claws were too clear before it lurched into obscurity once more, patrolling the ruins for whatever it could scavenge. My breath stuttered in relief knowing the harsh wind had stopped it sensing us.

'Croverns.' Emrys's voice was the barest puff of frosty breath.

Croverns. Shadow eaters and devourers of dead things.

'Croverns eat remains,' Thean observed quietly, slipping their shadow blade from the sheath at their thigh, their full attention on Emrys as they pressed closer to my side. 'They shouldn't still be here.'

Croverns feasted on dark magic.

Yet, all that was left beneath the debris was charred bone. The dark fires would have claimed any flesh. Any bodies that survived the chaos would have been devoured by scavengers years ago – their magic too.

Those croverns remained because they could sense there was more to devour. Just like the skelmor in Fairfax Wood.

Something was luring them here. Even after all this time.

Dark magic. The remains of it.

'It's here,' I whispered, my focus on the darkened path beyond us where the moonlight made the shadows shift between the ruins.

'Stay where you are.' Emrys gave the barest nod, the command was quiet as he pulled a blade from inside his coat. He moved into the darkness and out of sight.

A strange coldness lingered after his departure. How easily he shed the demeanour of a lord. Like a snake being free of an old skin. Of course. He'd fought in streets like this for years. The fight against the Mage King hadn't been held on a grand battlefield, but down cobbled narrow streets where the bricks were still chipped from the deadly spells they'd survived.

Emrys had once been Lord Commander. The most ruthless title to hold.

I should have focused on him and what direction he took – only there was something else on the wind, beneath the stagnant memory of death. Familiar and strange. Like damp earth, old scrolls and tobacco laced with hookers' weed. That trader's scent. Taunting me.

My skin almost burnt with the urge to change. To hunt.

I took the portal stone from my skirt pocket, not looking behind me as I forced it towards Thean's chest, barely having a moment to think of how tangled our fingers became. Too consumed with that scent, how faint it was in the wind.

'*Alma*,' Thean barely had time to snap in warning. It was the first time I'd heard my name from their lips – and it almost made me stay.

My beasts had other ideas.

It was a painful rush, a biting sting over every inch of me, a sinking inside of my clothes. Then there was just the world through different eyes. Too small and quick. The filthy ground too close, reduced to a blur as my small limbs burnt with exertion across the uneven terrain, following that vague scent. The ghost of a memory loomed as I plunged through the sharp stone ruins, small claws racing over damp wood and shattered glass, frigid puddle water biting into my fur.

The screeching howl of the forsaken monsters haunting this place echoed around me, but I ignored that danger, nose twitching. The scent grew stronger and stronger, leading me through a maze of destruction and towards a trapdoor at the back of a dilapidated house. A rusted chain curled around the handles. Wooden planks had collapsed across it, blocking the way as weeds tangled with brambles. There was a crack in those doors, a hole just big enough. One I rushed for.

Then I was falling.

I felt the air open up – and then I changed.

The stinging rush returned as my bare feet landed on damp wood, the impact jarring my knees enough to force me into a crouch.

Bitter, dead air licked up my naked back, making spikes cut through the ridge of my spine in defence.

I panted, breath misting before me in the moonlight, looking into the shadows only to find a face looking back.

A scream caught in my throat as I jerked backwards into a shelf, the jars rattling against my bare shoulder blades. Dust danced in the needle-thin streams of weak light. The remains of a withered corpse coated in dust sat behind the desk opposite me, cobwebs woven between the gaps in his grey teeth. The mangled face still screamed out in agony as the head hung oddly off its shoulders.

The trader.

I looked down at the shattered jars at his feet, the lumines-cent glow still clinging to the murky glass. Poison. Jars he'd kept to deter thieves.

Killed by his own bounty.

Good. It was what he deserved. My eyes fell to the battered, dusty leather coat holding his bones together. I pulled it from the tangle of his remains without hesitation until a thick plume of dust filled the air, making me choke and spit.

I shuddered, pulling on the coat and ignoring the stench of decay as I knotted the belt. The old leather creaked in protest. I brought my balled fists to my lips, trying to warm my numb fingers with my short, panicked breaths. Looking up at the low beams, the webs tangled between them.

How small this space seemed now. How forgotten. I'd stood here before. Tired and hungry. Aching from another beating. The thick hand of my Keeper on my shoulder. The sweat-and-ale stench of him.

Now a scuttling from the darkness made my ears prick. Then I smelt the matted fur and filth. Faeces and rotting meat.

Another beast. Its beady eyes gleamed as it hissed from the hole it had gnawed into the wall, small furry body trembling with the urge to attack – to guard its territory.

There was a sharp ache in my jaw before I bared long, sharp teeth, a horrid growl tearing from my throat. The creature's ears flattened as it sank back into its hiding place beneath the rotten boards and I jolted towards the shelves amidst rows and rows of dusty bottles and jars.

It was here. It was all still here.

A horrid weak sob burst through my lips. My clawed fingers dug into the soft rotting wood as a deranged, choked laugh escaped my lips.

'I did it, Kat,' I whispered.

A creaking of wood and a thump above made my hackles rise, turning me towards the remains of a crooked wooden set of stairs leading out of the basement.

'*Alma*,' a hissed curse, muffled, from somewhere above along with the scrape and drag of wood being moved off the trapdoor.

I used my cat-like sight to avoid the shattered glass hidden beneath the dust that carpeted the bare wooden boards.

'I'm here,' I coughed in response, scrambling up the rickety wooden stairs that led to the trapdoor, listening to them creak beneath my weight. Dust streamed down, burning my eyes as I heard the drag of chain against wood. 'It's chained this side.'

I squinted, the knot of metal above me a rusted mess where it was tangled around the handles. It was heavy as I unwound it and let it pool at my bare feet. Then came the stiff bolt. I slammed the heel of my palm against it three times. Hard enough to bruise but it did the trick. Then the door was thrown open with a crash, bright moonlight making me wince and move down a step.

The imposing form of Emrys was waiting, blocking out the light in an instant. Effortlessly, he dropped into the opening. Dark blood stained the cuffs of his shirt, a splatter marring the side of his throat. I could smell the foulness of it, as well as the rich potency of forsaken bark.

He gave me a quick, irritated assessment. Determining I was all in one piece, he sheathed his blade with one sharp motion back into his coat.

I waited for the reprimand, getting my fangs ready to bare at him. Only for him to duck past me down the narrow wooden steps and into the dark.

I didn't have a moment to school my emotions before Thean followed Emrys with a grimace.

'Wonderful,' they sighed, taking in their surroundings with mildly contained disgust, that sharp predatory gaze landing on the now crumpled remains of the trader slumped in the corner. 'A corpse.'

They dropped something at my feet, making me take another step down, only to realise it was my boots, my dress hanging carefully over their arm.

The voyav's gaze remained stuck on the trader, the smooth beauty of their feminine face making it hard to determine if it was in anger or boredom.

I made quick work of tugging on my boots, not bothering with the laces.

'There were jars of murgal worm venom. They must have shattered in the storm. He wouldn't have stood a chance with—' The words caught in my throat as I felt a gentle tug at my hair, only to see the voyav pull back their hand, a grey tangle of dusty webs caught in their fingers that they let drop in the damp air between us.

'Murgal worm venom.' They gave an irritated sigh, folding their arms and moving their focus to the shadowed form of Emrys investigating the darkness. 'That isn't alarming to anyone else?'

I ignored them. Especially their helpfulness in bringing my boots. It wasn't kindness – my feet bleeding all over the place would only alert those dark scavengers. I moved after Emrys as he scanned the rows and rows of shelves in the endless dark.

'The more valuable samples should be over there.' I nodded to the back shelves strung with cobwebs.

He gave the barest nod before vanishing into another row of shelves, the clinking of glass echoing back the only evidence he'd begun his search.

I moved to the other side. Knowing that even if the ravhorn sample hadn't survived – something would be here. Something useful. It had to be.

I tried to sniff it out, to depend on the beasts in my blood, but the scent of decay was overwhelming. Mingling together like an itch inside my nose. Frustration made a growl rumble in my throat.

Thieves' instincts took over as I rummaged desperately, fingers tangling with thick dust webs. Labels curled and cracked with time on the murky bottles, flaking away from the glass with the barest motion. It was hard to read but I let the feral urges in my blood guide me. Anything that sparked hunger in my fingertips. I grabbed the small vials and pushed them deep into the trader's coat pocket – extracts of herbs and scales I didn't recognise. But they'd survived this long, the glass that encased them practically vibrating with the magic they still contained, so they were coming with me. They shouldn't be left to rot here. Shouldn't be forgotten. Nor the creatures whose suffering they evidenced.

I was restless with my search, scales and fur rippling across my hands with irritation before a distant scream pierced the air. Wild and savage. Making my clawed fingers dig into the wood of the shelf. Pausing my plunder for the barest moment. One of those creatures had clearly discovered whatever Emrys had done to its companion.

'We don't have long,' Thean observed dryly, hand moving to one of the shadow blades sheathed at their belt as those amber eyes remained on the trapdoor.

If anything caught us here, there was no way out.

Yet, fear didn't accompany that thought. Not with the voyav standing there. Drenched in silver light. Reminding me of a knight from one of the ancient tales Kat used to tell to chase away the nightmares.

No. Not a knight. They were a rebel – and they were here for their own cause. One I was certain had nothing to do with valour.

Scales rippled across the back of my hand, aggravated by my dallying, wanting to fill my palm. Hungry. I followed the sensation into another row of shelves where larger vials sat, their corks more expensive, the wax seals blood-red in warning. One was covered in a dark film of dust, untouched longer than all the others. Right at the back.

Mortals do not play with what they fear. No, because cowardice was in their blood. Bred into them by the first who had come to these lands. By their bastard sacred saint.

I ran my thumb over the label, the uneven crumbling mess of what remained of the parchment. Trying to make my eyes focus. Trying to see the letters. To understand them. Only the longer I focused, the more the ink moved. Blurring and dancing into the cracks in the paper. Mocking me. The specs of gold and silver like winking stars in a night sky from where they threaded through what remained of the ancient scales contained within.

'Alma?' Emrys asked, suddenly at my shoulder. The forsaken bark scent of him was too hard to miss, stinging my nose with its potency. It should have been my first clue he was fucking Verr, and didn't just have a strange preference for poisonous bark as cologne.

My unsteady clawed hand offered it to him. Too afraid to even breathe, never mind hope this could have worked, that I could have fixed anything.

'What does it say?' I demanded, swallowing down the taste of dust and decay. Trying to calm the thunderous beat of my traitorous heart, so alive with hope.

'*Velnock*,' he answered, a softness to his voice. The ancient Verr tongue sent unease rolling through me. His eyes were suddenly the lightest shade of grey. That darkness in him abating for a moment. 'The ravhorn.'

I'd found it.

Chapter Four

Alma

The ravhorn. Great serpents of scales and poison, large enough to eat a man, but they prefer to devour the dark, burrowing deep where they sleep beneath the earth.

Insidious Theory – Myths of the Deep, 1145

'Thank the ancestors,' William greeted as he lurched to his feet from his perch on a low stool by the fire in the study, his bottom lip bruised from how much he'd been biting it.

'How is she?' Emrys demanded, pulling off his coat and tossing it on an abandoned chair filled with books, knocking most of them to the ground.

If the boy was alarmed by the dark blood splattered on Emrys's shirt and jaw, he didn't show it.

'Stable,' Gideon sighed from where he rested against the study door frame, shoulder stooped with tiredness as he rubbed the back of his neck, a rag thrown over his shoulder stained from whatever tonics he'd been mixing. 'For now.'

Then those sad blue eyes landed on me, nestled between Emrys and Thean. I could only imagine the dirt smeared across my face, dark hair a tangled mess around my shoulders. The wildness in my eyes from the change as the stolen trader's coat swamped me.

'Alma?' William took a cautious step forward, alarmed by the state of me. Probably the reek of me too.

Gideon's long strides cut through the space between us, halting William's approach. That strange energy he possessed practically thrumming in the air between us.

'Show me.' He held out his gloved hand and Emrys relinquished the sample of the ravhorn from his white knuckled grip.

Gideon turned the vial over, holding it up to the warm study light, twisting it so the grey scales inside gleamed, those gold and silver threads sending my magic biting ravenously into my bones.

Now. It seemed to growl deep in my chest. Ravenous with a hunger I hadn't felt since Daunton.

'This sample is petrified.' Gideon frowned, a light going out in his eyes as his gaze moved reluctantly back to his brother.

A sound slipped between Emrys's lips as if he'd been punched in the gut, but I couldn't focus on that. Couldn't stop. I snatched the vial from Gideon's hand, moving past him and towards Kat's desk.

'I never said I needed a live sample,' I called over my filthy shoulder, rolling the cool glass against my palm, feeling the sharp bite of scales around my wrist.

Now, it demanded but I kept moving. To the clear surface where Kat's things lay abandoned like some strange memorial.

Hating how faded the scent of her was. Missing it most of all.

I was cursed with value. One Kat hadn't even let Master Hale see. One I'd been used for before. Endlessly. All the things I could become, exotic and extinct. All the things that could be harvested over and over again. How they could make more just like me so easily. Use me until there was nothing left to take.

Just as they used all the others.

I pushed the stupid books, papers from the desk. They clattered to the ground, the house letting out a weary groan but I ignored that too as I reached into her bag for her healing kit. Letting the bandages tumble and unroll across the desk, the small vials and balls of cotton – creating a mess, but it was the clank of the healing knife that made me stop.

I grabbed it, hilt cold and heavy in my grasp.

My wrist was caught before I could make the cut, by fingers tipped with pure darkness, as if they'd been dipped in ink, spreading into thin veins up the back of his hand to his wrist.

'Alma,' Emrys cautioned, his hold inescapable, making me look up at where he towered over me. Feeling the strange cold sting of his magic against my skin, as scales rose under my flesh with the threat of his touch. Protecting me from whatever wrongness lurked inside him.

Verr.

How raw and pale he seemed with grief.

I wanted to hate him, but as I looked at the anguish in his shadowed face it was like looking into a mirror. I knew he was the only reason she was here now. He'd brought her back to me.

'Why can *you* be consumed by madness to save her and I can't?' I challenged, watching his jaw tense. The slightest flinch as my words struck their mark.

There was nothing but darkness in his eyes and I knew he wasn't protesting for me. He was protecting Kat, even now. Protecting her from seeing me in pain, even if she wasn't here. He might care for her, but she was my family. All I had. All I never deserved.

'I made her a promise.' My voice broke. I knew he'd understand that if nothing else as I wrenched myself free from his hold.

I wouldn't leave her. Not like this.

'If anyone would like to inform me of what the fuck is going on, I'd be most grateful.' Gideon came to a stop on the other side of the desk. Looking down at the mess I'd made with accusation.

I ignored him. Letting Kat's healing blade slice my palm in one swift motion, blood pooling quickly. Focusing on the familiar sting as I brought the vial to my lips. Biting down on the seal, cracking it and spitting out the cork. Ignoring the sour grimy taste the poison left on my tongue.

'Are you mad?!' Gideon surged forward. 'That could be the last—'

Emrys caught his arm with impossible speed, stopping the protest as I let the crumbs of the scales fall into my bloody palm. Curling my fingers into a fist.

Blood slid between my knuckles with horrid familiarity.

Heathen bitch, Daunton had spat during his torment. His favourite insult for me. I almost smiled bitterly at the truth of it. Just how unholy I was.

'Emrys!' Gideon barked, knowing what was about to happen, but it was too late. I'd destroy all that was left of that beast and I'd do it for her.

One.

Two.

Three.

I let the count calm me. Listening to the fire crack, the drip of the blood and the thrum of my heart. The gritty texture of the remains against my skin. How a biting chill had begun to spread up my arm.

Find it, came a hiss in my ear. The painful phantom press of fingers against my flesh, twisting into my hair. The reek of old blood and rusted chains. *Find it, little rat.*

I shook my head, flinching from the memory of the Keeper.
I tried to feel it. Tried to remember the story Kat had
told about the ravhorn. Remember the calm wonder in her
voice. How desperately I needed to hear it again. Hear her.
Make her real once more. So I could find my way back to
this form.

My breath suddenly pained. Throat too tight, a sharpness
there as if lined with ridges and scales. How my fear manifested to choke me, forcing me to submit to it.

There isn't a form I wouldn't find you in, Alma, Kat's words
like a ghostly brush of breath against the shell of my ear. A
promise. A tether to always bring me back.

Then breath slipped between my lips.

I could smell damp soil, old musty earth. Hear the drips
of water falling from stone, the endless cold that seeped deep
into my bones, burying itself right to the marrow.

I imagined the sharpness of those dark scales, felt them
ripple painfully beneath my skin. Each like the jagged slice of
a knife. Across the tops of my shoulders, the dampness of the
blood that would soak my skin. Heard a sound of alarm from
behind me but it was too distant. Too far for me to care as
I forced the sensation of the pain down my spine and to my
arm where those scales met the blood in my palm. Where
they could take my offering.

My breath caught, I screwed my eyes tighter, my palm
burning. Fingers trembling as I felt the sweat bead on my
forehead. I gripped onto the desk with my other hand, a
horrid sound tearing up my throat. My nailbeds split, fresh
claws digging into wood.

Old wounds opening on my forearms and down my thighs.
Skin slick with blood.

'Emrys!' Gideon ordered almost desperately.

36

The pain almost made me let go, my very bones seared with the intensity of it, trying to crack and change. Warm tears sliding down my cheeks, breath rattling in my throat. I didn't open my eyes. Wouldn't. Wouldn't give in.

Useless rat. How easily I'd made those words true.

No.

I'd done it before. Performed for food, for their pleasure, for their cruelty to stop. I'd done it for them so I could do it for her.

Nothing is ever going to hurt you again. The memory of a younger Kat whispered into my ear. A breathless sob escaped my trembling lips. Remembering the compassion in her toothy grin as she hooked our filthy, thin pinkie fingers together in the first act of kindness I'd treasured.

When she'd used torn bed sheets to bandage my raw wrists in the dead of night, kneeling on the brutally cold floor. Unfazed by what they meant. The truth of them. That I wasn't worth anything. The first time I'd been given something without a price.

Kindness.

She'd taken the beating the next morning, been forced to sleep on the hardwood floor for weeks after. Until her thin shoulders were bruised and too stiff to move.

She'd done it for me. Not understanding how little I was worth.

How desperately lonely she was to befriend a monster like me.

I'll keep you safe. Always. I held that promise close to my heart and I wouldn't lose it. Not as I lost everything else.

I pressed the knot of my fist against my stomach, dragging in a stuttered breath as the blistering torment of my curse shot up my legs, making them buckle. My knees slammed into the wood. Someone called my name but all I saw was darkness through serpent eyes as it bowed me over. I cried out from the madness of it. Heart beating too fast as it split apart and became two organs. Pressing too hard against my ribs, squeezing the air from my lungs before turning to one again. Bile burnt my throat as I spat it from my fanged mouth onto the hardwood floor. The wild thing inside me thrashed to get out. Clawing at my ribcage and filling my mouth with the bitter taste of blood.

I forced the agony of it down until it consumed my forearm. The burning tightness of it as I focused on the image of that beast in my mind, as I smelt sulphur and tasted that poison, acrid and sharp. Felt my tongue split like a snake's, brushing the inside of my mouth.

Someone's hands were on my shoulders, pushing me up but then they stopped.

'Fucking great, Barnabas,' came the breathless words from Gideon as the blurry vision of him sat before me, a horrid hope blooming in my chest as the pain receded enough for me to catch my breath.

Faces came back into focus as a thick silence took hold of the room. The cracking of the fire was louder than anything else. Even the drumming of my own heartbeat high in my ears. The healer was crouched before me, face pale, staring down at my arm between us as I gasped for breath.

Thick black scales, speckled with gold and silver, sleek as if covered in oil, surrounded my forearm where it lay exposed in my lap. The trader's coat sleeve torn away with the sharpness of them. A blue sheen beneath of the venomous coating.

You can do anything, Alma. Kat's words came in reward and despite all the sadness and suffering I wanted to smile. But her voice faded too easily from my memory.

Then came the tight pinch of fear that it could slip from my control. That those scales could vanish. I saw the healing blade glinting on Gideon's belt as he knelt before me. Hands hovering as if hesitant to touch me. His lips moved but I couldn't hear a word as I focused on the knife, short and razor-sharp.

I lunged for it, almost knocking him over as I dragged it from its hilt. In one swift motion I ran it down my arm, feeling each scale pull away, the intense sting of it as blue blood ran down my forearm to drip onto my bare thighs.

'Alma,' Emrys cursed as the knife clattered from my numb fingers. One arm across my shoulders to keep me steady as breath hissed through my clenched teeth. Emrys pressed a clean rag against my arm as spots danced in my vision. The pressure made it worse as my skin struggled to shift back.

'That's—' Gideon half stuttered, half sprawled on the ground, golden hair hanging limply across his brow. Stunned. How those scales glistened in the firelight, keeping their serpent form.

'*Gideon*,' Emrys snapped, bringing his focus back as the healer lurched into his role. Pulling a handkerchief from his pocket as he scooped up the pieces of me. The pieces of something that shouldn't be, curses slipping from his lips as he moved back to his own desk with urgency.

A pale William stumbled after him and awaited instruction. Poor William.

There was a tension in Emrys's jaw as he glared down at me, his arm across my shoulders the only thing keeping me up. The blood from my wound seeping into the clean white cloth too rapidly.

'I'm fine.' I pulled my arm back with panting breath, trying to take the rag from him but there was no strength in my fingers. My movements too slow and clumsy. Uncomfortable with his concern. Not knowing what to do with it.

'I'll do it,' Thean spoke, so commanding and fluid. Emrys's gaze turned to the voyav with sharp surprise where they leant casually against Kat's desk, ignoring the mess all around them. How my blood almost touched the tip of their perfectly polished boot.

As if they witnessed impossible things every day.

'Best not to leave the *drunkard* with the valuables,' Thean shrugged, pulling their hands calmly from their pockets.

I wanted the deviant nowhere near me but I could cope with Thean's disdain over Emrys's open concern.

All it took was the slightest nod from me as I pulled in a steadying breath for Emrys to relinquish my care to Thean. The voyav came around the desk, circling me like a vulture in the wastelands. I didn't have the energy to care as my shoulders slumped. Breath too harsh, nausea rolling inside of me as I stared down at my mangled arm. Letting myself fold over my own knees with exhaustion, swallowing back the urge to vomit again. To get the beasts out, let them crawl their way up my throat.

Please, I begged in the back of my mind. Knowing there was nobody to listen. There never had been any ancestors watching me. Nobody to care if it killed me.

Then I felt the tickling brush of something at my cheek, opening my eyes to see a cushion. The tasselled end almost waving at me. I could have lost my mind, or was it just the house mothering me?

I raised my head the barest inch, as the cushion slid beneath me of its own accord. Allowing me to rest my cheek there. A blissful chill from the fabric soothing something inside of me.

Safe.

I was here. Not there. Not in the past with the monsters I'd been forced to become.

'I believed you could be many things, darling; a fool wasn't one of them,' Thean drawled, their voice too soft. Too distant.

'Tell me when they're gone,' I half slurred. Unbothered by what the voyav thought of me as I listened to the clatter and chaos of them work. I just needed a moment. One moment to rest and I could go back to her.

I waited for Thean's sharp ridicule but it never came. No. That brandy and clove smell of them chased away everything else. So close I could feel the warmth from their skin.

'They're gone,' came their voice again and then I let the darkness of exhaustion have me right there on the study floor, imagining someone gently holding my hair back, to see my face. To count my very breaths as if they mattered.

Chapter Five
Kat

Chapter Six
Alma

Be wary of the beast with many forms for it is always on the hunt to consume one more.

A child's voice sang those words into my dreams, cruel laughter trickling through the warning. A child I'd never been allowed to be. Rhymes to mock and strip me. Making me desperate, to cling to the crumbs of my humanity. Wishing my claws could bury themselves deep into it. That my fangs could drink the merest moments of innocence dry.

That I could keep the parts of myself I used to be, but they cut them away effortlessly. With knives too sharp and skilled. Until I was just a girl with no name. Nothing but a pet.

A beast waiting to be fed.

Those memories sat heavy and sour in my gut like bad gruel. Then came the rattle of chain and the burn of copper down my throat. The snap of bone and the searing pain of my flesh as it peeled away to become something else.

I lurched forward, gasping away from the coldness of my nightmare's hold, only to find my wrists captured in soft, warm hands. Halting my escape.

'I must say . . .' Thean Page sighed before me, the usual cruel upturn of their feminine lip absent as they peered down at me. 'I didn't anticipate you having such a flare for the dramatic, darling.'

Their hair was uncharacteristically braided back from their striking face. Showing one of those ancient runes marked on their flesh, tucked behind their ear. Amber eyes gleaming like a calculating cat under their dark lashes, as their fingers curled gently around my forearms. The sharp smell of cloves coming off them that easily chased away the haunting stench of my dreams.

'What are you doing?' Slipped from their grasp, almost stumbling back onto the chaise, a tattered blanket discarded and tangled around my feet. A chaise that wasn't there before. Not in this study. One the house must have manifested.

I'd fainted. Only there was no space for shame as I pressed my clammy palms against my forehead, trying to ease the throbbing pain at my temples.

'Babysitting, clearly.' They turned, returning to their perch by the fire. Those long legs hugged in a pair of riding trousers so tight that it was a miracle the stitches were still intact.

I dropped my hand, only to wince as I moved my arm, finding it covered by a dressing gown sleeve. The fabric thick and luxurious, swamping me. I pulled back the sleeve to see my wrist. Expertly wrapped with clean, white bandages. The dark scales still protruding at the edge of the cotton, not fully settled back into my skin.

The cut across my palm was also wrapped neatly. The sticky sensation of healing balm as the pungency of mint and bitter healing herbs met my nose.

In the firelight I could see the small marks on my skin. My scars. Almost easily missed but I saw every one, the barest shade lighter. Every cut where they'd made me change and took something from me. Every nick of their blade that they hadn't bothered to heal. Allowed to be open too long, forming small divots.

I pulled my sleeve down. Refusing to remember as I looked to the window. Unable to hide my deep swallow of relief. It was barely dusk. I hadn't been unconscious long. Hadn't lost any more time.

'Gideon—' I turned back to Thean, seeing the voyav's elegant hand raised to stop whatever unarticulated rubbish was about to come spilling out from between my lips.

'He's still with the patient.' They rested their elbow on the arm of the chair, perching their chin perfectly on the back of their hand and pursing those full lips. '*You,* darling, had the fortune to be tended to by me.'

Something about being the centre of the voyav's attention felt dangerous as my fingers traced the edge of the bandage, how neat and careful it was. How they'd wrapped it further down my arm than was needed, covering up the mottled, scarred skin of my wrist. My shackle marks. Not out of pity, I was sure.

'I'll commend myself to save you the trouble,' they goaded at my silence. It was only then I realised I was in a dressing gown. Not the trader's coat.

'Who changed me?' I demanded, watching them closely for any hint of a lie. Refusing to be relieved the reeking leather coat was gone.

'Me.' They crossed one ankle over the other with relaxed ease, that smile softening. 'Don't worry, darling. I'm too old to get any enjoyment out of *voyeurism.*'

'Really?' I mocked. It didn't bother me. I'd learnt long ago this skin was nothing but another mask, one of many.

In a moment the voyav was up, across the room and before me again. Breath sweetened with brandy as it stirred the loose dark strands of my hair. That wild thing inside of me rising to the challenge of them. Delighting in it.

'I can slit a man's throat without a shed of moonlight to guide the blade.' That feminine voice was soft with seduction despite the cruelty lacing the words. 'I think I can manage putting you in a robe without looking.'

There was nothing but truth burning in those amber eyes. A smugness about it. As if knowing I wanted them to lie so then I'd have a reason for my anger. Instead, it simmered uselessly inside of me.

For the first time in my life . . . the beasts beneath my skin felt torn. Undecided if they should bite or play. Drawn in by the heady scent of the voyav and the taunting flutter of their pulse, the strong line of their throat.

I retreated before that fucking scent could draw me closer. Could make me stupider. Retreating to Kat's desk. Wanting to put her things back. Wanting to fix one small part of this mess. Needing to move. To be useful.

'No more colourful threats?' The voyav followed. Their soft laughter like a caress down my spine.

'I'm certain Blackthorn has given you enough.' I doubted even they could avoid the darkness of Emrys's moods.

I gathered up Kat's bandages and healing kit. Moving to put it all back in her bag. Only to pause when a small metal tin caught my eye. Her healing salve – her favourite one.

How often she'd dab it onto my kitchen burns. The peppery scent of it stinging my nose as she rambled about some cursed book she'd been reading.

My thumb dragged over the rough paper label, singed at the edges with more evidence of her carelessness with a flame. A knot of emotion threatened to seal my throat as I curled the tin in my fist, nails scraping against the metal.

'He's not as vicious as you, darling,' Thean continued. Making me turn to see where they peered over my shoulder, spying to see what had caught my attention. There was gentle curiosity hidden in their eyes. There were darker specks of amber there too. Like a cluster of autumnal stars. 'You had no chance of hiding that.'

'Alma!'

William's voice echoed down the hall and into the room. Making me jerk back from the voyav's lure. Cursing as I darted towards the door on unsteady legs, grabbing onto the frame to propel myself into the hallway only to almost collide with the boy. His eyes were wide, freckled face flushed and a bright beaming smile on his lips as his dishevelled hair knotted around his horns.

'Go and see.' He grabbed my sleeve, tugging me up the first three steps. 'Gideon wants you.'

I didn't allow myself to think. Bunching up my robe and taking the stairs two at a time, leaving the boy behind, I rounded the corner at the top. Only to skid to a halt as I found Emrys standing in the doorway of his room. Arm braced against the frame perhaps to stop himself from entering, a taut tension in his shoulders as if it took everything within him not to.

He pulled back at my arrival, the angles of his face sharper in the shadow of the hallway. An oddness clung to him, making me and the beasts beneath my skin wary once more.

Curse Kat. The one time she decided to take an interest in anything other than a bloody book and he was darkness incarnate. *Verr* – and probably a hundred other forsaken fucking things besides.

'Let me see,' he ordered quietly, moving towards me. His hand extended politely for my bandaged arm, fingers still black-tipped and veined with the evidence of what he was.

That thing I shouldn't trust.

'It'll be better soon enough,' I offered instead, tucking my arm carefully close to my side as he came to a stop in front of me. He didn't lower his hand. Just waited patiently. It was then I remembered something else, as I saw those horrid, bruised marks on his face I'd made.

Hate is a poisonous thing, Kat had said once, reminding herself of it after another cruel examination by the Council. Another attack she had no defence against. Another piece of proof of why this world wasn't worth saving.

I didn't hate him. Couldn't when I knew Kat trusted him. When she felt things so deeply for him. *Stupidly* perhaps.

But right now, I didn't like him. Nor the secrets he kept. Yet, if he was responsible for this then so was I. We both should have taken better care of her.

I gave him my arm. Pretending I didn't care how strange and beastly it was.

A thousand excuses cluttered my tongue but none could escape the tightness of my lips. 'Did it work?'

He gave the barest nod, his jaw tense as his eyes moved reluctantly back to the doorway he'd left watch of. 'Gideon sees an improvement but there is too much we don't know about the venom.'

'She'll make it.' The words felt childish from my lips. Impossible.

I could see the pain in his solemn grey eyes, how haunted he was by hope, the cruel temptation of it. How mortal he seemed with it. Despite how I knew he was anything but, how the room creaked with the warning of the cursed magic trapped beneath his skin.

I didn't know all the stories. Not of the Verr and the curses beneath. Couldn't understand most of them but I knew it cost

51

him to be close to that darkness. He'd paid it for Kat and I couldn't hate him for that.

Then my gaze caught on those unhealed marks made by my claws. The memory of William's desperate screams in my ears. Shame burnt through me, cold and sickly at the thought of all the horrid things I'd said. How they'd scraped at my throat on their way out as if splintered with glass.

'Here.' I held the small tin of salve between us, still curled in my other hand. The only peace offering I was willing to give. 'Those marks will upset her when she wakes.'

I wouldn't say sorry. I was too much of a proud bitch for that. No matter how my chest ached with the weight of my guilt. The discomfort from where it sat, heavy against my ribs.

The shame that I'd always bite before I'd listen. Something in me too broken to be fixed. Too sharp to be soft.

'She'll be waiting for you.' He took the small tin from me. His thumb tracing the label she'd written just as mine had. Not dismissing my gratitude but not accepting it either. Just leaving it there between us.

She'd be waiting for him too. Like the fool she could be.

A fucking *Verr* – of all the creatures she could choose to keep. Yet, how could I fault her. She'd kept me too.

He hesitated for a moment more. Fist curling around the tin, darkness seeping between his knuckles like smoke before he left me there. The house releasing a quiet, sad groan

I made it to the bedroom. A thousand thoughts racing through my head, a humming like bees trapped within my skull as I forced myself forward.

Finding the stern form of Gideon standing at the base of the bed, looking through a healing bag that lay open on the ottoman at the base. I didn't make a sound. Couldn't, and yet he still looked up.

52

'Miss Darcy.' He straightened, folding his arms behind his back.

'Emrys said you see an improvement.' I ignored his formality.

'Her pulse is stronger. No more tremors and she hasn't had an adverse reaction to any of the healing tonics.' His words were cautious, with a deep crease of worry at his brow. 'However, I doubt we're out of the woods yet.'

'We'll find something else then,' I answered too sharply for the peaceful quiet in the room. Not allowing him to dampen my hope. Not willing to accept just how fragile my grasp of it was.

He considered me for the smallest of moments and I refused to be ashamed by what he saw. A tired and lost creature. A madwoman with monstrous scales.

'As you said. We're not finished.' He dipped his head in agreement, running his hand through his golden hair, letting it curl between his gloved fingers as those sad blue eyes came back to my own. 'Have some time with her, and then we'll have another look at that.'

He nodded towards my arm, as he moved to leave the room.

'Thean and Emrys already—' I began.

'It's the least I could do,' were his parting words before he left me standing there.

The moment I heard the door click shut, I lunged for the bed. Reaching for her wildly, needing to press my trembling fingers against the skin of her hand. To feel she was real. Warmth brushed my fingertips, the barest flare of heat from her magic like a spark against my skin.

A sob left me, bowing me over as I took hold of her hand. Dropping into the chair next to the bed, tightening my hold on her no matter how it made the wound on my arm sting.

Kat.

Her cheeks were flushed. Breath sliding easily between her lips. The barest flutter of her eyelids, something new that made too many emotions rush through me, fuelling that burning hope inside my chest. Ribs tightening their hold on it like a startled bird so it couldn't escape.

I curled our pinkie fingers together. Holding hers so tightly as I kissed the back of her hand. I cried harder with relief, as I pressed her hand against my cheek, unable to stop the smile that came to my trembling lips.

She pulled in another breath, deep and steady. Each one chasing away the sadness that forever lingered inside of me.

'I'm here,' was all I could say as my head dropped onto the bed. Tightening my hold and hoping she could feel it – wherever she'd wandered to. Letting the sound of her breaths settle me, deep and greedy for life as I let exhaustion have me once more.

Chapter Seven

Kat

Tauria, guardian of the North. Who sang to the heavens and wielded the fire to cleave the earth.

Tauria who showered the world in chaos when she fell. She who burnt first. Teaching her blood that magic holds a price that the divine must pay.

The Ode of Tauria – Unknown

Tauria.

I hadn't given much thought to my death but I never thought I'd have to endure it being mocked by my own name.

There was no peace in the darkness of my dreams. Just that name, haunting me. In the blackness of that abyss came the short smears of colour bleeding through the gloom like an unfinished painting. Too much bitter, sour rot down my throat. Packed too tightly as if I was buried in a grave.

My own.

I could hear the rattling creak of wheelbarrows. Feel the wet press of mud beneath my fingers. Flashes of pallid, grey skin from the bodies hidden beneath Daunton Wood. The icy stiff flesh pressed against my own.

Live, my mother's voice commanded. Turning me to the brush of breath against my ear, only for agony to claw at my body once more – trying to drag me back.

The screeching scream of foul things followed, making me flinch away, only to be comforted by the sharp scent of beasam bark. The cool relief of his magic against my burning skin.

Emrys. I dragged in a breath, wincing as it scraped at my raw throat. Trying to find him in the abyss, curling towards the barest dim flicker of silver, demonic light. A weak grey smudge out of the corner of my eye.

Kat. He called my name so softly, like a blessing or a curse. The phantom brush of his magic around my wrists, weaving between my fingers. Holding on.

The ghost of a caress against my cheek guided me, made breath slip easily through my lips but too swiftly it changed into a vicious agonising bite. Sharp teeth scraping bone that sent an excruciating fire through my veins. My throat too dry to scream.

The copper tang of blood heavy on my tongue, sliding down my throat as I choked and gasped for air.

Live for us, Tauria. My mother's words found me. Joined by distant searching voices, calling my name.

I'm here. I'm here. I wanted to beg but nothing came from between my lips.

Beg. That monster's voice hissed into my ear, the stench of burning flesh so potent I could taste it in my mouth. A razor-sharp blow came across my back, a horrid animalistic sound filling my ears as pain raced up my spine – making my back bow as I lurched into waking, forcing myself to open my eyes.

Live. That command came again as I panted, eyes scanning the dim room. My fingers curled into the damp sheets beneath me. Desperately clinging to consciousness.

Nausea rolled through me as the room span and twisted. Murky smears filled my vision. The dark wood and navy fabric of the bed I lay in.

I rolled to free myself from the covers, only to tumble to the ground. The jarring pain of the impact shooting down my spine, muscles stiff and aching, but the cold polished wood was a relief against my burning skin as I gasped against the floorboards. Digging my nails into the cracks between the boards.

I glanced up through the tangled curtain of my hair, seeing the door blur in my vision. Hearing the muffled taunt of those voices. The gleam of light beneath the door too distant.

Searing heat rolled through me. My magic rising from its slumber with fury. Threatening to engulf me. To crumble me to nothing but ash, slipping easily between the floorboard cracks. Lost for evermore.

Sweat dripped from my temples. Every breath scraped against my lungs painfully. Darkness creeping into the corners of my vision.

I dragged myself forwards desperately. Tangled in my own damp nightdress, anything to reach the door.

Please. Barely a croak escaped my lips, my fingers fumbling with the turning of the doorknob. Needing to escape the nightmare. The door swung free on the third try, taking me with it. I tumbled forwards. Only there was no hallway.

No William or Alma waiting. No Emrys. Nothing but the endless foggy chill of night air. My hands pressed into marshy ground, muddy water sliding between my fingers as a rainstorm hammered down in relentless strikes. Small icy pinpricks against my burning flesh as I knelt in the boggy grass.

The darkness of Blackthorn Forest beckoned in the distance as I tipped my head back to the thunderous sky.

I greedily gulped down the night air. Pressing chilled fingers against my breastbone, letting the rain drip down my front, opening my mouth so the frigid drops could chase away the bitterness of blood and ash on my tongue.

Forgive me. My father's voice whispers against my ear, brought by the harsh winter wind. Then came the memory. The roughness of his beard damp with tears as the mud and grass beneath me shifted to wet sand.

The world broke apart before me, a mix of storm winds, dark smoke and memory. The trees in the distance shifted, bending and bowing like great waves. Until their silver bark became grey sea foam, briny salt thick on my lips.

The north sea. The shores of Tauria.

How viciously the rain pelted my skin – just as it had then, filling my bones with a coldness I'd never lost.

I saw the tall shape of my father in the distance, broad and bold. How effortlessly he moved through those thick waves to the small waiting boat. His hair drenched. The sharp point of his ears visible through it.

'Come back,' the words rasped from between my lips. I tried to get back to my feet but there was nothing but the curtain of rain as it pounded into the earth.

Tauria! The ghost of my mother's voice called behind me, broken with sadness, but I didn't listen as I ran, the sand wet between my toes just as it had been that day, only to stumble on weak legs and fall to my knees. Tumbling back into reality, cold mud biting into my flesh, plastering the fabric of my nightgown to my legs. Panting, I turned. Wildly looking for him through the downpour.

I needed to go back. To tell him not to go.

To stay.

A king's blood, for a king's awakening, came a dark, hissing voice inside my mind. A scream slipping from my lips as agony bit into my neck, making my wet fingers clutch it. I jerked around, waiting to see fangs and claws, yet there was nothing but the house behind me, and the dark night.

Blackthorn Manor was an imposing shadow in the distance with bright yellow light cutting a path through the gloom towards me like a clawed hand reaching out with spread fingers.

How far I'd run. How awfully my limbs ached. No beast from the pit lingered there. It was in my head. It was madness.

My nightmares had followed me here.

'Wake up,' I begged helplessly. Uselessly. Trying to pinch my own skin, but the rain made it too slick, the icy chill freezing me in place.

Then that rainwater simmered as it gathered in my muddy palms.

Murderer, screamed though my head, a sharp ache against my temples. Making me clutch my hair as I lurched backwards. Trying to escape, but the long-wet grass suddenly became charred hands that grasped and curled around my limbs. Pulling me down to the earth, trying to bury me whole.

I kicked and fought, rolling myself to dig my fingers into the mud. Only for a horrific weight to press into my spine, fingers gripping my hair to wretch my head back. The burning agony of the skin on my back from his brutality.

Foolish little troll.

A half-sobbed scream slipped from my lips as I fought to be free of that weight. Free of Daunton's grip. The phantom lash came against my spine, making me cry out like an animal. A sharp kick to the side rolled me across the wet earth until I landed on my back.

Kat! A voice shouted through the agony but there was nothing before me but darkness and the reek of demonic breath as the galmoth loomed over me in that pit, the press of that claw against my heart.

Kat! Emrys's voice screamed, desperate and real. I wanted to roll towards it but lead filled my veins, pressing me into the soggy earth as I choked on the taste of my own blood. Screwing my eyes shut, willing myself awake.

Tauria. The name came playfully. Soft and filled with the warmth of her love.

My eyes opened to the wooden beams and the thatching of the roof. No charred hands but the heavy warm covers of a bed weighed me down.

My head fell weakly to the side – and there she was.

Her smile soft and playful as she lay next to me, book open in her hands, waiting. Her hair a chestnut disarray. Thick lashes casting shadows against her cheeks. The orange light from the hearth illuminating her beauty. Sharp and inescapable as it made her eyes seem umber.

My mother.

'You're here.' The words were a croaked whisper between my chapped lips, smelling the lavender and healing herbs of her. She was real, she existed for the merest of moments.

She didn't answer. Yet she leant closer, her calloused fingers gently tipping my chin to lay a kiss against my cheek. There was a slight tremble on her lips. As if I'd broken her heart too.

You're not finished yet, my love. Her breath was suddenly as cold as the icy wind against my skin.

Live. I tried to curl my fingers into her hair, but all I met was grass and, in a blink, there was nothing but the bitter night before me.

Alone. The last place I ever wanted to be was alone. The vast bruised sky endless above me, illuminated by white flashes of lightning as the storm raged above.

I choked on a sob, rain running down my throat, thumping ruthlessly against my bruised skin. My neck burnt as if the fangs were still buried deep, the old scars down my back a searing torment of all my mistakes.

'Kat!' came my name again. The prince from beneath. But I couldn't see him.

Pain feasted on me as I curled onto my side, trembling as I gathered my knees to my chest. The barest movement stealing my strength until I became limp and still. That wishing stone before me tangled in the weeds, flickering weakly like a heartbeat.

Real. It was real but I couldn't reach it. Couldn't pull myself back from the abyss as the darkness bit into the corner of my vision.

'Kat!' Desperate and deep like thunder. His voice, just as it had been in that darkness.

I shook my head, pressing my forehead to my knees. It wasn't real.

Serus. Something whispered distantly in my mind. Calm with its darkness. Then I felt the soft bite of his magic brush my skin, curling around my forearms, until the sting of the rain couldn't touch me. Turning me gently – and then he was there.

The cool press of a leather gloved finger caressed my jaw. Tender and restrained. There was a stormy nature to his eyes, shadows beneath them, as was the tension in his jaw as he knelt over me. I was entranced in a moment, how the rain dripped from his hair, turning his shirt sheer as it clung to the muscled contours of him.

Another illusion. One I wanted more than all the others.

'Kat.' There was such agony in the quietness of his voice as his gaze desperately moved over every inch of me.

'I—' Words were too heavy on my tongue, throat too raw with the weight of them. Unable to draw in enough breath to say his name. To call him back to me. Grasping weakly at his shirt; wanting to feel the warmth of him. To hold onto him. Even if he wasn't real.

He pulled me into his arms, as if the sheer size of his form could shield me from the icy pounding rain. The warmth of his skin, the sharpness of that beasam bark scent as my face was tucked against the curve of his throat. Greedy for that promise of reality. That he'd come back for me.

Then I was up in his hold. The rain gone, just the dripping of water as the warm wooden walls of Blackthorn Manor rushed past me. My head lolling back against Emrys's hard shoulder. The ceiling so vast; wooden creatures peering down with sad, concerned faces as we moved through doorways; bells ringing as I was jolted, pain sharp and unforgiving in my limbs.

'Bloody saints!' William's pale, fear-stricken face stumbled into focus. Hair dark and curls flat from the rain as he peered down at me as we continued to move. 'Where was she?!'

'Get Gideon.' Emrys's response was terse in a voice not entirely his own. Every step jolted me with new agony as I winced, clawing at his shirt.

'He's . . . I think he's—' William stumbled over his words, eyes darting desperately to me as if for help.

'Get Thean to deal with him,' Emrys replied through his teeth, not lessening his pace as William vanished. Suddenly there were no hallways or trinkets, just the bed I'd escaped. Sheets soft and warm beneath me as I trembled, my grip on Emrys tight despite the numbness of my fingers. The surge of the fire in the hearth stinging my flesh with its intensity.

'Kat.' My name left him so weakly, weighted with such disbelief, as if I was the illusion and not him. His eyes watching every trembling breath slip through my lips.

'I-it hurts,' I half moaned, unable to stop shaking.

The quiet admission spurred him into motion, one arm still around me as he rooted around the bedside table, curses slipping between his lips. The soft thump of items hitting the floor and rolling across the wood before he came back to me. Coaxing gently with a hand under my chin.

He held a teacup to my lips that caught on my teeth with their chattering. I tried to drink what he offered, even if half of it dripped down my chin. The horrid earthy taste of it made me grimace, gritty on my tongue, but I swallowed. The warmth of it soothing the rawness of my throat. Chasing away the tang of blood and the bitterness of wet earth.

My fingers curled around his wrist, feeling the thrum of his pulse. The restlessness of his magic brushing over me. I tried to drag in a deeper breath, only for it to turn into a retching cough. A horrid rattling in my chest tugging on my ribs and making me wince. Emrys's palm became a firm pressure against my damp back to soothe it away.

A cloth suddenly appeared at my mouth as he wiped away the spilled mess. He was too cautious as he watched me with dark eyes, counting my very breaths until they settled once more.

'I need to get you warm.' A desperation lingered in his voice. It was unlike him. As were the troubled depths of his gaze, flecks of black deepening their colour with his worry.

I wanted to soothe him but I couldn't move. My muscles too knotted with pain.

'Kat?' he asked and it was then I realised he was waiting for permission.

I nodded weakly, trying my best to turn towards him. Then my wet ruined nightgown was gone with clinical efficiency, to be replaced with soft, warm towels against my skin, wrapping around me before I was buried beneath the heavy covers, thick socks on my feet as I curled into a ball beneath the weight and warmth of it all. My fingers moved, sluggish but greedy as I found his gloved hand beneath the tangled bedding.

The leather damp but I didn't let go. Desperate to stay here with him. With the sharp authority of his magic as it wrapped itself around my wrists, seeking more of me, pressing itself between my fingers.

I relished in the drag of it against my skin. Knowing nothing could touch me here. Even my own demons. He wouldn't let them. Just as he'd promised.

The fingers of his other hand tangled in my wet hair, combing it out from where it had knotted around my neck. I let my head turn on the pillow, looking up at him as he leant over me, like some ancient wyvern guarding a prize. A flare of my lavender pierced the pitch-black of his eyes. The shadows played against the sharp angles of his handsome face.

'You came back.' His words were so soft I almost missed them in the crack of the fire.

'You—' The dryness of my throat stole the words, but under the rawness of emotion in his gaze I forced the rest out. 'You asked me to stay.'

How tense the strong line of his jaw was, how weighted with pain his expression had become as he looked down at me. Unable to stop touching me but hesitant at the same time.

'Kat.' My name slipped from his lips, his resolve crumpling as his forehead came to rest against my own. Breath unsteady as his fingers curled gently against the nape of my neck. As if I was something too delicately precious.

I wanted him to be real. Wanted to say a hundred things to him in this dream. This strange gift from the ancestors. A moment of calm in my agony.

His touch numbing that pain inside of me and putting my demons to rest so I could sink into the warmth of the bed.

You came back. His words followed me into the peaceful quiet of sleep but my mother's voice was there too. Waiting, as if fearful I'd forget.

Live, Tauria.

Chapter Eight
Kat

Serus.

The first prince of the dark, created of the depths of the Old Gods' magic and moonlight. Manifesting with pale, forsaken demon fire. Who wielded an ancient shadow sword, the only blade that could challenge the fire of a Kysillian's. The King who never was. The Old Gods' weapon.

Myth of the Old Gods – Unknown

Serus.

Tales that never mattered before haunted me now. The Verr histories they said were nothing but dark fairy tales. All the things that should never have been forgotten.

My moments of consciousness were a fleeting blur. A tangle of dreams and madness. Alma's rumbling purr against the crook of my neck from her feline form. The rustling of pages and the endless stories of plant herbs and common weeds echoed into my dreams from William. Then there was the annoyed grumbling of a voyav as if bored with the drama of my death.

The image that came most clearly to my mind was the dark form of Emrys slumped in the chair at my bedside. Head bowed, dark hair falling onto his brow. Hand still resting on the covers as if he'd been holding my own. Those dark-tipped fingers, shadows weaving between his knuckles. That small crescent moon at his index finger. How he was reaching out for me in the moonlight-drenched bedroom – just as he had in that pit. Pressed flat against the bloody ashen earth, reaching for me, desperate and pleading.

Stay and forgive me.

Please.

The pain in that plea. I wanted to reach for him, to wake him, but this was still a dream. So I used the last of my strength to slide my fingers so gently between his own. That dark power brushing my skin in comfort as if to hold me tighter.

'Shh.' The groggy sound left my lips as those shadows sank contentedly back into his pale flesh and exhaustion dragged me down into my dreamless sleep once more. Where that name lingered the most.

Serus.

It was almost on my lips, pulling me back into the discomfort of waking hours later. Limbs too sore and heavy as the dim winter morning light filtered through the window, too much for the pain at my temples. Making me wince as I rolled deeper into the sanctuary of the covers with a muted groan. I expected to see the worried imposing form of Emrys from my dreams. Or Alma. To hear the comforting tones of William's voice.

However, it appeared my misfortunes would continue.

Thean Page was the first thing I saw, slouched in a wing-backed chair next to the bed, feet up on the counterpane as they rubbed an apple on the lapel of their pristine, fawn-coloured hunting coat. Short auburn hair brushed back from their handsome face, eyes heavily lined with dark make-up despite the masculine form they'd chosen this morning. The white shirt creased and unbuttoned halfway to reveal their sun-kissed skin and the runes painted there.

'Maybe you should check your heritage.' They smiled sharply enough to show fangs, unsurprised to see me awake despite the fact I was certain I was dead. 'I didn't believe Kysillians were this resilient.'

We aren't. The distant memory of a stormy night in the long grass came back to me, uncertain if it was last night or days ago. Emrys's anguish and William's worry, the biting cold and the madness.

'What do you want, Thean?' I groaned, my head resting heavily on the pillow.

'I'm merely here for curiosity,' they answered with the biting crack of the apple, 'to see how long this madness can last.'

Madness.

Kysalor. The power of one word to remind me so vividly of every failure. Shame rolled through me. I'd lost control.

How that seal had shattered like delicate glass beneath my bare bloody feet. That dark smoke forming claws. Pulling me down and clawing at my flesh. Refusing to let me go. Starved of its vengeance.

Tears burnt my eyes as I focused on the midnight fabric above the bed, the dark wood and the intricacy of the carving. Noticing this wasn't my room, the strong scent of beasam bark and the familiar seductive chill of the remnants of his magic. Making something uncertain swoop through me.

The memory of falling into the same bed. The cage of Emrys's body around me, the seductive drag of his lips up the curve of my throat.

This was Emrys's room.

Thean continued with their apple, unbothered by my sudden flush of memory. I turned my head, wanting to tell them to leave. Only to see their attention on the fire, revealing a horrid purple smear of bruising on their sharp jaw.

'What happened to your face?' I frowned and tried to prop myself higher up on the mound of pillows behind me. Those sharp eyes turned back to take me in with barely contained annoyance.

'Ask your dark prince.' Irritation flashed in their expression. Fingers gently tracing the injury before falling back into their lap. 'He clearly isn't amused by my humour where you're involved. Then again, if you were attempting to lead him into madness, rolling around in your nightgown in the rain certainly worked.'

Their smile was wicked, as their head fell back against the chair so they could shift their focus to the open doorway.

It was then I realised they hadn't been waiting for me to wake up. No. They'd been waiting for someone else.

A moment later Alma appeared in the doorway. Her dark hair in unfamiliar disarray.

'What are you doing?' A stack of towels dropped from her arms with her surprise of seeing the voyav. Landing in a heap at her feet, she ignored them, gathering up her grey skirts to stumble over the mess, striding right for Thean. A menace in each step that I knew too well, a flush on her darker skin.

'Helping,' Thean reassured her, folding their arms as if excitedly readying themself for whatever performance she was about to offer. That the claws beginning to sprout from her fingertips were for amusement, not warning.

'You can't be in a ladies bedchamber!' She leered over the voyav's larger masculine form, hands braced on her hips.

'This is *Emrys's* room, darling,' Thean pointed out wryly.

'It's improper.' Scales peppered her cheeks at the challenge.

Thean's grin sharpened and in the mere blink of an eye, their male form shifted easily until the female one took its place. Long luscious hair cascading over their shoulders as they

69

fluttered long lashes, the low buttoning of the blouse almost revealing full breasts.

'Better?' they asked, eyes gleaming with delight as Alma's face only got redder, bumpy green ridges rising at her throat.

'If you want to be *disembowelled*, carry on,' Alma ground out between fanged teeth, one finger pointed in a warning that ended with a deadly sharp claw.

'Careful, darling, you might arouse me,' Thean teased, and I saw a slight tremor up Alma's spine. As if she was about to leap out of her dress and make good on her promise.

'Alma.' I reached for her across the covers.

She froze. An unsteady breath slipped from between her lips before she turned cautiously, hesitant as if she could have imagined my voice. The barest tremble in her hands where they fell limply to her sides as those bright green eyes met my own.

So human and lost. How she stared at me blankly for the longest moment, as if she didn't recognise me. I felt like she wouldn't. As if I'd been unmade and pushed back together in all the wrong places.

'Kat.' It was the barest whisper. I felt the sting of my tears, the tremble of my lip as I tried to smile. That broke the spell over her as tears rolled down her own cheeks.

'Kat!' She tripped over Thean's sprawled legs as she grabbed my hand and clambered onto the bed. Not giving me a moment before she crushed me against her chest. Sobbing softly against my neck, her whole body shaking in my weak hold. She'd lost weight, too small and thin in my arms.

'You bloody bastard madwoman,' she wept. I felt the sharp dig of her claws into my back. Not caring for the discomfort. She was here.

Stay right here with me. Another command I'd followed long ago from her lips.

70

A memory coming to the forefront of my mind. Alma's small face covered in soot and blood. Filthy hair singed as she shivered in the darkness of the burning wood. Fat snowflakes clinging to her lashes as she pressed snow against my burning flesh.

Go, I'd begged, knowing they'd come after I'd killed Daunton. That it wouldn't be long until they found us. How they'd never let us go.

How she'd huddled over me, shielding me from the snow in nothing but her nightgown, letting my head rest in her lap. How tears made tracks across her filthy cheeks. The map of bruising across her skin up to her brow. So thin and small.

I'm staying right here with you, she'd answered. Her fingers finding my own, despite what my hands had done. How my skin still burnt.

How easily I'd killed them. The last time I'd lost control of my flame. When I'd turned our nightmares to ash.

The memory made emotion burn in my throat. How ruthless I'd been then. How foolish I'd been now. How she'd remained all the same. How easily I'd ruined everything once more.

'I'm so sorry, Alma.' My voice broke.

'Never leave me again,' was her answer as she laid a kiss on my tear-dampened cheek. Not a threat or a command. A gentle request as she pulled herself back the barest inch to look over her shoulder at Thean, whose gaze was on her backside, which was in their face.

'Make yourself useful and go and fetch something,' she snapped, wiping at the tears on her cheeks with irritation. 'Master Swift or some food, perhaps?'

Thean scowled in response, then gracefully got to their feet. Looking down at our display of affection with a blank expression, lips parting probably to deliver a cruel remark but Alma's attention had returned to fretting over me.

Thean vanished without another word.

'You need to rest. Gideon said it's been centuries since anyone has been treated with ravhorn venom.' Her hands ran down my arms, as if checking to see if I'd sprouted new ones. It was then I realised I was wearing a clean nightgown. Part of me wondering if the storm had been another dream. But as I looked at my fingers I could see the remnants of dirt in the creases between my fingers, beneath my nails.

Real.

It was only then that the words she'd spoken pierced my thoughts.

'Gideon?' I frowned.

'Healer Gideon Swift. Emrys brought him back to the house to help. Bloody bastard is—' She cut herself off, shaking her head as she gently tried to press me back onto the pillows. 'Never mind that. It's best you lie down. I don't know if you should be awake. I'll get you some—'

I noticed the hesitation in her movements, the shadows beneath her eyes, and the bandage peeking out from the sleeve of her dress. Then her words penetrated my tiredness.

Ravhorn.

The ravhorn was extinct.

'Alma.' I reached for her arm, turning it so I could see it better. The bandage covering the remains of what she had become. The violent bruising around it. 'What did you do?'

She pulled easily from my weakened grip, tucking her arm behind her back, turning to the bedside table, struggling to find anything to distract me with.

'Alma.' I leant forward despite the pain in my ribs that shortened my breath. 'What did—'

'It's nothing compared to what you did.' Her eyes were filled with tears but burnt with the intensity of those words.

Stilling me. That hollow pain in my chest of all the things that should have never come to pass. Why she was afraid of changing. Why her magic was hard to control, because they'd made her fear it. Used it to hurt her.

Yet she'd changed. Changed into something too dark to speak of. She'd done it for me.

'You could have been hurt,' I whispered, unable to stop the rawness of my fear as it consumed me. The thought of her being something so dark. That she might not be able to find her way back. Forever lost in one of her forms.

'If you wish to blame anyone for that recklessness . . . blame yourself. You taught me.' There was a steel to those words. Unbreakable. I taught her friendship. Taught her kindness too. She'd always said that. From the start.

Nothing will hurt you again. My promise to her that now filled me with sorrow, because I'd lied. I'd hurt her.

'Alma.' My voice broke around her name.

'I was so scared.' The words were raw from her lips as she pulled in a stuttered breath. 'I didn't know what to do, Kat. I'm not smart like you.'

I reached for her hand, barely having to as she half fell into my arms. 'That's not—'

'I didn't know what to do,' she admitted again and all I could do was hold her. Hold her as her perfectly formed defences crumpled. The admission was so small yet filled with so much fear.

'I'm sorry,' I breathed into her hair, sadness clawing at my heart as I ran my hand up and down her back. 'For all of it. But you're wrong. There isn't anyone as clever as you, Alma.' I ran my fingers through her dark curls as she pulled back to see me. So she could see the truth of it in my eyes.

I wasn't her saviour. Alma had saved herself and she'd saved me too.

A shiver went through me before she could argue with my declaration, her fingers instantly running around the collar of my nightgown – jolting her back into action.

'You must have had night sweats again.' She pursed her lips. 'Let's get you cleaned and changed.'

I instantly regretted my stubbornness in forcing myself to sit up. Clearly deceiving her into thinking I had more energy than I did. She untangled me from the covers and moved me to the edge of the bed, quickly laying out warm towels, and brought a steaming bowl of water. Then she set about getting me out of my damp nightgown.

I sat obediently, ignoring the horrid sudden cramping sensation in my middle as my fingers curled into the sheets and I let my eyes close. The motion of just sitting up exhausted me. Too weakened by everything that had come before.

'I'll get you another tonic.' Alma ran her hand through my hair before she quickly braided it to stop it tangling.

I could only nod weakly. Numb fingers trying to catch hers in the barest brush of thanks. How effortlessly she took care of me despite how foolish I could be. Fatigue wearing too heavily on my limbs. Understanding the pain was another way for my body to tell me how far I'd pushed it. Almost punishing me for my recklessness.

She managed my clumsy limbs effortlessly as she towelled me off only for my focus to fall to my bare thigh, seeing the curving streak of scar on the delicate inner skin. A vicious mark, still puckered from healing. My fingers dragged over the raised texture. How strangely cold it was.

Kyvor Mor. That creature's voice hissed in the back of my mind. The glee in its torment. The phantom agony of its claw digging into my thigh making me wince.

The warmth of Alma's hands gently brought me back as she tried to put me in another nightgown, only for her to see where my focus had fallen.

'It looks better than it did,' she reassured me. 'Emrys stopped the bleeding, but he had to revert to mortal practices. He was too fearful there were shards left inside.'

A grief clung to her words as she pulled the nightgown over my head. Perhaps it was a mercy that I didn't remember any of it. Yet they all did. What Emrys had done to try to save me.

My fingers moved to the side of my throat, feeling uneven, cold skin there too. Remembering the ache of where the galmoth had bitten me.

Alma caught my hand, curling it into the safety of her own grasp. 'The galmoth left a scar. It's better than it was. Emrys said it should be less noticeable in a few weeks.'

Her reassurance was small and weighted with too much grief. Grief I'd given to her.

'He isn't here.' The words slipped too painfully from my lips. A crushing weight to them. Remembering he was calling for me.

'He was,' she sighed, worry creasing her brow as she fixed the nightgown around me, before gently bullying me back under the covers. 'Get comfortable and I'll try to read some of those hideously boring soil books William left.'

I wanted to laugh, but a small broken sound escaped my lips as she tucked the covers around me.

'I'm sorry,' I whispered. Sorry for my foolishness. For making too many mistakes. For being incapable of keeping her safe.

'Enough of that,' she chided, brushing her lips against my forehead. 'You're here. You're safe. That's all that matters.'

Yet as exhaustion weighted my limbs and consciousness drifted away, fear dug its claws into my heart that those words were a lie. They had to be.

Chapter Nine

Kat

The dark calls all things back in the end.

I could taste bitter earth. Feel the phantom sting of a blade across my throat. The agony as it cut to the bone. The burning scrape of that darkness against my skin.

A horrid scream.

Emrys.

His roar of agony as that darkness tore him open.

The warm splatter of his blood. Claws ripping through his heart. Seeking something within.

You thought you could keep him, Tauria? A dark voice hissed against the shell of my ear. Lurching me into waking once again. A horrid repetitive fate I'd found myself in. Nothing before me but the darkness of the night. Alone in this room.

Moonlight seeped through the curtains, casting strange dark shapes across the floor that seemed to move out of the corner of my eye. My heart pounded, sweat dripping from my temples as my fists clutched the sheets. Seeing things that weren't there. Haunted by the phantom sting of a blade across my throat. The agony as it cut to the bone deep in that pit. All the fey that had died there before. Every single one remained with me even now. Just as those in Daunton had.

The covers suddenly felt too heavy. Trapping me.

I pushed them off, my legs almost folding beneath me as I slid off the bed. Reminding me just how weak I'd become.

Thankfully, the house took pity on me. The lamps in the room flared to life with a comforting glow. Chasing those shadows away as my fingers curled around the bedpost. Pressing my forehead against the cool wood, trying to steady my breath.

'Thank you,' I whispered, dragging the robe from the foot of the bed and pulling it on, having to take two breaks on my short walk to the door. But I needed to move, to prove to myself I could get away.

The house groaned and creaked in question.

'I'm fine,' I smiled weakly, ignoring the twinge at my ribs as I made my way to the door that the house opened without complaint.

However, instead of the hallway, I entered a room I'd never seen before. One the house clearly wished for me to see now. Small and circular as if it sat at the top of a tower. Thick wooden beams above me, with dried herbs hanging from rope as if we were in the garden of a witch's den. The air thick with potent magic and fresh ink.

One large table sat at its centre, cluttered in the same manner as all the other tables in the house; the walls lined with shelves stacked too high and bookcases bursting with dusty tomes and scrolls.

My gaze fell on the books left open on the table. The dark shadows painted on the page. Verr stories and ancient symbols all tangled together within the illustrations. It was in my hands before I could think better of it, cracked leather cool beneath my palms as I considered the words written there. Writings of witchcraft and the dark arts of their alchemy.

The princes of beneath. Nightmares and endless darkness hungry to feast.

The sound of someone clearing their throat made the book slip from my palms, crumpling the papers on the desk as I turned to see an unfamiliar figure filling the doorway behind me. His dark blonde hair tousled, a frown on his strikingly handsome face as if burdened with worries beyond his age.

A coat was draped over one arm, his white shirt wrinkled and untucked, his hands filled with leather-bound volumes. There was something familiar about him. About the inquisitive sharpness of his magic. The sad, almost otherworldly nature to his haunting blue eyes. Eyes I'd seen in the portrait hanging above the stairs and a face I'd seen in the Council records. Wondering if now I was seeing ghosts too.

'Gideon Swift.' The name slipped carelessly from my lips, lingering in the quiet, magic-singed air between us.

'Miss Woodrow,' was his simple, unsurprised and inexpressive greeting. As if we'd met before, or he had stumbled upon half-dead women in their dressing gowns all the time. 'You shouldn't be out of bed.'

I picked up the book I'd dropped, smoothing the papers with my trembling fingers. 'Nobody stopped me.'

Liar. Alma would have skinned me alive – and from the sharp look the healer gave me, he knew that.

'I should be surprised you've got the energy to try to escape again but Kysillians are known to be . . . unyielding.' He dropped the books he carried and his coat onto the table between us with little care, a low stoop to his shoulders. 'Even when faced with the challenge of death, it seems.'

'I don't feel unyielding.' No, the taste of failure was bitter on my tongue as another sharp cramp came at the base of my spine, making me brace my hands on the table's edge.

He eyed me with something between concern and irritation as he pushed the hair back from his forehead. Only his hand wasn't made of flesh. . . but golden metal.

It was intricately carved, a faint glow bleeding from between the gaps in the small mechanisms that made up the finger, knuckle and wrist joints.

Blessed metal. The same compound that created Kysillian steel from beneath the sacred mountains high in the north called Lae'mor. Its golden hue was unmistakable. My magic rose inquisitively in response, just as it would for my sword. Sensing something so familiar.

'That's blessed metal.' I instantly regretted my curiosity as he flinched, his whole body going rigid. He dropped his hand, trying to hide it behind his back, his eyes scanning the mess of papers between us before they landed on a discarded glove that had seen better days.

'Sorry,' I added quickly, shamed by my prying.

'*Car Lorve.*' The Kysillian word fell easily from his lips as he pushed his hand into the glove, flexing his fingers before pressing it close to his side. As if he could conceal the truth of it. 'Came in quite handy when I lost my arm and half my leg in the north fields.'

I winced at the ease of how he said those words. The north fields massacre had been the last of the Mage King's battles.

Car Lorve – metal weaving in Kysillian.

'All the magic smiths have been dead two centuries.' I frowned, the last Mage King had tried to revive the art in order to take the north from rebel hands, to reach the northern mountain pass and the fey elders that resided beyond, with all the ancient magic they guarded. Imbuing metal or any natural resource with magic was a dangerous art and one that had deadly consequences – consequences most of his men discovered too late.

'Emrys sourced what was needed and found the final parts in the cellars beneath the house. Blackthorn lords have a useful tendency to hoard, it seems.' He rolled his wrist, the slight whirr of the metal muffled beneath the glove. 'He did his best but the mechanisms tend to misbehave.'

'I didn't know there were cellars beneath the house.' I frowned, only for a drawer in the sideboard behind Gideon to bang as if the house was excited.

'I wouldn't get curious,' Gideon warned, pressing his knuckles to the drawer to stop its rattle, as if silencing an overexcited child. 'The old witch who made it left traps down there and I'm certain some of the locks are due to expire in the next century.'

'That doesn't worry you?' I grimaced as a tugging ache came at my ribs. Making me wonder if I was due another tonic.

'You seem to be in some discomfort,' he observed, ignoring my question.

'I'm fine,' I lied. No matter the discomfort. I didn't want to go back into the dark of that room. Not to sleep. Not to see all the things I couldn't change. 'Thank you for your concern.'

He considered me with mild irritation. As if he was tired with my presence but didn't have the energy to dismiss me. However, he was mistaken in thinking his annoyance was the worst I'd experienced. 'I see from Thean's *irritating* observations you've a habit of causing trouble. I wonder what great offence my brother committed to be burdened with such a problematic partner mage.'

'I received my partnership on merit, Master Swift,' I corrected. No matter how much I doubted the truth in my own words.

'Of course.' He smiled, eyes falling to the stone around my neck that had tumbled free of my dressing gown.

My hand itched to move and hide the gift, but I curled my fingers into the fabric of my dressing gown instead. Refusing to be goaded. Ignoring the pounding of my heart, and the flutter of something in my stomach at the memories of Emrys giving it to me. Seeing its light reflected in his eyes as he'd kissed me in that bed.

'That stone once belonged to Asterin Everard. She was the first witch of the Blackthorn. The one whose soul created this very house to keep those of her blood safe.'

A flush of embarrassment came to my cheeks. At the importance of it, and why Emrys had given it to me, but I swallowed down the emotion, refusing to be lulled into more foolishness.

'Some records refer to it as the Blackthorn star. Quite an impressive gift to bestow on a simple *partner mage*. Wouldn't you say, Miss Woodrow?'

'You can call me Kat.' I tipped my chin, refusing to be provoked. 'Emrys decided I needed all the help I could get.'

A humourless laugh slipped from his lips. 'You'll find most protections fickle in the presence of my brother. You can take me as an example.'

Brother? Only it didn't seem real. Especially since this man looked nothing like Emrys, acted nothing like him and neither did his magic. It was uncomfortable, sharp and prodding. Demanding to know things with its irritable pinching.

He dropped into the only chair in the room not cluttered. 'How do you feel? Magic madness is said to have consequential effects, especially on the mind and control of blood magic.'

'Fine,' I answered. Not trusting myself to say more.

His frown deepened with his frustration. 'Surely a woman as intelligent as yourself knows not to lie to a healer, Miss Woodrow.'

'Kat,' I corrected again, getting the sense he was using the formality to annoy me.

Gideon muttered to himself, and began to tidy the table before him. 'Refrain from using your summoning flame for the *foreseeable*. We're uncertain of the limits of the venom, or if your blood will fully accept the healing.'

'If it doesn't?'

'As Emrys and your *vicious* little companion say, we'll find something else.' There was a heavy weight of exhaustion to his words. He held out two vials he uncovered from beneath a stack of papers. They looked like the ones Emrys had given me for Alma.

'What are these for?' I frowned, letting the warm vials roll across my palm.

'Miss Darcy – Emrys did a fine job of complicating the incantation Emmaline wrote. That should settle Miss Darcy's changes more efficiently and make them easier to recover from. Also . . . it should speed up the recovery of her arm.'

Her arm. I almost flinched thinking of how much pain she must have been in. Pain she'd endured for me.

'Thank you.' Shame made my voice thick. At all the trouble I'd caused. 'Thank you for helping her.'

'If you wish to repay me, go back to bed.' He rubbed his jaw with his gloved hand and leant back in his chair. 'You're troublesome enough without wandering the house. Emrys is due to return from another futile attempt to distract the Council. I don't think I can face another evening of his scolding . . . especially fucking *sober*.'

How easily I'd forgotten what had passed, lost within my own nightmares. The Council, Lord Percy and Fairfax. My stomach plummeted with dread. 'Distract the Council from what?'

'*You*.' His reply was so matter of fact. So simple and yet it was like a sharp slap to cold skin. Unease straightened my back as I reached for my magic inside myself but instead found nothing but that endless silence. It saw no threat here and I wasn't in a rush to rouse it from its slumber.

'Gideon!' William's voice shrieked into the room. Spinning me towards it with such speed I almost tripped over my own feet. Gideon lunged from his chair, reaching across the table to grab my bicep just as the stricken boy came skidding into the room, panting for breath with rosy cheeks and knocking a small stack of papers off the sideboard with his hurry. 'Kat's gone mis—'

His wide brown eyes landed on me, going impossibly wider as he straightened. Pressing a hand over his heart and sucking in a deep, relieved breath.

'I appear to have located her,' Gideon answered wryly, releasing my arm. 'Against my will.'

I don't think William heard him.

'Bloody saints, Kat.' The boys smile wobbled on his lips as he looked over me with disbelief, before throwing his arms around me, his breath not quite steady under the crushing pressure of his embrace as we tumbled backwards a step. I couldn't help the small laugh that slipped free – no matter how it tugged painfully at my ribs – as I pressed my palms against his back, holding onto him.

'Hello, William.' I used my finger to untangle a curl from around his horn, finding a small dry leaf stuck there from his work.

He tipped his head back, tears in those warm brown eyes as his smile wobbled on his lips. 'You're back.'

I swallowed down the emotion building within me. How stupid I'd been and how he deserved to suffer none of it.

'I feel much better. I just wanted to stretch my legs.' I ignored the weight of the lie as he pulled back, rubbing his cheeks with an embarrassed flush, realising my state of undress.

Only the minute William stepped back to release me, a weakness ate into my bones, almost buckling my knees.

'Easy!' William cried out, arms coming around me as if I was an oversized doll he was attempting to carry.

'I'll be all right.' I flushed, grasping onto his shoulders and trying to find my balance.

'The bloody house shouldn't have let you out,' Gideon cursed, striding around the table. The floor raised to trip him on his way to help William, forcing him to stumble as he took my arm once more, the cupboards rattling as the jars inside clinked as if in reprimand. 'Fuck's sake,' he cursed again at the floor. 'Behave.'

'Come on. Let's get you back to bed,' William huffed, taking a firm hold of my other arm. 'Gideon, don't fight with the house. It's still annoyed about you ripping up the east flooring.'

'Why would you do that?' I demanded, turning to look at the healer. Concerned as to why he'd go so far out of his way to annoy the house.

Gideon kept his gaze ahead, jaw tight with displeasure, clearly keeping his disagreements with the house to himself. I wanted to press for more but then I realised they were both guiding me back into the hall. Back to bed.

You gave your blood too freely, little troll. A dark, horrid voice mocked in the back of my mind. The memory of that pit, waiting to devour me as I slept.

'I don't want to go back to bed.' Panic tightened my throat, making the words sound like a squeak from my lips. I was too scared to go back to the nightmares. To remember, digging my heels into the hardwood floor – jarring them both.

'You need to rest, Kat,' William tried to reassure me as they continued to guide me through the door.

'The house also needs to stop—', Gideon choked on his words. 'You *interfering menace!*'

I looked up. We weren't in the bedroom. The house had taken us to the study.

A relieved breath escaped me before I filled my lungs again with the familiar and comforting smell of books. The stacked bookcases. Pointed arches and decorative carvings instantly putting me at ease. How low the fire sat in the hearth, the wooden carved griffins peering down from the beams above in curiosity.

Home.

'Let's sit you down anyway,' William offered nervously, eyes moving to Gideon whose jaw was clenched so tight I worried if he'd have any teeth left as he glared at the ceiling.

William dutifully guided me to a chaise before the fire – one that had never been there before and was oddly cleared of any clutter.

'I'll be fine here for a little while,' I tried to reason as William helped me sit. The cushions rearranged themselves behind my back at the house's command as a thick blanket slid off the arm and across my lap.

'I'll be the bloody judge of that,' Gideon huffed, moving to rifle thought his desk like an ill-tempered thief.

The house gave a clatter of the desk drawers in answer. Clearly unbothered by Gideon's annoyance.

'You do look pretty awful, Kat,' William added, biting his lip anxiously as he fussed with the blanket on my lap.

'Thank you, William.' I grimaced, as another biting twinge consumed my side. Then Gideon was back in front of me, a murky vial of liquid in his hand.

'Drink all of it.' He uncorked it, making me almost retch at the stench, like rotten eggs. Even William went a bit green. The healer's eyes narrowed, anticipating resistance from me.

I could have refused, only I had a horrid feeling Gideon Swift would have no issue with plugging my nose and forcing the mixture down my throat like I was a petulant child. I decided to save William from the harrowing sight.

I took the vial and did as I was told. Thankfully, it tasted far better than it smelt. Finding the mixture sweet on my tongue.

'Well done, Kat.' William grinned. 'I can make you some nettle tea, that'll help with—'

Only he didn't get to finish.

A gentle teasing shiver ran down my back, like fingers tracing my spine. The light of the fire dipped. A rush of footsteps turned us all to the doorway.

And there he was.

His hair was in dark disarray, shadows cutting across his jaw. There was a breathless dishevelment about him, his coat half-unbuttoned. As if he'd run all the way here. That rich scent of beasam bark filled my lungs in an instant – or maybe it was simply the memory of it.

Emrys.

A sadness lingered in his features – and it broke my heart. He was alert, as if some great threat was about to befall us. Endless dark eyes focused on nothing but me.

Tauria. The softness of how he'd called my name made a quiet sob come to my lips. I could see the image of him pressed flat against the bloody, ashen earth, his arm reaching for me as his mouth moved, desperate and pleading. Screaming something over that firestorm.

Me. He was calling for me.

'William, I think you left some west herb stewing on the stove.' Gideon cleared his throat.

'No, I didn't—' William barely finished before Gideon took the scruff of the boy's shirt, pulling him towards the door in a forced march, a clumsy scuffle that Emrys didn't seem to notice.

No. Nothing broke his focus on me. Such a stillness to him I didn't think he even dared to breathe.

You thought you could keep him, Tauria? That dark voice came back. Filling my memory with the torment of his screams. Panic made me try to move, fingers curling over the arm of the chaise.

'Emrys.' His name came broken from my lips as I felt the dampness of tears on my cheeks, breaking the spell over him, and in the blink of an eye he was before me, his gloved hands capturing my face so gently. Thumbs brushing away my tears. Looming over me as I grasped the sleeve of his coat. Desperate to make him reel.

'Kat.' His gaze traced every inch of me. Unbelieving. One hand moved to cup the side of my throat.

Such deep emotion burnt in those eyes as they flicked from black pools to stormy grey. Breath slipping unsteadily from his lips. I held onto him. Desperately.

'You're here,' I half sobbed in my quiet hysteria, forcing myself further into his arms as I pressed my face to his chest and dragged in deep breaths of his forbidden scent. Allowing it to calm that small part of me that still didn't believe it.

'Croinn,' was his only answer, breath unsteady as he crouched before me and wrapped me in the strength of his embrace.

Croinn. The gentleness of that word soothed over some raw place inside of me. The soft reverence of it.

Real.

He'd found me again.

'You should be in bed.' His voice was so hoarse. Pained.

'I want to stay here,' was my muffled response, not wanting to move. As I trembled with exhaustion.

'We can stay here.' His words were soothing, but I couldn't stop the brutal pounding of my heart as panic spiked inside of me.

Serus. That darkness had called. The hunger of it. How viciously it had wanted him.

I pulled back the barest inch to see him. 'H-how long—'

'Thirteen days.' I knew by the raw hurt in those eyes and the tension in his jaw he'd know every moment. Every second if I asked.

Devastation ploughed through me. All that time. How silent my magic was. My hands shook and his shirt slipped from my grasp.

'Kat.'

'I've ruined everything.' The words broke apart on my lips. Breaths too short with terror. What the Council would do. All the things I'd failed to hide. 'I should never have come here. You and William—'

'Don't.' He captured my face once more, so gently. Hurt shadowing his features as if my words were a knife I'd driven into his heart. As if I could mean it. 'Don't say that.'

I shook my head. He needed to understand. 'It's all my fault.'

'No, it isn't, Croinn.' He brushed my lose hair behind my ear as if it was something priceless.

'Gideon said the Council—'

'You don't have to worry about that.' He shook his head, a coldness creeping into his eyes that told me he'd be having words with his brother. 'The Council are too busy trying to find evidence that isn't there.'

'Fairfax . . . the seal.' My fists curled into his shirt.

A soothing sound slipped from him. His fingers curling into my hair. That dark gaze didn't break from my face, seeming to watch every breath. Cautious, as if they could stop at any moment.

'The chamber collapsed. The house with it.'

It couldn't be that simple. My sins couldn't be concealed so easily.

'Was anyone hurt?' I shouldn't care. Not about those horrid people, and yet I couldn't stop.

'You,' he answered without hesitation. As if that was all that mattered. Settling me further into his arms as I dragged in another beasam bark breath, feeling the shy brush of his magic. Cautious as if I wouldn't want it.

A warmth pooled in the pit of my stomach from the tonic as my limbs became weightless.

Kat. My name from his lips. How he had called it over and over. I remembered it. Remembered it tethering to something deep within my chest.

I curled my fingers into the hair at the nape of his neck.

'I heard you. You were calling for me,' I whispered, my words feeling slurred. My tongue too heavy as my eyes kept drooping shut.

'I was.' His voice was quiet, almost unsteady.

Because I'd asked him to. Even if he didn't know the power of that word. He'd done it all the same.

Something in that made me sink back into the warmth of him. The shadows not so dark and the oppressive weight of my fears no longer lingering.

You thought you could keep him, Tauria? That voice kept coming back. Bringing with it the truth that clawed at my heart. How desperately that darkness wanted him. How I knew there would be nothing left of him if it did.

I held him tighter. Feeling the gentle thump of his heart against my cheek and the reassuring brush of his magic.

Real. Here.

He was here with me.

The thought settled me, enough to close my eyes for a moment. Only then I couldn't open them again as I rested more heavily against his chest, but he didn't move. Just kept hold of me.

'Stay,' I whispered instead. 'Stay here with me. Please.'

Here where it was real. If only for this moment.

'Where else would I be, Croinn?' He pressed those words against my temple in a whisper of a kiss. His finger tracing the shape of my ear as he had once before. Seeming to be drinking in my scent as I devoured his.

'*Tauria.*' It came so softly, the brush of a kiss against my brow, but as I turned towards it, sleep pulled me back, and there was nothing waiting for me in the darkness of my dreams. As if they were too fearful of him to linger.

Chapter Ten

Kat

There were once vicious beasts in the north. With scales thicker than any Kysillian armour and teeth as sharp as blades. They hunted for treasure and ruled the wildlands. Only for their greed to lure them further beneath the mountain. Gluttonous and old, they grew too tired to fly, and so they rested.

Only they rested too long, becoming nothing more than another piece of stone that formed the great mountains. Then how easily those treasures were stolen from beneath those once powerful wings that made even the kings in the north cower.

The Northern Ballad – Unknown

My father told old stories of the winged creatures in the north. Great powerful beasts who grew greedy with their conquest.

Gluttony led them to an endless sleep. Bested by their own mistakes. That tale now taunted me that I'd rested long enough. Allowed my fears to consume me. Weaken me. A truth that chased me from my slumber just before dawn. Waking confused as I found myself still in the study, curled up on the chaise. Emrys slumped in the chair next to me as rain pounded against the stained-glass ceiling from a storm that rumbled above.

My heart stuttered at the sight of the dishevelled lord sleeping before me. His head held up by his fist, dark hair falling across his brow, which furrowed even in sleep as if troubled in his dreams too.

Troubles I'd caused. I rolled onto my back, watching the streaks of rain slip across the glass above as the weak morning light seeped through the dark clouds.

Too late, came another dark reminder. All I'd uncovered against my will. How close that darkness was. How awfully the fey had suffered and how little the Council had done.

All my studies. The Institute. How it led nowhere.

I let my eyes close only to see jaw bones and teeth scattered in cursed soil, the glisten of magic still trapped in their marrow. Fey bones. Just how many there had been in that pit. How many the Council had let them kill.

Anger rolled through my limbs, heating my skin. The blanket suddenly oppressive as I pushed it away and sat up. Thankfully not feeling any discomfort as I turned my attention to the large bay windows that had appeared – the study had rearranged itself, bookcases moved aside so we could look upon the blackthorn wood. A cushioned bench beneath waiting with a steaming cup of tea on a small tray as if wishing to lure me closer. I managed to get myself up without waking Emrys, moving to the window, relieved that most of the aching in my legs had abated.

I picked up the cup, letting my fingers curl around the warm porcelain. Watching the rising sun cut through the rain, making the grass glisten.

Tauria. How vividly I'd heard my name in that wilderness. Guided by nothing but madness and memory. I let my fingers drag over the mark at my throat where the coldness from the galmoth's bite lingered.

Too late. The demonic memory of that voice mocked. A sadness clung to my throat and I downed the tea in the cup to chase it away. Even if it burnt on the way down.

Putting the cup back on the tray and pushing the window open, I was thankful for the frigid morning as it brushed against my skin. Ignoring the wariness in my bones, how unlike myself I felt.

One recovery spell could have altered it. Made me believe it hadn't been so bad but I recoiled from the thought. I needed to remember. Remember I was strong enough to heal, bold enough to wander the wilderness of this world. Resilient enough to survive my own mistakes.

Only . . . as I stood in the study's silence, I couldn't find her. The girl that had taken the next step. Who had been driven by curiosity. Who had led me here. Wanting to solve this agony.

All that dwelled in me was sorrow and a bone-weary tiredness.

I waited for the visions to return, the briny taste of the sea and the distant shape of my father walking through the waves. Waited for the echo of my mother's voice to come. But there was nothing. Nothing but the distant chatter of birds, the patter of the dissipating rain and the ruthlessness of the wind.

It hadn't been real. None of it. Not my father's sacrifice or the stories he kept so sacredly close to his heart.

How had that darkness remained and yet he was gone? In the absence of fear, and the anguish of my grief, a simmering rage consumed me. One that used to linger in the tips of my fingers, the burning promise of my magic and the chaos it brought. An ancient anger that seared itself into my very bones.

Quiet, demure and still. The words Master Hale had given me. The instructions for survival. How pitiful. Nothing but another lie I'd gorged myself on.

I looked down at my trembling fingers only for my eyes to catch on the small table at my side. A stack of papers baring Emrys's messy handwriting. Seeing the words he'd written, Kysillian letters in a wobbly hand, unfamiliar as he was with them.

Simple sentences. As if he was trying to learn.

Then I felt it. The soft brush down my arms, cautious and seeking. His magic. I turned into it, letting it guide me as the draft from the window stirred my loose hair. Seeing him watching me from his chair.

'I should know better than to expect you to be where I left you,' he sighed with soft reprimand. A caution in him as he rose, as if I was nothing but a creature formed of morning mist. Able to disperse at the barest of movements. A witch of the wildwood from the fairy tales.

His white shirtsleeves were rolled up, his shirt half unbuttoned to show the strong column of his throat and the expanse of his chest. Scars appearing silver in the morning light.

My heartbeat grew unsteady remembering all the things left unsaid.

Serus. The word taunted from the back of my mind. And just like a maiden from a dark tale about ancient folk and the temptation of demons, I waited, meeting his cautious gaze as he came closer, that forbidden scent calming my thunderous heart.

'I didn't want to wake you.' I curled my hands at my elbows where his magic lingered. Comforted by the sensation of it against my skin. The cool inquisitive nature of it as it slipped through my fingers.

'Remind me to have a word with the bloody house. Especially for it leading you outside.'

I wanted to smile, only for those storm-filled eyes to trace every line of my features. His brow furrowing with concentration as if trying to work out the thoughts plaguing me. Cautious and quiet.

His gloved hands curled into tighter fists at his sides. Too still with a tension as if it took everything in him not to move.

'I don't know if you remember everything.' He swallowed. Wary. As if I wouldn't remember. Wouldn't remember the last thing I'd wanted.

Him.

That he'd come for me.

'I remember,' I whispered, that answer bringing back the horror of that darkness, of the beasts in the pit and all the things I'd done to contain it. The hollow ache of my magic inside of me, as if it too were haunted by the truth of what we'd seen.

Yet then my eyes moved to the table, where those Kysillian letters remained.

'You're learning Kysillian?' I asked, unable to stop the strange warmth that swooped through me at the thought. That he'd try where nobody else had before.

'I thought it might settle you,' he answered quietly.

I wanted to smile at the thoughtfulness of it. Yet all that remained was guilt. Those fey murdered beneath that house. For nothing but madness; for stories and lies. A war that had torn my life apart. Cost my parents their lives. All for peace so it never happened again.

'They lied,' I whispered. After all those wars and death. After losing everything, this darkness remained. Unrelenting and I couldn't see a way out. 'Nothing changed, did it?'

His jaw tightened as if with the urge to deny it.

I cannot lie to you, Croinn. Only now it didn't feel like a comfort, but a curse. When all I wanted was lies. To be told it would all work out. That all my fears were wrong.

'I never anticipated this. I should have.' His brow lined with the weight of his thoughts. How easily he blamed himself, despite being the only one trying. 'The Council are scrambling for a reason for their anomalies.'

'Anomalies,' I scoffed, wincing as the motion pulled at my tender ribs. I pressed my palm to them, taking a seat on the bench. The cushions moving of their own accord behind my back to support me.

'Lord Percy is still in hiding. Denying all charges.' Emrys's tone darkened, watching me closely, especially how I guarded my right side.

I shook my head, hating the burn of childish, useless tears in my eyes. The agony of that truth gouged too deeply into my chest. 'They won't do anything to him. Not for any of this. Master Hale lied.'

My anger felt like a poisonous knot in my throat. The world was falling apart, and yet Master Hale had said peace was possible? That my indenture in that horrible place would be worth something. That fey would gain something from it.

No. They'd died in a pit in those woods. Brutally and without anyone to even remember them. Just like Daunton.

He should have let me go. Yet he'd kept me. Trapped me like a pet in a cage and now I didn't know the way out. Smothered by the pretence of safety, because in the cocoon of those lies I couldn't see. Didn't allow myself to feel what was now burning in my blood.

Vengeance.

'Kat.' Emrys's voice pulled me back, still here with me, yet out of reach. Hesitant. His expression unreadable as a new fear bloomed in my chest.

Another memory of fire and rage. Of the chaos I'd summoned and how easily it had rendered everything to ash.

'Are you afraid of me?' The words slipped so quietly from my lips.

'No.' He crouched before me instantly, so close, catching my chin gently between his finger and thumb. The leather of his glove cool against my skin. 'Never, Croinn.'

Breath slipped more easily between my lips as I watched the colours shift in his eyes, the paleness of them to the depths of the black at the rim.

There is a prince that sleeps beneath the earth. Serus. The ancient hymn echoed through my thoughts but I pushed it away.

I'd felt the evil of this world, the bite of its cruelty, and I knew that monsters came in many forms. Most just as simple men. As I looked at Emrys now drenched in that soft morning light, I knew those stories were nothing but lies.

There was nothing evil in him, not when the barest brush of his magic chased every fear from me. Made me wish for nothing else but the comfort of him.

I caught his hand before he could let it fall away.

Amartis. I'd said those words. I'd meant them with every fibre of my being. Known they were true the moment I'd seen my father's hilt in his grasp. That it had allowed Emrys to summon it.

I turned over his gloved hand, running my fingers against the soft leather. 'Why are you wearing gloves?'

His fingers curled automatically, capturing my own as if to stave off my curiosity.

'It—' His voice broke, his fingers tightening around my own as if fearful I could slip away. 'I made it worse.'

There was a wounded quietness to his words, almost lost in the rustle of the wind.

His head bowed, a devout worshipper seeking salvation, shoulders slumped in complete surrender. 'Touching you made it worse.

'I've been trained to endure many things. Have endured them all without hesitation, but . . . I couldn't endure that,

Kat.' He barely shook his head, breath seeming almost painful as it slipped through his lips. 'Not hurting you. Not with what I am.'

Verr. The word he didn't say.

The impossibility of it, yet I'd seen the truth. Only, it didn't feel like the stories. Not a great dark evil snapping with deadly jaws. No. He was just Emrys, quiet and burdened.

There was a lie somewhere. Only I knew it had never been spoken by him. It had been spoken long ago. Long before us.

I looked over the scars on his cheek and jaw. The slight pink tinge to some marks as if they were new. I let my thumb brush over them. Remembering how viciously the dark had tried to devour him. Feeling him still beneath my touch, tense.

'Do you think that matters to me?' I asked, knowing what it was to be feared. To be made into a monster, when all you wished for was to belong.

'It has to, Kat,' he answered but didn't pull away.

Had to because we were opposites in every way. Deadly and followed only by death. Yet I didn't wish to be anywhere else.

I gently pulled the glove from his hand. Until I saw the dark magic lingering at the tips of his fingers, how thin veins of it ran across his palm. Then removed his other, letting the gloves slip to the floor.

My magic was content. Quiet with nothing but a pulse of curiosity at my fingertips as I pressed our palms together and fit my fingers into the space between his own. As he'd done for me, when I thought I'd never feel safe again.

When I'd told him the worst thing I'd ever done and he'd just held me. How he'd crawled across that cursed earth, reaching into flames that could turn him to ash. Because he promised he wouldn't leave me.

'Tell me all of it.' Fear quieted those words from my lips. That his silence would prove there was nothing here. Nothing left in the chasm between us. That his choice was made. 'Please.'

'Just give me another moment.' He swallowed, jaw tight, but those eyes remained on me, taking in every inch of my face, savouring it. 'Another moment like this.'

As if one word from his lips would change everything.

Then all I was left to wonder was who put that fear in his eyes. Then a different type of sorrow began to bloom between my ribs. For everything he never wished to be. For the spy and the war hero he never wished to be.

'The Mage King . . . in his madness began to indulge in—' Something close to disgust cut across his expression. His gaze moving to the window. To the stormy morning sky. 'Rituals to try to summon the Old Gods from beneath. To give them mortal form again. To raise Verr to his cause using fey girls who had no choice in it.'

I'd heard of ancient mating sacrifices, blood rites and dark worship done by many kings obsessed with the dark. Each becoming obscener than the king before.

His gaze remained distant as if he couldn't bear to see my expression or how I'd process his words. 'My mother was one of them.'

Icy horror coiled tightly in my gut.

'Lady Blackthorn—' I frowned but he shook his head.

'No. I was just a cuckoo in her nest. A well-placed curse.' His eyes came back to me, filled with nothing but anguish. 'My birth mother was fey. One of the few kept to endure the rituals. A pet of the Mage King.'

I'd heard those stories of lords' obsessions with fey girls. Depraved and cruel. Using them to produce mortal-passing heirs to bring magic into their bloodlines. Mostly whispered in Daunton between the older girls. Then in whatever pages of the Crow's Foot that found their way into the Institute. To spit and sneer at lies fey told. Only I knew they weren't lies at all.

Nightmarish tales worse than mere mortal men hungering for fey girls, to appease their predatory appetites. This was different – worse. Seeing them as nothing but a vessel. A lamb to slaughter.

'The lords who were working against the King got her out. Moved her to a safe house.' He drew in a pained breath. 'I was born there. Blackthorn was there. They knew she'd die from the birth, that containing such darkness for so long would weaken her with how corrupt the summoning had been.'

A hideous ache took up residence in the centre of my chest. The bitter memory of that pit. The pain that had pressed against my flesh. How they'd sacrificed others.

'They could have saved her the agony of it but the promise of finally gaining a weapon against the King was worth more to their uprising.' He looked down at his hand entwined with my own, dark hair falling across his brow. 'The creature she'd birth was worth more than her life.'

Creature. The certainty of that word from his lips broke my heart.

'Blackthorn gave his own newborn son over as a decoy – along with my mother's body once it was done. The boy was a failed attempt to awaken Serus or any of the other princes from beneath the earth.'

A sharp talon of dread clawed its way down my back as I remained in horrified silence.

'Gideon was the decoy. He was labelled another failed bastard and returned to Blackthorn to ward. Safe in a lord's house who swore loyalty to a mad king.' Emrys grimaced.

Gideon was Blackthorn's child. It was why he looked familiar to that portrait on the stairs.

'I stole his life.' Emrys nodded as if seeing that realisation slip across my expression. His smile was cold and self-mocking as he stood abruptly, breaking my hold on him as he turned to the window. Running a hand through his dark hair. Pulling at it as if he could free himself from the burden of his thoughts. 'I don't even know where they buried her.' Such a quiet confession, almost lost to the wind. 'Blackthorn said he didn't remember.'

Didn't remember. As if Emrys's mother was nothing in that tale. Just another fragment of a myth that didn't matter to them. My heart broke for the boy who'd asked. For never knowing.

A shudder moved through him, darkness flashing beneath his skin before it settled once more. There was a new tension in his body as I saw that darkness curl beneath his skin, just beyond his shirt's collar. Marks I'd glimpsed before, only fainter. I told myself it was nothing more than a play of the light.

'You've been repressing it,' I said. Understanding how easily he could have known I'd been doing the same.

He nodded almost reluctantly, looking down at his own hands in mild disgust. '*To summon such darkness is to be consumed by its hunger.*'

The warning from one of the old texts came so easily from his lips, as if he'd repeated it often.

He shook his head, curling his summoning-stained fingers into fists. 'I've been taking beasam bark since I was twelve. When the summoning began to manifest within me. It was poison at first. Unbearable. But I gathered it was no more than I deserved.'

His words punctured my heart. He was a child.

'Do you believe that?' I rose, coming to his side. That he was a monster. Some foul thing from an ancient text, no better than the galmoth in that pit, or the gobrite that had crawled out of that book.

Such a hopeless sound slipped from his lips. 'I've seen what I do, Kat. Blackthorn brought a curse into his house and his family paid the price.'

I shook my head. Knowing he was Verr and yet understanding that part of him was fey too. I shortened the distance between us but he wasn't finished.

'Blackthorn used me to try to find more. I found others in the west. Hidden in villages and slums. Verr that had survived the sealing of the earth centuries before. Nothing like me. Settled and hiding amongst the fey. Traders, innkeepers and maids. Normal beings trying to live – mortal-passing, even.'

His words froze me in place. Verr. Amongst us all this time. It didn't seem real, and yet I knew it was truth from his lips. It could be nothing else.

Serus. That name came again. He may be part Verr . . . but I was something equally as vicious. Something else that perhaps shouldn't exist from the destruction I'd wrought and the ancestors before me.

We were two sides of an ancient coin. Two things that should be dead. Too dangerous to exist. Only we'd found our way here.

'You weren't the only one with secrets, Emrys,' I challenged quietly. Reaching for his hand again, seeing the darkness beneath his skin he'd been hiding, muted and fading. Ancient strange marks that belonged pressed between the pages of ancient tomes or deep within my imagination.

How his fingers tangled with my own, still marked by the darkness he'd summoned. That crescent moon at the knuckle that I dragged my fingers over.

I won't leave you alone to that darkness, Kat.

He hadn't. I wasn't alone. It was me who'd left him, sleeping in that bed as I'd wandered into that nightmare and nearly got him torn apart. How ravenously and how he'd screamed out from the agony of it.

'In that darkness . . . I forgot my own name.' My voice broke with those words. Remembering the brush of death's breath, how close I'd allowed it to come. 'But I remembered yours, Emrys.'

Even in the depths of my pain I remembered his name.

That he was there. Waiting. That he would call me back.

'You asked me to stay,' I whispered, knowing I'd made my choice in the pit. His hands captured my face, thumbs wiping away my tears. Breath unsteady with restraint, but I tightened my grip on his forearms. Holding him to me.

Knowing it haunted him as it haunted me.

So much had changed but I didn't want this to change. Not this fragile tangle of threads between us. He touched me as if he couldn't resist, his fingers brushing along my jaw, the arch of my ear and then the curve of my throat. As if the flutter of my pulse against his fingers was the most important thing in the world.

'I didn't know what I'd do if you didn't come back.' His voice was like gravel, breaking ever so slightly as his fingers trembled against my flesh. 'I thought I knew fear. Then you were so cold in my arms, Kat.'

'I'm here.' I pushed myself up, rising onto my tiptoes to brush those words so gently across his lips, done with the distance and all the things unsaid.

I may have been broken. Too many sharp pieces pressed together inside of me but there were spaces between the cracks. Spaces I wanted this strange forsaken thing between us to fill.

'I'm wrong, Kat.' His fingers slipped into my hair, moving gently through the strands. Hesitant but not pushing me away.

'Kysillians burn, Emrys.' My fingers curled into his shirt. The Kysillian curse: to be consumed by our own fire. That was the story of my blood. The price of my magic. A fate I should have followed. 'If we're nothing but our stories, then that is mine.'

'No, it isn't.' There was a firmness to his denial. So sharp and sure I couldn't help but smile.

'Then this darkness isn't yours.' I brushed those words hesitantly against his jaw, breaking the stoic spell over him as he pulled me the rest of the miniscule distance to him. So his lips could claim my own. Soft and devout, as if we'd been allowed time to court. As if there was nothing beyond us. This thing burning more wildly between us than the flames in my blood.

And for that moment, there was nothing but the warmth of him, the tentative brush of his magic and the swelling of emotion in my chest as I dug my fingers into his strong back. Wanting him closer. Wanting him to never retreat again. To have all of him. Darkness or no.

An icy blast of wind came through the window, causing a shiver to move through me. He pulled back the barest inch. Breath uneven.

'You're cold,' he observed, worry creasing his brow. 'Let's get you a tonic before Gideon reprimands me again.'

'I'm fine,' I countered, but his hand slipped easily into my own as he guided me through the study and to his desk. Ignoring my small protest as he began to look through his things. 'Gideon came back?'

'I didn't give him much choice.' His smile was grim as he found the vial he was looking for.

'William's pleased,' I noted, resting myself on the edge of the desk as Emrys uncorked the healing tonic and held it out to me. Thankfully this one smelt like burnt sugar.

'That doesn't say much. William thinks Thean is pleasant company,' he observed dryly, making a small breathless laugh escape my lips. The sound seemed to startle him for a moment, as if it was the last thing he'd expected to hear.

'Rebels seem to be the least of our worries,' I pointed out, my smile small and self-mocking but it captured his complete attention none the less as I quickly drank the tonic. Wanting it out of the way so maybe he'd kiss me again.

'I couldn't agree more, Miss Woodrow,' came a sharp male voice I didn't recognise, my magic rising in alarm at a presence it didn't know. The surge of it painfully stealing my breath and making me choke on the remains of the tonic in my throat. The vial slipped from my fingers to shatter on the floor as Emrys went rigid at my side. The shadows in the room darkened, muting the morning sunlight.

A thin man stood in the study doorway, wearing Council-issued hunting leathers. The insignia of the boar on his collar as he grinned, showing crooked gold front teeth. His fingers curled into the collar of William's shirt, the boy white as a sheet in his clutches.

'Blackthorn. A tricky man to get hold of these days,' he drawled with cruel amusement, but he didn't need to say anything. I knew by that smug glint in his hateful eyes – my time avoiding the Council was finally up.

Chapter Eleven

Kat

William was pale with worry, his apron lopsided on his shoulder as if he'd been manhandled. The hunter was clearly smart enough to release him in Emrys's presence, sending the boy stumbling across the threshold towards us.

'Oi!' William snapped uneasily, a flush staining his freckled cheeks as he tried to straighten his shirt. 'They—'

'It's all right, William.' Emrys laid a reassuring hand on the boy's shoulder as he nervously wrung his muddy hands.

Emrys's predatory focus moved to the uninvited guests as the house groaned in warning.

'My house isn't fond of intruders, and neither am I. What would hunters be doing so far north?' Emrys asked, voice edged with lethal calm. Hands pushed into his pockets, a relaxed ease to his shoulders but I sensed the darkness in his tone. Could feel it simmering in the air.

'The title is *Steward* now, Lord Blackthorn. Surely you remember that?' the man said as two other hunters shifted behind him. Hands on their blades, leaning casually against the wood panelling awaiting instruction.

Stewards. What the Council called their guard, despite most of them being nothing but the King's old hunters given new titles and rank. Who led the persecution of the fey in the north, who still arrested fey, claiming any they caught were rebels. Hunters I knew Emrys had run into before, when he'd freed fey from their false charges in his reports.

'I'd answer my question,' Emrys warned.

The hunter grinned. 'Haven't you heard? The western road fell last night.'

Emrys froze. A surprised noise came from William next to me but I couldn't focus on anything except the tension in Emrys's back. The western road. The only path from north to south. So Elysior was divided once more and I had a horrible feeling something inevitable had begun.

'The rebels blew up half the west bridge and set the mortal towns alight.' The steward tutted at Emrys's answering silence, straightening the fall of his tunic, the ostentatious gold buttons catching the lamplight. 'It seems the rebels are painting quite a story about your recent . . . *escapades*, Lord Blackthorn.'

The steward's eyes moved to me, lingering too long. 'About your . . . nefarious *companion* too. The Kysillian has an appointment with the Council.'

'I've already spoken on the matter,' Emrys answered. A perfect image of contained restraint.

'*Unfortunately*, your lordship, they require *her* presence.' The man moved forwards with purpose as if he intended to take my arm by force. Like a prisoner to be led to the pyre.

Quicker than I believed possible, Emrys moved. Seizing hold of the man's wrist. So tightly I could have sworn I heard the creak of bone.

'If you touch her, your men will be dragging your body from this hall.' There was a lethal calm in those words. The house creaked with pleasure at the threat.

Then as quickly as he'd grabbed the man, Emrys sent him stumbling backwards into his watching companions. What little, lesser magic those hunters possessed simmered in the air with warning.

'Are you so *possessive* of all your partner mages, Lord Blackthorn?' The hunter half sneered, rubbing his wrist with indignation. 'Or just the pretty ones?'

'You have already manhandled my ward.' Emrys stepped forward, forcing the hunter to take another step back, his men shuffling with unease in answer. 'Be grateful you're still in possession of those rotting stumps you call teeth.'

'Now, Emrys, let us not murder guests before lunchtime.' The amused words echoed down the hallway as Gideon appeared, pulling on his gloves. Golden hair swept back from his face. A fine navy coat buttoned and matching cravat in place as if already warned of this horrid appointment.

The hunters turned, positioning themselves as if sensing the new threat.

'Healer Swift.' The main hunter at least had the courtesy to bow his head in greeting, those hate-filled eyes shifting uneasily. 'There were . . . rumours you'd resurfaced.'

'Let's hope my jilted lovers haven't heard just yet. I could do without cock curses being sent my way.' Gideon smiled, a charming offering, but I could see the sharpness in his eyes as they landed on William's rumpled shirt. 'William, I believe there is a messenger at the service door that requires your attention.'

The boy hesitated behind me for the barest moment but I felt the brush of Emrys's magic. The silent command as if it sought to push the boy with invisible hands. William slipped away obediently, the house materialising the stairs just to our right and, in a blink, the opening was gone. William with it.

'The Council demands the presence of Miss Woodrow,' the leader repeated, lips curled with annoyance.

'And you attempted to drag her out in her dressing gown?' Gideon asked with a sharp smile. 'Who knew the old bastards were so *perverse.*'

'You'll show the masters of the republic respect,' the hunter bit out in response. 'Her presence is *not* a request.'

No, because the Council hated lose ends. Hated the barest tendrils of truth slipping free of their grasp.

Emrys tensed. His magic sharper in the air than the winter wind had been. 'I told the Council—'

'If they seek my presence, then they shall have it,' I answered, making Emrys's back go rigid, as I curled my hand gently into the crook of his arm. His attention turned to me immediately, Gideon shooting me a dark, wary look.

Only there was nothing but calm in my answering expression. The creature those Council members had trained me to be. Quiet. Demure and still.

The Council sought me, as they always had. To discredit and mock. To act as a scapegoat for their failures, only it was their last mistake.

For I'd found my vengeance in that darkness. Found it in all the fey they'd silenced, and just like them, I'd be silent no longer.

Emrys's dark grey eyes ran over every inch of my expression, seeking my fear or apprehension. Only when he found none did he relax ever so slightly.

'Very well,' he relented, a muscle moving in his jaw.

Surprise flickered across the hunter's face before he hid it behind a scowl. The two behind him shifting uneasily at my forwardness.

'If you'll give me a moment. I'll need to make myself presentable,' I offered, excusing myself as I moved towards the stairs.

'I'm certain you gentlemen won't mind waiting with me at the portal entrance,' Gideon said behind me.

'Your presence isn't required, Healer Swift.' The hunter's words were sharp and mocking with his irritation. 'You can return to your grave, or whatever whorehouse you've been hiding in.'

Gideon's answering laugh sent a cold streak of fear down my spine. Feeling that ruthless energy humming around him.

'Miss Woodrow is suffering from summoning sickness, caused by exposure at Fairfax Manor, as the Council is aware from my report,' Gideon replied, a hard edge to the authority in his voice. 'She is under my care; therefore, I'll be accompanying her.'

That thankfully gave the hunter pause as I climbed the stairs, and I was almost to the top when Alma came charging around the corner, clawed fingers gripping onto the banister as she glared at me.

'Where in this fucking cursed earth have you—'

'Shh.' I pressed my hand over her mouth, forcing her back against the wall. 'Council hunters are here.'

She dragged my hand away but didn't let it go. Those eyes reptilian in a moment. 'What for?'

'Me,' I answered reluctantly.

She half choked, shaking her head furiously. 'You can't go into the Council chambers. You were almost dead a few nights ago.'

'I don't think there's another choice,' I argued, despite knowing she was right. I felt like a wrung-out rag, and I doubted sitting in bed would stop that.

'Kat, they'll—'

'I know what they'll do,' I cut her off. What they'd done every time before. Ridiculed me. Abused me. Anything they could. The worst pain of all was that I'd let them. Drank the poison of their lies gladly. Let those fey die.

The truth of that would have cowed me, only now it stiffened my spine. Now I understood – I'd survived worse than them.

With a settling breath I pulled back and made for my room, the house jangling some small fairy bells to show me it had moved the door nearer to the stairs. However, as I entered, I realised I was back in Emrys's room.

'My clothes aren't here,' I complained in the direction of the floorboards. Only for the wardrobe doors to burst open, to see my dresses rattling on their hangers within. Many more than I'd come with, and I wondered just where on earth all the rest had appeared from.

I ignored the forwardness of the house. It was my own fault. I had willingly entered Emrys's bed. I couldn't be annoyed at the house's clear delight at the debauchery I offered it.

'What are you going to do?' Alma demanded, closing the bedroom door. 'You're still too weak to be going and—'

I caught her hands again, stilling her panic for the barest moments. 'Emrys and Gideon will be with me and if we're going to solve this and help anyone . . . I need to answer this summons.'

I needed the Council off my back. I needed to be free of it once and for all.

I didn't know what she saw lingering in my eyes but whatever it was settled her enough for her to pull in a harsh breath, for those scales to slip back beneath her skin and for determination to spread across her features.

'If you come back with the barest *scratch,* I'll kill you myself,' she snapped, turning for the wardrobe and rifling through the options available.

'I don't doubt it,' I laughed softly, cutting it short when it still pulled at the ache in my ribs. Remembering the hunters had interrupted me taking my tonic.

'Wear the black lace. That'll really piss the bastards off.' She draped it on the bed, scowling down at the fabric as if the barest crease had caused her some great offence.

'That'd normally worry you,' I observed, earning myself an annoyed glance.

'I'm confident Blackthorn will probably kill them all before you can get a word in anyway,' she added dryly, pulling me towards the dressing table to start on my hair. It worried me more how pleased she seemed by the idea.

Chapter Twelve
Kat

The sanctity of the grand halls should never be breached, nor any harm befall the mages who defend the purity of magic. To save it from the corruption of beneath. From beings with little control, who bring chaos and entice the world to fall back into the way it should never have been.

The Saints' Compendium, 19:1–11

Those warnings had been written in dusty texts by fools. Lords who knew nothing of fey magic and cared little for anything but themselves and what they could take, what profit could be made or how high they could rise. The stories they could spin and lies they could tell to justify the murder of magic and the beings it belonged to.

I fidgeted with the high collar of my dress, making sure it covered the bite mark at my neck, the pale scar I'd glimpsed in the mirror as Alma did my hair, vicious and ugly with how it pulled at the thin skin there.

The lace at the collar of my dress was severe, making the golden hue of my skin stand out. I ran my hands over my skirts, anything to keep them busy as I followed the large forms of Emrys and Gideon as we moved through the hallway.

The echo of the hunter's footsteps matched my panicked heartbeat. Like a war drum.

The Council portal door was waiting, making me wonder how the hunters had managed to open it. From Emrys's tense form, it was a shared thought. He'd pulled on his coat and buttoned up his shirt but the air of wildness still hung around him as we passed through the portal doorway. It littered my skin with the familiar sting of the strange magic but our steps didn't falter as we moved through the curved hallways, the clicking of our boots against the sterile marble.

The Institute.

So much hatred lingered here. How they hated me for knowing too much. Ignoring that they'd locked me away for half my life with nothing else to do but learn.

Disregarded my voice and only made me strive to be louder so maybe they would listen.

Perhaps I was a monster, but I was what they made me.

I ignored the depictions of the past mages on the portrait-filled walls. Their white robes and golden spell books. Carried on past the depictions of the ancient beasts they slaughtered, listening to the whispered mutterings of the students who lingered. The mages finishing their classes paused at the sight of me and the maids scurried away as they always had.

I'd walked this hallway before, scared and burdened with guilt. Constantly glancing over my shoulder, waiting to disappear like all the others before me. Another victim to this world, a body for an unmarked pit, a lesson for other fey to learn.

I breathed in the harsh bitter saint smoke that lingered in the air after their morning prayers, letting it stoke the painful rage in my gut.

Lies. That voice hissed in the back of my mind. Just more lies.

A darkness crept into the side of my vision, a weakness crawling up my thighs, threatening to buckle my knees, but

I kept my focus on the broad expanse of Emrys's back as we reached the mage's doors and the hunter turned on his heel to give orders.

'You'll give us a moment.' Gideon smiled tightly, as he fixed the cuff of his pristine sleeve at my side. The hunter gave a moment's pause before nodding to his men, then moving through the chamber doors with relaxed ease.

Gideon waited only a second for the door to close before he whirled on me, reaching into his coat pocket and pulling out a vial filled with the familiar iridescent liquid of a healing syrup.

'Drink it before you collapse,' he commanded, forcing it into my hand.

'She's just had one.' Emrys interjected.

Gideon glowered at him. 'Calm down. A second tonic clearly won't maim her, and let's remind ourselves she should still be in fucking bed.'

'I'm feeling better,' I countered, ignoring his disbelieving glance and the fact I sounded like a petulant child before I did as he said. Hating the numbness the syrup left on my tongue.

Gideon – satisfied I wasn't in mortal peril due to my own foolishness – turned his annoyance on his brother, a gloved finger pointed in accusation.

'Montagor is up to something.' His words were quiet, not wasting a moment of breath.

'We'll worry about that later,' Emrys sighed, running a hand through his hair, stormy grey eyes surveying me quickly for any harm. As if some great injury could have befallen me on the short walk here.

'*Later?*' Gideon snapped dubiously, claiming his brother's attention once more. 'I doubt they've ordered a summons to serve us tea and fucking scones, *Emrys!*'

'I'm well aware of that,' Emrys growled back as the shadows that lingered in the corridor lengthened in response to his dark anger. Gideon, however, was not deterred. This was a darkness he knew all too well. Understood better than me. How Emrys could walk the very fine line between Verr and lord. Blurring the two together seamlessly.

'There is something you aren't telling me, brother.'

Emrys's jaw was tight with irritation, his eyes moving over his brother's features. Trying to give himself time. Of course. He couldn't lie.

'Don't play the fucking mute, *Emrys*,' Gideon seethed, stepping closer until their boots touched. I could see the wariness in his eyes, the concern. 'Answer me.'

'Later,' I cut in, making the brothers ease apart with the command that had no weight in it. Gideon turned his glower on me but the stone around my neck fluttered in panic, barely giving me time to prepare.

'Katherine,' came the breathless worried words of Master Hale behind me.

I turned, either out of habit or surprise, but any other emotions were stuttered as his pale sickly fingers curled around my wrist too quickly. 'What are—'

I looked at his familiar grubby navy robes, wiry beard and sallow skin with those deep laugh lines etched into it.

Liar. A dark voice hissed, reminding me of the path that had led me here. Led me to my own death, a sharp phantom pain slicing into my neck where the mark of that bite remained. My breath caught and as if he could hear it, I felt Emrys's magic rise in response.

I pulled myself out of Hale's hold, too weak and panicked to contain me as I stumbled back, only to be steadied by Emrys.

'Katherine?' Deep concern laced Master Hale's words. Worry that turned my stomach.

Suddenly the hallway was too big and small at the same time. The air close and my magic too ravenous. Only there was no satisfaction with the surprise that flickered across the old man's expression. Not as my anger simmered so close to the surface.

'What have you done to her?' Hale demanded, looking me over with furious concern. As if I was a book that had been borrowed and returned with torn and creased pages.

'What did *you* do?' I demanded back before Gideon or Emrys could answer. My voice a hollow thing cutting through the space between us. Watching him take a step back from me. The first time he ever had. As if I was a stranger, a changeling in his midst.

Nothing. That dark voice mocked. He did nothing. Not as those fey had died, not here or in Fairfax's land. Not as the Council mocked and trapped me here. Not as I cowered under his mercy for the grace of letting me simply exist.

Suddenly I didn't know if it was that healing tonic or the viciousness of my own anger. I pushed past him, straight for the Council doors.

'Katherine—' Hale called but I ignored him, striding into the main chamber, finally ready to be rid of it all. The assistants struggled to catch the door as it banged against the panelled wall. The chatter was silenced instantly, only the dramatic scrape of chairs and rustle of pages remaining.

They gathered as they always had behind their desks. Ainsworth at the centre, his hateful glare relentless as always. They sat in a semi-circle as if around a stage awaiting a performance.

It seemed I was finally ready to perform.

'Council men, I believe you wish to speak with me,' I addressed the room, taking my place at its centre, lacing my hands carefully before me.

Then came the press of Emrys's magic, a solid comfort at my back, cool and authoritative. I wasn't alone. Not anymore. Yet despite my boldness, the childish fear of these old men remained, clinging to me like morning mist.

'Your presence was requested two days ago, Miss Woodrow,' Master Ainsworth reprimanded, spittle flying from his chapped lips. 'The disobedience of your dallying cannot go—'

'A studying mage under partnership is allowed three days to respond to summons.' My interruption was sharp, making him choke on the rest of his words. 'Under the Investigation Act, 1812.'

'Blackthorn assured us your absence was *necessary*,' Master Grima interrupted, flushed with his surprise at my presence, or at Master Ainsworth's rage – I couldn't tell.

I saw the trap, the pristine silver robes, the milky eyes of the creature that sat at the end of the table as that orb sat before them. The pink scarring at their throat from the markings to worship their saint that would go all the way up across their bald scalp hidden beneath their hood.

The Truth Seeker.

The reason for the audience. For the hunters. It was all a performance. To make an example of a fey who pulled too far on their leash. A Truth Seeker to pry words from my lips.

'Lord Blackthorn was gracious enough to grant me time to recover.' I nodded respectfully. 'I'm certain he's provided you with sufficient information in my absence.'

Something moved out of the corner of my eye. Dark and swift, turning my attention to the large arched windows, draped with their banners. Nothing there. My heart began to race, the grip on my own fingers painful as my nails dug into flesh.

Emrys's magic grew cold and vicious as if sensing my distress. Curling around my waist as if to pull me back but I didn't go.

Here. A dark voice mocked, whispering against the shell of my ear. Turning me a bit further until I saw it. The warning came too late.

Sat in a column of shadow at one of the tables in the far corner, legs crossed and hands braced casually on his knees. As if this was no more than a hound race for coin in one of the lower arenas.

Montagor.

His dark uniform of the commander tight to his form, that horrid gleam in his dark eyes and the hint of amusement on his lips as he peered at me down his thin, regal nose.

'I wasn't aware you'd been granted Council robes, Montagor.' Emrys stepped forward, arms gathered behind his back but I could see the tightness in his shoulders, how it strained his coat. The tension in Gideon's jaw as he stood like a disapproving golden pillar at the other side of his brother.

'As the leading defence against chaos magic and the rebellion, Montagor's knowledge is imperative to the investigation,' Ainsworth interjected, his smile too sharp with deceit.

'To be held in a higher regard than a founding house?' Emrys asked, not removing his eyes from Montagor. From the bastard son of the King. His brother in some regard.

That truth sent a cold chill down my spine. Then I understood why Montagor was a bastard too. Why the Council kept him so close.

Horror clawed at my insides. How unsettled Emrys was.

There wasn't just one prince beneath the earth, and I feared Montagor was another summoning. The dark tongue Emrys had used in his presence.

'When a member is accused of *impropriety*. Yes.' Montagor practically preened, looking down at his nails with feigned boredom.

'Shouldn't you be busy investigating the western road?' Gideon interjected coldly.

Montagor sat forward, his smile cruel at the challenge. 'We already hanged twelve rebels at dawn. Fey are easy enough to catch. The true culprits . . . guilt will draw them from their nest soon enough. I'm sure.'

As if it were nothing but one of their grand hunts. A game to catch deer for a feast.

I felt that healing tonic threaten to crawl its way back up my throat.

'However, we have more pressing matters. Such as a dead lord,' Montagor continued, that smile never wavering. 'Suspicious is it not, Miss Woodrow, how the destruction at Fairfax is so similar to the chaos that consumed Daunton's estate? How peculiar that you were present for both events.'

I heard the mutter of the masters, felt the burn of Gideon's suspicious gaze on the side of my face. Could do nothing, not even allow the brush of Emrys's magic to calm me as fear pierced its talons into my heart.

Smoke filled my nose, bitter with the stench of burning flesh. *Murderer.*

'I'm certain I don't need to remind the Council the punishment for wild magic. For lying to this Council under oath. I can assure you it's far worse than a simple cleansing, Miss Woodrow,' Montagor continued, relishing in what dregs of my fear he could sense.

The orbs that sat in the room remained white. Truth. Although I didn't need the orb, I knew the price. It was death.

I ignored the thunder of my pulse and how my palms became slick with sweat. The trap they'd set and how I'd let my anger walk me right into the centre of it. Just as they predicted.

'I'm not in possession of wild magic,' I replied. Truth – but there was no relief to be found from it. Not when I knew I possessed something far worse.

Kysalor. Fire that eats the world. What lived in me wasn't magic. It was too old to possess a name.

'I'm also certain we can agree Daunton received what was deserved in the end.' I kept my voice level, ignoring the bile that built at the back of my throat as his name slipped between my lips. 'Death by fire is still the punishment for torturing beings with curse casting, is it not?'

There was no comfort in that truth. Not as I said those words aloud for the first time. Admitted what he'd done. What I'd allowed him to do to me. Felt the turbulent rage in Emrys's magic. Saw a few of those lanterns splutter out as if disturbed by a deadly wind. The sun slipping deep behind clouds high above us.

Those scars on my back almost ached with the memory of it, as if I could feel the groove of each one he'd burdened me with.

I returned Montagor's stare. I was finished with my fears. As I stood burdened with all the things I'd never said. The weight of my guilt like stones in my pockets.

I'd felt the pain of those fey. Saw their deaths. Tasted the foul tang of it. The bitterness of that fear that would never leave me.

I hadn't saved them and everything in my blood would mourn them until I was no more.

Only fear can bind your hands. I'd allowed it to do more than bind my hands. I'd allowed it to gag and smother me. Drag me down into the foulness of cowardice.

Master Ainsworth cleared his throat impatiently. 'Miss Woodrow—'

'You wish to hear my testimony.' I eyed the orb again, ignoring the sharp stab of my apprehension. Remembering every other time they'd subjected me to such things. The exhaustion and cruelty of it. 'Did you seek Lord Percy's under the watch of the Truth Seeker?'

'As protocol dictates,' Master Grima drawled, tapping his quill on the waiting parchment before him. The powder on his face congealing around his temples with his sweat. Unfortunately, the globe before him stayed a clear white with truth. 'He had some . . . *interesting* allegations to report.'

'Miss Woodrow is in no condition to—' Master Hale began to interrupt.

'Very well.' My voice was a knife through his attempt to defend me. He'd never bothered before. Not here. Not as they'd clawed through my thoughts. Undeterred by my fear. By how small and lost I'd been.

It is what they need, Katherine. No matter that I was too young to have my mind dissected like it didn't belong to me. Agreeing because my fear of what they'd take if I didn't was greater.

I moved to the desk and pressed my palm to the glass orb. Never breaking the Council's stare.

I felt Emrys's lethal power simmer with displeasure from the distance between us. The lanterns dimming as Montagor's smile grew cat-like out of the corner of my eye. Seeing me as a mouse in a trap. Probably expecting me to gnaw off my own limbs to escape.

Only I was their last mistake. They'd kept me too close. Let me see all their flaws and there was no escape for them. Not now.

'This Council has been made aware of alarming allegations against yourself and your partner mage, Miss Woodrow. Lord Percy has stated—'

'I think Lord Percy has forgotten, it was *he* who made illicit advances,' I interrupted. 'Heated comments I made relating to his *impotency* might have upset him.'

I watched the white smoke dance, listening to the hissed outrage move through the mages as if we were in the company of snakes.

Gideon let out a choked sound that I could only imagine was a laugh he'd been surprised by.

They began to splutter, seats creaking. Trying to deflect from things they couldn't discuss. Lies they couldn't keep.

'Speaking of breaches. You bring us to the next point of *contention*, Miss Woodrow.' Grima flipped through his short stack of parchment before he pulled another free to read. 'The removal of a serving fey without authorisation from this Council. An indentured maid has been removed from these premises.'

No.

A churning, inescapable fear burnt through me. Taking me back in an instant to the small creature I'd been. Begging and whimpering for mercy.

Master Hale surged forward, meaty palm on the desk with outrage. 'Miss Darcy has been working with Miss Woodrow for—'

'The maid signed her agreement to the Council halls, Master Hale. Not your private house. Nor Miss Woodrow's who, I will remind you, is unable to own *property*.'

Property.

Alma wasn't their misplaced possession, nor their property.

'The maid's housing cost this Institute and she has not paid back the debt of it.' Madame Bernard practically preened under my distress.

Alma never would be able to free herself. How could she when they didn't pay her at all?

'Miss Darcy's debt to these halls has been paid by the Blackthorn accounts.' Emrys's voice didn't sound his own.

Too dark and tightly pressed with his anger. 'It seems you're behind with your records.'

My heart stuttered in my chest. Turning me foolishly towards him. The imposing form of him, just as he'd been the first time we'd stood before this Council.

His deadly stare focused on the Council who seemed to shift with unease under its might.

He'd paid for Alma's freedom. When? Too many emotions ploughed through me. My heart pounding against my ribs.

Master Grima choked, rifling through his papers. 'No agreement was made—'

'You bound a child to an indenture and forged a guardian's signature to make it so.' Emrys's furious gaze dragged over the bench, landing for a longer moment on Master Hale, who had gone quite pale. 'Her boarding debts have been paid, so she is no longer your concern.'

Hale had never done that. No matter how close the Council had got to her. How many burns she'd acquired or abuse she'd endured from the maids. When exhaustion made her bones wary. He'd never once suggested it.

No matter how I'd begged in the end.

She's safer with you, Katherine. No. He'd made her nothing but a chain to bolt me in place because Daunton had taught him one truth – I'd never leave her.

A strange hum began in the back of my skull as I sank further into my body. Allowing the sharpness of my magic to rise closer to the surface. A deadly calm settling over every inch of me. Reminding me of something this Council should never have forgotten – how deadly a Kysillian is when challenged.

'*Taelacor.*' I straightened my spine, ignoring how it pulled at the base of my back. The ache of the old wounds awakened by everything I'd been forced to endure. The reminder of everything they'd allowed.

'You dare invoke the—' Master Grima began to stutter, only for Ainsworth to silence him with a raised hand.

Taelacor. Their saints' word. An ancient demand for truth. To speak without interruption.

One they couldn't challenge.

I'd allowed them to humiliate me in this very room, the sharpness of their words stinging more venomously than any lash.

Only fear can bind your hands. Finally, I understood the weight of those words as they became true. Guiding me. How the time had come to speak it. To speak of all the things still tethered to my chest. To let them go.

I wouldn't allow them to tell me who I was. Not anymore. I could feel Emrys's eyes on me, urging me to look at him as if he could sense it within me. The mercilessness of my rage.

'Make it quick, Woodrow,' Ainsworth sneered.

'Did you know?' I asked. Quiet and demure. Exactly how Master Hale commanded me to be. Saw the paleness in his face as he realised before the rest of them. The trap the Council had wandered right into. One made of their own web.

They wished to trial me under the laws of their treaty. Yet what if they broke it long before I ever could?

Ainsworth frowned as his bench sat a little taller and cleared his throat. Unsure if I was asking a question or making a statement. 'You have to be clearer in your—'

'Master Daunton was accused of the mutilation of four fey girls in the village of Telvor,' I continued, listening as sudden silence consumed the room. 'He ran the Council's peace efforts from that outpost, did he not?'

Madame Bernard's choked stutters were barely audible. 'Vicious rumours of—'

Master Grima cleared his throat. 'There was . . . an *accusation*.'

'Before he was moved to Daunton?' My voice faltered, not with fear but with rage as I swallowed down the taste of smoke. 'To further his calling to your *saint*?'

I focused on the vibrations of the magic within the orb beneath my palm. Alive and seeking lies. Lies it wouldn't get from me.

'Miss Woodrow, I fail to see why this is—'

'A fey girl named Lara Delvern escaped Daunton's confines – she reached the village of Farrow. Her arm was shattered, her nose broken, and her flesh covered in spell burns.' I kept my gaze focused, but I saw Gideon's flinch out of the corner of my eye. Of course. As a healer he'd understand that pain. The torment of it. The inability for spell burns to heal. How deep and foully the magic would seep into the victim's blood.

The madness that could follow.

I didn't need to look at Emrys. I could feel his energy. The ravenous fury of it, just as it had been the night he'd felt that pain on my skin.

A cavernous silence followed my words.

'She was also covered in lash marks. They'd begun to fester and she'd been assaulted.' My finger dragged across the orb, watching the white smoke dance so peaceful, so disturbingly serene compared to the horror of the truth that seeped from between my lips like poison finally freed from a wound. 'This Council reviewed her claims and returned her to Daunton – declaring her insane.'

'I don't see how—'

'He broke all of her fingers with a contortion charm.' My words pierced through the silence and any lies they could muster. 'Made her say a devotion prayer for each one. For the ten promises you hold to your saint.'

To be good. To be pure. To be quiet. To be true.

'He beat her to death with forsaken iron.' I could hear her even now. The distant desperateness of her screams. How they caught in her throat with her tears. How fear had locked every one of my limbs in place as I trembled in Alma's arms. How her taloned fingers had dug through the thin fabric of my nightdress. Hidden by nothing but shadow in the freezing dorm.

I let my fingers slip from the cold surface of the orb, reminding me too vividly of how cold Lara's flesh had been in death. How cold all of them had been.

'She's buried between the gnarled roots of a yew tree. One-hundred and eighty-four steps from the back gate.' I remembered because I had buried her. 'Her body was covered in spell burns. She was broken by Master Daunton and I know because I saw him do it.'

I watched the white smoke swirl inside the orb like a flurry of snow. Bright and undeniable. 'I didn't see the others, but I saw her.'

It didn't matter that I hadn't seen the others. That I'd only heard it. They mattered. She mattered. Lara Delvern mattered. With her wheat blonde hair, small white curved horns, brown eyes and kind hands. She mattered and I'd done nothing but hide in those cold dorms. Nothing but hide in this very Institute. I let the record of her sit in those bookcases collecting dust, let her linger there like a ghost.

'Her last word was *please*.' I'd remember that until I died. 'He enjoyed it most when you said please.'

To prove he'd broken you beyond repair. Knowing it didn't work. That in the end not even begging could stop a monster. The power it gave him. How desperately Daunton wanted it to be mine too. Tried to pry it from my small, bloody lips.

The room was so quiet, the air thick with an oppressive tension as if thunder was about to crack.

'So, my question is . . . did you know you sent a monster into the east woods to take his pleasure?' I demanded, voice firm with my defiance. Staring down these monsters in mortal form. Filled with hate and the greed for power, just like all those that came before.

'No. We—' Ainsworth's words were halted as that orb started to glow red.

Liar.

'There were complaints—' That smoke continued to churn, dark as blood, and something inside me settled. A sharp pain that had been a discomfort for too long. Knowing how evil they were but refusing to let myself accept it. Refusing to see everything because surviving was more important.

'You have nothing to ask me.' I pushed away from them, grateful my strength didn't falter. 'No rights under that treaty. Not when you broke it yourself over twelve years ago.'

'This hearing is not—'

'Protection for the beings of the land. Both own blood and magical. United in desire for peace. *Your oath.*' My words seared through the silence, through the oppressive chill of Emrys's magic.

They'd killed us for nothing all this time.

I let them see the vengeance burning in my eyes, feel the heat of my magic roiling with sadness and fury. Watching Montagor give the barest flinch as if he remembered the potency of my flame upon his skin.

'There is no treaty to keep. There never was. So how can any fey breach it?' I'd signed a lie. Been bound by a falsehood – and perhaps that was the most painful part of all of this. How easily I'd devoured those lies, hungry for anything to ease the agony of my own grief.

129

My gaze moved to Master Hale, saw the paleness to his features. The depth of hurt in his eyes and that was when the agony began. As I looked at the orb before him, stained with that bloody darkness like all the others.

He'd known too.

He'd known and done nothing. Nobody had come. They'd left us there and I wouldn't torment myself with it any longer.

Murderer. Yes, I was. And I'd do it again.

'How easily you've spoiled their fun, Woodrow,' came the bored voice of Montagor, only . . . he was still smiling.

It was then the pain came, straight in the centre of my chest. Searing hot, stealing my breath. I reached into the collar of my dress, tugging the chain of my wishing stone so it came tumbling out. Blinding light emitting from it, stinging my eyes. My chest unbearably tight, as if my heart was trying to crawl up my throat.

Run. That mocking voice came again. A warning that came too late as that odd sensation consumed me again. Too cold, too sudden. All the air being pulled from the room in a moment.

Intense agony bit into my neck, a helpless cry left my lips as I gripped my throat, as my knees made brutal impact with the chamber floor.

'Kat!' Sharp with warning, raw as if it hurt to even speak my name.

I turned my head, Emrys already moving towards me, the darkness spreading across his skin.

But I didn't get a chance to see his eyes before the room exploded in fire.

Chapter Thirteen

Kat

There was a ringing in my ears, a dryness on my tongue that threatened to choke me. My name came muffled through a horrid rumbling sound. Too close. Too loud in the darkness. A flickering of bright white light before me, stinging my eyes as I tried to open them.

Slowly, the wishing stone came into focus, blinking wildly like the irritated flutter of a dust sprite's wing.

Danger.

I reached for it with aching fingers, palm meeting nothing but shards of stone, blood coating my fingers as I pushed myself to my elbows, sharp rubble digging ruthlessly into my forearms. I coughed again, blinking the burning smoke from my eyes.

There was a horrid, muffled wailing, turning me towards another wall of acrid smoke only to realise it was the warning bells echoing through the gloom. The world was upside down, the room too hot and the air too thick. Dark smoke curled before me, flashes of bright orange and red concealed within it.

The stench of burning flesh cloying.

Murderer. No. My magic was silent. I looked at my hands, no illumination from a summoning in my veins. No bite of my flame. This wasn't me. Couldn't be me.

It was something else.

Then I remembered Montagor's smile. His taunt. The agony of the warning from the wishing stone. He'd done this.

Something crashed inside the smoke, the ground shaking with the force of it. The sharp bitter smell of a magically ignited flame burning my nose.

'Emrys!' I choked out, desperate as I spat grit from my mouth.

All that answered were the distant moans of injured, the rumble of destruction. A familiar shape lay in the dust and debris just before me. Master Hale's cane.

'Master Hale?!' I stumbled to my feet, skidding as rubble caught under my boot, forcing me sideways into a fallen column. I tripped over my ruined skirts, trying to clear my vision as the room seemed to sway beneath my feet.

Through blurred vision I saw a sprawled form in the rubble through the smoke, a half-destroyed desk trapping his legs. Master Hale.

'Master Hale.' I pushed the desk aside, listening to his grunt of pain as I took hold of his shoulder. A horrid paleness to his blood-smeared face. He groaned, blinking up at me with distant confusion.

'Stay still,' I commanded, tearing at my skirts for anything to stop the blood, pressing it against his temple but his clammy hands grabbed for me. His hold too tight, eyes too blood-shot and pupils too large.

Another boom cut through the chamber. A scream followed as I curled into myself and heat flushed my skin, unable to make sense of anything with that acrid smell burning my nose.

'Kat!' the echo of Emrys's voice came to me, making me turn, but there was nothing but a wall of smoke.

'Emrys! We're over—' I tried to call, but Master Hale tugged me closer, almost brutally, forcing me to look at him.

To see as he frantically shook his head, clawing at the sleeve of my dress, trying to drag me even closer.

'Master Hale, you need—'

'Kayin,' he begged, wheezing and coughing, only it was too wet. Blood slipping through his teeth and onto his lips.

Kayin. One word that froze me in place.

A name I'd never spoken.

One he couldn't know.

A horrid sound slipped from my lips as a sharp talon of fear pierced my heart. *Kayin.* My father's name. After the ancient Kysillian king. The endless sun of the north.

Magic flickered in my veins, not powerful enough to fight the terror chilling my blood. The wishing stone fluttered against my breastbone.

Master Hale shouldn't know that name.

Couldn't.

His grip tightened. Nails digging into my flesh. Shaking his head as if willing himself silent.

An animalistic sound slipped through his cracked lips as he hunched over. A wheezing rattle as his back heaved. 'Couldn't. Couldn't find him.'

The room groaned in warning, the sharp snap of flames, the distant crash of something else collapsing. Another scream, but none of it mattered.

Things I shouldn't have forgotten filled every space in my mind. Hale's reluctance to talk about the past. The impossibility of him finding a creature like me.

His unwavering kindness. His need to see things right.

Lies. That voice hissed once more and I knew it to be true.

'Stop.' I tried to pull myself back from the nightmare, but his nails dug in like claws refusing to let me go.

'Kat!' Emrys called out to me through the smoke.

I needed to move but I couldn't stop staring at those horrid blood-coated lips.

'I didn't mean to tell them where he was!' he begged, shaking me wildly as a wailing moan escaped him.

All warmth was sucked from my flesh.

'Katherine, *please*.' His grip was too tight, fingers too cold. 'Forgive me.'

Forgive me. My father's voice whispered against my cheek. In that moment all I could see was my father's face, the sadness heavy in his eyes and the tightness of how he held me. Knowing he wouldn't come back. Knowing he couldn't.

Knowing they'd kill him.

Quiet. Demure and still.

I looked down at the creature before me, in the ruined Council hall, blood coating his teeth and revulsion rolled through me, the burning sting of rage in my veins.

Looking into the dark eyes of Master Hale, understanding what I had been all this time to him.

A pet to soothe his guilt.

Useful. All I'd ever been to him.

The stench of burning flesh filled my nose, coated my tongue. Hale had made me beg and grovel for his affection. Made me ashamed of who I was. Made me a spectacle.

It was all a lie.

With a sharp tug he dragged me closer, until his breath brushed my ear. Until I could smell the coppery tang of blood that coated it. A choked wretched sound coming out of his lips. It was then I realised he was laughing. Demonic, dark laughter.

Then he wasn't Master Hale at all.

'She was alive when you burnt her, *little troll*,' he spat, bloody spittle hitting my cheek as his nails became dark claws.

Sinking into my flesh and taking gouges out of my wrist. 'You killed her!'

I screamed, wrenching myself back as his teeth snapped like a feral beast. Elongating. Too big for his mouth that cracked and split. Blood spraying my throat as he bit through his own tongue. Eyes full black, that darkness spreading outwards as his bones began to twist and crack. Becoming something else. Teeth chattering as the darkest laugh crawled out of his throat.

I twisted and thrashed. Screaming with rage or fear, I didn't know. They'd woven themselves too tightly together. My wrist bloody enough to slip from his clawed grasp. As I fell back against the sharp rubble.

'You killed her!' The creature gnashed its teeth, bones popping as it tried to escape his mortal flesh.

'Stop!' A feral scream tore from my lips. Fire tore itself from my bones, lethal and wild as it slipped through my veins. My magic tearing itself from its slumber at the bottom of my soul. Just like the dragon should have in that tale. Vicious and starved as it tried to force itself out of my hands.

The stone around my neck flickered and pulsed wildly. The creature that was Hale lunged but before those claws could reach me, bright white light shot from the wishing stone. Straight through the thing's throat. Just as it had in that pit. Black blood pouring as its eyes rolled back in its head, slumping onto the ruined marble floor. Its body cracking and twisting, a gurgling hiss from its lips as it began to reform.

Move, I commanded myself. Unable to let the words out of my trembling lips.

A crash sounded through the smoke. Screaming. A hissing skittering followed by a roar. Dark things claiming the dead's souls. Debts come to be collected. And I was in the centre of it.

Then there were hands on my forearms. I screamed, kicking out, but those hands didn't let me go. They turned me abruptly so I was looking up at Gideon. His blonde hair falling in disarray across his brow, covered in dust. Jacket sleeve torn to reveal the golden metal of his right arm. Dark blood smeared across his cheek, pale blue eyes almost glowing with rage.

'Up!' he commanded ruthlessly, hoisting me to my numb feet with hands under my armpits like I was a child.

He half dragged, half carried me over the debris. Moving faster and faster, the roaring collapse behind us, the licking flames, blinding smoke and screeching of dark things being awoken in mortal flesh. Another rumble threatened to take my legs from beneath me as Gideon curled his body over my own, stone bouncing and skidding across the ruined marble.

Thick dark smoke curled around us, streaked through with bright white light, abating the flames and making us a path through the chaos to the main doors. The familiar cold bite of that magic.

Emrys.

We stumbled into the hallway, fragments of rubble meeting my boots as the wardens lay bloodied and dust-covered in the foyer. Smoke curling around the high arched ceilings, the door nothing but shattered wood.

Students screamed and ran past covered in blood and dust. Clutching at patches of seared and burnt flesh. Gideon pushed through them effortlessly as the warning bells continued to screech.

He forced me back into an alcove out of the commotion. I panted, each breath tasting of blood. That wishing stone glowing between us, satisfied by what it had done.

Master Hale.

My stomach knotted and I had barely a moment before I vomited in the small space between us, splattering Gideon's boots.

'For fuck's sake,' he hissed, pressing one hand against my shoulder to keep me upright against the wall. Then his brow furrowed, looking down at his metal hand covered in bright red blood where he'd touched me.

He went rigid, eyes dropping to my arms.

'Fuck,' he tugged the cravat from his neck, the stitches popping, but he gave little care as he tore my sleeve to see the wound. Pain I'd forgotten about in the aftermath of everything else.

Deep gouges wept blood over my forearms. Too much blood. Gideon's fingers slipped against my skin as he worked quickly. Tearing the fabric into long strips as he bound my forearms with it, the white cloth turning red too quickly.

'He – Hale changed,' were the only words I could get out as another set of demonic screeches came from the room beyond, making me flinch. The smoke-filled hallway suddenly ominously empty.

'They sold their souls,' was Gideon's terse answer. Of course. I'd forgotten that. Sworn themselves to the mad king. Sworn their soul too. Emrys had told me that.

Emrys. I needed to say his name. Needed to call him back.

My lips parted only for a roaring rumble to come from the crumbling Council room, as unnatural screams filled the air. I pressed back against the wall, the wishing stone fluttering wildly.

'What is that?' I demanded.

'Emrys,' Gideon answered with short annoyance.

Then I felt it. The brush of Emrys's magic but different. Sharper, almost wild in its movements across my skin. Colder than before. Consuming.

As it had been in that pit, rising within Emrys. Shadows leaked into the hall, only these were not made of fire smoke, they were like tendrils of ink spreading across a page. The same ones that had guided us through the fire.

Darkness bled from the chamber doorway, or what remained of it. As if one of the ancient Old Gods had been awoken, dragging his dark cloak across the sky to summon the night. Only the creature at its centre wasn't a fable, a story or an old malicious god.

No – it was Emrys, bathed in that strange white ethereal light to match the glow of the wishing stone around my neck. The darkness curling around his limbs as if it was an extension of himself.

His shirt was torn, face splattered with blood, but his eyes were pitch-black, darkness spreading beneath his skin like vines. He strode towards us, that strange shadow slipping from him like a cloak as it faded from his pale skin once more. I didn't move. Couldn't, as an awful trembling consumed my body.

'If you're quite finished making a *spectacle!*' Gideon barked with all the authority of a perturbed housekeeper. 'She's hurt.'

Emrys didn't falter in his path to me. A barely contained wildness to his movements. The demanding, probing touch of his magic made the pain recede enough to breathe.

His cool palm cupped my throat, fingers stained black with the evidence of his summoning. He was here. The relief made me droop. A sob escaped my lips. Fingers curling into the ruined remains of his shirt. Every breath I gulped down lined with the sharp scent of beasam bark, every one taking that ache away from my lungs.

'Kat.' His hands captured my face, forcing my hair back to see me, but I could only shake my head.

'He lied,' I gasped, chest too tight, tasting nothing but my own tears. 'He lied.'

'Hale changed,' Gideon offered quietly, wiping his bloody hands on his trousers. 'We need to come up with a fucking plan to get out of here.'

He lied. A voice in my head mocked. Like a shard digging into my chest. Nothing could stop it burrowing deeper. Not even the strength of Emrys's hold as he held me to his chest, as my blood soaked into his shirt. His lips pressed against my temple, my panicked breaths brushing his throat still marked with that darkness that lingered within him.

'They're here!' a voice cried through the thick smoke. The dishevelled dusty form of Finneaus shouting down the hallway as he appeared mere feet before us.

Footsteps rumbled in the distance. What remained of the Council hunters looking for us, but I cared for none of it. Didn't hear the curse slipping from Gideon's lips or the lethal cold of Emrys's magic as I pushed from his arms with ruthless strength.

Feral wild fury tore through me as I barrelled straight for Finneaus. He didn't have a moment to react as I slammed the full force of my body into his. Knocking him to the ground.

'Lying, vicious bastard!' I screamed, pinning him beneath me, a horrid crack as my fist smashed into his face with all my strength. Two sharp blows. Something white and bloody skidding across the dusty marble with the force.

His teeth.

He screamed and twisted like a trapped fish beneath me as my nails tore through the skin of his cheeks like paper. I roared into his face. Going for his eyes.

'Kat!' Emrys's arms circled my middle, lifting me easily. My hands curled into fists, Finnaeus' blood sticky between my fingers. He scrambled backwards, palms slipping in his own blood as it dribbled from his shocked, parted lips.

'*Norac!*' The feral scream clawed its way up my throat.

Coward. The Kysillian word was nothing but an animalistic roar of fury from between my lips. The fire from the walls surged for him at my will, molten jaws wanting to devour at my command as he screamed. The stench of singed hair and burning flesh permeating the air.

My breath was heavy through my clenched teeth. Only no screams could compete with the roaring chaos inside my head.

Emrys went rigid at my back as something changed in the chaos. Something new. I felt it shift in the magic that curled around me. Harsh and vicious like a snarling beast towards a threat. That skittering from my nightmares, the sharp drag of claws against stone at the end of the hall.

Dark and bony as it moved through the smoke, all sharp angles.

Then I saw them. Dark towering creatures. Leathery grey flesh sagging from their bones. Arms too long and thin, dragging against the floor. Maws open to show sharp, narrow fish-like teeth. As the flames continued to crawl up the tapestries around them, devouring the paintings and the books in their cabinets.

Manifestations. Demons summoned from the death in the room beyond.

Emrys moved me behind him, my trembling bloody fingers curling into the back of his shirt. Knees threatening to buckle as my magic churned within me, unsatisfied. Seeking more vengeance. Burning for it.

'Dear Emrys,' Montagor smiled as he appeared between the creatures. Tendrils of darkness curling around his form as he fixed the cuffs of his coat. Unbothered by the destruction. Or Finneaus's blood beneath his boot or how the boy kept scrambling backwards pathetically. 'It appears you've run out of bargains.'

'This madness won't end well for you, Varin,' Emrys warned. 'Your sire should have taught you that.'

Varin. That name. One of the princes from beneath. *Where Serus brought honour, Varin brought wrath and ruin.*

'*Our* sire,' Montagor replied without even a blink of hesitation, as I saw the darkness curling across his skin, pressing against it like insects scuttling beneath.

Another one of the King's summonings. Montagor was made like that too.

The fire pulsed and twisted from the walls. My magic feral in its need to consume. To finish off Finneaus and the rest of them.

'You killed them,' I panted, fingers curling more tightly into Emrys's shirt.

'Did I?' Montagor's smile was predatory, his eyes filled with dark mirth as they met my own. The creatures behind him screeched and gnashed their teeth. Held back only by the slight twitch of Montagor's dark-stained fingers. So similar to Emrys's.

No. They weren't similar at all.

'They want your little pet, Serus,' he warned, coming a step closer, smearing Finneaus's blood across the ruined marble. 'And they aren't pleased you denied them their feast.'

Feast. That was all that pit had been.

I was torn from the horrific thought as more screeching came from the opposite end of the hall. The Council chamber. Wild and demonic.

He hadn't killed those lords in the chamber with the explosion. The dark had just come to claim them.

'You think you can outrun your fate?' Montagor mocked, a darkness rippling between his fingers, and I hated how familiar it seemed. 'How strange it always guides you back to me, brother.'

'He isn't your fucking brother,' Gideon sneered, a lethal nature coming over his features, a charge of magic simmering around him.

Witch casting. There was only a moment before chaos reigned again and then I learnt why they called a witch's aether *havoc*.

Gideon's fists glowed pale blue with aether, crackling in the air with the sharp static of it. It had no rhythm, wild and sharp as it twisted up his forearms. As his eyes burnt with it.

'Move!' Montagor commanded but it wasn't quick enough as those demons screeched, saliva dripping from their fangs as they surged to charge.

Gideon thrust his aether forwards, it slammed into the supporting columns of the arched hallway. A horrid crash, the ground shook. I was pressed down with the weight of Emrys wrapping around me. Stone clattering against marble but between my fingers pressed over my face and through the white cloud of ash and dust, I saw the hallway collapse.

Over the chaos came the skittering of demonic claws. The howl of something hunting. I twisted in Emrys's arms, seeing the other end of the hallway, dark shapes stumbling through the smoke like reanimated corpses. More souls the darkness had stolen.

More creatures Montagor had summoned.

This was a trap. It had always been a trap.

One of Montagor's making.

My fingers dug into Emrys's forearms; by the bite of his magic around my skin, he felt it too. Saw the new threat.

'Fuckers,' Gideon coughed, the blue glow of his aether weaker than before.

Focus. I wasn't trapped. I wasn't a pet to be contained. I turned, scanning the remains of the hallway as Emrys untangled himself from me, rising to assist whatever destructive plan Gideon was concocting.

Then, through the smoke, I saw the shape of the narrow stone stairwell. Once hidden behind the tapestry now aflame on the stone floor.

The annex stairwell. One that lead to the fey quarters. I lunged towards it, fingers digging into Emrys sleeve as I dragged him with me through the narrow stone arch.

'Gideon!' he barked. Then the three of us were pressed tight in the narrow stone passage.

'Tell me again about my dramatics, brother,' Emrys snapped at Gideon, who pushed his filthy blonde hair back from his brow. Both casually ignoring the roaring darkness just beyond us.

'It got rid of the bastards, didn't it?' Gideon fired back, those eyes burning bright with witch light.

'Up,' I panted, listening to the hollow roar from the hallway. 'We need . . . up.'

The grit of stone and dust caught on my tongue. That ringing in my head as the shaking stopped, only for the distant rumbling of dark things.

'Up!' I commanded again. Pushing at Emrys's broad chest with my trembling hands. He didn't seem pleased but took my hand, sticky with blood, and moved up the stairs.

The ground shook beneath my feet, threatening to send us both tumbling. A horrid screeching howl from behind, sharp claws on stone.

Emrys pushed me in front of him, a steady hand at my back forcing me up the twisting stairs as I slammed my toes into the steps. Blue flashes of Gideon's aether caught my eye but I kept moving despite the spots dancing in my vision, despite how my hands slipped on the stone in my own blood, until the doorway appeared into the fey quarters.

I staggered into the passage, not stopping before I barrelled straight into my old door, the sheer weight of my body breaking the flimsy lock. I staggered across the stone floor, managing to catch myself on the stone chimney breast.

'Kat.' Emrys's hands were at my waist, turning me towards him as I fought to catch my breath. Still trying to cough that horrid acrid smoke from my lips.

'Yes, let's hide in a cupboard,' Gideon hissed scathingly, rubbing his head from where he'd caught it on the low beams.

'This was my room,' I panted, pressing my hand against my ribs to stop the terrible ache in my side.

Gideon's angry expression became appalled for the barest moment before he hid anything else behind another curse. I didn't dare look at Emrys. Not with the cool simmering power still radiating off him. There wasn't time. I moved out of his hold and towards the bed. Sad and narrow, where I'd huddled with Alma for any warmth. I pushed it to the side as I dropped to my knees. Fingers running over the worn wooden floor, finding the loose floorboard. Pulling the plank away and letting it clatter to the side.

I rifled through the pathetic collection of contraband. Alma's rust-speckled sweet tins, storybooks and teacups – Alma was like a magpie, collecting treasures. Her favourite blue cup sat abandoned in the dust.

'Here.' I pulled the string of the waxed bag from the hole. Tipping it so the items inside tumbled free. Salvaged from the ruins beneath and collected over the years. Amongst it all a vial of black travelling salt. My palms braced on the rough wooden floorboards as dark spots danced across my vision. Emrys's hands came about my waist to help me to my feet, not letting me go.

Gideon looked to the small empty hearth.

'Let's hope William's left the receiving grate open,' he huffed, just as another boom echoed down the corridor.

Demons on the hunt.

Alma was going to kill me.

Chapter Fourteen

Kat

Mortals swore their souls to the creatures beneath under a King's command. Desperate to be imbued with the power of the Old Gods they gave worship to. Only the moment their hearts stopped, darkness poured forth into their veins – becoming as the Old Gods always intended. Nothing but a plaything to devour this world.

Relics of Elysior – fey Compendium Records

Despite the quiet of the study, the distant ringing of the warning bells wouldn't leave my ears. My hair hung free around my shoulders, ends knotted. The ache of my magic unbearable where it bit into my bones, making my limbs tremble.

A horrid taste lined my mouth. Reminding me cruelly that I'd been sick. Blood still sticky as it dried between my trembling fingers.

The barest crackle of the fire seemed too loud. My heart pounding too painfully against my ribs.

She was alive when you burnt her, little troll. I winced at the memory of those words, how tightly they seemed to constrict my throat.

'Kat,' Emrys's cool hands cupped my face, making me look at him. At the darkness in his eyes. Endless. How it curved along his jaw, the sensation of his magic hesitantly brushing

145

my forearms, trying to seek the source of the pain. But it was burrowed too deeply inside of me. Ash still clung to his dark hair. Smeared on his cheek and neck along with dark demonic blood. The blood of what those lords had become.

Monsters hiding in mortal flesh.

'Well. Council meetings appear to have become more eventful.' Thean's voice was sharp with accusation as the voyav lounged in the study doorway, hands pushed deep into their pockets. 'You can hear the Council warning bells all the way to the west hills. What on earth is going on?'

'They're dead.' Gideon tore off his ruined jacket, tossing it carelessly against the sideboard. 'Montagor made his move.'

'What?' Thean's relaxed demeanour quickly forgotten as they moved further into the room. 'Tell me *exactly* what happened.'

'So you can decide to be useful, *parasite*?' Gideon bit out, such malice in his voice I flinched.

'The Council members became what they sold their souls to. Montagor also summoned *Scavengers*.' There was a harsh reluctance to Emrys's words, a tension rippling around him. As if something else could claw its way out from beneath his skin, causing the fire to flicker wildly.

'The Council chambers are miles from the nearest seal or even breach—' Thean's words were calm and assertive with fact but Emrys was already shaking his head.

'Montagor has a *relic*, and now no laws of summoning can stop him,' he interrupted, a dark warning in his words that let a chill slip over my skin.

A relic.

The dark held weapons of their own. Weapons even the old Kysillian's flame was no match for. The warning sang though my mind, unable to remember who had spoken it to me. Montagor had used something demonic to tear that chamber

146

apart. Something so ancient the tales had forgotten it existed. To form a perfect deadly trap.

A sinking feeling consumed the centre of my chest, as if a soft bank of earth was slipping away from a cliffside within me. All these things and none of them made sense.

This darkness wasn't just back, it had never left.

'What's hap—' a familiar voice began before it stopped.

Alma.

I hadn't realised until that moment that my heart hadn't finished breaking. Until I saw her in the doorway, the concern in her deep green eyes and the worry at her brow.

'Kat.' She crossed the room to me in an instant. 'I bloody told you—.'

The barest brush of her fingers against my torn dress sleeve, but I recoiled like a wild thing. Unable to bare it.

I stumbled back against the shelves. The books rattled but the house settled them quickly, creaking with worry. Either for the state of me, or the sudden panic that seemed to be encasing my heart.

'I'm fine.' I tried to push my arms behind my back, only for the pain to stop me. For it to shorten my breath.

'Kat.' Emrys came closer at the same moment Alma did.

'You're bleeding,' she replied, a sternness coming into her words as she tried to reach for me again. To manage me as she had before. Only I wasn't the Kat of before and I was fearful I never would be again.

She was alive when you burnt her, little troll. That creature's words seared through my mind, the flash of Master Hale's face covered in blood.

Murderer.

'I'm fine!' I sneered, baring my teeth as I gripped one of my injured wrists. Feeling the wetness of my blood against my palm as it seeped through Gideon's makeshift bandage. Feeling the stinging rush of magic burning in my veins.

The fire roared in the hearth, almost singeing the books that rested on the mantel.

That vicious pain in my neck came back, making me grip it, bowing me forward.

'I see things aren't going to plan, dear Emrys,' Thean drawled with almost boredom.

'You knew he was close to finding a relic.' Emrys's voice was steel, eyes darker than the night. 'And your master knew it too.'

Thean's master – the Countess.

Of course, because if the Council fell to ruin, Elysior would be vulnerable once more.

'Are you angry at me for not telling you, or that you couldn't sense it yourself, *my lord*?' Thean inclined their head, but I could see the concern buried in those amber eyes, dulling them. 'That you've allowed yourself to become second to a monster?'

Second. Serus was the first son of the Old Gods. Varin . . . Montagor was the second.

The other few names that had survived record: Acarus, Duar, Than and Orus. Then Serus' shadow – his sister in the tales. *Acara.* Queen of the Damned, seer of the night.

My knees almost buckled, the pain at my ribs tightening my chest. The house groaned, movement on the bookshelves behind me as if the books themselves wished to flee the room as the bitter cold bite of Emrys's power rose. Dark shadows moving between his fingers like blades.

'As much as I commend it, Emrys . . . killing the voyav doesn't help us.' Gideon moved between them. Hands resting on his hips, the golden fingers of his right catching the firelight, speckled with the red of my blood. 'We should ward the house and—'

'Someone tell me what on earth is happening?' Alma snapped, hands clawed as if anticipating a threat. The hurt in her expression and the depth of her confusion were plain as her eyes found my own once more.

I'd never felt further from her, too far from what I was supposed to be.

'Montagor attacked the Council,' Gideon answered.

'Bloody saints!' William clutched his horns, mouth agape since he had entered the room, apron still on and speckled with flour.

'I assume they're dead then,' Thean offered with the barest interest. 'Or claimed.'

Claimed. Turned into the demonic creatures they'd worshipped when they followed the King.

Emrys gave the barest of nods as a shocked curse slipped from William's lips but it was all background noise as my eyes met Alma's and I saw the panic and the weight of her heartbreak. Saw it in the shadow of scales at her jaw.

'Master Hale?' she asked so softly and all I could feel was the blood between my fingers.

Kayin. My father's name on Hale's lips. The truth of it. All this time he'd known.

I didn't mean to tell them. He knew. He told them. He made my father leave. Let me carry this guilt in my heart. Let it burrow into my very bones. He knew all my secrets and how ruthlessly he wielded them against me.

Told me to forget Daunton. Told me its victims were best left to rest in the past. As if this pain in me would only make them suffer more.

Liar. He was a liar – and how easily I'd devoured those lies. I turned away from it, the horrid hissing inside my skull as I pressed my fingers to my temples, desperate for it to stop.

Tauria. You did not listen. The voice clawed at my mind. I shook my head, tears running down my cheeks. It was like something inside me was ripped in half. Shattered so easily.

Only for Alma's hands to take hold of my face, stilling me. The familiar rough scrape of the scales forming at her palms.

'He lied.' The sob clawed its way up my throat. 'He knew. All this time he knew and he lied.'

All I could see was the red smoke in the orb before him. Of the things I'd done, how little it was all worth, when fey had died anyway. Died for nothing.

'I don't—' Alma shook her head, looking to Emrys for any help before those eyes came back to me.

'I trusted him with you,' I wept. It was a raw animalistic sound from my lips. I trusted him with Alma. With the only fragments of myself I had left. 'He knew.'

Daunton. What he did. What he would do. Those girls' faces flashed into my vision like pages flipping in a book. Small and bony. Desperate and weak. I could hear them, screaming endlessly. The taste of smoke filled my mouth, coating my tongue.

Then all I could smell was the bitterness of saint smoke. The blood and bruises on Alma's flesh. Could feel nothing but the damp coldness of the night mist, of the bodies beneath wet soil.

'He knew.' My magic rose, sensing my panic as a threat, biting painfully at my bones. I saw Alma's eyes widen as she felt it, as she snatched her hands back from my face as if I'd seared her skin.

A scream was burning in my throat. The house gave a wary groan and Emrys called my name.

The stone around my neck fluttered like a panicked heart-beat. A horrid pained sound escaping my lips. Unable to bear it, I pulled at my hair, dust and grit beneath my fingertips. I heard the hearth roar in answer and I couldn't stop it. Couldn't survive the fury of my magic.

'She shouldn't summon!' Gideon warned too late.

'Outside!' Alma ordered. On command the house raised the floorboards beneath my feet. Sending me sideways only instead of falling against the bookcases, I stumbled into the space that opened up like a doorway between them, out into the bitter cold day. The low winter sun stung my eyes, as grass tangled around my boots. The vicious wind stirring my ruined skirts where the house had sent me into the wilderness.

Just as I'd wandered through those nightmares. The cold wind whipping around me as the first drops of rain brushed my cheeks; nothing compared to the endless flow of my tears.

I'd killed them. Killed those girls in Daunton and fooled myself into believing they mattered. All that time, I'd suffered it so they would matter. But they didn't. They never would.

There was nothing but the darkness of the wood in the distance. No memories. No voices calling me back. How far I'd wandered and yet how this pain remained.

A scream clawed its way out of my throat the same moment my fire burst from my palms. Rain sizzling away as I was engulfed in the inferno of it. It swirled and danced around me. Vicious and ruthless as it roared. My dress became ash, floating away on the wind of my own making. Leaving me in my slip, unable to be consumed by flames because Alma always enchanted them.

Always took care of me. Always. Even when I failed her.

The agony of my grief kept clawing its way out of my throat. As I screamed my fury towards the bruised sky, at the ancestors for not showing me a better way. For leaving us. For allowing them to suffer it. For never saving them.

Forgive me. The memory of my father's voice whispered so gently as if in comfort . . . but I feared there was no forgiveness left in me.

Then, as quickly as the fury came, it was gone, simpering and weak within my bones. Leaving me with nothing but ragged useless breaths. Exhausted with its rage until all that was left was the consuming nature of its grief. The earth was scorched beneath me, left to nothing but ash.

I fell to my knees, rain pounding against my skin until arms came around me. A soothing bitter chill of magic that the ruthlessness of my own submitted to. The sheer size of him curling over me, blocking me from the storm.

Emrys.

He said something against the curve of my throat but it was lost within the taunt of those voices in my mind.

Tauria.

My sacred Kysillian name that the dark shouldn't know. The thing I should never have let out.

Then the darkness took me back.

Chapter Fifteen

Kat

To burn is the cost of our fury, Avaya. *Our fury can end this world, that power must be feared. The kings burnt to save us, but perhaps . . . they burnt to save us from themselves, as much as that darkness beneath.*

Greed and power are never far apart – no matter what the stories say. For even those heroes never wished to fall, Tauria.

The roaring crackle of fire filled my ears now, lurching me into waking as the reek of smoke filled my nose.

Avaya. That name followed me into waking. A word of fire and smoke. What my father had called me to show his love. It meant starlight in Kysillian. Because he called my mother *Aya*, which meant little flame. How easily I'd forgotten that.

The smell of books, old magic and the lingering scent of beasam bark chased that memory away. I was in the Blackthorn study. It was drenched in orange light as the sun sank across the wood beyond the window.

Home. I pressed the heels of my palms against my eyes, realising the smell of smoke was coming from me. I was still in my slip – the only thing that had survived that fury within me.

I looked at the bandages across my wrists. Gideon's cravat had burnt away with the ruthlessness of my summoning.

But someone had washed and dressed my forearms in clean bandages. A glass sat waiting on a small table next to me, a healing tonic too.

My trembling fingers rubbed the fabric at my wrists. How brutally my fury had hollowed me out. Most of it a blur. Just the memory of Alma's quiet broken reassurance left. The strength in Emrys's hold as I'd been moved to the chaise as if he remembered that I hadn't wanted to go to bed. Didn't wish to be left alone in the dark.

A horrid taste lined my mouth and I reached for the healing tonic. Sick of my weakness before I picked up the glass, drinking deeply before I pressed the cool glass to my forehead, trying to steady myself and find some sanity.

'Please,' I whispered to nobody. The small table next to me rocked slightly, nudging against my knee, offering some small comfort.

A murmur of voices reached my ear, coming from beyond the room, from somewhere down the hall. Probably everyone trying to work out what to do next, while I'd fallen apart so easily.

'Pull yourself together,' I sighed as I untangled myself from the blanket, seeing my enchanted bag abandoned on my desk. I rooted through it for my training attire, only for pages of my notes to come out. All my scribbled workings on incantations and research into wild herbs.

Notes on the saltorvarious pox. The thing that had brought me here in the first place. How easily I'd forgotten that desperation to fix something. To see the world right.

How easily I'd believed I could. Write a paper good enough to graduate. Find Alma a home. Find some useful position and live the life I'd dreamt of: helping fey.

Only it was a lie. They'd been dying all this time.

Everything that had happened . . . I believed it had to be for a purpose. To graduate. To be the first. To prove them all wrong.

Only the bitter reality was impossible to deny. It was all for nothing.

My gaze blurred with tears of frustration as I pushed the papers away and tugged out my training clothes, only for the clatter of something hitting the floor to stop me.

The hilt of my father's blade, glinting in the dusk light.

A flare of memory made the training clothes slip from my fingers. Remembering how the sword had clattered against that seal. How Emrys had touched it, brought it to me.

How it had come to me, despite all my mistakes in leading us to that horrid place.

With trembling fingers, I picked it up. Letting my thumb run over the scratched and tarnished metal.

'I shouldn't have let you rest so long.' Guilt raked at my bones. How long I'd left the thing in disuse, how long my muscled ached for the strength they once had.

Too long pretending to be something I wasn't. Mortal. A simple girl with no ambition or choice.

Again, Tauria. My father's soft command brushed my ear, making my breath catch as the hilt almost slipped from my numb fingers.

Tauria. The name the darkness knew. Knew I was here. Knew the power in my blood to awaken it or seal it. A realisation that only deepened my panic, my throat too tight as I sank to my knees.

'Please.' The word was too small from my lips as I looked down at the hilt curled in my fist. The smooth warmth of the blade so real.

A Kysillian is never beaten. Never marked by the viciousness of this world because the kings in our blood bow to no other.

Words from the ancient texts I'd found in the abandoned Fifth Library. Those scars on my back burning like a brand. I'd been beaten. Marked. I'd let them scar my very soul. I'd lost, over and over again.

Imperfections that I knew meant I was unworthy of the Kysillian name my father had given me. Unworthy of the fire in my blood. How the ancestors would see me as a disgrace. A weakness.

'Forgive me,' I whispered. Too small and pathetic for a creature that held the right to wield an ancient blade. I pressed the hilt against my brow, bowing forward as the emotion cracked me open.

Knowing only one truth: I'd always be my father's daughter. That he'd love me . . . no matter what I'd done, or how foolish I'd become.

Always. A word whispered in my mind, a word from my mother's lips with the ghost of a kiss against my cheek. The barest hint of memory as I took myself back. Back to that beach. To the day I'd said goodbye. To all the things I'd allowed myself to forget.

The crashing of the waves, high and rough as they always were on the north sea. The briny taste on my lips. The bitter cold bite in the air. How I'd tumbled down on that wet sand, only for my mother to kneel in it with me.

'Tauria.' Her hands took hold of my shoulders as the storm raged around us, plastering her dark hair to her cheeks. How perfectly beautiful she was, even in her grief.

'He has to come back!' I cried, breaths uneven with my sobbing. Using my small fists to rub my eyes, stinging from my tears.

'He will, my love.' She brought my sandy fingers to her lips, her smile weighted with sorrow before she presented the hilt of my father's

sword to me, letting it rest across her palm as the rain puddled around it. 'Do you think he'd leave this behind forever?'

A small offering. A hope between us. A promise and a lie.

'No.' I shook my head as she wrapped my hand around the hilt so we both held it. Still warm from his touch. From the chaos in his blood.

'It's your job to keep it safe. Just as he taught you.' One arm came around me to bring me closer, to wrap her cloak around my shoulders, the other hand falling to her very pregnant stomach between us.

'He loves us very much,' she averred, her brown eyes filled with such endless love and hope. Even then. 'Never doubt that, Tauria.'

I curled myself into her arms as she kissed my tear-stained cheeks as my hair tangled with hers in the harsh wind.

'No matter how far this world takes him from us, he loves us beyond anything else.' Her voice broke with the pain of her grief but I felt her smile against my skin. 'That truth remains. Aest'rea. Always.'

Always.

Aest'rea. A promise in Kysillian that mortal words had no equivalent. A love eternal. In every life.

I watched my tears splatter onto the blade now. Saw the murky reflection of myself in the golden metal. I knew the depth of their love because I felt it in the weight of my grief. How it had changed me forever. A small darkness in my heart that would never leave. One no joy could erase.

My first blessing was to be their daughter. To be loved.

Always.

'Isn't this a depressing sight,' came the silky, irritating voice of Thean Page.

My head shot up, turning to see the voyav still in male form in the study doorway. White shirt rolled to the elbows and creased as if they'd been hard at work. Their strange auburn hair left long and tied back at the nape of their neck. That dark make-up lining those sharp amber eyes. A furrow at their brow with either disgust or confusion but I didn't care.

I wiped the tears irritably from my cheeks and got to my feet. Clearly the voyav had somehow survived Emrys's temper.

'If you want to end up back in your deathbed, you're going about it the right way, darling,' they sighed, as if my mere presence was exhausting.

'Unless you missed it . . . it appears I'm rather difficult to kill.' I flipped the blade, letting it shift to become a throwing knife, glinting in the firelight. Ignoring how my hand trembled with the barest motion. 'I'm fine.'

Thean inclined their head. 'Is weeping on the floor a recent hobby you've decided to indulge in? If so, you should know it's quite . . . pathetic.'

'What do you want?' I demanded, reaching down to snatch up my training attire.

'I was looking for your handsome dark lord.' They shrugged, moving closer, keeping to the shadows cast by the shelves as if the weak sunlight could render them to dust.

'Not here,' I answered.

'Maybe roll around naked in the rain again. That seemed to summon him quickly enough,' they offered dryly. 'Besides, you should be counting your blessings.'

'What blessings?' I snapped, annoyed I was being goaded so easily.

'That he's not here, otherwise you'd have to lie and we know just how much you hate that.'

'Lie about what?' I demanded petulantly, despite the sinking feeling in the centre of my chest.

Their fanged smile was so cruel. 'The things the dark told you.'

Serus, that mocking voice called. That darkness was calling his name. Reverent in its hunger.

What the dark wants, it never let's go. Emrys had spoken those words and now the memory of them struck like a fist to my chest.

The thought of it made the wound at my neck sting. I flinched but refused to touch it. Not needing any further warnings against my own foolishness.

'The dark does like to mock before it bites.' Thean's smile taunted me. Treating me just like the idiot I was. 'It knows, doesn't it?'

Yes. That word wouldn't leave me, sticking to the roof of my mouth. The dark knew Emrys was there, and it was seeking him out.

It wouldn't stop.

'You knew that seal was down there,' I accused. Remembering all their taunting at Fairfax, how unsurprised Thean seemed. How could they not when they were made of that same darkness. 'You didn't warn us.'

'Now, where would be the fun in that?' The voyav's lips pursed with mock sympathy.

Heat flushed my veins, my grip tightening on my blade and then it awakened something else inside of me. 'You didn't tell me.'

'You didn't *listen*.' The voyav shook their head. 'It appears you're nothing but another Kysillian drunk on their own importance.'

My grip on my blade became white-knuckled, the voyav's smile sharpening with the threat. Heat rolled through me. My magic seeping into my limbs, building strength it knew I'd need. The house sensed it, giving a weary creak, before every table, chair and desk were pushed to the far corners. Creating a clear space between us.

'Shut up,' I snapped. Trying to find my sanity. The hilt in my hand changed to a sword in response to my anger.

'That's what you should have done . . . before you broke poor Alma's heart so carelessly.' There was a hard, cold nature to their eyes.

Alma's face flashed in my vision. How carelessly I'd told her the truth. Told her of Hale's lies. Of his death.

My rage was a wild thing tethered inside of me that snapped free in a moment as I swung my blade. Only the voyav was quicker. Summoning shadow blades in their palms, meeting my blow and trapping my blade between their own.

Their fangs gleamed. 'Careful, darling, that antique looks quite sharp.'

I bared my teeth, forcing my weight into Thean so they stumbled back into the panelling of the study walls, having no choice but to release my blade. I swung again, only for them to twist out of my reach. Their speed only fed my anger. Anger at myself. At my own stupidity. I attacked, over and over again. They met each of my strikes with the efficiency of the killer they were. The challenge of it would have given anyone else pause. All it did was fuel my rage. Awakening that ancient part of my blood that needed victory.

I became nothing but a vessel for my strength, blow after blow. Ducking and weaving, every limb remembering its purpose like a well taught dance. Again and again, I struck out at the voyav with deadly blows. Grunts and cries leaving my lips, bursts of emotion I rarely let out. A side of myself they'd mocked too long. An aggressive, monstrous thing – and I revelled in it. Relishing in the tension lifting from my limbs with each strike and blow. The impact of hitting the ground, rolling and surging back to my feet, listening and feeling Thean's blows cut through the air. The brutality of each one and being able to match it no matter how hard or fast it arrived.

No matter how weak I'd allowed myself to become.

Sweat stuck the lose strands of hair to my brow, breath panted harshly through my lips as my slip stuck to my back. My limbs burnt from exertion, the weight of the sword more noticeable, making my footing clumsy as I was backed against the sideboard, raising my blade just in time to keep Thean's from my throat.

'Tired darling?' The voyav taunted, barely panting, their eyes alight with the promise of a fight.

'Shut up,' I spat. I didn't want to listen but those words dropped into my murky thoughts like stones into a lake. Settling too easily.

I was so tired. Too burdened by my own lies.

'I clearly overestimated your intelligence,' Thean laughed, dark and mocking, peering down at me with disdain.

'You don't know anything about me.' I ignored the frustrated burn of tears in my eyes. The flare of panic from the silence of my magic, the hollow echoing inside of me where it should be despite how my body surged to fight, despite the power of the blade I wielded.

'No darling, you don't know anything about yourself,' they corrected so softly, as if addressing a child.

I bared my teeth, surging forward but Thean was ready. They were always ready. Pushing me too easily. Moving too quickly, every strike rattling through me. Too strong. My grip too weak.

I clung to my fraying pride, that after all this time, I still remembered. My body remembered every lesson my father had given me. Barefoot in the field beyond our cottage, feeling every groove and divot of the dry earth beneath my toes for balance. The smell of dry cut grass, the sweetness of the flowers crushed every time I was knocked onto my back.

The rough texture of his hand as he pulled me back to my feet.

Again, Tauria, he commanded softly in my memory. The sword warming in my grasp as if it could hear those words echo through my memory.

I went faster and harder, letting the blade guide me. Thean's eyes went wider with surprise, struggling to match my new bloodthirsty pace. Good.

Only, just like my magic, I burnt too quickly. Each turn and block slower. My limbs sluggish as if moving through water.

When I met the voyav's eyes in the fury of our spar, I didn't see hate or disgust. No, they were studying me closely. Trying to pass a message without words. Where they knocked my leg to correct my stance, or hit the underside of my arm to strengthen my block when they could have used my weakness against me.

I tried to focus. Tried to see it, and that was my mistake. It slowed me enough to almost miss a block, to stumble and let the voyav's foot knock me to my knees.

I panted wildly, winded as I stumbled back to my feet. Surging just in time as Thean's blade slashed passed my head. My sword too loose in my hand, the blows reverberating through my bones.

I was losing. I was done.

'Stop,' I commanded, fear taking a vice-like grip of my heart as weakness spread through my limbs.

'You think *they'll* stop?' The only sign of sympathy came from the sharp arch of their brow as they pulled back, not to release me but to strike another blow. Harder than all the others.

Who? I wanted to sneer but I was done.

My legs gave way, knees slamming into the floor. A horrid weak sound leaving my lips as my body failed me. As the blade slipped from my grasp, sliding across the floor. Leaving me to my fate.

Only no blow came. A worse fate – a smug voyav crouched before me.

'Feel better, darling?' A dry laugh slipped from their lips, elbows on their knees, blades loose in their grasp between their legs. A mocking gargoyle.

'Smug bastard,' I panted. Rage still simmering too closely to the surface in me. Mostly at myself. That wild Kysillian part of me wanting the fight. Wanting it to hurt so I'd feel something other than this guilt.

'We can tell dear Gideon you're not at risk from blood madness at least,' they answered, sheathing their blades once more. 'Since neither of the Blackthorn boys were brave enough to test it themselves.'

Those words nestled sourly in my gut, pausing me as I tried to get back to my feet.

Blood madness. Inability to control chaos magic. I could take the whole house down. Incinerate it with the barest flick of a finger, and myself with it.

Thean had been testing me and I'd tumbled into their trap so easily. Another concocted scheme of theirs. But they'd revealed something in their persistence to help.

'Emmaline asked you to keep him safe,' I repeated their own words back to them, only now I understood the truth in them. 'Did she mean from this?'

From Varin. From the power of that darkness. From the Old Gods beneath. From all of it.

Thean's jaw tightened, eyes glinting with an emotion I knew they'd never express with words. 'Once again, darling, you're cleverer than I'd like.'

My lips parted wanting to know more, when a strange

sensation rippled over my skin, a fluttering from the stone at my chest and a sharp pain from the bite at my neck, as the house clattered the sideboard cupboards loudly.

Thean jolted to their feet as if they felt it too.

Then William's cry echoed down the hallway.

Chapter Sixteen

Kat

'Fucking saints!' came the echoed scream, the house's doors slamming as I darted into the hall the same moment Thean did. Tumbling into the wood panelling as I used it to push myself further down the hall just in time just to see William appear at the other end, hands over his horns as he ducked low. Diving to slide across the tiled entryway.

I skidded to a halt. Thean slamming into my back.

A dark fiend came scuttling around the corner at the other end of the hallway. Its bony body made of dark grey smoke with glowing red eyes and lethal, long, gleaming talons. It screeched, flapping two thin pairs of beetle-like wings. In moments it formed into pallid grey flesh instead of smoke, covered in markings. Archaic rune-like carvings on its body as if it had freed itself from an ancient text and imprinted the words on itself during its escape.

It was unlike any fiend I'd seen before.

I felt the house groan as it swung one of the high beams down, swatting the beast into the wall with a crack of plaster. It screamed, claws cutting through the wood to free itself. I saw the darkening at the corners of the hall as shadows gathered, felt the brutality of Emrys's magic. Cold and vicious. The dark creature recoiling as if sensing his threat. Too late.

A long shard of Emrys's summoning shot past mine and Thean's stunned forms. Burying itself in the creature's chest as it fell and curled into itself with a screech. William let out another panicked shriek. Scrambling across the tiles towards us.

'Gideon!' Emrys barked from where he'd appeared from a doorway just down the hall, eyes jet-black and shadows crawling up his forearms.

Only I didn't hesitate to finish the job as I sent my power rippling down the blade in my grasp, waiting until the fiend leered and screeched, neck extended.

One swift fury-fuelled turn. Fast enough to miss its claws as I cut off the fiend's head, spraying the hallway with thick black blood. A loud squelch as the remains hit the tiled floor. A sizzle; dark smoke curling along the length of my blade.

Silence consumed the hall only to be broken by the pleased creak of the house, and then the shocked gasp of Alma as she rushed up from the kitchen stairs to my left. Wiping her flour covered hands on an apron.

'Bloody bastard,' William panted as Alma knelt to help him up, checking him for injury.

'Does nobody know the fucking meaning in—' Gideon came to a skidding halt on the stairs landing above us. Lips still parted in the beginning of whatever lecture he was about to give, a pair of spectacles perched on the end of his nose as he took in the chaos and now the reek of demonic blood below.

'Bravo, darling.' Thean gave a slow clap as they slouched against the staircase banister. 'Gideon, you should recommend decapitation to all your patients. It seems to have cured dear Kat marvellously.'

'That's a blood seeker,' Gideon replied sharply, ignoring Thean as he came down the stairs. Pulling his glasses off as if he didn't trust them.

'A salvek,' Emrys agreed darkly as he examined the remains with a cold expression, suddenly at my side. Then his dark gaze found my own, ran over the entirety of me. It was then I remembered I was only in my slip, worse for wear since Thean's impromptu sparring session.

'It came in through the bloody greenhouse window!' William swallowed, looking peaky.

Salvek. The name of a demonic blood seeker. A beast from beyond.

It had flown here – been summoned nearby.

'That's not possible,' I whispered, watching black blood drip onto the hardwood from my father's blade. Yet even as I said the words I knew they were a lie as a shiver raked its way down my spine.

'Montagor has a relic. The full extent of such a weapon is not known,' Gideon continued, speaking to nobody in particular but more to unburden the thoughts from his mind. 'Records have been lost to time and—'

Gideon's focus dropped to see my state of undress and my sweaty dishevelment before he turned that sharp, annoyed gaze to Emrys. 'What the bloody fuck have you two been up to?'

'Nothing,' I snapped, ignoring the heated flush on my cheeks as I fixed the strap of my slip.

'I don't recognise any of those markings,' William frowned as he leant over the remains of the creature hesitantly as if it could lurch back to life at any moment, mercifully dragging everyone's attention back to it.

Emrys pulled off his coat and draped it over my shoulders. I slid my arms inside instantly, clutching the lapels closed. Suddenly cold as the potency of my magic abandoned me. Slipping my father's hilt into the pocket.

Then he moved to the creature, crouched down and ran his finger across the flesh, the ink smudging and coming away. 'Summoning ink.'

'We're beyond fucked, Emrys.' Gideon glared at his brother over the still-twitching corpse.

'I'm aware.' Emrys sighed, rubbing the back of his neck in thought as he got back to his feet. A deadly silence left between the two.

'Why?' Alma asked, her dark curls tumbling over her shoulders as her assessment then moved to me. Partially in undress and probably in a worse state than how she left me.

Only those green eyes also moved to Thean, her nose twitching as her eyes narrowed. Of course, nothing got past Alma.

'Every record of ancient darkness no longer exists. Thanks to the purging during the peace treaties.' Gideon let out a frustrated breath, his metal fingers curled into a fist. 'Even the fucking mad king didn't go this far.'

'Montagor has nothing to lose,' I corrected. No kingdom to impress, no lords to keep quiet. No, he just had that hunger. The madness.

'Something must have survived.' Alma wrapped her arms around herself, the bitter truth of how dire the situation was like a ruthless chill. 'It isn't like they kept their word.'

'Wonderful, just what I need. A cursed fucking treasure hunt,' Gideon snapped, making William flinch with the venom in his tone. Earning him a sharp glare from Alma but before her claws could interfere, Thean stepped into the fray.

'Yes, because you have so much else on your plate,' the voyav drawled, earning themself a dirty look from the healer which they seemed unbothered by. 'Let's not ignore the fact your dear brother, Emrys, has allowed his senses to dull so much he couldn't even sense a relic until it was too late.'

Something dangerous shifted in the air between the voyav and Emrys. The beasam bark had suppressed his magic, but also suppressed his natural senses. Suppressed the predator that all Verr in those dark tales had the potential to be.

'Couldn't sense that Montagor would be present in that Council hall. Or what dangers he carried on his person.' Thean grinned. 'Now Montagor is ahead and awakening ancient relics this house swore to silence. So, what are you going to do about it, *Blackthorn?*'

I heard the challenge and felt the wrath in Emrys's magic as it darkened the hall. The Blackthorns were the last keepers of the dark, of all it could do.

'We need to find out where he made his summoning from,' I intervened, trying to ease the worry in the house and William, if for nothing else.

'And how do you propose we do that?' Gideon snapped.

'All dark things return,' Alma answered, turning all eyes to her. The one story we all knew. Yet her focus was on the remains of that creature, the leathery flesh covered in blood.

I saw the thought in her gaze. Saw the remains of the bandage still around her wrist.

'No.' The word left me sharply. Guttural, recoiling from the danger in the mere suggestion of it.

'That creature came from a summoning, which means the others were summoned too. They can communicate with each other.' She put it together quickly, rolling her shoulders as if she could slip into the beast's form at any moment. 'So it will remember where it's been.'

Remember how to get back to its master.

'Theoretically,' Gideon offered.

Alma took a step towards the remains but Thean suddenly blocked her path.

'I wouldn't do that, darling.' The voyav's words were short. Almost as if they cared and were repulsed by the fact. 'I doubt you want that thing crawling around in your pretty little head.'

'Concerned?' she mocked. 'You said they were summoned, so wherever they were resting, there could be something else there.'

'Alma—' I began but then those sharp feline eyes were on me, burning with fury.

'Something *useful*,' she added sternly.

'No.' The word slipped free before I could control myself.

She bristled, her furious gaze now pinned on me. 'That isn't your choice, Kat.'

'You've never changed into anything that dark,' I snapped, heart pounding painfully against my ribs with my panic.

'Haven't I?' she challenged, so stony and distant that for a moment I didn't recognise her.

Haven't I? Then I remembered the barest impression of scales on her skin the first night we'd met, so large and dark that she wouldn't let me anywhere near her. Not until they faded. How she'd curled herself around them as if guarding a treasure. She never spoke of them again and I'd never seen them since. In all her forms. I'd never seen them, as if I'd imagined it.

'If I can connect with that beast, we'll know where they've been and where they're going next,' she continued, her voice too distant for me to work out her thoughts, her expression too hidden.

'Why not? Considering the torture was so fun to stomach last time,' Thean threw in dryly, their arms crossed and lips pursed in annoyance at the idea.

'It worked.' Alma bared her now fanged teeth.

'What is your plan when those creatures also remember you, darling? When they hear you crawling around in their mind and tell their master. The girl who becomes beasts.'

Alma stilled at that, a flare of panic in her eyes for the barest moment before her expression slipped back to annoyance.

'Alma, it's *dangerous*.' I interjected before she lacerated the voyav. It sounded like a plea, soft and desperate as I moved closer to her. Blocking out everyone else until it was just us. So those very human green eyes could meet my own. Clear and filled with her iron resolve. She'd made up her mind and there was no unmaking it.

'This is *my* curse, Kat. I will be its master.' The unwavering weight of those words struck me like a blow. The painful truth pressed between them. Shame coursed through me at my attempt to stop her. She was right. How much agency she'd been denied that I had no right to take more from her.

No matter how scared it made me. She'd been caged long enough and I knew the madness of it. Her eyes didn't even flicker in Emrys's direction, nor Gideon's. She needed no permission. She never had.

'William.' She held out her hand patiently, the boy going pale, eyes moving to Emrys, who gave the barest of nods. He wouldn't forbid her. Not as those words hung true between us.

William reached into his apron and pulled out his sharp small shears and a knife.

Alma ignored the knife, taking the shears as she gave him a small reassuring smile. Moving to where the fiend still twitched.

There was a horrid crunch as she cut off the thing's clawed finger, straightening before making her way to the study and giving us no choice but to follow. Moving straight to my desk, turning over her sleeve, revealing the webbing of scars that bit into her flesh. Paler than the rest of her skin. Rolling the fabric higher to where the small white marks lay from other extractions. All the things she never spoke about.

'Miss Darcy, if you—' Gideon began but Alma ignored him, already making the cut with the small healer's blade I'd left on my desk.

The barest slice just at the base of her thumb, enough to bead against her skin. Then she smeared that dark foul blood from the beast's finger across the wound. Let the talon drop from her hand to thud against the desk; a small puddle forming of dark liquid and smoke.

Her back straightened as her eyes fluttered closed. Nothing but the weary groan of the house and our own breath.

She was so silent, so still for the longest moment. I'd seen her change before, but never like this. Never with such focus.

'Is she all right?' William whispered out of the corner of his mouth, before huffing when Gideon elbowed him in answer.

Alma didn't even flinch, not a twitch. Slowing until her chest stopped moving, her stillness becoming deadly.

Too long.

Unease rolled through me as I moved the barest step forward. Missing the curl of Emrys's fingers in the back of the coat I wore as if to wrench me back.

'Alma?' I asked cautiously, reaching out for her arm. The house groaned. Desk draws rattling as if something was trying to escape. Then the fire went dead in the hearth.

Wrong. A voice mocked in the back of my mind. Alma's eyes opened. No green to be seen. Only black. Endless as the night. A flash of darkness moving beneath her tanned skin.

One minute she was mortal, beautiful and familiar. The next she was nothing but talons and smoke. Lurching right for me with a feral scream of sharp yellow fangs in a demonic jaw. Forcing me back as we tumbled over the desk in a tangle of limbs and black vapour. Papers and books raining down as I hit the floor hard. Not having a moment before those fangs went for my face.

'Alma!' I screamed, hands on her monstrous jaws as putrid breath and saliva dripped onto my throat. The weight of her claws against my ribs squeezed the air from my lungs. Only they didn't pierce Emrys's coat. Or whatever charm he'd worked into the fabric.

Thankfully Emrys's powerful forearm came beneath the creature's chin, stopping its attack as it screeched into my face. Strange leathery skin too hard to hold.

'Gideon!' Emrys roared. Blue summoning light in the corner of my eye, only we didn't get a chance because then the creature that was Alma formed wings.

The strength of them manifesting threw Emrys and Gideon backwards, crashing into one of the bookcases as paper ruptured skywards.

'Fucking saints!' William shrieked from somewhere in the commotion.

'Alma!' I snapped, trying to push her back. Only for her horrid sharp teeth to catch my hand between my finger and thumb, making blood flow. 'Stop!'

I forced my knee up and used the momentum to throw her demonic form off me and into the sideboard. Breaking its legs and making it collapse, artifacts littering the floor with heavy tomes.

Only as I rolled and got my knees back beneath me, turning in defence, did I notice she was gone. Nothing but smoke curling where she should have landed.

'Bloody fucker,' Gideon cursed, blue aether crackling in his metal fist as he and Emrys regained their feet. Emrys's eyes were pitch-black, veins of dark magic crawling up the side of his tense jaw. As if he was resisting summoning.

'Don't kill her!' William cried, his hands buried in his unruly hair to grip his horns from where he crouched low as if anticipating attack.

'Nobody is killing anyone!' I snapped, trying to drag air into my lungs as I turned, watching the eaves, waiting to see from what direction she'd attack next. To sense her. My hand stinging from where she'd bitten me.

'It's still too early in the evening to make promises, darling,' Thean pointed out, completely unconcerned, lounging against the shelves with folded arms. Of course – because the fiend form of Alma didn't appear to be coming for the voyav.

My gaze shot to William, who was also unharmed. Despite the fact he'd been in the hallway with one of the things. It hadn't bitten him. No. The creature had been desperate to make its way down the hallway . . . towards—

I looked down at my hand, blood dripping between my fingers. Blood.

My heart stopped, sinking into my gut.

Salvek hunted blood on command. And Alma was hunting mine – just as the creature she took that claw from had been.

Maybe it was Thean's smug smile that made the idea materialise as the house began to groan and creak. A warning that she was coming.

I lunged forwards, right for the voyav, dragging my bloody hand across their face. Smearing it red as a curse slipped from their lips. Before they could push me off, I was already diving for the floor. Just as Alma swooped in from the shadows above for another attack. Taking Thean down instead of me.

The voyav swore, becoming nothing but a jumble of limbs as the creature roared and tucked its wings tight.

I lunged, locking my arms around Alma, holding onto my wrists. Her folded wings trapped between us, talons at the top digging into my chin but my Kysillian strength held her. My call for it the strongest it had ever been.

'Kat!' Gideon barked, lurching forward to help as Emrys grabbed the voyav under the arms and dragged him from beneath Alma's claws. The front of that ridiculous frilly white shirt torn.

'Alma!' I cried desperately. Her strength in this form almost too much for me to hold.

Then Emrys's dark summoning wrapped around us, holding her in place. The cold ferocity of it biting into my flesh.

'*Le Mev*,' Emrys commanded, his voice darker than I'd heard it, but that word made my magic flare in challenge.

Yield. A command in the old tongue. Something about the darkness of his magic against the smoke and strange pallid marked flesh that formed Alma. Making her shudder. Curving into herself with submission, a strange keening sound slipping from that demonic sharp mouth.

Sensing her withdrawal, Emrys's magic slowly released her, but I felt it curling between my fingers as if trying to get to my palm. To see where I was hurt.

I felt Alma's smooth cold demonic flesh start to warm, felt her returning as her body began to shudder in my arms. I let her go, watching as she supported herself on her forearms, her demonic whine morphing into deep uneven breaths as bones began to crack, the smoke slipping from her flesh.

'Here!' William called, tossing one of the blankets over her, draping it across her as those limbs cracked and twisted back into human form.

'Will she be all right?' he asked quietly, crouched next to me as I tried to gather myself. Too out of breath. Unable to answer when I didn't feel like anything would ever be all right again.

Alma let out a pained moan, a tremor moving for her as her skin returned to its familiar warm hue, those dark curls in disarray as her mortal body trembled from the exertion.

'Alma.' I reached for her but she flinched away, her lips moving, gaze distant. Then she clutched the blanket around herself and was on her feet. Stumbling to the table by the bookshelves where the maps always lay scattered. Emrys and Gideon averted their eyes, William went scarlet but Thean didn't break his glaring stare at me. Shirt torn and my blood still smeared across the voyav's perfect face like warpaint.

'Damp stone ruins. Runes on the walls. Carved too deep. They went too deep. There was an altar, crovern weed grows there. Evergreen in the darkness.' The words were too quick from Alma's lips, a tremble to her limbs as she fought to stay upright, gaze crazed like a madwoman.

'Alma.' I took hold of her shoulders dragging the blanket up to cover her better. Yet she didn't stop talking, didn't stop trembling as her eyes raked over those maps, as her clawed fingers rifled through them desperately.

'Crovern weed only grows in the south,' William half stammered.

'It's following.' She twitched, those horrid oily scales running down her arms. A crack and twist of bone before she shook it away, a hiss slipping through her lips with the pain. 'I need her.'

She shook her head, dark hair falling around her as another tremble coursed through her and she grabbed her head as if pained.

'Alma.' I held her tighter. Then her head shot up, eyes wide as she met my own.

'*Kyvor Mor*,' she said. Repeating the word uncertainly.

Kyvor Mor, that voice mocked in the back of my mind. The fear driving deeper with every flinch and twitch of Alma. She broke my hold, lurching towards Emrys's desk.

Then she flipped through those books and maps, eyes wild. Until one single long, horrid claw had buried itself into a map at the centre of his desk.

'*Near*.' The word was a demonic hiss from her lips. As if her tongue was still too long for her mouth.

I felt a presence at my back, expecting Emrys but it was Thean, watching like they'd never seen her before. The woman unashamed by the brutality of her magic as she stood in nothing but a thin blanket, meeting their stare.

A wild, uncaged thing.

I looked down at my palm, blood weeping from her demonic bite. The house could move anywhere but Montagor could find me within it. Yet they'd struggle to find where I'd bled before. Where old blood lingered.

'We need to move the house,' I said, trying my best to keep my voice steady. 'Dark beasts don't hunt the same ground twice.'

I needed to be somewhere Montagor believed I'd never go.

I moved between the shelves, heading for the Portium door. Everything that had led me away and yet I still found myself back where I never wished to be.

Someone called my name but I didn't stop. Not until I moved that crystal and gave the door my command. Until it hummed and began to work with a spark of my magic. The wheel stopped its clattering, and the house – seeming to confuse my unsteadiness for excitement – opened the door.

The blast of cold winter air was a sharp slap across my face. Sharp enough to distract me from the fear that turned my insides out. The sharp stone ruins of Daunton protruded like charred bones from the decimated earth.

Daunton Wood.

Chapter Seventeen
Kat

It is a blessing to exist. Therefore, the very pain of this existence must be a blessing too, for the ancestors have willed it so. They have walked this world before and will walk it once more. We pray not to worship blindly, but to seek the purpose of our path. To challenge what we deem unwise. For the ancestors listen, and we too will be ancestors one day.

Ode to the Ancestors – Songs of Kysillia

The old story kept repeating itself in my mind and all I could think was that maybe it wasn't a blessing after all. Maybe the fates of old, the creatures said to guide the ancestors' will, were just like most creatures in this world. Cruel.

Emrys, Gideon and Thean had left to hunt down the summoning. Leaving me and William to get Alma into bed. Gideon had quickly assessed that the darkness of her transformation hadn't caused her any damage.

He took her trying to bite him as he attempted to check her pulse as a positive sign she was herself. Exhaustion had claimed her shortly after.

I tried to keep myself busy while watching over her as she rested. Reading up on dark summonings to try to refresh my memory. To understand what relic Montagor could possess but I found my focus kept slipping back to Alma curled up beneath the covers in the bed.

Her defencelessness unsettled me. Reminded me too much of the past. Of all the things I couldn't change.

Craving normalcy and to be finally rid of the stench of smoke from my skin, I retreated to the bathroom and scrubbed my bloody and ash-smeared skin until it was pink. Pulling my nightgown on before swallowing down a stronger healing tonic. Tired of the ache of my recovery. Yet found myself pulling Emrys's coat back on, the scent of it soothing the small fluttering panic in my chest as I took up watch again in the chair by Alma's bed.

Worry weighted my thoughts with the darkness of her change. Exhausting me enough as I slipped in and out of sleep. Only to be roused when cool night air dragged over my skin, to find the bed empty, covers rumpled and no Alma.

I jolted upright, seeing her standing before the open window staring distantly out at the night.

'Alma?' I called softly but she didn't even flinch. Just kept staring out into the darkness. Her thin nightdress stirred by the breeze. Her thick dark hair falling down her back, curls wilder with her sleep.

I so rarely saw her in undress. In any other form than her pristine dresses, covered neck to wrist. Now the firelight washed over her, showing the tiny scars, line after line. Some too deep, puckering the skin. What they'd taken.

My heart ached at the memory of how tender the wounds had been when we'd first met. Red and angry, some opening back up too easily.

'Alma?' I gently reached for her. Startling her. Those feline eyes wide, taking in every inch of the room as if for a moment she didn't recognise me before she mouthed my name.

'It's all right,' I tried to soothe her. Her trembling clawed fingers coming to rest over my own.

'I just needed some air.' She shook her head, chin dipping so those dark curls concealed her from my view for a moment, scales shifting over her bare arms, like a reassuring caress.

How close her creatures sat beneath the surface. The wildness of her magic so tame, how at ease she seemed with it. So different than usual.

She'd come back from the darkness of that beast. No tremors or sickness. Just a lingering tiredness. Something I'd never seen before. Never even dared to hope was possible.

'I've never seen you change that easily.' No, it was always a curse. Something she fought and repressed.

'It's an old trick.' She shook her head. Words too short as she returned her attention back to the dark window. To the distorted reflection of us.

She'd always told me it was beyond her. That her magic was cursed. Only then did I see my mistake. I'd never asked when the curse began. She'd been thirteen when I'd met her, and I'd never thought of those thirteen years. Of all the secrets that she could keep. All she didn't speak of and how a nameless girl had found her way to Daunton.

'How old?' I asked, unable to fight the spike of fear in my heart. Of all she hadn't told me.

Then I remembered what lay beyond the window. What had captured her attention. Woods I wouldn't forget as long as I lived. A maze of tight-pressed trees, undulating with ancient roots and moss. Daunton Wood.

I reached for the curtain, hating that we could see it, but Alma caught my wrist. Fingers still clawed and skin still rough from the change. Her damp dark hair clinging to her cheeks as if fell over her shoulders.

'It's just a wood, Kat. I'm fine.' Her voice was hoarse from the sounds that had clawed up her throat. A stiffness to her spine as if faced with an opponent. Refusing to back down.

I ran my fingers through her thick hair. How the firelight brought out a warm sheen hidden in the darkness of it.

'Let me take care of you.' I slid my arm around her shoulders to steer her closer to the fire. Where William had left a plate of biscuits and some mint water. A little vase of bright blue povets – the healing flower.

'What a worrisome idea,' she huffed and I almost smiled as I eased her into the chair, turning to pour her some water but it was then I saw the small box's remains in the fire. The one Master Hale had given her. The ones she'd kept more preciously than any gift.

Her chocolate box.

I crumpled before her, down to my knees. My hands came to rest on her knees. A sinner repenting.

'I'm sorry, Alma. I didn't mean for you to find out like that.' Find out that it was a lie. That I'd led her on the wrong path.

He'd meant something to her and I'd shattered that hope so carelessly.

'It was the truth,' she shrugged. How much I still wished it wasn't. That someone cared without a price. 'I suppose if you want something enough, you can convince yourself of anything.'

'I'm sure—'

'Don't make excuses for him, Kat.' She twisted her fingers between my own. 'He isn't worth it.'

No. All this time he hadn't been worth it. He'd kept us there. Used Alma to keep me in place. Used my love for her to form another bar in my own cage. I hadn't seen it because I hadn't wanted to.

'I thought if I worked hard enough it would all be worth it in the end.' I shook my head. All those hours and all that time trying to be perfect. Trying to become something they'd accept. 'That if I could beat them at their own game, I'd make it better.'

I couldn't stop the tears then as I was consumed by the bitterness of my own failure.

'I wish more than anything that it worked that way, Kat.' Her voice caught with those words.

As I finally understood there were some things even magic couldn't fix.

'This isn't what I promised you,' I whispered. Late into the night in that forbidden dark place. I'd told her stories of the northern shores, how we'd see them together. How we'd be safe away from all of this. Yet, instead I'd led us to the centre of a dark storm and I feared more than anything . . . I couldn't fix this.

She pulled back to smile at me. 'You promised we'd stay together.'

'Alma, this is beyond—'

She tightened her grip, leaning closer so I could see nothing but the bright, vibrant truth burning in her mortal green eyes.

'I promised we'd stay together too. Don't take my promises from me, Kat.' There was a steel in her voice sharper than any blade. 'No matter how far we go, or what creatures we have to become. We stay together.'

Always. That word wrapped itself around my heart.

'I'm sorry that—' I began but she slid from the chair to sit with me on the floor. Her finger rough against my lips as she silenced me.

'*We* fought for our freedom, Kat. Tooth and nail. Never apologise. Not to me. Not for a moment of it.' Her eyes burnt brighter with the rebellion of her words as her forehead dipped to rest against my own. 'We fight. We survive. That's what we do.'

What we'd been forced to do and I wouldn't guilt myself with it any longer. I wrapped my arms so tightly around her. The way I had that first night. Tucking my face into the curve of her neck. *Home.*

Her claws formed fists in Emrys's coat at my back as I curled her closer to me, as I brushed my hand over her curls. Smoothing them as she held onto me.

'I'm sorry I bit you,' she mumbled, making me laugh.

'I'm certain I deserved it.' I smiled, my palm barely aching now the healing balm had sealed the wound.

I was certain I deserved worse for what I'd put her through. Only now the most important thing was holding her. Offering her that safety as the fire sank in the hearth to the barest embers and she sagged in my arms, finally accepting her exhaustion. Finally resting once more.

The house creaked, the edge of the rug next to my leg rising to tap my thigh gently to claim my attention.

I turned to find Emrys standing in the doorway, mid-step as if he'd been looking for me. His hair damp as if he'd been caught in a rainstorm, coat missing because I was wearing it, shirt untucked.

'You're back,' was my quiet greeting. Alma didn't move in my arms, too deep in her sleep.

'Montagor appears to be quite lazy in sourcing locations for his summonings,' he answered, coming into the room, the concern in his gaze running over every inch of my face before it dropped to Alma in my arms.

'Is she all right?' He frowned.

'She was restless but I think she's finally out now.'

'Let's get her back in bed,' he offered, carefully taking her from me as if it was the most natural thing in the world. To handle Alma despite the fact she'd tried to bite Gideon twice.

I moved around him to pull the covers back on the bed so he could put her in. Tucking her in tightly as she curled automatically into her small pile of pillows. Then Emrys guided me back to the doorway as if cautious of disturbing her.

'She says she's fine,' I sighed, feeling my shoulders sag with my worries. 'It's late. I should leave her to rest.'

Alma always was too light a sleeper and my presence probably wasn't settling her as I wanted it to. Not when those creatures beneath her skin guarded her so closely. When they could probably sense the unease in my own magic.

'You don't believe her?' he observed. Easily able to read me.

I worried about the things she wouldn't say. How heavily they haunted her. Then I remembered what happened in that Council chamber. The tight overwhelming emotion that bloomed in my chest as I looked at his beautifully stoic face.

'I shouldn't have told her about Hale like that. She – she burnt the chocolates he gave her. I didn't think.' I ducked my head, hating how I'd hurt her. Shamed by my thoughtlessness.

'Kat.' His fingers came beneath my chin, gently coaxing me to meet his eyes again.

'You didn't tell me. About what you did for Alma.' That he'd got her away from the Council, done it without a second thought.

'She should never have been there,' he answered so effortlessly. No. None of us should have been. He pulled back slightly to pull something from his pocket.

'Here.' A torn piece of cloth lay across his palm, stained with ash and blood. My blood. What they must have taken from the Institute after that creature in Hale had attacked me.

'It was in an old cemetery just beyond the Institute grounds. One of the old lord's mausoleums had enough Verr artifacts to make the summoning.'

Blood summoning. One of the oldest offerings.

I pressed down my unease of Emrys being so close to the Institute again. So close to the remnants of Montagor's attack.

'It'd be safer if you destroyed it,' he offered, jaw tense. Unsettled.

'Surely Gideon won't be pleased by that.' I took the blood-stained rag from him and moving into the hall where the house had thankfully put my room – or his room – just next door. I went to the fire. My magic rising quickly, the rag combusting against my skin, rendering it to ash as I let it drop into the orange flames.

'I think I've had as much of Gideon's opinion as I can stomach for the evening,' he commented darkly from behind me.

I turned, listening to the creak of the house as if it was taking a deep, relieved breath. Settling with all it cared for under its roof. Emrys considered the fire next to me with a tired, distant expression.

'Do you want to be left alone?' I was cautious of his emotions. Of the whirlwind that had been his life since I'd entered it. Also – that I'd stolen his room. Or the house had.

His answering smile was small. 'Not by you, Croinn.'

He lifted his hand to push the hair back from his brow and it was then I saw the spotting of blood on his shirtsleeve, how the darkness shifted beneath his skin as if to catch my attention, shadows dancing over his knuckles.

'You're hurt.' I crossed the space between us, hating the tension that came over his limbs as I reached carefully for his hand. The slight flinch, his eyes too alert in an instance.

'You won't hurt me, Emrys,' I reasoned. Pulling back his sleeve gently to see the curved slash beneath. Not too deep.

'Those back claws of the beast were surprisingly sharp.' His brow furrowed, as if he'd forgotten he had the wound at all.

'Those *claws* could have anything on them,' I corrected, looking at the wound more closely for any other sign of contamination.

I tugged him from the fire to where healing supplies lay scattered on the desk. The house materialising a bowl of steaming water and cloth without command. I made quick work of cleaning the wound and soaking a cotton ball in healing tonic as he perched on the desk's edge like a well-behaved patient.

'You're lucky Gideon didn't see it.' I scolded him playfully, listening to his small huff of amusement. 'Has he always been so . . .'

'Difficult?' He finished as the shadows cut across his pensive expression. 'He has his reasons. Witch blood isn't the kindest curse to possess.'

No. Most of the witches in the tales of old were driven to madness with the weight of their gifts. Most witches were renowned not only for their powers, but their prickly dispositions. Why most of them were dead – having crossed the wrong foe.

'Lady Blackthorn was a witch then?' I frowned, finishing cleaning the wound and moving onto applying the balm.

'Of a long ancient line. One I doubt even she knew the full truth of. She was raised in the rebellion. Used by them. Even Emmaline was nothing more than a creation of their meddling. One of the Countess' breeding experiments.'

Unease shifted through me at those words. My father had warned me of that. How the rebellion had its own breeding practices, mixing magic to raise more potent warriors for its battles. Horror stories I'd wished were just Council exaggeration.

Only the saint worshippers had to get their ideas from somewhere, and it was the ancient fey that had favoured purity of blood first. That had put the survival of their own magic above all else.

I wrapped his wounds in a thin, clean bandage. Watching the shadow of his magic beneath his skin, twisting as if intrigued by my touch. Deep shadows lingered beneath his eyes, a strange tension in his limbs. As if small tremors were moving through him.

'You're in pain.' I pressed my palm against his cheek, expecting to find he had a chill, only his skin was perfectly warm.

'I can't remember not taking it. The bark.' Shame coated his words. How quickly he curled his hands into fists. How close to the surface that darkness was.

The beasam bark. The suppressant to his magic.

'You've stopped.' I hadn't even contemplated what the withdrawal from it would be like for him. With just how potent and temperamental the bark could be.

'I can't sense things I should with it. Fairfax wouldn't have happened if—'

'That wasn't your fault.' I ran my thumb across the sharp line of his jaw. 'Not everything is your fault, Emrys.'

Those solemn dark eyes watched me with such caution. As if trying to find the lie. Disbelieving it didn't bother me as his fears told him it should.

Those eyes became pitch-black as they took me in. Standing before him in disarray, in my nightgown that had seen better days, still wearing his coat.

'What you said in the Council chamber.' His tone was gentle but quiet. Haunted. As if every word I'd said in that chamber lingered for him even now. 'Did he ever hurt *you* like that?'

What Daunton had done. The sharp claws of fear buried themselves in my heart, threating to shorten my breath but I refused to be cowed by my memories. Not here. Not with him.

The importance of what he was asking me. Why he was asking. What nobody had bothered to ask before. Would rather pretend it hadn't happened at all.

'No.' I shook my head.

His eyes ran over every inch of my expression as if seeking out the hint of a lie. 'You'd tell me?'

Something sparked in my chest at the depth of emotion in his eyes. It mattered to him. Everything about me mattered to him.

'I'd tell you.' Truth. I knew I'd tell him because those words were safe in the small space between us.

Then came the cold brush of shame against my skin. For not telling the truth sooner. For never speaking of it.

'Kysillians don't bear scars. It's a shame to hold a mark on your skin, a reminder that you were bested by a lesser being.' The words rubbed uncomfortably against my throat on the way out. Seeing that darkness in his eyes harden with wrath. His thoughts going to my back, at just how marked I was. 'I thought it was punishment from the ancestors. That I was weak. Why they hurt Alma. Why they cursed Master Hale.'

A harsh breath left me as the weight of those fears finally escaped the confines of my chest. Emrys's hands had come to rest gently at my waist, my own finding their way to his forearms. Holding on as if fearful I could fall apart.

'I believed it for so long.' My eyes came up to meet his dark ones. Seeing the burn of my lavender reflected there. Seeing the harshness of his features with his worry for me. As I looked at his own scars that had never bothered me. Never made me see him any differently.

'Only now I know, none of it was my fault.' My hands slid up until they rested at the side of his neck, over those marks on his own skin. How he came closer, as if trying to shield me even here. As his hands slip around my back. The strong warmth of his touch comforting me.

'None of this was your fault either, Emrys,' I whispered, as I brushed my thumb over the scarred side of his cheek. Seeing that shift of darkness beneath his skin. 'It doesn't frighten me . . . to see you as you are. Nothing about you frightens me.'

Just as it didn't frighten me to see Alma in all her forms.

I'd seen the evil of this world. Felt the callous cruelty of it as I held onto him. As I felt that magic brush across my skin, I knew there was none of it in him.

My thumb dragged across the rough stubble of his cheek. As I saw the tiredness in his features, the weariness in his shoulders with his exhaustion. 'You need to rest.'

'I don't think the house has given me a choice on that,' he answered dryly, leaving me to peek over his shoulder and see the door had vanished.

A nervous laugh bubbled from my lips. Making his decisions for him.

'Will you come to bed?' I asked quietly, ignoring the sting of heat at my cheeks. It was only sleep after all.

Where I thought I'd see amusement, he was looking at the bed. Pensive.

'I promise not to debauch you,' I blurted out like a fool, remembering the last time we'd both been in this room. Realising maybe it was too forward. Too much. 'You don't have to if—'

'All right, Croinn.' He pulled me closer, the ghost of a kiss brushing my forehead before he withdrew gently, reluctantly. As he slipped into the bathroom, I took a moment trying not to panic as I moved to the bed and turned down the sheets before combing my hair into a loose tangle down my back.

I tried to find my nerve. Obviously I'd shared a bed with Emrys before. However, reminding myself of *that* wasn't settling my nerves. No – it made my magic *surge*, making my skin too warm. Playfully excited.

'Behave,' I hissed as I pulled off his coat, hanging it up neatly. Fidgeting as I tried to sort out the side table still littered with healing items. I should have rifled through his coat pockets when I had the chance, I might have found something interesting – something to talk about.

'Kat,' Emrys half cursed, startling me as I turned to see he'd come out of the bathroom. Pinching the bridge of his nose, his shirt missing. His hand flexing slightly, as if he was holding on very loosely to his control.

The muscled contours of his chest catching the firelight, that scarring running from his jaw all the way to the waistband of his trousers. A path my fingertips had trailed before.

'Is it paining you?' I asked, frowning as I looked at the bandage on his arm. Knowing the healing tonic should be working.

'Can you get under the covers please?' he sighed as if in discomfort. 'There is only so much of you in that nightgown I can take.'

I laughed, tugging up the strap of my nightgown where it had slipped down my shoulder. 'There is nothing *alluring* about my nightgowns.'

Frumpy and too large considering they never made them long enough for me.

'You haven't seen you in them.' He turned to see to the fire, which was perfectly fine without his inspection.

Ease settled through me as I climbed into the bed. Pulling up the covers, a shiver moving through me at the cold sheets beneath.

'Better?' I asked, putting all my attention into straightening my pillow. Ignoring the fact no part of me was averse to him right now. Tired or not. Especially not my magic, which swooped through me with strange flutterings. The wishing stone around my throat thankfully better behaved as the house was nice and quiet.

Then I noticed the shadows beneath his eyes as he got into the bed, the tiredness in his gaze as I settled on my side. Curling my hands beneath the pillow to fight the urge to reach out and touch him, knowing I wouldn't be able to stop.

Unable to deny that there was something so natural about lying in this bed with him. Close enough to feel the warmth of him sink into my skin. To feel the brush of his magic.

'What keeps you awake the most?' I worried.

'Too many things,' he answered. 'Mostly the things I can't change.' A log snapped in the hearth, making shadows play across the handsome angles of his face. 'Some nights I can hear them.'

His words were cautious, as if hesitant to speak that truth. So I remained silent and still, wanting him to share this burden.

'Voices that are too distant, as if they're speaking in another room and I can never make out the words.' He scrubbed his palms over his face, his sigh filled with defeat. 'Then sometimes a woman is singing, hymns of the Old Gods. A wind calling my name, small and soft as if trying to rouse me.'

'Why I'd read anything, study anything. Wander all the way across Elysior to avoid the restlessness of sleep.' Then his head turned on the pillow, eyes so pale and light. 'Maybe it's just madness. An impossible strange thing.'

All I wanted to do was comfort him, but I didn't wish to give him empty words, just like I'd never given them to Alma. Never truly able to understand the depth of that pain . . . but wanting them to know I'd always be listening. Always be here.

A impossible strange thing. That was what he'd called himself.

'You're not strange to me.' I moved closer to his warmth. Wondering if some of my own truths would comfort him, would make him feel less bare. Less alone. Something to take his mind from it.

'Should I tell you a story?' I asked. He didn't answer, just waited. As if anything from my lips would capture his attention entirely.

'My father was born in the midlands. His mother was of ancient blood, a rare female that they bred with one of their elders before she was barely of age. Only, she never came into her flame. Was never able to wield it. So, despite eventually falling pregnant, they deemed any child of hers to be unworthy. A bad omen – so they cast her out.'

'I thought Kysillians guarded their own fiercely,' he asked, moving closer. His fingers absently pushed my hair back from my face, tucking it carefully behind my ear. Tracing the shape of it with such reverence.

'They value Kysillia's flame above everything else. To be powerless is to be impure in their eyes,' I answered, glad his hand didn't fall away. That his fingers curled absently into my hair. 'Why they hate half-breeds, because most cannot summon.'

'My grandmother was a storyteller. She knew all the myths of old, all the songs and histories of the fey. Even the Old Gods from long before.' I reached for his other hand that rested on the mattress between us and ran my fingers over his knuckles. Remembering the warmth in my father's voice when he spoke of her. The grief too that haunted every story he told. Because perhaps he wished only to hear those tales from her lips. 'She made a new life performing, travelling and teaching my father on the roads of Elysior. Just the two of them. Free in the wilderness of the world.'

A peaceful, simple life. Perhaps the type of life I could have envisioned for myself once.

'Then came the King's raids.' The Mage King's father. I felt Emrys tense, because that would be his grandfather. Another monster in a different tale. Who'd drenched the wetlands in blood for nothing but sport. 'My father was thirteen when the attack came. His mother made him promise to get the fey villagers out, to protect the children and take them deep into the western wood. To the fey ruins there.'

Emrys's body eased but his attention on my face didn't waver. As if he needed every word.

'My father did as she said. Only, she didn't follow.' No. Because she was Kysillian, even if those elders didn't value her as one. She would die for her child. Die for the beings we were formed to protect.

'She was captured and taken to the mines in the east. The Kysillians soon turned up to find my father hiding in the wood. To act as saviours in the aftermath. The elder who had sired my father saw his flame and claimed him. Took him deep to the north mountains and swore to find his mother. All my father had to do was complete the training of his blood. If he became the perfect champion – his mother would be returned and her shame forgotten.'

It was then I knew that grief could pass through families. That it could linger in magic. How painfully my magic grieved. For the woman that had borne it.

'Every day my father asked of her. Every day they told him they were looking.' As they locked him in training rooms, made him endure their trials and tests. 'He was seventeen when he bested his sire and won his blade. When he left to find his mother deep in the east.'

My breath caught with the weight of it. Emrys hand slid around my waist, bringing me closer as I braced my hand on his chest, feeling the steady beat of his heart beneath my palm. 'He was three days too late. She'd died taking a beating for another prisoner.'

She'd held on for him. All that time she'd held on. Knowing my father would make it back to her. That he'd find her – because she'd called his name.

'Her grave was marked with Azenia, the everlasting bloom. The sign of a true warrior.' A blessing from the ancestors to grow where she had fallen. 'So much of the flower grew, it drifted through the air like snowfall. As if the ancestors themselves wept for the cruelty of it.'

When the ancestors cared. Or perhaps they were simply shamed into caring.

'My father burnt down the entire mine. Freed the fey and took back the east field with nothing but his will and sword.' The mortals called it the firestorm of the east, blamed the rebels for another sabotage of their trade.

Only there was no victory in it. No justice. Justice couldn't exist. She was gone, and all that remained was pain.

'My father never forgave those Kysillian elders for leaving his mother there. For lying.' I saw the darkness seep into Emrys's gaze, his anger at the pain in my words. Reacting to it as if it was his own. I smiled. Smiled because the memory of her was a beautiful thing my father had gifted me.

'Her name was *Tauria*.' With golden hair, a soft smile and a kind, gentle nature she'd gifted my father. 'The elders gave her that name to mock her with everything she could never be.'

With the fire she could never wield. With the Queen's

name she could never hope to honour.

'My father gave me that name so if those elders ever found me, they'd know that I was made by her. And like her, not one part of me belonged to them.'

My fingers traced the edge of his jaw as I looked into his stormy eyes. Weighted with too much emotion.

'So perhaps I'm an impossible thing too.' A deviant of fate. Perhaps we were equal in that. Emrys didn't reply, just ran his fingers through my hair, the soothing motion of it making me rest more heavily in his arms. Pressing my cheek to his chest so I could listen to the steady beat of his heart, as it soothed my magic, it was only when I was in his arms he finally slept.

Chapter Eighteen

Kat

Beware the dark of the wood. Where demons linger in the shadows of the ancient pines. Luring maidens with sweet promises and handsome forms. For an old god's desire is forever, and your soul will pay the price of their lust long after death, fair maiden.

Curse of the Old Gods – Unknown

Those old fables seemed to mock me as I turned another page in the book before me. Fingers dragging across the rough, age-spotted paper. Another tale of Mort. The first mortal king. The first saint. He who had brought civility to a land of cruel beastly fey. Who had taught the other saints all they knew. As they huffed in their toxic smoke and justified their cruelty. As they stripped this land of its magic and tried to meld it into their own blood. By any means necessary.

What had started all this mortal madness, hunger for power and for fey blood. What had fed them first. Such strange dark tales spread before me, illuminated by soft buttery light that seeped through the barest parting in the curtains as I sat at the desk in Emrys's room. I was always too easily awoken, my thoughts too loud to rest so I'd returned to the familiar comfort of books.

I'd always thought the Old Gods to be no more than stories. That's what this world had diminished them to. Only now I wondered if there was a reason for that. The same reason the Council and the mad kings had diminished Kysillian power, and all the ancient fey before us. Rendered us nothing more than children's tales, so the horrid things they did wouldn't seem so horrid at all. Because for my own ancestors to lessen Verr into nothing more than myth was to reduce their power too – reduce the threat they could hold. For why would mortals hunger for it so? Kysillians would never admit they could be beaten. That they'd never conquered anything – never set anyone free.

My father had turned his back on the Kysillian elders, and I couldn't help but fear this was why. Because their lies had led us so easily to our own demise.

I sat back in the chair, raising my hand and letting the smallest summoning free. Watching those dull lavender and blue flames twist between my fingers. Performing for my attention.

I feared I'd come into my flame too early. That I'd damaged something, causing its ferocity. Only Kysillia's flame wasn't the same as other summonings. It didn't arrive at puberty when you were best prepared. No, it came when Kysillia willed it, when it was needed.

Then came the fear, of what exactly she saw for this world – to grant me such devastating power and the endless hunger that came with it. That its limit was set simply by my own conscience.

'Croinn, please tell me none of those are cursed texts,' came Emrys's sleep-roughened voice from the bed. My flame extinguished with a flick of my fingers as I turned to see him up on one elbow, his other hand pushing the dark messy hair off his forehead. The movement making the definition of his bicep more apparent. Air a little harder to pull through my lips as my eyes traced where the covers had fallen to his waist.

'Good morning.' I smiled tentatively, rising and making my way over to him. 'Do you feel better?'

'You should be resting,' he cautioned, his suspicious gaze moving back to the desk as if anticipating a fiend or a cursed illustration was about to burst free.

'I think I've learnt my lesson where cursed texts are concerned.' I tugged the sleeve of my nightgown back up where it had fallen off my shoulder. 'I feel much better. Besides, I have a lot of catching up to do.'

He caught my hand to rub his thumb over the ink stains on my fingertips, where the scribbling of my notes had got away from me.

'You shouldn't be anywhere near this.' His voice was still rough from sleep but the warning was soft. I knew he didn't just mean those forbidden tales, fiends or seals. He meant himself.

Only this warning was different. Different than just a lord with a fey. This was blood. Verr and Kysillian. Two creatures that had torn the world apart.

There is no worse fate than a girl who lures demons to her bed. Only those warnings couldn't turn me from the memory of him. Reaching for me across that cursed earth. Calling my name as if he'd want it to be the last thing on his lips. He'd come for me, even knowing that darkness would take him too. He'd kept vigil at my bedside. Driven himself to madness to see me well, fighting the Council at every turn – even thinking I wouldn't want him like this. That his darkness would be too much.

He was giving me a choice. Even now.

'It's where you are,' I answered without hesitation. I'd made my choice in this very room. It hadn't changed. 'I'm not afraid, Emrys. Not of this.'

Not of him. Not of the things that came before, or what I'd done. I *was* my choices, my mistakes.

I'd always choose this delicate thing between us. No matter the punishment. No matter what came next.

Only in the tense silence an odd vulnerability overcame me as I stood before him in nothing but thin cotton and disarray. Worry made me bite my lip. Shrink slightly inside as I dropped my gaze. 'Unless you—'

Only for him to catch my chin between his thumb and forefinger. Demanding my eyes, seeing that his were now pitch-black.

My breath caught. 'Emrys.'

His other hand slipped around my waist, tugging me closer until I fell into that bed with him. As he gathered my face between his hands, dark veins spread across his skin with how close that magic had risen.

'I thought you were a dream.' He pressed those words against my pulse. The confession so soft as his fingers curled into my nightgown, desperately. 'You've ruined me, Kat.'

'You sound entirely too pleased about that.' I wanted to tease but I was too breathless with that strange desire that only he could stoke.

He answered with a kiss. Gentle but commanding. My fingers curled into his thick hair, greedily. Relief making me sink into him, deepening that kiss, as I quickly found myself pressed against the pillows with the warm solid weight of him on top of me.

I arched closer as my nails dug into the strong contours of his back. Sliding greedily over him. Needing more.

A crazed sound slipped from my lips. Emrys responded to it with his own low hum of hunger in his throat as his hand curved around my waist, pulling me into the hardness of him. His lips drifting to my neck as I arched desperately for more of his attention, gasping wildly for breath.

My hands running over the strong lines of his bare chest as I'd hungered to do last night.

The stutter in his breath. The torment I'd caused him broke my heart. So I tugged his hair, bringing his lips back to my own.

Real. We were real.

There was a craving in it. A desperate need to be devoured. His hand ran up the thin fabric to brush my breast, lips tracing the curve of my jaw. Drawing another wanton sound from between my lips as his tongue dipped to trace my collarbone.

I panted, driven mad by the drag of his stubble across my sensitive skin. My nightgown slipped down, almost exposing my breast and his lips followed.

I curled my fingers into his hair, keeping him in place. My thighs brushing his side as I brought them up to cage him. He took the invitation, his rough hand cupping the back of my bare thigh. My skin too hot and too tight. Wanting the thin cotton gone. Needing nothing but him.

'Emrys,' I pleaded before he tortured me with another deep kiss. A sound of desire rumbled in the back of his throat, making my stomach swoop with anticipation as his hand found its way between my thighs.

'Bloody fucking saints!' The frantic, too-high-pitched words cut through the room, making Emrys go rigid before he whipped around towards the door. Cold dread washed over my skin. Shame burning my cheeks as I clung to Emrys's biceps, hiding beneath the sheer size of him.

'*William!*' Emrys snapped, detangling from me in a blur of movement. The covers thrown over me as he got off the bed.

This couldn't be happening.

'You could have locked the bloody door!' There was a crash and a bang, as if William had run head first into the wall in his desperation to escape.

'*It wasn't there to lock,*' Emrys answered through his teeth.

Flustered, I tried my best to untangle myself from the bed sheets, stumbling out of the other side of the bed, trying to fix my nightgown where it was tangled around my hips. Twisted around my body with the insistence of Emrys's touch.

Emrys's bare broad back blocked the doorway. The creaking of the wood of the door frame telling me the house was beyond amused.

'Bloody bastard,' I muttered as I grabbed my robe from the foot of the bed, pulling it on as I went to the doorway to save William from Emrys's annoyance. Where the boy sat stunned on the hallway floor

'Emrys—' I began, only to stop when I reached his shoulder. To find it had got worse.

Alma stood there too, come to get me ready for the day. One dark eyebrow raised.

Bollocks.

'I'd . . . we—' Useless sounds tumbled from my lips.

'This isn't the worst thing I've caught you doing,' was all the mercy she offered in her dry, slightly exasperated tone as she helped a flustered William back to his feet.

'*Alma*,' I hissed, cheeks burning but her irritated eyes slid to Emrys.

'If there aren't ghouls under the bed, there are usually cursed papers beneath her pillow,' she warned, taking hold of William's arm to steer him away from the door. The boy looking at the ceiling as if praying for the house to somehow take away his memories.

'Good luck, my lord.' She smiled wickedly.

'That was *one* time,' I leant around Emrys to call after her.

'Gideon is looking for you two,' she threw back in warning as she shepherded a still-spluttering William down the corridor.

I suppose it was a mercy to be found by William and Alma. I didn't think my ears could take the exclamations from Gideon.

'I hope you're feeling better,' I called back, still worried after last night – but her devious smile as she turned the corner put me a little at ease. At least she seemed more herself.

The hinges of the door squeaked like a demented mouse's laugh next to us.

Emrys shut it with more force than necessary. A curse slipping through his lips, frustrated annoyance on his face as he pinched the bridge of his nose and pulled in a deep breath.

I couldn't stop the laugh that escaped my lips at the ridiculousness of it. Emrys pulled his hand away from his face, those eyes pitch-black as they looked down at me.

'You should probably put a shirt on.' I smiled, pressing my palm against the hard muscle of his chest. Especially if we needed to hunt Gideon down before he came to find us.

His hands were suddenly on my hips, as he headed me back against the closed door.

'Emrys.' Anticipation swooped through me as he ducked his head.

'In a moment, Croinn,' he answered, lips brushing the curve of my cheekbone before they found my own.

Moments later – once the house had allowed Emrys to find his shirt – we found ourselves downstairs, Emrys taking my hand to pull me into a room I'd never seen before. Large bay windows let the morning light stream in, the space dominated by a grand mahogany table with high-backed chairs. Walls decorated in navy and gold wallpaper of ancient flowers and patterns. The chandelier had small crystal birds perched next to the candles.

Gideon slapped the pages of *The Crow's Foot* shut before letting it fall to the table where he sat at the head. A pot of tea steamed next to him with a selection of breakfast scones.

'Here I was fearing you'd slept in,' he greeted, voice far too cheery considering his greeting glare as his gaze ran over his brother's dishevelled appearance. 'I hope William didn't *interrupt* anything.'

'William is scandalised.' Emrys's words were cold with anger.

Gideon let out a small amused huff, his eyes falling back onto the pages of *The Crow's Foot* with boredom as he brought his teacup to his lips. 'Good. It's payback for what I caught him doing with the messenger boy.'

Surprise jolted through me as Emrys looked to the ceiling with a wince. Clearly this wasn't the first time the little deviant had been caught.

'There isn't anything wrong with that,' I objected. William could do as he pleased with who he pleased. My protective words were met with a further glare from Gideon as I took a seat at the table.

'I'm not opposed to the act. I'm actually quite fond of it. However . . . I'd rather not witness it in the stables before I've had my coffee,' Gideon added.

I found myself shocked there were stables.

'What were you doing by the stables?' Emrys frowned, seeming genuinely confused by the prospect of his brother doing anything so mundane.

'I tried going for a *walk*.' Gideon grimaced at the word as if it were something foul. 'Since you've forbade me from indulging in my usual *thrilling* activities, I don't have a choice.'

Emrys took the seat next to me, forming a blockade between me and his brother. 'I didn't *forbid* you.'

Gideon scowled over his teacup. 'I'm pretty certain there was an implication of bodily harm.'

Ignoring the brothers' prickly exchange, I dug into the breakfast that covered the table. Suddenly ravenous as I moved the sliced ham, cheese and a pastry onto my plate. Emrys poured me a lemon tea before I realised I needed one. Then added another pastry to my plate as the brothers continued to bicker mildly.

Only it seemed the drama of the morning wasn't over just yet.

'Isn't this cosy?' Thean greeted as they entered the room wearing breeches that left little to the imagination. A corset sinched over a large white shirt that made their waist appear miniscule and forced their breasts up. Displaying a summoning rune on the curve of their bosom.

'What do you want?' Gideon scowled. Much to Thean's delight.

'I wouldn't mind a crumpet,' they grinned, sitting down next to Gideon, taking two crumpets off the plate and reaching for the butter.

It was only then I realised their familiarity. Gideon knew Thean just as well as Emrys did. Of course – Thean had known Emmaline too.

I was disturbed from that line of thought as William entered the room with a rattle of the tea tray, catching my attention, still flushed.

'Good morning, William. I thought I heard a racket upstairs.' Thean smirked.

'Poor William walked in on Kat dressing,' Alma added sharply as she followed behind him, giving the voyav a look that could have flayed skin.

'A locking charm wouldn't have gone amiss,' William grumbled, taking a teacup off the tray and holding it out to me. 'Here, Kat, I made a new nettle healing tea.'

'Thank you.' I swallowed my mouthful of breakfast and took the cup from him. Anything to make him forget what he'd seen.

I took a tentative sip; the taste of soil hit my tongue and I almost retched.

Bloody ancestors.

I painfully swallowed the sour gritty chunks. William's hazel eyes were watching me cautiously.

'Perfect.' I smiled painfully, hoping the mixture wasn't smeared on my teeth. William let out a relieved huff, starting to plate up his own breakfast.

Emrys's fingers slipped around mine as he raised the cup to his own lips, blowing gently for a moment before taking a sip. The strange intimacy of it made my cheeks burn as those dark eyes never left my own.

'Is there mud on my teeth?' I whispered quickly while William was distracted asking Thean for a scone.

'No Croinn.' His eyes were soft with some amusement as he pulled away. Giving me the teacup back, ignoring the chill across my fingers with the absence of his touch. I looked down to see the liquid less murky. I took another sip, this time it was sweeter and I could taste other, more pleasant herbs in the mix.

'How did you do that?' I asked as he leant back, draping his arm across the back of my chair.

'Witchcraft.' He smiled. 'Drink it, Kat.'

Puzzled at what incantation he'd used and annoyed he wouldn't share, I drank the healing tea.

'Well now, you're here. We need to start correspondence with the lords that held loyalty to this house.' Gideon pulled an envelope from his jacket pocket and tossed it onto Emrys's empty breakfast plate. 'I've written down the ones still alive, and the others barely clinging to sanity.'

William choked. Emrys went still and Thean let out a short breathless laugh.

The lords. The lords from the houses that formed the uprising against the King almost two decades ago.

'I see you've chosen violence this morning, dearest Gideon.' The voyav dropped a lump of sugar into their tea.

'They haven't cared before,' William added around a mouthful of scone.

'Indeed. Let's summon them so they can sit idly back once more?' Emrys's voice held a warning edge.

'Their souls are on the line, Emrys,' Gideon offered. 'Your bargains to keep them from being possessed by the promises they made to that darkness are void if Montagor has a relic.'

'I'm aware,' Emrys's response was terse, a darkness rippling beneath his skin before his hand tensed and it ceased.

'How can you stop them being possessed?' I frowned, setting my teacup back on the table.

'Verr are territorial, darling. Didn't your ancestors teach you that?' Thean mocked. 'They submit very quickly to a creature far more powerful than themselves. A simple summoned demon wouldn't stand a chance against our dear Emrys's wrath.'

Serus, even. Why the Council had cowed under Emrys's mere presence. Why that gobrite had. They needed him, because without him to keep those demons after their souls at bay – they'd become the dark creatures they worshipped.

'The lords came together in the end,' Gideon added. They'd come together for the uprising, at the end of all things.

'Father saw to that,' Emrys challenged.

'Then you'd better channel the bastard and make them remember why they did it in the first place,' Gideon fired back, undeterred by the shortness of his brother's temper, or how many shadows had crept into the room.

'Those lords probably think I blew up the fucking Council.' Emrys drained the cup of tea before him in one irritated swallow.

'So? You should claim you murdered those lords in the outer territory too,' Gideon added, something like amusement dancing in his eyes. 'Fear might make them all more cooperative.'

The murder of Lord Septimus and Lord Huntington that had been reported in *The Crow's Foot* before Fairfax. The memory of it seemed to prod me.

'What use would I have for a lord's blood?' Emrys answered with barely contained irritation.

Gideon shrugged, stirring his tea once again. 'Drink it? I don't know. Be creative.'

Emrys glowered at his brother.

Blood, a hissed distant voice mocked in the back of my mind. A sharp flash came from the wishing stone. Like a phantom, prodding finger, insistent to get my attention.

Just like it had in the Council chamber. Warning me.

Blood. That's what the creature in the pit had been after. My blood. But it had started long before that. Finneaus with that book in the Fifth Library. How desperate the book was to be opened. The cloudy, fearful confusion in his gaze. Why Finnaeus would be working with Montagor. Why he'd need that boy's blood.

The compendiums.

I stood so suddenly my chair toppled over behind me.

'Kat.' William leapt to his feet, worry carving deep into his features, knocking over the stack of crumpets. Probably fearful I'd lost my mind once again. I couldn't blame him. I felt like I had.

'Where are those copies of *The Crow's Foot*?' I demanded, unable to steady my breath. Too many thoughts pressing too tightly against my temples.

'These—' Gideon began, pointing with a metal finger to those scattered across the table.

'No. Before,' were the only words I could let escape my lips, my heart hammering viciously against my ribs.

'In the kitchen,' William answered reluctantly. 'Why do you—'

I was already moving, Emrys's voice a distant call as I raced into the hall and almost threw myself down the kitchen steps that manifested to my right. Skidding to a halt only when I came to the table at the centre. Seeing the stack of William's collection beneath a bowl of highly polished green apples.

I lunged for them, rifling wildly, hearing the commotion of everyone following. I turned, Alma and William pressed into the narrow stairwell as Gideon elbowed his way through them. Emrys already before me.

'Lord Septimus.' I thrust the pages at him, only his focus didn't stray from my face as the pages remained pressed against his chest. 'Lord Huntington.'

The murdered lords. Who'd been deprived of their blood. The ones that had set Emrys on edge.

'He was hunting them.' I tapped the pages as Emrys took them into his hands.

That Montagor was seeking the power he could take from them. What if that power was compendiums or relics? Items that could only be awakened with blood. Just like when Finneaus opened that book.

'He needed their blood. To open the compendiums they left behind. That was why Finneaus was opening the book in the Fifth Library. He didn't want to be there. Montagor must have forced his hand,' I continued, prodding those lords' names on the page to emphasis my point. 'That's how he got the relic. He found a compendium that took him to it.'

'The Septimus lords didn't have a compendium.' Gideon ran a hand through his blonde hair, the metal of it glinting in the kitchen's firelight.

'Their bloodline must have crossed somewhere with another house. Whatever he's looking for has to be old.' I shook my head, the lord lines were known to marry into one another. Anything to keep the blood pure. Only maybe they'd been keeping it pure for another reason. To keep their secrets hidden.

'There was a tale many dark things could be hidden in books that old,' Thean began, voice almost disinterested, but their eyes were too sharp as they peered down at the abandoned copies of *The Crow's Foot* spread across the table. 'Why the lords were hesitant to relinquish them after the wars. Why they bound them to their bloodlines.'

'Relics?' I pressed.

'I've seen many things in my years,' Thean nodded, turning around the papers with a distasteful glance. 'Hiding one object within another is an old trick.'

'Fuck.' The word was a soft curse from Gideon. Emrys had gone very still, those dark eyes scanning over the pages before him. 'Relics are from the old ages. Before the seals.'

'If Montagor has a relic, he can find a seal. Those bastard compendiums probably lead the way,' Thean added without emotion. Of course – because all dark things return in the end. They always know their way back.

'That's why he wants her.' Gideon nodded in my direction. 'Why he sent that beast after her blood. Why he set the trap at all. He'll also be needing more than one relic to accomplish anything.'

I hadn't considered that. Just as relics could guide the dark to a power source, the magic in my blood could do the same – guide it to the seals it protected. Because Montagor knew there was a seal beneath Fairfax. He knew it was gone. And he knew I was the reason for that.

'He's going to open a seal.' I felt heat flare in my veins with panic as my eyes met Emrys's. 'There are other Kysillians. Others with lesser blood. It isn't just me.'

No. I wasn't special or chosen. That poor girl and all those fey had died in that pit for nothing and Montagor would do the same. Find anything remotely close to Kysillian to try to get what he wanted.

'No. But you present a challenge I'm certain a primitive part of Montagor's nature is quite obsessed with,' Gideon offered, giving Emrys a dark look.

Of course. Verr were territorial. I flushed. Montagor knew mine and Emrys's entanglement and he'd use it to his advantage. Anything to claim power over another. In challenge, an opponent needed to find a weakness . . . and Montagor had found one of Emrys's.

Me.

William worried his hands. 'It makes sense why Montagor has been after you and your role within the Council, Emrys. You have enough compendiums and dark artifacts here.'

Gideon let out an irritated huff of breath. 'As entertaining as this revelation is, we still don't know where to start.'

'Ainsworth's compendium,' Emrys and I said at the same time, startling Gideon.

'It's already open,' I finished. 'They wanted something from it.'

'Why on earth would it be open?' Gideon asked, looking slightly unnerved by the thought. 'Where the fuck is the gobrite from inside it?'

The house clattered the pans in the corner in excitement before something crashed into the kitchen table. Sending the apples bouncing from their bowl.

There, rattling in the cage I'd trapped it in, was the gobrite. Only it didn't look the same. It had shifted itself into something far less grotesque. Like a small wyvern as it curled in its own sheddings, hissing at us as if annoyed by the disturbance.

Small onyx scales glinting in the hearth's light.

Why had Emrys kept it? I looked at him but his annoyed gaze was focused at the ceiling, hands on his hips.

'There it is!' William beamed, but he still took a few steps back from the creature, standing on Gideon's foot. 'Kat captured it in an old chandelier.'

'Of course she did,' Gideon grumbled. Then those blue eyes were back on me, hard with annoyance. 'We could have asked the little Ainsworth twat about the book and saved ourselves all this bother, if Miss Woodrow hadn't clawed his fucking eyes out.'

'When?' William croaked, mouth agape.

'Should have gone for his throat,' Alma muttered darkly, making William go paler.

'Finally, you've decided to be interesting, darling,' Thean mocked me, amber eyes practically gleaming.

Gideon – thankfully – ignored them all and finished. 'Now, we have to deal with the bastard lords.'

'I can check the inventory for which compendiums we have and which were destroyed. Which books belong to which houses. That will narrow down the missing ones and any Montagor might be interested in,' William offered, turning to see where Alma was still lost in pensive thought. 'Alma, do you want to help?'

'I don't read well,' she offered with mild irritation, her cheeks flushing.

'You should be thankful I have nobody better to torment,' Thean sighed with barely controlled boredom. 'I read *excellently*.'

Alma's lip curled back as if resisting the urge to bare her fangs.

'We need to summon the lords,' Gideon interrupted, voice sharp with authority.

'That won't be necessary,' Emrys corrected, turning to William. 'William, was there any post this morning?'

The boy frowned before looking in his apron. 'Only this. I didn't think the fire post was still open.'

He held out a simple letter, no name on it and singed at the corners. But something in it must have been familiar because Gideon tensed as he saw the blue wax seal.

'You bastard,' he seethed.

'I'm certain we'll find all the answers we need at the east dock.' Emrys smirked, a teasing darkness in his eyes as he met his brother's annoyance head on. Then I saw the depiction of a ship's anchor at the wax seal's centre.

'What's at the east dock?' I asked.

'The Lady of the Reavers,' Thean Page answered darkly, a threat lining those words. 'You'd better understand the game you're about to play, Blackthorn.'

Chapter Nineteen
Alma

They say the clever thief is one that is never caught. The thief that never existed at all. No stories to whisper on the wind, no names to chase.
  That's why you're perfect, little rat. You never existed at all.

Sometimes I had memories, but they never felt like mine. As if I'd slipped inside someone else's skull. The pain of trying to piece together what was lost was worse than the loneliness of never knowing. So, whoever I was, it didn't matter. Who I wished to be was all I had.

And I never wished to be a fool.

He lied. The memory of those words from Kat's lips, the raw pain laced into them. How deeply they lacerated inside me still.

Master Hale had lied. Just like all those who had come before. How easily I'd worn his leash. Believed this time it would be different. I looked down at my hands, how they still trembled. Rage was too potent in me, like over-steeped tea.

I couldn't blame Kat for trusting too easily. She hadn't seen the things I had. Didn't know this awful world as I did. We shared Daunton, that cruelty was insignificant compared to all that had happened to me before.

I should have known better. I should have seen Hale's trap. I'd been in enough of them.

I wrung the cloth a little tighter in my hands, letting the soapy water rush through my fingers. Still getting no relief, no matter how tightly I twisted the fabric. The washed cups stacked next to the sink gave a concerned rattle.

'Shh,' I hissed. Not in the mood to entertain the house and its mothering. Not in the mood to admit all my mistakes. Chafing too close to the bone. Too true.

And I knew just how venomously I despised the truth. Changed and morphed into anything else to avoid it. Why the beasts beneath my skin were so fucking unsettled.

He lied. An irritated pained growl slipped from my lips. How I'd performed. Smiled and cared for the old bastard. How I'd worried for him.

With an irritated snarl I tossed the cloth and retreated to slump down onto the bench by the kitchen table, pressing my face into my damp, clawed hands.

I hated stopping. Hated the stillness. Hated having to think. Yet, a putrid bitter smell still stung my nose. Like coal tar. Repugnant and stifling. A smell that remained from being that beast and I didn't know why.

My beasts never lingered. Not like this. I raised my head to watch the black flames lick at the stone of the hearth. The sour smell from where I tossed the remains of that demonic clawed finger into the fire nearly turned my stomach. Needing to be rid of it.

I don't know why I'd kept that finger, why I'd viciously wanted to, like some cursed trophy. Maybe I'd lost my mind.

Why I hadn't given any protest as Kat demanded to go with Blackthorn and Gideon to the east. Despite how close it brought her to the Reavers.

Gideon looked like he wanted to carve his own eyeballs out with a kitchen spoon at the suggestion – but one glare from Emrys had silenced him. Thankfully.

I should have talked her out of it. Talked her out of going deeper into another deadly game none of us should be playing. Considering the state she'd come back in from the Council chambers.

Instead, I'd hidden once again in the kitchen. Like the coward I was, only to be faced with *The Crow's Foot* as the papers lay scattered across the table before me, the violence and riots that had already begun across Elysior. The uprisings that had erupted against Montagor's vicious new rule. As his hunters sought any rebellion they could find.

They'd taken cursed venom again, turning them into vicious monsters who moved faster and could kill quicker. Just like in those wars as fey fled further north. As their villages were purged. How quickly their façade of peace had crumbled. How ready their cruelty was.

Unease clawed at my skin which still stung from the change or from the vicious scrubbing I'd done in the bath earlier. Not feeling clean. No matter how much soap I used.

I'd always remain like this. Dirty.

We were all made to be used, little rat. You're a liar for telling yourself any different. The memory of the Keeper's drunk slurred words only soured my mood further. How right that monster could still be, even after all this time. How true Master Hale had made those words.

A hand waved in my vision, making me jump. Seeing William's worried frown as he stood before me, clearly speaking to me.

'Sorry, William.' I shook my head, rising from the table, but his kind brown eyes dropped to the back of my hand, where I'd scratched the skin red raw.

'Does changing irritate you?' He frowned at the mark.

'Sometimes.' I shrugged. Reluctant to admit how it felt like I lost something every time. How this power had been so tightly woven with my pain. How they'd twisted this gift into a curse. Made me remember everything I wished to forget.

Kat would have made me something, a tonic, maybe? She would have stayed if she'd known but I wasn't her burden.

'It's hard to feel . . .' The words seemed to stick to the roof of my mouth. Claggy. 'To feel clean afterwards.'

Something that seemed like understanding crossed his expression before he moved to one of the kitchen shelves, coming back with a small metal tin in his outstretched palm.

'Here. Mirtle wood. That'll soothe it.' His offering was so simple and yet it made a brutal mark across my heart. That he'd care enough to even think of it. To help something as wrong and strange as me.

'Thank you, William.' I squeezed his hand. His warm smile like a reward. Then I saw the strange markings scratched on his fingers.

'What happened?' I frowned, wondering if he'd got carried away with his thorn tonics again.

His cheeks flushed as a small line furrowed his brow. 'It was that bloody gobrite. Horrid little bastard. I only tried to put it back.'

'Why would Emrys keep it?' I unscrewed the lid and rubbed the balm on my raw flesh. Feeling the irritation ease instantly.

William shrugged. 'Who knows. But I wondered if you wanted to go over the compendium records.'

The offer was gentle, coaxing. Perhaps afraid I'd withdraw further. I tried not to be unsettled by that. By someone caring so much. Too used to hiding in kitchens, store cupboards or shadowed stairways. Hiding from all the things I couldn't change.

'Where does Emrys keep the compendiums?' I asked, something within me seeming to raise its scaled head at the question. My curse's interest never usually led to good things.

'In the cellar,' he answered with a shudder. 'It's . . . *strange* down there.'

'Strange?' I frowned.

'Magic doesn't like to be contained, and it likes to misbehave when Emrys is out of the house.' The boy shrugged, pulling at his curls.

Of course. Emrys was Verr. The mere presence of his magic would be enough to tame more feral manifestations. Why he didn't seem to have an issue hunting dark fiends. They probably came to heel easily enough. Why the lord had unsettled me upon first meeting, despite doing nothing to warrant my suspicion.

Something in me must have sensed that threat. Even if I didn't know what it was.

'There was . . . a strange scent. When I changed, I could smell something. Kat said dark beings can track dark magic.' I wondered if that was why it still stung my nose. As if trying to catch my attention, the darker side of my nature trying to help for once.

'They can.' He nodded, weighing my words.

'I wonder if I could sense if there was anything similar in the other compendiums. Something created at the same time.' That if I even went near them, would the creatures in my blood be able to sense it.

'We . . .' he began, but before he could answer, the storeroom door opened, revealing a stone set of stairs leading down. The house clearly making the decision for us.

'It's rude to listen to people's conversations,' William grumbled at the wooden-beamed ceiling as if the house's presence was no more than a bat hanging there. The only response was the door rattling in annoyance.

'All right, we're coming.' William crossed to the door and I followed. Slapping irritably at my skirts. Not used to being in a light simple dress rather than the confining heavy fabric of my maid's attire, but relieved the house and William had given me a distraction.

I was desperate for a distraction.

Even if that distraction was at the bottom of a drafty and twisting stone stairwell. Steps so narrow I had to watch my feet, fingers dragging over the cold, damp walls. All warmth seeping from the air, as if the house's comforting magic couldn't reach down here.

William paused in the gloom at the bottom of the stairs which was no more than an archway leading to endless darkness. My nose twitched, rough scales forming on my palms as if in anticipation of touching something.

'Sorry. It has to be the old-fashioned methods,' he sighed, pulling down a torch from the wall that was strung with cobwebs and dust, as he rummaged in his apron and pulled out a small box of matches, handing them to me. 'Magical flames don't do well down here.'

Thank fuck Kat hadn't found this place then.

I quickly lit the torch, stuffing the matches back in his apron as the cavernous space was illuminated. Large stone arches greeted us, solid wooden doors spaced evenly all the way down the hallway. The remains of a red carpet clung to the stone floor as gargoyles peered down from perches above.

As if we'd wandered into ancient ruins from one of Kat's history texts.

'What would you two be up to?' came a sly, smooth voice from the shadows.

'Bloody fuck!' William hissed, almost jumping out of his skin as he struggled to keep hold of the torch.

'Language, dear William,' Thean drawled, only there was no amusement on the voyav's face. Just that sharp annoyance where they stood at the base of the stairs, one arm braced on the wall, peering down at us in striking female form.

'Why are you creeping around in the dark?' I demanded, refusing to acknowledge the strange play of my magic over my skin in their presence. The wildness in me not knowing if it should preen or bite. Of how the richness of their scent chased away everything else.

'Why change the habit of an eternity?' The voyav shrugged a graceful shoulder, that beautiful auburn hair catching the torchlight as they ran their fingers idly through it.

'You're not that old.' William frowned, sucking his finger where he'd burnt it on the torch. 'Besides, Alma wanted to see the compendiums.'

William winced slightly, clearly realising he probably shouldn't be telling a rebellion voyav that information.

Thean didn't seem to care, those troublesome eyes coming to land on me instead. 'Of course this was *your* idea, little nightmare.'

'I don't see you helping.' I crossed my arms, feeling the sharpness of fangs against my gums. My treacherous body wanting to mimic them. Ignoring the stupid name they'd chosen to bestow upon me.

'Perhaps I'm not in the mood to take a beating from a dark lord after rummaging through his cursed collections.' Thean leant back against the damp wall, apparently unbothered about ruining their outrageous suede jacket.

'You shouldn't have said anything about Kat's breasts then,' I snapped. Remembering how frighteningly quickly Emrys had moved at Thean's taunt and how brutally his fist had made contact with the voyav's grinning face. Thean not having the chance to hide within their more feminine form.

I doubted it would have saved them. I knew Emrys wouldn't hit a woman – hitting a *Thean* was a completely different matter.

The voyav leant forward, a sly smile upon those full lips. 'Don't fret, darling, if I was interested, I wouldn't have said anything at all.'

I snorted. I didn't care what the voyav said about Kat's breasts. Or if they thought about them at all.

Their smile grew sharper as if hearing my treacherous thoughts. Although those amber eyes mercifully left me and drifted to William. 'Lead the way, dear William.'

'I don't think you're allowed to be down here.' The boy shuffled nervously, looking down the dark corridor as if waiting for the house to respond. Only for silence and dead air to greet us.

'The house has clearly made the decision on Blackthorn's behalf.' Thean came closer to me, bringing with them that bastard scent that I dragged in too willingly. Anything to get the demonic stink out of my nose – or so I told myself.

I saw the only open door next to us, a gloomy dilapidated room that appeared to have once been an office. A perfect place to wait.

'Give me those matches,' I sighed, grabbing the box out of the boy's apron. 'I'll keep an eye on them, William.'

I pushed the voyav's very firm shoulder so they had no choice but to move into the side room with me. Ignoring how easily they went at my command despite how much taller they were than me.

A sad-looking chaise was in the centre of the gloomy room. One end stacked with crates of books long forgotten with dust gathering on their leather covers.

A grimy lantern sat on an abandoned stack of tomes; the fireplace was bricked up but the mantel remained, covered in candles that had all melted, dripping wax down the chipped bricks. I busied myself lighting them all, drenching the depressing space in warm orange light.

How old and stagnant it was, the air thick with dead magic. Leaving a bitterness on my tongue. Unsettling me, but I turned to find the voyav sat on the chaise.

'It must be my lucky day.' Thean grinned, baring those fucking fangs that made my gums ache to do the same. Luring my beasts to play.

'What do you want?' I was too tired to even think about fighting with them.

'To see if you decided to get any more mad ideas.' They shrugged, the motion moving their shirt to reveal more of those forbidden runes marked there. Blood marks. Evidence of their devotion to the rebellion. To the witch that puppeted them. 'Or if you were finished licking your wounds?'

'Because I'm a beast?' I sneered, though the voyav never reacted to my anger the way I wanted.

They inclined their head, thoughtfully. 'No, because self-pity isn't like you, love.'

'Sod off,' I sighed. Pressing my fingers against my brow. Hoping the motion might soothe the dull ache in the back of my skull from the presence of something else within me.

Something I'd let in. That horrid sickly feeling still against my skin.

'Some things are not worth your worry,' the voyav cautioned, leaning forwards so their elbows rested on their knees. The most casual gesture I'd seen the creature make. Perfect bow lips pursed as if with concern.

'You saw the state of Kat.' It worried me more, how much more of this she could bare.

'She should have been resting,' they offered gently as if cautious of my mood. 'Unfortunately, Blackthorn is too bewitched to see reason where she's concerned.'

I should have hissed or bitten out a curse but I found myself stuck in silence. Kat was impossible to reason with even when she was of sound mind. Reluctant to give the voyav a victory, I childishly turned my attention to the candles. Hoping like a vicious spectre they'd vanish with the lack of attention.

'A Kysillian will never be told what to do. Stubborn as an ox, even when faced with a foe as vicious as you, darling,' they reasoned softly, and if I wasn't smarter, I'd convince myself I heard an edge of concern in their voice.

'We're generalising everyone by blood now?'

'Am I wrong?' They rubbed their jaw, the collection of golden rings on their fingers catching the candlelight. 'You might be in love with her but surely you can see her faults, darling?'

A sharp laugh escaped me at the ridiculousness of the statement. Echoing off the stone around us. 'I'm not in *love* with Kat.'

I ignored the bite of curiosity that had lingered in the voyav's words. Why the accusation would leave their lips. Why a being like them would care for such fickle emotions at all? 'She's half of me in a way I wouldn't expect *you* to understand.'

Like a limb, it was a familiarity I was dependent on. So close to my heart it didn't have words. As if our stories had begun on the same page, even if I knew that wasn't true. Even if the nightmare of mine had started long before.

No. I wasn't demented enough to be in love with Kat. Blackthorn could suffer that fate alone.

'Have you met many Kysillians?' I frowned, finding myself against my better judgement turning to fully face them.

'A few.' There was a guardedness to those eyes. As if not anticipating my curiosity.

Tough. They should have been cleverer in their games.

I blew out a frustrated breath. 'Do you answer any questions?'

'Perhaps you aren't asking the right ones, darling.' They tilted their head, revealing more summoning marks up the strong column of their throat. So many. Almost sadistic in their abundance. A testament to how tightly such a creature needed to be bound, as if Thean's will was too wild to be contained with merely one.

Or perhaps their master just enjoyed the sight of them too much. My fingertips brushed across the mottled skin of my wrist, fur rising beneath my touch. The creatures beneath trying to comfort me.

'Why are you even still here?' I demanded, pushing my hands behind my back. Turning my own anguish to anger like flipping a coin.

Thean seemed to preen under my irritation. 'Maybe the question you really want to ask is why it bothers you so?'

It doesn't bother me, I wanted to snap, but the slipping of scales over my spine with a shudder I had to repress told me otherwise. Every sense in my cursed body was on alert in their presence. Beasts too curious.

Flustered, I turned my attention to the abandoned items in the room. The oddities that littered the sideboard behind me. Jars and strange dried herb mixes. A peculiar, small metal orb sitting amongst the mess. Odd runes carved into it. I reached for it only for the voyav to suddenly be next to me, catching my curious hand. The warm brush of their body making my breath catch.

'I wouldn't touch that,' they warned, their fingers strangely soft.

'What is it?' I frowned, looking up to see them eyeing it suspiciously. How they tugged me away ever so slightly.

'A vorg,' they answered, gently releasing my hand. 'A way of transporting summoned fiends.'

I reared back, appalled. 'Why would you want to transport them?'

'Hungry creatures do well in battle.' Their eyes remained on the orb, cautious of it. All their humour gone. 'What do you think made a mess of Emrys's pretty face?'

Horror ploughed through me at just how hideous this world could be. No mortal or lesser fey could have survived such an attack. The brutality of it. Only it was their lack of surprise at anything that had unfolded to do with those relics that caught my attention. Their lack of surprise at any of this.

'You've seen a relic before,' I accused. They'd said as much as Kat read over those *Crow's Foot* pages. Unsurprised by the development.

'How clever you are.' Their fanged smile gleamed with predatory delight – back to their games so quickly.

'Don't mock me.' I bared my teeth.

'Little love, I wouldn't dream of it.' Their hands slipped so easily into their pockets – taunting me with their relaxed ease. Making me ponder how many of their perfect teeth I could knock out in one hit.

'Tell me,' I demanded. Knowing I had nothing to offer in such a bargain. Hoping that if they had any pity left in them, they'd allow me this answer at least.

Those sharp eyes dragged over my tired features. If they were repulsed by my dishevelment, they didn't show it. No, they considered me as if weighing up what price they'd ask for.

'*She* has one,' they shrugged but I didn't miss how a coldness crept over their expression. How they rubbed at that summoning mark at their collarbone as if it irritated them.

The mere mention of the Countess coated my veins in ice. My beasts rippling beneath, making me clench my fists and turn my attention to those candles flickering weakly on the mantel. My nose suddenly filled with a cloying stink of roses. A repugnant sweetness mixed with the distant scent of decay.

'Why would she need a relic?' I asked.

'How do you think she holds her flock to their blood oaths?'

My gaze shot back to them, falling to the mark that was poking out of the edge of their shirt.

Of course. There was no fey summoning that dark. No magic that would trap a being as ruthlessly. Why the menageries were full of Verr worshippers, why they used forsaken iron to chain us, drank our blood in some perverse amusement. Our pain an aphrodisiac. The other dark incantations to make us do their bidding.

You already knew this, little rat. Did you forget?

I bit the inside of my cheek. The Keeper's taunt wasn't real. The ghost of him wasn't here. I'd made that voice up to torment myself.

Dark magic was the only power that could suppress fey. Why it could now only be found in the vilest corners of the world. Why those mortal kings had craved it above everything else.

'Those relics have been out there all this time.' I swallowed. Being used on fey and the Council had never cared.

'They hold power. Just like the one your Kysillian keeps.' Those sharp amber eyes watched every one of my breaths, just like the predator they were. As if waiting for some dramatic emotion from me.

225

'Kat doesn't have any power like that.' Her blade. A sword this creature before me should know nothing about, but whatever game the voyav was playing – they had no clear interest in Kat's secrets.

They wouldn't be lingering here with me if they did.

'If she stopped pretending that blade doesn't belong to her . . . she could.'

Kat didn't seek power. No, she wanted to be left alone to read her books, to study and heal this world. Only that dream of a simple life had been taken from her.

I wanted to deny it. But Kat had always called it her father's blade. As if she was simply minding it. Always hidden it. Knowing the brutality of such a weapon and what it meant.

I shuddered, remembering the stories the keepers had whispered. Of vicious Kysillian beasts who seared creatures' bones for nothing more than sport. Why I'd recoiled from Kat the moment we'd met in that dank dorm room in Daunton – seeing those violet eyes. Because my keepers had taught me that fear well. Because the monsters we were taught to fear as children took different form depending on who was telling the tale.

'You shouldn't know about that blade,' I wanted to snap but my anger exhausted me more than I cared to admit.

'What will you offer for my silence, sweetheart?' Then came the slight sultry lift of their lip.

Everything. Nothing.

'None of this scares you?' I bit back. Surely a voyav – a Verr like them – should be more worried about the chaos Kat could unleash. Of what Montagor's madness meant. Of relics and seals being brought to light. Of all the unrest that was bound to follow.

'On the contrary, I'd enjoy the view of this world burning down.' There was nothing but truth in the handsome angles of their face as the candlelight flickered across it. 'For what has it done for me, darling?'

Nothing. A little voice answered inside of me. My eyes reluctantly moving back to the marks across Thean's skin. Evidence they were owned.

And from how long they lingered here, they couldn't be *that* good a spy, not when it appeared they had no desire to leave. Not when all they did was taunt a worthless creature like me.

'Found them,' William announced, making me jump as he appeared – out of breath, with crates in his arms that looked like they'd been used to carry vegetables in the past, a small lantern dangling from his fingers, an ink smudge at his chin as he smiled.

'These are open so we can go through them to start. I need to ask Emrys where he put the rest.' He strode to a sideboard that was less cluttered than anything else and put the basket down, picking up the first compendium and handing it to me. The leather peeled and cracked, rough against my palm. A shudder rolling through me at the unpleasant sensation as I brought the yellowed spine to my nose. Smelling the sweetness of fey magic mingled with the sharpness of decay, making me recoil.

'Anything?' William frowned.

I was aware of Thean's presence right over my shoulder, the soft scent of brandy and the spice of their cologne. The creatures in me more curious of the voyav's proximity than the cursed books before us.

'The leather is made from wyvern hide and the pages are fey skin.' I pushed the book back to William. Bile burning the back of my throat.

'Bloody saints,' William cursed, looking down at the thing in horror as it fell open between his palms. I expected a retort from the voyav but, as I turned, I saw those amber eyes were focused on the text. Eyes moving across the cracked page with an intensity that unsettled me.

The beastly magic within me almost wanting to growl in warning.

'How can they be hidden in books?' I demanded, suddenly the focus of those strange, beautiful eyes. Feeling their body brush against the length of my own. Only their focus was still stuck on those pages and the books William had brought.

'The same magic that forms a Kysillian sword. Which I know you're familiar with.' The words were short and businesslike, but their eyes were moving too fast, as if a thousand thoughts had consumed them. Knowing something they didn't say. 'Between here and nothing.'

'Why would Verr use Kysillian summonings?' William mused.

'You think Kysillians came up with it all on their own?' Thean snorted. 'The conqueror always writes the history of the conquest, darling.'

Thean flipped the book between us, dust rising from its pages, to the centre. As if they'd read it before, landing on the middle page as it was spread before us.

On the revealed page were no words.

Just an image. Sketched like the tapestries of old I'd seen in the Institute. Only older. Darker.

Women holding children, bowed over. Clutching their young to them as fire rained down from above. Using their bodies as shields. Their mouths open as if they were screaming. As they cowered on the ground. Dark marks on their skin, showing they were Verr. Golden flames shaped like ravenous jaws surrounding them.

Large forms painted in gold holding swords to smite them. No matter how small and defenceless they were.

The Kysillians purged this world of the darkness that could end it. The story echoed in my memory. Only there was no darkness on this page. Just innocent beings. Punished for something they couldn't change. Their blood.

'If they were monsters to be purged, then perhaps we are too,' Thean added so softly, the words barely brushed the shell of my ear. Making it twitch as if my beasts were listening too. 'Are we all born cursed? Or have we simply forgotten who made us that way?'

Verr were monsters forced beneath. I'd seen the fiends their magic created. Yet as I looked at that picture . . . they'd been beings. Just as Thean stood before me now. Just as Emrys existed.

Not fiends, shadow beasts or monsters. Women and children. Beings that looked just like us. Like fey. It didn't make sense. I couldn't process the horror of the image before me as I slammed the book. My uselessness led too easily to defence as my heart pounded against my ribs but not with rage. Some strange emotion I couldn't understand, but before I could ask, the voyav stepped back.

'I'll leave you to your reading.' They straightened their jacket and moved to leave.

William startled. 'Thean—'

'Where are you going?' The demand slipped out before I could swallow it.

'To call in a favour,' they replied from the doorway, hands tucked carelessly into their pockets. 'Worried I'll meet a gruesome end?'

Thean lifted a mocking brow, smile sly and calculating. My heart fluttered and I told myself it was in irritation, from whatever form my anger wished for me to take.

'Only that you'll deprive me of the pleasure of doing it myself.' I smiled sweetly, turning back to the books William had gathered. Ignoring how the boy's gaze shot between me and the voyav. Ignoring the voyav's quiet laughter as they left. Somehow knowing they'd won.

I didn't hate the image of their smile that came to my mind. Not with how rare they seemed to be. Like a strange gift I shouldn't want.

'Should we let them wander the house?' William asked out of the corner of his mouth, nervously as if the voyav was still listening. Wiping his hands on his apron as if the compendium had dirtied his hands with the sorrow it contained.

No, Thean was gone. I knew by how my beasts settled and curled within me. Bored now.

'We have bigger problems than a bothersome voyav,' I sighed, dragging the crate closer to peer inside. 'We need to find whatever bastard bloodline those lords share.'

Whatever Thean was up to, they meant no harm. My beasts might have been vicious but they'd warn me of that. They always had. Even if I'd never had a chance in how their vengeance came.

William pulled a stained scroll from the basket, brandishing it like a sword with a grin. 'I found this family tree of the old houses. This should narrow—'

Only the scroll unfurled from his fingers at its own will, the page snaking across the table, knocking books free. Then onto the floor, rolling and rolling until it slid out of the door as if it were trying to escape.

William's mouth hung open, looking down at the endless lines and lines of names. Centuries' worth. 'Bloody saints. It's going to take forever.'

Forever was something I feared we didn't have.

Chapter Twenty

Kat

The wild winds claim the east. Reavers through the underground move fey to the northern shores. Their numbers unknown and their intent dubious. Mortals and lesser fey are involved. The docklands are unsafe territory for those loyal to the civil republic of Elysior. Three patrols have attempted to secure the region yet supplies dwindle and retreat is our only option. For how should we fight a faceless enemy even the rebellion seems hesitant to conquer.

Council report from the eastern fields

Gulls screeched above on the unforgiving sea wind. Coating my lips in the taste of salt as I kept a tight grip on my hood. Thankful for the light mist of rain giving me a reason to conceal my ears. But the poor gloomy weather didn't disturb the bustle of the markets beyond. Packed tightly with both fey and mortals.

A maze of stalls lined the great sea wall. The east coast of Elysior, known for its fishing and island trade. A fey haven, the Council having too much need of the items made and traded in the east to cause trouble here. One of the places I'd considered safe for Alma in my plans after the Institute. Yet the maps and stories had never done it justice.

The hiss of distant steam engines caught my ear, ready for their cargo.

Then came the traders' shouts carried on the wind as women scurried past with buckets and baskets of wares. Young boys with hooved feet sold pies from shop doorways.

So much normality it put me on edge, where I lingered in a narrow alleyway. Right where Emrys had left me, in the company of Gideon – and his disapproving scowl – standing opposite me.

Much to the healer's annoyance. The harsh winds disrupting his golden hair – he hadn't bothered to pull up his cloak.

He'd protested my coming. Stating it was best I was left in the house. Emrys hadn't said anything, he'd given me the choice and despite my track record with foolish decisions I didn't want to stay put. I needed to fix things. Needed to learn. Needed to help.

Kysillians healed by training, moving, and hunting. They didn't do well sitting still. Besides, if Montagor could send another blood seeker, I'd rather face it in the open than have it run into William or the house first.

I pressed myself back against the chipped brick, returning my focus to the beings that bustled past the mouth of the alleyway, the wind bringing the smell of roasting nuts and hot wine. The shriek of children playing and dockworkers laughing as they hauled rope while girls sold flowers from small crates.

How strange such peace was to me. How it threatened to drag me back to the memories of my own childhood that now only stung like an open wound.

'You must have impressed someone,' came Gideon's dry voice from next to me, making me jolt with surprise at how silently he moved. 'That's quite a striking likeness.'

He was still studying the market, but he held a piece of paper out to me, torn where he'd pulled it from the notice wall at the alley's end. I took it, oddly not surprised to find my own face looking back at me.

Katherine Woodrow.
Rebellion accomplice.
Wanted on suspicion of murder and arson.
Full reward to be paid after capture.

Thankfully the artist who had constructed my likeness hadn't been employed by the Council. If they had been, I was certain I would have had fangs and claws.

No. Master Hale had paid for the artist for my Council file a few years ago.

Repulsed by the memory of him, I pushed the paper deep into my pocket. Another act of charity to soothe his own guilt.

'You weren't raised with Kysillians?' Gideon asked, the question too short as if he had no desire to ask it but also didn't enjoy the silence.

'My mother was mortal. My father wished to protect us from Kysillian scorn.' I answered. Why we settled in the north. Where beings didn't care for the sin of impure blood mixing. 'If only he knew how futile the endeavour was.'

The words slipped free until I could fully contemplate the weight of them. The horror of everything that had followed as I left the north.

How strange it was to have such secrets free after winding them around my ribs for so long.

'I'm sorry that you were there.' Gideon's words were almost lost in the wind. Genuine sadness in his profile. The hint of regret in the tight press of his lips as he considered the market beyond.

Daunton. Of course, Gideon wouldn't have known until that Council chamber.

'I'm here now.' I smiled despite myself.

Those sharp eyes came back to my face, lips parting as if he wanted to say something else. Only to be distracted by nearing footsteps. The dark form of Emrys slipping into the shadow of the alley, his grey coat catching on the breeze as he ran his fingers through his damp hair. Jarring me by how those scars down his face stood out more in the daylight.

'What were you doing?' Gideon demanded, voice low as if being left in my company was a taxing punishment.

'Making myself seen,' Emrys answered.

'You could have said that.' Gideon muttered, moving closer to the mouth of the alley as if to watch for a threat on the streets. His arms folded tightly across his chest, that metal of his arm groaning.

Emrys came to stand before me, presenting me with a small brown paper bag. 'For Alma,' he offered. I didn't need to open it – by the weight and the feel I knew it was chocolates.

He'd remembered what I'd told him about her others. I couldn't help but smile as I caught his chin with my thumb, bringing his face closer so I could kiss his cheek in thanks.

'Ancestors deliver me,' Gideon grumbled like a petulant chaperone, despite his back being to us.

'I can grant that wish,' a female voice spoke. Emrys went tense as his attention and mine turned towards that voice.

She stood exactly in the middle, somehow there despite making no sound. Four cloaked figures behind her, blades glinting and faces obscured by dark masks.

Reavers.

The woman was unmasked. Although dark paint was smeared around her eyes as if she'd been wearing one, metal studs through her nose and lip in decoration. She was tall and broard, her dark skin damp from the mist of rain. Blonde hair braided back as the pale white horns that curved back against her scalp caught the weak sunlight.

'Gideon Swift. I heard a rumour you were back from the dead.' She folded her arms over her fitted leather jacket, her blonde braids falling over one shoulder.

There were ink designs across her knuckles that had nothing to do with magic or summoning. As sharp teal eyes ran over our small gathering with displeasure. 'From the looks of things . . . you should have stayed dead.'

'We have an invitation, Sigrid.' Emrys moved in front of me, holding up his hand, and there between his two fingers was a folded piece of paper. Like a street urchin performing a magic trick.

'Do you remember the name of all the beings who've tried to kill you, Blackthorn?' She took the letter from him.

'Old habit,' Emrys offered darkly.

Those words made my magic rise within me like a summoned beast. Awakening something primal within my blood, at the mere threat of them. The woman called Sigrid scanned over the letter, before a muscle moved in her jaw.

'This female will be the death of me,' she muttered, folding the letter with a sharp slap.

'Back to your positions,' she threw the command over her shoulder. The cloaked figures had the barest hesitation before they slipped back onto the streets and into the bustle of people at the market stalls. A shifting of light above told me more had been perched on the roofs above. Neither Emrys nor Gideon seemed disturbed by the prospect. Anticipating it.

Of course, none of this was new to them. Elysior had been in conflict for longer than it had been at peace.

'Shall we?' The female turned to lead the way. It was perhaps unwise for her to give us her back, but the broadsword strapped there seemed to be a taunt. That she'd enjoy bringing down anyone foolish enough to attack her.

She turned to one of the damp, brick walls that had penned us in. Only then did I notice the scratches on the stone. Faint rune marks in the shape of a narrow archway.

She tapped twice on the red brick, the wall peeling away with a clatter of stone and dust to reveal a short passage, resembling something a servant might use.

What greeted me was the smell of hay, dry wood and sweat.

'Brilliant bloody idea as always, brother,' Gideon griped, fixing the sleeves of his jacket, his eyes darted around, as if needing to know every exit. 'The Reavers are clearly *thrilled* to see us.'

'Quiet,' was Emrys's dark command as he – thankfully – went first, despite the fact I was certain every gentlemanly urge in him fought against it. With Gideon cursing at my back, I had no choice but to move forward, at least thankful to be out of the wet gloomy weather and to be able to take down my hood as I pushed the small packet of chocolates into my skirt pocket.

The stone passage led past tall archways and inside what appeared to have once been a theatre. I'd never been in one but I'd seen pictures. Viewing boxes, extravagantly decorated walls – only now the paint was chipped and peeling. A once-grand chandelier hung above reflecting the dim lamplight. Only the stage was now gone, and instead a large fighting pit took up the space. Surrounded by wooden benches, some men gathered, smoking pipes and handing around betting slips.

What would the Reavers be doing gathering by a fighting pit? The stories my mother told me were of the Reavers being freedom fighters who worked the streets and villages. How they kept fey and mortals safe though an underground movement. So at odds with the version before me now as we moved further through archways until we passed through thick velvet curtains to an office at the back.

Greeted by bookcases and an assortment of shelves holding what appeared to be shipment scrolls. The smell of tobacco hit me first. Eyes moving to where smoke clouded. Coming from the rouge-painted lips of a beautiful woman sitting behind a large, ornate dark wood desk.

Her warm brown skin was only marred by creases around her golden eyes as if she smiled often. Dark hair was arranged perfectly on top of her head, her red nails tapped on the leather desktop where it was littered with papers and silver coin. The excessive frills of her expensive silk shirt making me certain Thean would be jealous of the monstrosity.

'You are as clever as I remember, Blackthorn,' came her hoarse voice as smoke seeped from her lips. She took another drag of her thin cigar, leaving a red stain at its base. 'I knew you wouldn't waste time on those old bastards still calling themselves lords.'

'I told you *one* a day,' Sigrid warned, as she pried the thin cigar from the woman's delicate hand and placed it in the ashtray, which appeared to be made of a bejewelled human skull. Those gems throwing multi-coloured shapes across the floor between us in the lamplight.

'With a Blackthorn on my doorstep it appears I'll be dead long before the smoke takes me, my love.' The woman behind the desk grinned, her attention moving to me. Or more my unease at her choice of human remains as decoration.

'Don't worry, my dear, he deserved it.' She tapped her red nail against the skull's socket.

Emrys's face remained impassive, his hands sliding casually into his pockets at my side. 'Lady Ramsey.'

237

'We both know that title means little anymore, Emrys.' She waved her ring-covered fingers dismissively. 'However, it is good to see such a handsome face. Even in such dismal circumstances.'

'Troublesome times don't seem to have affected your business,' Gideon offered dryly, eyes moving over the shelves filled with scrolls and small money pouches left unguarded on the sideboard. As if anyone would be foolish enough to rob this woman.

'Not yet,' the Lady countered, her attention remaining on me. Running from my damp skirts to cloak-covered shoulders. Where my hair had slipped free to curl around the sharp point of my ear.

'Montagor was swifter than I anticipated,' Sigrid said as she moved to stand behind the Lady, her face grim and tense as if anticipating an attack. 'It appears madness is guiding him.'

'To remove the Council suggests he's set on following the Mage King's legacy. Hunting a way to free the darkness from beneath,' Gideon answered.

'I was about to reach out to Lord Farrow for you, Emrys. Since the bastard has eyes all over the southern lands.' The Lady nodded as she took a sip from a glass of port on her desk, leaning back in her extravagant chair. 'However, he became . . . *reluctant* to correspond once he heard Gideon Swift was back in the fold.'

Her golden gaze seemed to gleam with amusement.

'A piece of advice, dearest Gideon. Next time you decide to insert yourself into someone's *marriage*, maybe make certain we don't actually need their help afterwards?'

'The bastard and his wife invited *me*. It's not my fault they both became quite obsessed,' Gideon replied, making the lady's grin widen. 'Besides, if you're lecturing anyone on dangerous entanglements, *Priscilla*, surely it's my brother you should be speaking to.'

Gideon's eyes drifted over me with mild annoyance to make his point clear. Sigrid gave a short, amused snort as Lady Ramsey's prying eyes found mine once more.

'*I'm* not married,' I snapped. Cheeks burning, unable to think of anything else to say to fill the awkward, tense air.

'I doubt it would stop him if you were,' Gideon added wryly, as Lady Ramsey's laugh filled the small office. Only heightening my embarrassment. Emrys didn't even blink to rebuke the remark.

'Always the scoundrel, Master Swift,' the Lady chuckled.

'You have many ships in the harbour headed to the eastern isles.' Emrys's words cut through the Lady's mirth. Her eyes flashed with surprise before he continued. 'Your traders like to talk.'

That's what he was doing at the markets. Seeking information. Listening.

'Maybe they need to be reminded of the consequences for a loose tongue,' Sigrid offered, folding her arms tightly over her leather-covered chest.

'There have been sightings of large fey groups moving this way. However, the inns and lodges appear relatively empty. The surrounding villages and healing houses too,' Emrys continued his ruthless line of questioning.

There were stories in the build-up to the uprising of Reavers moving fey on ships. To the ancient islands surrounding Elysior. To places only the fey knew, that only their magic could access. Why my parents had chosen an island in the north.

The rebellion branded Reavers cowards. Nothing but street urchins, lower fey. Running when they should fight.

'Maybe they vanished into the mist like in the stories.' Lady Ramsey traced a finger around her glass, eyes calculating.

No. She was moving them to the eastern isles. Just as the Reavers always had. No matter the consequences from the rebellion.

'Maybe they did.' Emrys nodded in agreement, a strange truce as he perused the map laid across the Lady's desk with ease. 'Your Reavers have already been spotted at the south borders.'

'I thought you'd be here to discuss the massacre on the western road,' Sigrid interjected.

Emrys rubbed the back of his neck. 'Unfortunately, I'm too familiar with a creature like Montagor, and his motives. The western road was a distraction, to spur the Council to gather. He's up to something else.'

Lady Ramsey gave a small unamused laugh. 'Blackthorn really did train all his weapons to be as sharp as himself.'

She cleared a pile of coins off of the map before her with one movement of her hand. Revealing a patch of Elysior marked with red blots of ink.

'Montagor's men have begun mining. Only broke ground a few days ago,' Lady Ramsey finished, all humour vanishing at the same time my heart began to climb up my throat. Breath slipping uneasily through my lips.

Mining. The mines and the fey indentured to work in them had been the reason behind Elysior's wealth for the upper classes for centuries. Only where there were slaving mines, there were always Reavers destroying them. How most of the skirmishes had begun during the Mage King's purging of the east. Mines like the one my grandmother was murdered in. The one my father destroyed. Mines that were supposed to be outlawed – should have been for over a decade.

'With who?' I demanded, forgetting myself.

'Prisoners. Rebellion sympathisers. Suspected Reavers,' Sigrid answered tersely, her gaze pinned on my face as if the flash of pain across my features made her curious.

'Montagor has gathered himself quite a little collection under the Council's watch.'

'The mines were destroyed.' A darkness lingered in Emrys's words. The bite of his magic seeming to hum in the air. As if he'd seen to the task personally.

'It seems Montagor wishes to return things to the *good old days*.' The Lady shuddered, using the desk to get to her feet, hands planted on its top as if she needed it for support. 'I'll never understand fascists' obsession with the past. If only we could send all the righteous fuckers back there and be done with it.'

'He's looking for something beneath.' The words escaped my lips before I could fully understand the weight of them. Why Kysillians had been captured and forced into mines. We could sense the darkness of Verr magic. They'd tried to use us to find it.

'We've sabotaged as many of the new mines as we can, but it won't take long before his work begins again,' Sigrid spoke, words clipped with her disdain.

'The rebellion won't take kindly to your meddling in fey affairs,' Gideon interrupted, his expression stern as if we'd tangled ourselves in a trap. 'She'll see it as a challenge.'

Of course. Speaking to the Reavers was working against the rebellion. The rebellion who didn't forgive and especially didn't forget.

'Fuck her rebellion,' Lady Ramsey answered, picking up a bejewelled cane from where it leant against her chair and moving from her desk with some difficulty. 'These beings are mine to protect and I can deal with the Countess's games.'

Her attention drifted back to Emrys. 'Strange how the moment the Council crumbles, you come to *our* doorstep, Emrys.'

'The Reavers have always had the support of my house.' His words didn't surprise me – I knew Emrys had been helping fey. However, assisting the Reavers was a level of treason against the Council's false peace efforts I was glad of.

'Yet they're untrusting of you. Your dealings with the Council haven't put you in good stead,' Sigrid added, her eyes narrowed in suspicion.

'The Council were a necessary evil. They've finally paid their due,' Gideon added, arms folded tightly across his chest in Emrys's defence.

They'd paid it being consumed by that relic. Destroyed by their own greed.

'A Kysillian in your ranks might sway their opinion,' Lady Ramsey offered, eyes running over my features, amused by something.

'Miss Woodrow isn't a pawn to be moved about your board, Priscilla,' Gideon warned, startling me with his defence. Only the Lady didn't seem to care for his tone.

'You seem familiar to me,' she mused, both hands on her cane. Curious but coming no closer. Something unsettling in her expression. In those sharp gold eyes, as if this woman knew too much and you had no hope of keeping any secrets in her presence.

'It's probably all her "wanted" posters,' Gideon answered quickly, shooting Emrys a warning glance.

Thankfully, Gideon's comment was enough to steal her attention once more. Focusing it back on Emrys. 'What do you want, Blackthorn?'

'We believe Montagor has turned to blood summoning. If he's digging, he's looking into the past. And he's also seeking lords' blood for his summonings.'

'Why on earth would he need that when the houses have no power in these lands?' Sigrid snorted, only Lady Ramsey didn't share in her amusement.

'He's seeking a relic then?' the Lady assessed. Despite her youth, I noted how heavily she leant on her cane. How pain rippled across her expression. 'Which means you're looking for something of my father's?'

Lord Ramsey. I knew the house name. Knew them for being so closely entwined with the King's missions in Elysior. Not a member of the lords' rebellion. No, he was a sadistic brute. Crimes that spanned chapters of text. Mass graves left in his wake, signs of his devotion to his saint, and his king.

'The old bastard kept many dark secrets,' Gideon answered. 'What is your price?'

The Lady smiled, something wicked flickering in her eyes as they ran over the three of us and, for the first time since stepping into this room, I feared we'd walked into a trap. 'If you wish to *trade*, I usually like a demonstration of goodwill. To test loyalties. It's the Reaver way.'

Gideon gave Emrys a side glance, but Emrys remained still at my side. Waiting.

'I'm a fighter short,' she offered. 'I have a miroc bull that needs teaching a lesson. Rumours are you've gone quite . . . *soft* in your later years, Emrys.'

Confusion furrowed my brow, only for an unamused sound to slip between Gideon's lips. 'Pray do tell what *we* get from this?'

'What you'll be needing. If Montagor is coming east, he's looking into the past. Only he doesn't know what for. Not yet.'

'And you do?' Gideon demanded.

Sigrid went tense at his clipped tone, however the Lady laughed, another soft and genuine sound.

'My father was the Mad King's favourite advisor. What wicked things they'd whisper to each other in bed. Many have come to me seeking the things my father knew. And none of them have been seen again.'

'Montagor?' Gideon frowned.

'You think that mad weasel would ask a woman anything?' The Lady quirked a brow.

'You already knew we'd end up here,' Emrys demanded, a darkness lacing his tone with warning.

'I didn't survive this long with beauty alone, gentlemen.' She leant back against the panelled wall. Head tipped in challenge. 'The moment that Institute fell I knew how this would play out. My father had a journal he kept, filled with pieces of his madness. He handed it off before he was killed. Whatever he knew will be concealed in those pages.'

Gideon swore, probably at the prospect of another doomed hunt. 'To whom?' Emrys demanded.

'Lord Turner. Rumours say it was buried with him, kept safe for when they could resurrect the bastard with one of their dark summonings.'

'Where?' Gideon demanded, a sudden urgency as his aether flickered in the space between his fingers.

'I failed to ask my father before I drove a dagger through his eye.' She nodded, opening her desk draw before pulling out a thick gold coin. The old currency from before the wars. 'You'll be needing this to find it.'

'You've never looked for it?' I asked, unable to ease my doubt that the answers could be this simple. That she would be this helpful. That the answers could be lying in a grave somewhere. Waiting.

'I have no desire to read the monster's ramblings. I lived with them long enough.' Pain laced her features as if remembering something before she tucked the coin into her skirt pocket. 'Some dark things are best left to rest.'

I noticed then how unsteady she was, how Sigrid came closer upon instinct. Emrys seemed to sense her tiring as well, but where I thought he'd use it to his advantage he simply nodded, almost out of respect of all she'd shared. Of course, these dark histories were something they had endured together.

'Very well,' he answered as he began to shrug out of his coat. The Lady laughed, excitement flaring in her golden eyes as she grabbed the small bell off of her desk. Shaking it.

'What are you—' I began as Gideon cursed next to me. Only for a young boy to arrive in the doorway. A small trut, earth-born fey with bark-like skin, and dull green hair.

'Simon.' The Lady smiled. 'We have our fighter. Tell Mr Briggs we'll begin shortly. Bring the patrons.'

'Sorry ma'am, he says he's not happy with the prize money for the delay. Wants an increase,' the boy stuttered, wringing his flat cap nervously between his palms.

Sigrid stepped forward as if to sort out the issue but the Lady lifted a graceful hand, her smile wicked. Those golden, amused eyes coming to my own.

'Tell the bastard we'll throw in a kiss from the Kysillian girl who burnt down the Institute as an extra reward,' she grinned. Gideon swore and Emrys's magic became a deadly static in the air. 'Just to sweeten the deal.'

Bollocks.

Chapter Twenty-One
Kat

Smoke curled thickly in the air, the stench of body odour mixing with the reek of tobacco. Rowdy men from the docks wearing flat caps with rolled up sleeves sat on benches below, sipping from flasks, wedged around the fighting pit. Small messenger boys shook bags of nuts or betting slips frantically trying to catch a buyer's attention.

Then there was the ethereal faded flicker of white light in the shadowed corners. Spectres lingering. Fey that had died here. Probably in that very fighting pit.

Damn Emrys.

I curled my hands more tightly around the viewing rail on the second floor. A box Lady Ramsey had moved us to after Emrys had vanished to play his part in this awful, stupid plan.

'Stop fretting,' Gideon ordered from where he leant next to me against a pillar covered in peeling, floral wallpaper. Emrys's coat slung over his arm for safekeeping.

'Follow your own advice,' I snapped back, unbothered about keeping my voice down. 'You don't have to *kiss* anyone.'

Gideon let out a grunt of amusement, but his eyes remained fixed on the ring below.

'Emrys has had worse fights than this. For far lesser stakes,' He offered. Making me wonder if those words were to comfort me or himself.

'*He failed to mention that.*' I bristled, sounding more like a perturbed alley cat in my annoyance.

'He didn't get the Council to fear him by writing incantation papers and chasing ghosts,' Gideon added as he watched the waiting crowd gather before turning to where Sigrid counted betting slips in the corner of the room. 'Put one hundred on Emrys knocking him out first round.'

Lady Ramsey smiled, stirring her tea where she sat in an extravagant wing-backed chair. Unbothered by all the chaos she'd created.

'*You're absurd,*' I hissed, unable to believe he was encouraging this. Mirocs were dangerous. Especially ones that apparently loved beating other fey to death in that very ring for coin.

'You're right.' Gideon frowned, turning back to Sigrid. 'Make it five hundred.'

If I didn't have more restraint I would have hit him. Instead, I tightened my grip on the rail and tried to find some patience. This was mostly my fault after all – my foolishness setting us on this path.

There was a roar from the crowd as the first fighter appeared. The miroc and my apprehension began to spiral. Emrys was an imposing form, but the miroc was a huge hulking mass as he entered the fighting pit, stomping hooves covered in coarse blonde hair just like most of his bare barrel-like chest. His horns were short and sharp. The ends tipped with silver studs that did little to calm my dread.

Gideon went tense. Finally, he was taking this seriously. His energy seemed to crackle around him. Making the hairs on my neck stand on end.

'Now you decide—' I began but he was already turning.

'*You bitch,*' he seethed. Aether practically vibrating off him as he glowered at Lady Ramsey. Sigrid moving forwards to block his path.

'Watch your tongue,' Sigrid snapped, hand moving to her blade.

'That's *Regus*,' Gideon spat the name, aether curling up his arms, making his eyes glow.

'Never agree to a bargain until you've read the fine print.' Lady Ramsey continued to sip her tea as if she hadn't a care in the world.

'Who?' I frowned, my eyes moving from the ring and back to our suddenly tense gathering.

'The Countess's fighter.' Gideon tugged his fingers through his golden hair in frustration. 'Which means she's here, doesn't it, *Priscilla?*'

Fear clawed at my insides. My gaze shooting to the other viewing balconies that faced this one. But I couldn't see anyone. And down below, the crowd was pressed too tightly together.

Beware the witch that bargains in blood. For those she takes never return as they were. Puppets on a monster's string.

'Why?' Gideon demanded, coming to stand before me, blocking me as if the room was suddenly filled with nothing but threats. As if he wanted to pace like a manticore protecting territory.

'Because she can fucking do whatever she wishes, especially now Montagor has removed the only defence keeping her at bay,' Sigrid challenged.

The Council. The Countess wasn't brazen enough to start a war, but if given the opportunity . . .

'Emrys asked for this meeting,' Lady Ramsey snapped, her cool composure dissolving. 'His timing is as poor as ever. You came to *me*, Gideon. That miroc beast has killed good fey for sport. All for her to teach *me* a lesson.'

Because Lady Ramsey offered fey a different choice. A choice the Countess didn't wish for fey to possess. Not if they could be of use to her. The Reavers didn't prioritise ancient and more powerful blood, no . . . they treated everyone equal. Mortal, fey and lesser beings.

'You could have warned us.' Gideon's temper didn't waver, yet I could hear the hesitation in his voice. His reluctant understanding.

'What warning did we have?' the Lady scoffed, sadness burning in her golden eyes. 'Favours have a price, Gideon.'

'I'm aware of slipping into bed with vipers, Priscilla,' he replied, but the words weren't as cold as he intended.

A useful pawn in all this madness. A willing traitor, an easy whore and a brutal killer. The memory of Emrys's admissions settling uneasily inside of me. The things they'd been forced to do to win. And now how fleeting that victory and peace were as we verged on the abyss of another war.

'If you think I invited that blood-bitch here to kill my fighters for her own perversions . . . you're very much mistaken. Our rations dwindle. The border crossings grow more deadly . . . and my Reavers pay the price. She wants these lands and I'll do whatever it takes to keep them.'

Despite the pain in her words, it didn't settle the sharpness of Gideon's aether.

'Kat.' He reached for me, as if his only priority was seeing me out of that room.

'You're not leaving, Gideon,' Sigrid commented from where she blocked the door. Making him pause. His hands curling into a fist. The metal at his joints creaking. 'Bargains are to be kept.'

We needed what Lady Ramsey knew. We needed her help. Emrys knew that – it was why he was down there. Why he'd sought to come here at all. Something only she could give us.

I glanced at Gideon, seeing a muscle tense in his jaw as he kept his eyes on the ring below. He knew that too.

An excited roar came from below, bringing my attention back over the balcony as Emrys entered the fighting pit. Bare chested, his eyes dark as pitch with focus.

The miroc male grinned, raising his meaty fists to rile the crowd up further. Yet, I was more focused on the broad set of Emrys's shoulders, how he turned revealing the defined muscle, the path those scars made down to the low rise of his trousers. A path I'd followed with my very fingertips.

Behave. I flushed, curling my hands tighter around the railing. Feeling shamed at the strange heat flashing through me. It wasn't the time nor the place to be distracted by the temptation of Emrys.

Not when he was about to get pummelled by a miroc for an old coin and the barest hope it could lead us to where we needed to go. Not when the Countess was here somewhere. Watching this disaster too.

'I can't imagine the Countess is pleased about your numbers, nor the territory you've secured,' Gideon pressed, making me reluctantly turn my attention back to Lady Ramsey.

'She isn't,' Sigrid answered, considering Gideon like the threat he was despite the finery he wore. 'She's been quite keen on handing over any Reavers she catches right into the hunter's claws.'

Horror swooped through me at the thought. Of what happened to rebels caught by the Council hunters. Staged hangings as magic-mad lunatics wishing to disturb the Council's peace.

'They're on the same side,' I reasoned. Why couldn't they see that?

'Are they?' Lady Ramsey tilted her head in contemplation as she took another sip of her tea and another roar of excitement erupted below. 'When the rebellion wins, who do you think will rule?'

Fear bloomed inside of me at the thought. The reality I'd ignored. What my father had warned me of. Why he'd woven the rebellion so tightly into his cautionary tales. Why so many fey were hesitant to challenge the Council's control. If the

Council were gone, they'd only be feeding themselves to a worse beast if the tales were to be believed.

The Countess. A witch who bound her members with blood and lies. Who used them as a child would dolls in a playhouse. Who saw only a very select few as valuable. Mortals were nothing but parasites. Lesser fey only a disappointment to be left to rot. Mixed bloods like myself something to be purged.

'And the Reavers?' I asked, unashamed of the challenge in my voice.

'We've been allies to the mortals for centuries. We're striving for a true republic. No blood oaths,' the Lady continued, giving me mercy from her attention. 'Superiority and ancient blood have led us to our ruin too many times.'

'That's a fairy tale.' Gideon's face was stern as he continued to watch the ring below. Flinching slightly as his jaw tensed, almost making me turn to see what had happened.

Then Sigrid stood taller, a softness coming to her features as she met Gideon's stare. 'Emmaline believed in it.'

A light went out in Gideon's eyes. His face nothing but a cold mask. Hiding every emotion beneath it. *Emmaline.* Their sister knew these people. Despite the fact she was fighting for the other side.

'Look where it got her,' he replied. Voice so empty and cold it didn't sound like his own.

Bound to the Countess as Emrys had said. Bound until she was dead.

A sadness seemed to ripple across the Lady's features. Softening her for the barest moment. 'She'd hate to see it torment you so.'

'Then she should have been less fucking reckless,' Gideon snapped but it was tinged with pain. A younger brother who missed his sister.

'Reckless is believing you can avoid the Countess's attention forever, Gideon.' Lady Ramsey's voice was calm. 'The bitch doesn't like to be left in the dark.'

'Strange. Considering that's where she chooses to linger.' His words were as sharp as any blade, those eyes alight again with a different type of fury.

'I knew I missed you.' Lady Ramsey grinned. Then the cheering grew below. I gave into the temptation and looked over the balcony as another roar filled the room.

Emrys's shoulders rolled, the muscles moving as the sheen of sweat on his skin caught the afternoon sunlight that came in through the old theatre's high windows. A thin trail of blood down the scarred side of his face from a cut above his eyebrow.

How gracefully he moved, how the muscles of his back shifted and how each sharp movement pressed the fabric of his trousers tighter against his legs.

The hay was disturbed, the miroc panting wildly, doubled over before it lurched again. Deadly precision in its strikes, but Emrys met each one. Movements sharp and the responding blows biting, the thud of flesh meeting as the miroc was forced to give up space between them.

A vicious bloody dance. Then Emrys faltered, turning wrong. He left his side unguarded. The bull saw it, my lips parted to shout the warning but then Emrys moved faster than I thought possible. The miroc charging into his trap.

Three efficient bloody blows, two to the ribs and the final to the jaw and the bull was down.

The crowd reached a crescendo of cheering. Emrys didn't waste a moment, barely out of breath as he caught a rag someone threw into the ring. Wiping it over his face as one of the men raised his arm in victory. Yet those dark eyes fixed on the balcony.

Fixed on me. A slight boyish smile on his lips as if sensing my concern. So I scowled my answer, beyond unimpressed. However, that only seemed to heighten his amusement.

None of this was *remotely* amusing.

'Montagor will also be looking for the sword.' Sigrid's words cut through Emrys's haze, turning me once more.

'What sword?' I asked, noticing Gideon's lack of reaction as he met Sigrid's eye.

'The blade of the Old Gods,' Lady Ramsey answered.

That darkness crafts blades with demon fire. They gleam and shatter seals. How cold they burn and decimate the fragility of fey magic. Too powerful to exist, even to their own kind. That story. From the hymn of the Old Gods. Such weapons couldn't be real.

Only I couldn't deny the relics existed – so why wouldn't those weapons? My enchanted bag at the belt of my skirt felt suddenly too heavy, holding another object that shouldn't exist. My father's blade.

'He'll be looking a long time,' Gideon offered darkly. The air in the room suddenly too close with an unspoken threat. 'Maybe he should start with the children's fairy-tale tomes. That's the only place such a blade exists.'

'Of course.' Lady Ramsey's smile was soft as she flicked that coin and it tumbled through the air for Gideon to catch in his gloved fist. 'Your reward.'

It all felt too easy and I should have known better as the flutter of that wishing stone began beneath my dress. The chamber door burst open. The small messenger boy from before stood there, panting with wide eyes.

'She's coming,' he stuttered.

There was barely a moment. Gideon moved closer, almost forcing me back against the rail. A strange energy filling the air, how still he went before me. How all mirth and teasing guttered from Lady Ramsey.

Two men entered the box, nondescript and wearing fighting leathers, both with summoning runes on the back of their hands like Thean's. Yet it was the next one that stilled me in place, as my gaze met a pair of lavender eyes.

A Kysillian. His dark, thick hair was pushed back from his face. Falling in a wild tangle down his back. His ears prominent and his darker skin had the classical Kysillian golden hue. Eyes ringed with lavender. The shadow of stubble at his jaw. He couldn't have been more than a few years older than Emrys. But with a Kysillian's more graceful ageing it was hard to tell.

As I considered the bulk of the warrior before me, I almost missed someone else appearing in the doorway. That was the strange thing about creatures from tales. You always expected them to be *more*. Grander than words could say.

She was dressed in a luxurious dark suede jacket and breeches, a simple dagger sheathed at her side. She wasn't tall or striking. Her beauty was subtle, lethal in its peculiarity. A sharp rose perfume penetrated the air, tanging nauseously with Lady Ramsey's cigar smoke and the stench of sweat.

Her age undeterminable, thick brown hair slightly curled and brushed with grey – but there was something ancient in her eyes, a chilling blood-red colour to her irises. A testament to her power.

A blood witch with a cruel curl to her dark painted lips. One I had a feeling Thean had impersonated.

'Secret meetings, Priscilla.' Her voice was deep and smooth and there was a regal air about her, a practised ease to every motion as she came to stop in the centre of the box. 'You wouldn't be trying to hurt my feelings now, would you?'

The Countess.

Chapter Twenty-Two

Kat

Beware the witch in the west who makes promises in blood. With no age or name. Who cares little for the world, only for the power she can drain from the beings who wish to save it.

A blood witch who cares little for her soul in her bargain for power. Why she lives eternal, to never face the ancestors for her crimes.

Warning from the western shores — The Crow's Foot, 1856

Gideon slipped his hands into his pockets, despite the tension in his limbs and the faint sting of his power against my skin. As unsettled as the wishing stone beneath my clothes.

'In my bounds, my company is my own business, Countess.' Lady Ramsey smiled as she took another sip from her teacup. Those golden eyes hard and cold, filled with nothing but distaste for the creature before her.

'For now.' The Countess's mirth was slow and predatory. 'Still a cripple I see, Ramsey. Not enough coin for a good healer?'

Sigrid straightened and I could swear I heard her teeth grind.

'To what do we owe the pleasure of your interruption, Countess?' Gideon offered before Sigrid did something to turn the already tense room into a bloodbath.

I noticed the Kysillian remained still, those eyes pinned on me as if I was the last being he expected to see here. We had that in common at least.

'Gideon, you're supposed to be dead.' The Countess pulled the leather gloves from her hands, holding them out to one of her rebels who took them obediently. Her fingers decorated in jewelled rings, but her skin stained red up to the knuckle, her nails long and tinged black. Marks of blood worship.

'I tried my best,' Gideon offered darkly.

'Still tempestuous.' Her answering laugh was small and seductive but it pulled too tightly at the corner of her mouth. As if a spell had been brushed on her flesh so it didn't crease. 'I thought some of your mother's meekness would have rubbed off on you. Alas, I think Blackthorn's arrogance won that battle.'

'Lucky me.' Gideon's answer was dismissive but I didn't miss the weight of her words.

She knew Gideon was Blackthorn's. Apprehension prickled inside of me, at just how much she knew. Only I should have saved my worries for myself as those blood-red eyes focused on me.

No matter how rebellious you wish to be in this life. No matter how many fey you seek to save . . . that witch isn't the saviour of anyone, my love. My mother's words came into my mind. Another warning come too late.

'I've never seen a Kysillian female,' she noted coldly, her attention like an unwanted caress over every inch of my face. 'I thought you'd be prettier with all the fuss you've caused.'

The slight glanced off me. Having *troll* hissed at you most days had that effect. Yet my lack of reaction didn't stop her assessment.

'Females are quite rare, aren't they, Callen?' she asked, making a jolt of surprise move through me before I could control it.

Callen was a sacred name. Of Kysillia's line. One of the ancient king's names, one of the wielders of the sacred blades.

The Kysillian's expression remained blank, his arms folded before him with little interest. 'Quite.'

What was a Kysillian doing at the Countess's heel? Only the question felt like a betrayal. The same question I should have asked my father. He'd been in service to her too. Once. An impossibility.

The Countess pursed her painted lips, running a stained finger along her own jaw in contemplation. 'Quite a mess Emrys made in those Council chambers, Gideon. If rumour is to be believed.'

The wishing stone fluttering against my breastbone and it was then I saw it, the ring on her finger. So out of place amongst the gold ones. The dark metal carved with small ancient runes, a blood stone in the centre.

The pinching sensation. The wrongness of it. An object from a different time. She was wearing a Verr relic. Everything in me wanted to recoil, yet my magic bit viciously into my bones in response to the threat. In a way that it had never responded to Emrys.

'I'm certain Montagor deserves more credit than Emrys,' Gideon answered indifferently, but every inch of him remained tense.

'I wonder what the King's two bastards could have been fighting over?' Her lip curled as if knowing everything but wishing to see us squirm. 'I hope dear Emrys isn't losing his control, Gideon. You know how I'd hate for us to have to have a . . . problem.'

'What do you want, Countess?' Gideon demanded.

She turned that ring over on her finger. The two men by the door gave the barest flinch as if they could feel it.

Callen remained stoic but it didn't fool me into believing he was unaffected. 'The late Lord Blackthorn gave me his word Emrys would be useful. Then again . . . Emmaline's use ran out quite quickly.'

Even if I could only see Gideon's profile, it was impossible to miss the pain that cut deeply into his expression. The groaning of his metal fist beneath his glove.

Emmaline's use ran out. No. She was dead and this creature cared nothing for it.

'Let us not forget your mother's years haven't been fulfilled.' The Countess threw the words over her shoulder as she moved around the small space, surveying the side table and shelves for any secrets they could hold.

As if it was her own territory.

The threat was clear. Gideon owed her, or his blood did. This creature had plans; nothing had changed them. Not the suffering of the fey or Montagor's activities. She didn't care.

'You need to train your fighters better, Countess,' came the dark, terse voice of Emrys as he entered the room. The rebels at the door shifted to lay a hand on their blades but he ignored them. Callen gave not even the barest flicker of interest. No, he watched only me still, waiting. As if sensing the threat in me. Sensing the fire that slumbered in my bones.

Emrys's shirt was open, clearly not bothering to button it in his haste to get up here. Making me wonder if he could have sensed this from below. How the thin fabric clung to his damp skin. Blood glinting on his knuckles as he moved towards Lady Ramsey, snatching her untouched glass of port off the table and draining it in one.

'Since when did you involve yourself in fighting pits, Emrys?' The Countess's smile was filled with dangerous delight as she moved across the room with a dancer's grace. Close to Emrys as he dropped the empty glass back on the table.

So close her fingertips rested against his abdomen, her long nails biting into his skin ever so slightly as if to keep him in place. My magic burnt in my fingertips, forcing me to curl them into fists. To let my nails bite into my palms. A strange feral urge moving through me and then I was the one grinding my teeth.

This was worse than that awful Lady Lovell. My magic coiling deep in my gut, willing me to strike.

'A new hobby,' Emrys answered, peering down at her with such cold boredom. Just as I'd seen him deal with the Council.

'Is collecting dangerous beings another?' She raised a brow, turning her head to see me, her eyes filled with disinterest. Only my magic's focus was on how fractionally lower her fingers on Emrys's skin had slipped. Almost playfully near his waistband.

My jaw ached with the urge to bare my teeth. Territorial urges I wasn't familiar with rising in me too viciously. My flame flushing my skin.

'I'm certain there isn't anything about Miss Woodrow you don't already know,' he answered, easily.

'Such formality.' She tutted, only I saw the ripple of whatever magic enchanted her flesh. The barest flash of her displeasure.

She didn't know as much as she wished, because my father knew this monster and he'd hidden me well.

'I doubt the elders in their far mountains know about you.' She thankfully let her hand fall away from Emrys's chest. 'They're quite fond of their females, I hear. Despite your . . . *inadequacies* to save your own kind. Isn't that right, Callen?'

I ignored the slight. Kysillian lack of fertility was a well-known fact. If she wanted to hurt me, she'd have to be more creative than insulting my useless womb.

The lamps dimmed ever so slightly, a cold biting at the air with Emrys's anger, but I didn't need him to save me. Not from this creature.

'Indeed,' Callen answered, voice deep and empty.

As if sensing that resilience in me and the fury in Emrys, the Countess moved closer, folding her arms as she considered me. 'However, the barren creatures always do make the best playthings.'

She would know. This creature who played with others' lives as if she were a god.

Then she reached up to brush an imaginary strand of hair from her face. I thought she wished for me to flinch, anticipating attack. To be unnerved by that Verr relic in the space between us – but then I saw the bracelet slip down her wrist. The gold chain gleaming. Only it wasn't the chain, but the small discs that hung from it. Each marked with a rune I knew better than my own name.

Ralmev. The marks of the ancestors. Runes that decorated the seven sacred blades gifted to the Kysillian kings by Kysillia. My heart sank to my boots, my magic churning with confusion inside of me.

The hilt in my bag practically vibrating against my hip. Willing itself to be summoned.

I could have sworn I saw Callen give the slightest wince but I couldn't be certain when the Countess had captured my attention so completely.

She had three ancient blades around her wrist. Only not in a form she could wield. No. They'd been given to her; Kysillians had bargained with this creature. Given over their ancestors' treasures so easily.

My own blade in the bag at my waist suddenly felt like a dead weight. Sensing the others in the set it belonged to.

'*Kneel.*' The command was soft and mocking from her lips. So consumed by the horror of what she possessed I almost missed it.

The room went silent. The lamps around us guttered out, the wooden floor beneath me groaning and I knew it was under the force of Emrys's repressed summoning. My own magic raged inside of me at the word. A command it had heard before from different lips. How I'd burnt them to ash.

A command she gave me because she owned those blades. Owned three Kysillian bloodlines. Only I wasn't born of one of them and she wished to prove it to herself. Wanted to know whose I was.

'I have business to attend to, Countess,' Lady Ramsey sighed. 'You can play another time.'

The Countess's dark eyes narrowed slightly on me, paying Lady Ramsey not a moment of her attention. I met her gaze, the strange lifelessness of that red. For a reckless moment, I wanted her to see my father in me. To know she'd failed. That her weakness was right here before her.

She didn't own my blood and she didn't like it.

'Brave little thing.' Her head tilted ever so slightly. 'Not one of mine then. Yet those hunters and Montagor think you are.'

Hers. As if she owned them. Owned Kysillia's blood. As if she could bring the ancestors themselves to heel.

'Their mistake,' I answered. Voice unwavering as I swallowed down the taste of smoke on my tongue. My rage. Yet I knew she could see it flickering in my eyes. A flash of power that would have sent any sane fey back a step. Only this blood seeker leant closer, as if relishing the warmth.

'Careful, little Kysillian. Even your great King of the North swore his oath to me in the end.' She turned that chain over at her wrist. Playing with those small golden disks, as if they were no more than a jewel. '*Mal Tarour.*'

Mal Tarour. The Kysillian from her lips made unease stir inside me. An ancient vow. A mark of trust. *No king of my blood.*

Only the inflection was wrong. The vow was no kin of my blood. Not *king.* A promise to never produce another that would see them harmed. A vow my father would have given her to be bound, only . . . he'd given it wrong.

Kayin. King of the North. My father. He'd survived this blood witch with his blade still intact. Evidence that she wasn't as powerful as she thought she was.

My eyes darted to Callen where he continued to watch me. He'd know that vow was wrong too, and yet no emotion flickered across his stoic face.

It appeared the Countess wasn't as clever as she believed. That some things would always be beyond her control.

'He isn't here now. Did you misplace him?' My focus moved back to the Countess. Making a fool of her claim to power. She might have the three swords, but they were nothing without the creatures to wield them. Something she could never do because they would remain in that form without a true heir – because she hadn't earned their power. Wasn't worthy of it.

I saw the barest twitch of Callen's lips but it was the crack in the Countess's mask I was focused on. Skin too tight and smooth from too many enchantments to retain her youth. She didn't like the challenge as she pulled back. Too unfamiliar with it.

She turned from me, to where Emrys had moved closer, his eyes full black.

'Montagor is quite eager to obtain her, Blackthorn. He's put a steep price on her head. Alive – strangely enough. He must want to play.'

'I didn't know you and him were so . . . cordial with one another,' Sigrid snorted in answer. As if knowing Emrys would only say something to make this whole interaction worse.

How those dark eyes tracked the Countess like a predator on the hunt.

'Your payments, Countess.' Lady Ramsey let a heavy purse fall on the edge of her tea tray, calling an end to the exchange.

The Countess took her time turning on her heel. In no rush to take her prize. 'Don't make me collect them myself again, Ramsey. I'd hate for me to have to cripple your other leg.'

Lady Ramsey's golden gaze was hard with hate as she refilled the port glass Emrys had used. 'Always a pleasure, Countess.'

I hoped this creature would leave as swiftly as she arrived, only I should have known better than to hope.

'Oh and Blackthorn . . . tell Thean he's to return to me.' The Countess held out her hand as she reached one of her rebels who offered her gloves obediently. 'I tire of his games.'

'I don't know why you think we'd be harbouring your pet,' Gideon interjected, clearly not trusting Emrys to say a civilised word. However, his carefree tone didn't hide the threatening hum of his aether.

The Countess shrugged, suddenly bored with our company as she slipped her hands back into her gloves, covering up that cursed ring. 'He always did enjoy sniffing around dear Emmaline. Even her ghost, it appears. My patience wains. Pray you're on the right side when it depletes.'

'Your fighter needs treatment,' Sigrid commented, eyes pinned to the Countess as if each of her movements was a threat.

Her fighter. The miroc in the ring who had relished in harming fey. Of course, the miroc was under the Countess's control. Another puppet on a different string.

'He's outlived his usefulness. I have no time for failure.' She straightened her gloves before she moved to the door. 'Keep the scraps.'

Her men left behind her. Callen gave the barest pause, eyes sweeping over all of us before he exited, a tension in his shoulders that hadn't been there when they'd entered.

Only when the door closed did my magic settle inside me. Emrys was instantly at my side, his magic curling around me as if hating every inch of distance that had come between us.

'I almost forgot how abhorrent she is,' Lady Ramsey sighed, taking a deep drink from her glass of port.

'You don't fucking say,' Gideon snapped. 'You tell us next time you need help, Priscilla.'

'I'm afraid it'll be sooner than you like.' She sagged heavily, fingers massaging her temples. 'Take the Portium door back. The boy will show you the way.'

Sigrid moved to the door to summon the help we needed, as Emrys took my arm, eyes still dark as if unable to control his temper as he made to leave.

'Emrys,' Lady Ramsey called, hesitant and filled with sorrow, making him pause for a moment. 'I'm sorry there wasn't another way.'

Chapter Twenty-Three

Kat

The house – seeming to know the trouble we'd got tangled up in – decided to dump us in Emrys's room, much to Gideon's grunted annoyance. The smell of Lady Ramsey's tobacco following us back.

'Get yourself cleaned up before you give William a bloody fright,' were Gideon's parting words as he dumped Emrys's coat on the desk and strode for the door, muttering something at the coin in his grasp.

I pulled my cloak off as Emrys perched on the edge of the bed. His head bowed in contemplation as his bloody knuckles rested on his knees. A shudder rolling through him with a flash of darkness across his skin before it settled again. As if it had taken everything in him to hold it in.

'Here.' I pulled my bag free of my belt and tipped the contents onto the bed next to him to find my healing kit. Thankfully, the house materialised a bowl of hot water and a pitcher. As well as a small pile of clean towels.

'At least the house is being helpful.' I wet and wrung the cloth quickly, moving around the bed so my skirt filled in the space between his spread knees. 'It must have sensed your idiocy in going against a miroc.'

He tipped his head back so his troubled gaze could roam

over my face as I worked on his knuckles. 'Lady Ramsey enjoys harmless fun.'

The splits in the skin looked worse than they were. By the pale scarring beneath the wounds, Gideon was right. This clearly wasn't Emrys's first fight.

'Harmless?' I raised a brow as I reached around him for the milky healing tonic from my pack. 'This is the best one I have.'

The last one I had, which meant I'd need to brew more. When the world stopped falling apart. Ignoring the dread of that thought, I pulled out a ball of cotton, soaking it quickly before pressing it against his split skin. The healing tonic stung but Emrys didn't even flinch, despite how his magic shifted beneath his skin, as if in discomfort. I watched the angry cuts settle and stop bleeding before quickly swiping some thick balm over each one.

'You left your side unguarded,' I admonished quietly as I pushed the shirt from his shoulders, letting my fingers trail over the faint bruises beginning to bloom across his shoulder and his side, just below that strange crescent moon mark over his heart. My fingers moved to the scratch across his pectoral, wondering if it was from the miroc's sharp horn as I pressed the cloth to it. How solid and warm he was beneath my hand.

I dragged the cloth downwards to wipe at some stray blood. Then over to where the Countess had touched him. Foolishly. Drawn by nothing but strange primal urges. As if my magic could sense her on his skin. Emrys caught my hand, stopping me. Probably a good idea considering I was apparently intent on scrubbing him raw.

'Croinn?' The bastard inclined his head. Almost teasing.

'Don't smile at me.' I let the cloth drop. Flustered that I'd been caught. I snatched up my tin of balm, pushing back his hair to put some over the cut above his eye. 'The Countess isn't someone we need the attention of.'

'She's occupied with Montagor for the moment.' He rolled his neck as if it ached. Good. He deserved the discomfort.

'She seemed far more occupied with *you*,' I snipped, irritated by the fear coiling in my gut.

Once the cut above his brow was beginning to mend, I turned away from him. Needing something to do with my hands. To process all the things I didn't understand.

'Kat.' Emrys's fingers hooked into my skirt, halting my retreat, and despite all my strength, the barest tug sent me stumbling back into the warmth of him. His hand resting easily at my hip.

I turned my head, hearing the depth of that concern, seeing the crease at his brow. How he knew me well enough to understand. 'The Countess has the blades of the old kings. Three of them. On that bloody bracelet.'

Her holding Kysillian relics unsettled me. Enraged me more than I'd admit. Hating the feral noise in my head at the sight. The thought that perhaps I was the vicious creature the Council always feared.

Emrys went so still, those eyes pitch-black in an instant as I turned in his arms.

'You didn't know?' I asked.

A frustrated breath slipped from his lips as he shook his head. 'No. I thought they were just another relic. She's had them a long while.'

If she controlled all seven blades, she controlled the elders' will. Kysillians were ruled by the conquering of blades. The last to hold all seven was said to be Kysillia herself.

A testament of power; and Kysillian power was dangerous enough in our own hands . . . but in the Countess's? I shuddered at the thought. Emrys's arm becoming firmer around my waist as if sensing my unease.

Then another thought occurred to me. 'That ring on her finger—'

'A dark artifact. Some say she's held it for decades,' he answered without hesitation. 'It's how she seals their vows. With dark magic. Nothing else is as powerful.'

Because no magic was as dangerous to fey as that of the dark beneath. It was why the Kysillians feared it so, because it took no purity of blood to wield it. Why they all had those same marks on their flesh.

'How can she claim to be different from Montagor if she uses the same power?' I demanded. Hating that they had no choice but to follow her. That the fey desperate enough had no choice.

'Dark magic corrupts. I don't imagine this is how she thought her rule would go. How desperate her hunger for power would make her when she began.'

No. Because we never learn.

'Callen is a sacred name. One of the Kysillian kings.' I couldn't help my confusion at that Kysillian's presence. How it chafed against everything the Kysillians were supposed to believe – how he could be in her service. Yet so was my father, and perhaps it was that truth that made me the most uncomfortable.

'Callen has been under her control for over a decade. The Kysillians owed her a debt, so they traded a warrior they had no need of.'

How easily they'd traded their own blood. Showing how far the Countess's reach had stretched. So even the fey elders were playing her games.

Then something occurred to me. Something I'd missed. My eyes fell to where my father's hilt gleamed amongst the bedcovers where it had slipped from my bag.

'You're not surprised I recognise those sacred blades?' That I'd know them so well despite not being raised by the elders. Would know them because I wielded one the same.

'No, Croinn.' His smile was small. Knowing. 'A sacred blade is hard to miss.'

Of course, because he was Verr. He would have known it upon sight. Yet . . . it hadn't changed anything. He'd never asked about it. How he'd just accepted that piece of me. Even knowing what darkness had created him.

'It didn't bother you?' That I was Kysillian. That I held a blade that promised to end Verr.

His thumb dragged over my cheekbone. 'You could have chosen to drive that blade right through my cursed heart and it wouldn't have bothered me at all, Kat.'

My breath caught with the depth of that confession. My fingers tracing the line of his jaw. This beautiful foolish man.

'Tell me you're all right?' He bent his head, lips moving gently across my cheekbone.

I couldn't – I wasn't. Not since I'd seen how far the lies had run.

'Master Hale said my father's name,' I answered, unable to bear the pain of it, like a bruise on my heart, any longer. 'He knew it. All that time he knew it because—'

My hands slid up to rest on his shoulders. Anything to steady myself. Emrys's hands gently captured my face, as if I was something delicate between his palms.

'He made him leave somehow.' I opened my eyes to see the darkness of his own. Darkness that I knew was in reaction to my own pain.

'Kayin,' he answered softly and, unlike when Hale said it, there was something comforting about Emrys speaking my father's name. As if making him real again for the barest moment.

'Did you ever see him?' I asked childishly, holding out the smallest hope for any truth in all of this.

He shook his head, a worry at his brow as if he wished to tell me something else. 'I was never that far north. There were stories. The lords made bargains with many elders – Kysillians included – to protect the seals.'

'I know he's dead.' I swallowed. I knew it deep in the marrow of my bones. 'Maybe one day I'll accept it.' Accept that his death would be a mystery that would elude me. Torment me so differently than my mother's had, where I was forced to witness every last one of her moments. Helpless.

He seemed to sense the depth of that grief in me as he brought me closer, pressing a kiss against the hair at the side of my head.

'If I told you the number of times I anticipated Emmaline walking through that door, you'd think me mad.' His fingers played with the loose ends of my tangled hair as if lost in the thought. 'Wondering what she'd make of all this. Of what she'd make of me.'

'I'd think she'd find you quite remarkable,' I answered against his chest, letting my fingertips trace the muscled contours of his back. Dragging in the faint beasam bark scent, chasing away everything else. Calming me for the barest moment.

'Did she kill Emmaline?' I asked, knowing I'd hate the answer but needing it all the same. I'd known the tales. The Countess was vicious, and her amusement was fickle.

He was still for the longest moment before he answered. 'We'll never know for certain but Emmaline started to amass support. The rebels trusted her. Would follow her anywhere. The Countess saw that and I suppose we'll never know the truth of what came next.'

Because they were all bound, just as Thean had warned me in Fairfax Wood. All the things they could never say. Yet I couldn't shake the way Callen had looked at me. Almost as if waiting.

The Kysillian troubled me more than I wanted to admit. Seeing him beneath the Countess's rule unnerved me. Made me wonder how my father had been in that predicament and how he had got free of it.

'Can many stray from the Countess's control?' I frowned.

'If they're clever, but it's never for long.' His gaze was distant and I knew he was thinking of Emmaline. 'She trades in money, blood and land.'

'There is no saving them, is there?' The question was too sad and too small from my lips.

'Considering the bitch won't die. No. And destroying a relic is harder than it seems,' Emrys finished darkly, his thumb running over my knuckles before something else crossed his expression, dark magic flashing beneath his skin as those eyes became full black. 'I felt your fire, Croinn.'

I flushed, dropping my gaze. 'I didn't like her touching you.'

It felt hard to admit those words, to give into the territorial urge of them I knew was in my blood.

Emrys captured my chin, forcing me to see him once more. To find the handsome, wicked creature smiling. 'You're shamed by that.'

'I didn't feel . . . in control of myself.' Not when I wanted to render her to ash. To pour flame down her throat for nothing but spite.

'Good, I need company in my madness.' His lips pressed a teasing kiss against my jaw, my fingers digging into his shoulder as I tipped my head, offering him more, as his kiss found my pulse.

'M–madness?' I stuttered, wondering if I was supposed to be affronted.

'There is nothing controlled about the way I feel about you, Croinn. And nothing is more seductive than your fury.' And he sealed those words with a kiss.

A kiss I was hungry to return. Perhaps restless to claim my territory. Emrys pulled me closer. Equally as desperate, as if every breath of space between us was wasted.

Then the door crashed open, William half-hanging off the doorknob with one hand braced on the frame.

'Sorry, but—' the boy panted before his eyes went wider. 'Where are your bloody clothes?'

'William,' Emrys half groaned, his forehead falling into the curve of my neck.

'Thean's back . . . and they have a witch's finger,' the boy blurted out.

Emrys went deathly still. The floorboards beneath us gave a wary groan. Then he raised his head, his expression murderous.

Chapter Twenty-Four

Kat

Thean did in fact have a witch's finger. A half mummified, rune-covered witch's finger that had clearly been dug up recently or kept under some preservation enchantment. How Thean would know a witch that old or where they were buried was a mystery I didn't have the mental capacity to solve right now.

The house creaked and groaned, clearly unsettled by the sudden stench of rot that filled the study where we all gathered. Rain hammered against the glass dome above us, the fire flaring to paint us all in orange light as if doing its best to chase away the storm's chill beyond the windows.

I couldn't help but feel camaraderie with the house's unease. Witches had been regulated and historically hunted far more harshly by the King's regime than the fey. Mostly because witches were the most mortal-passing creatures. Also, their blood was potent. One drop in a bloodline lasted for centuries. They were outcasts with most of their summonings deemed a curse.

Even fey were mostly unsympathetic to witches, seeing them closer to Verr in their otherness and the endless unnatural powers they could amass.

With those rune markings, the finger was old . . . and so was the brutality of the magic encased in such a creature's flesh. Withered or not.

'You're being too helpful, *voyav*,' Gideon grumbled, eyes narrowed as his aether gave a threatening snap.

Emrys remained quiet at my side – still deprived of his shirt – the only part of the day I wasn't complaining about.

'I'm always helpful, darling. You're just too proud to see it,' Thean goaded from where they sat in the chair by the fire, swinging the finger that hung on an old knotted string like a strange pendulum. 'A totem will come in useful, will it not?'

'Stop fucking waving it around,' Gideon snapped. Clearly disturbed. I remembered Emrys's warning about witches. How the power of their own kind unsettled them too. 'That *totem* has the potential to wake the dead.'

'The dead?' William squeaked.

'Scry for the location, Gideon,' Emrys intervened with a strong pat on his brother's shoulder. Whether in comfort or command I couldn't tell.

Of course, with the old coin, and a witch's totem, it should lead us right to the location of Lord Turner's resting place and that diary. That didn't seem to settle Gideon. But he begrudgingly snatched the offending item off Thean.

'Put some bastard clothes on,' Gideon groused over his shoulder at Emrys before he went to work at his desk.

Emrys's lips twitched but clearly thought better of showing his amusement and excused himself. The same moment William decided what would make this whole situation less tense would be a tray of tea. A clatter from the bookcase told me the house agreed.

'That's the second time today he's been in a state of undress. You should give him a break.' Alma crossed the room to me, her shirtsleeves rolled up and dark curls perfectly pinned – green eyes sharp and serpent-like.

I couldn't help the laugh that slipped from my lips. 'I had no part in *this* instance of undress.'

'You're all right?' She took hold of my forearms, eyes running over me as if some great injury could have befallen me. Grateful perhaps that the only thing currently wrong with me was my windswept nature, and unease about the things I'd learnt. 'You look flushed and you reek of . . .'

'Tobacco?' I winced.

'Amongst other things.' She wrinkled her nose as if I'd caused it great offence. 'Where in the ancestors' name did they take you?'

'To a fighting pit.' The words came out too quickly, making her eyes go wider before I saw that crease at her brow which was usually the starting point for her fury.

'I'm fine.' I dug into my pocket and pulled out the small brown paper bag for her. 'Here – Emrys got them for you from the market.'

She took the bag cautiously, weighing it. Her eyes swirled to mortal as her bottom lip dropped slightly with emotions I knew she wouldn't show.

Gideon grumbled another curse to himself, making a different type of worry line her brow as her head came up to quietly consider the now-working witch. 'The healer appeared to be in a foul mood long before Thean started waving fingers about.'

I rubbed at my temple. Suddenly exhausted and knowing the day wasn't over. Not with the new gauntlet we'd been set. 'We had a run in with the Countess.'

Alma's body went taunt, her scales flashed across her cheek almost in pain before they sunk away. As if fearful of being seen.

Strange. I thought she'd erupt. Bite and spit. Maybe shift into something that could do more damage. Her stillness was

275

something I hadn't anticipated. How that paper bag slipped from her fingers that trembled ever so slightly. Not a claw in sight.

'Alma?' I frowned, reaching for her, but her attention darted from me to the packet on the floor. Almost as if she'd been wrenched back into her body from wherever her thoughts had taken her.

'Clumsy,' she snapped, her voice too hoarse as she snatched the packet up. Blinking, seeming to struggle to remember why she had it at all. 'I'd better put—' She didn't finish, leaving the room. Not even the barest flush of scales at her cheek to tell me what thoughts had consumed her. Her name was on my lips as I turned to follow but I didn't get that choice.

'Why was she there?' Thean asked, startling me from where they still remained by the fire. Those amber eyes fully focused on me, apparently on every word of mine and Alma's exchange.

'Since when did the mad bitch need a reason,' Gideon muttered from behind his pile of books.

Only Thean didn't seem appeased by the answer. Their jaw too tight as they turned to look at the hearth. Revealing where their own marks could be seen beyond the collar of their shirt. Whatever dealings the Countess had in the east, the voyav didn't like it and if Thean didn't like it . . . it felt like a greater threat than any fiend or cursed object.

I moved closer to them, arms wrapped about myself to try and settle the unease biting deeper into my bones.

'I think she's after territory in the east,' I answered. Thean didn't flinch, didn't even blink.

'No.' Their smile was small, almost in sympathy at my stupidity. 'What she's after and what she's doing are seldom the same thing.'

Of course. Thean would understand her. If a creature like that *could* be understood.

'Why would she reappear now?' Why come out of her lair? She seemed too obsessed with her own legend to rise for nothing more than to antagonise Montagor, to want any part in this brewing conflict.

No, she'd appear at the end when everything was settled. A saviour in the ashes the fey had no choice but to choose.

Then Thean stood, tall and lean as they towered over me. Only there was no threat in their proximity, or the way they dipped their head so I didn't miss a word from their lips. 'You speak as if she's ever stopped. Poison needs time to spread. Her type is long and agonising. Her roots are deep, and she'll do anything to win.'

There was such hard cruelty in those usually warm eyes, imploring me with the rest of the words I knew they couldn't say. My eyes moving to that mark on the side of their throat.

'She wasn't there for any other reason than to see how her game is playing out,' Thean answered the question. As if we were all pieces on her gameboard. Even if we wanted no part in the play.

'*Mal Tarour,*' I barely breathed the ancient words, scared they might bind me the same way they had bound others. Thean's attention was suddenly rapt on my face; they went as taut as a bow-string, waiting.

'She held the King of the North for a time,' I finished, all the pieces slotting into place. My father served that monster with the blade I now carried, a blade a creature like Thean wouldn't miss. They knew who I was.

Yet they hadn't spoken a word of it. Had kept that secret without being asked. Despite what they could gain. Only they stood here with me, because there was no power to be gained from the Countess's favour. She took, consumed. But she never gave. Not even mercy.

'She doesn't hold him now,' they replied, voice so soft, lost in some memory. Confirming what I didn't need to ask.

My father had been bound. He'd unwound himself somehow from that vow and Thean knew it. All this time. They'd stayed for Emrys, for Emmaline, but perhaps for themselves too. To try. 'You asked me to forgive you.'

Only for what, I didn't know yet.

They looked back to the fire, dismissively. A mask sliding back across their features. 'It hasn't happened yet.'

'When it does, I'm sorry I didn't have the answer.' The words felt too broken from my lips by the regret of the truth in them. Seeing the flash of pain in their amber gaze. 'No matter what she makes you do. I'll forgive you.'

Just as Emmaline had. As if knowing sending the voyav on this path would lead them here. That they needed us just as much as we needed them. Even if their help was fleeting, even if their will was never their own.

'Tea,' William announced, turning me to the boy. Noticing Alma hadn't come back with him. Too many loose threads I couldn't catch.

She wasn't there for any other reason than to see how her game is playing out. Thean's words sat uncomfortably inside of me. A warning I felt it might be too late to receive.

While William brought some semblance of peace back to our gathering with a pot of tea, Emrys re-emerged, washed and changed.

Then after three irritated attempts at scrying, Gideon found a location for the Portium door.

★

Any hope I had that the next steps in locating what Montagor was looking for would be easy were lost as we were greeted by a night bitter with frost, thick fog curling over the crooked tombstones and the lumpy frozen dirt path that curled upwards towards the hollowed-out abbey just beyond. Nothing but shards of rock held together with ivy and hope that the wind didn't blow too strongly in its direction.

Fat snowflakes fell from a bruised night sky, every tree withered and twisted. A strange gloomy silence that accompanied most forgotten places.

Relmort Abbey. One of the saints' most prized places of worship where it sat on the cliffs in the west. The wind was sharp and lined with salt, stinging my cheeks, making the snow dance before us.

The stained glass was long gone and the saints' emblems worn from the stone, the faces of the statues chiselled smooth by fey – but I could imagine the grand depictions of their Elysior kings. How they'd brought civilisation to these lands and culled the beasts who once called it home.

Nothing but a tomb itself now. Forgotten and alone. A fitting end for their tyranny.

Small glimmers of white flashed in the corner of my eye. Roaming spirits lost across this unhallowed ground.

I pulled my cloak tighter against the night chill. Alma butted my thigh with her snout in her new dog form. Her dark, curly fur catching the snow. William had been thrilled at her choice in creature for this evening. Something about her sudden decision to shift made me think she was hiding though – and, because she was Alma, wondering just what she was hiding from was a hopeless endeavour. Her secrets woven too tightly around her ribs, stored deep like small nuts for winter. I'd never asked for them. Knowing that her secrets were part of her defence. Her safety. No. I didn't need her secrets. I just needed her to know I'd be listening, even if it took her decades to let one slip free. I'd be here. Waiting.

I let my fingers run through the soft fur at her head before she darted off with a bark.

'I told you we should get a dog.' William grinned, skipping slightly to keep up with Alma's trot as she sniffed at the overgrown weeds lining the path.

'Not this again,' Gideon grumbled, digging his hands deep in his fine grey suede coat pockets. Snow clumping on his tense shoulders, his eyes scanning the graveyard before us.

The pale light from the Portium door in the dilapidated mausoleum behind us illuminated the path, making us cast long shadows across the terrain.

'I didn't think there were any necromancers left,' I whispered, tucking my hands deeper into my cloak as I looked up to Emrys as he kept pace next to me. No more relaxed than his brother.

'There shouldn't be,' he answered, looking at where my cloak was wrapped about my body as if concerned it wasn't enough to deal with the damp, winter air. 'The more worrying thing would be how Thean has kept a necromancer from the Countess.'

He eyed the voyav where they led our small party to the centre of a cluster of worn stumps I assume used to be grave stones. A voyav that had remained aloof since their warning by the fire.

Necromancy. A magic that valuable would turn the rebellion's tide against the Council. To tell the Countess would be to enslave that being with the same blood vow that Thean seemed to chafe against. A necromancer was old blood – old magic – and whatever loyalty Thean Page had, they seemed to respect such a being's freedom. Or perhaps they were simply waiting for their usefulness to run out.

'Bloody bastard couldn't be buried indoors?' Gideon griped as he came to a stop, shooting another hateful glance at Thean. 'You could have found the bastard yourself.'

'My skill is murder, little witch, not scrying.' Thean shrugged, but their amusement had dissipated with the statement, making me unsure if they could actually have done it on their own. The being was still as much a mystery as the unfortunate night we'd met them.

Rooting in his pockets, Gideon pulled out the worn coin. It now emitted a strange ghostly glow. He flipped it, letting it drop to the frozen earth. It spun for a moment before it rolled and jumped. Settling finally on a low mound where a small sad stone marked the place, as if nobody had bothered to remember the burial plot.

'There he is,' Gideon sighed, turning to hold his arm out to William. 'If you wouldn't mind, William.'

The boy nodded with determination, stepping forwards and kneeling next to the coin as his palms glowed green and he pushed his fingers into the lank, frosty grass. He closed his eyes as his summoning grew, making his fingers glow green too, a small rumbling coming from beneath our feet before a harsh misted breath left his lips.

'There are slabs on top,' William huffed, sweat at his brow despite the cold. His fingers flexing as the ground rumbled from the roots he summoned to assist him.

'Someone doesn't want him dug up,' Thean observed dryly from where they leant against a grave, clearly unbothered by who they stood on top of. Alma gave a small growl. Probably at the voyav's commentary that might distract the boy.

'They do it so they don't walk after death,' Emrys answered, brows knotted with thought.

The warning in his words sent a chill down my spine. And that was the last warning before the ground shook and William gave another heave as the roots pierced the frozen earth.

Alma let out a bark, clearly deciding she wanted a better view as she leapt and shifted into a crow, perching on the boy's shoulder.

The soil shifted, undulating and spilling until the rotten casket rose. Willaim recoiled, landing on his backside as he panted with bright rosy cheeks. Alma gave a disconcerted squawk from being jostled around.

'Well done, William.' Emrys smiled tightly as he stepped forwards and used the heel of his boot to knock the remains of the coffin's measly lid off.

A skeleton lay inside. The innards of the coffin gleamed in the moonlight, covered in a strange waxy substance – I assumed it was the remains of the lord's body fat that had decayed. I'd read a paper on how grave robbers sold it to traders to extract the residual magic for unsupported healing tonics in the outer markets. A shudder moved through me at the thought, at how desperate this world had become.

Rusted blades and other trinkets appeared to have been dumped with little care. A rustle from the stray papers left at the bottom of the coffin, worm-eaten.

Alma hopped onto the edge of the coffin and then inside, picking through the remains. I knelt in the loose soil, gathering up the pages I could salvage.

'They look rather useless,' Thean cautioned with boredom.

I took hold of the pages. The corners were charred, the paper coated in bright white ash from a summoning.

'They destroyed it,' I murmured to myself before I allowed my palms to heat ever so slightly, remembering the lyrical mix of the incantation at the back of my mind, a song that didn't need words to be formed. Slowly, with a crack and the lavender hue of my magic, the pages were fully restored between my palms.

Pages of Lord Ramsey's scribbled madness.

'How the fuck did you manage that?' Gideon was suddenly perched over my shoulder, eyes moving too quickly as if his thoughts wouldn't catch up.

'I made a reformation incantation.' I offered the diary up for his consideration. He carefully turned the page, gloved finger running over the scrawl inside.

'The bastard is talking about the knights' trove; about the Alder Kings.' Gideon pointed the words out to Emrys, whose eyes seemed to darken in answer.

The Alder Kings, rulers of the endless dark. Ancient demons with no form. The rulers of this land long before stories had existed. Old stories, too old for me to understand.

This was far darker than my worst fears. Unease curled within me at how little I knew, how useless all my knowledge had become.

'I suppose we have much to discuss then.' Emrys pulled the witch's finger free from his pocket before turning to his brother with one raised dark brow. 'Just an awakening command?'

'This is my first venture into necromancy. However, the bastard will be compelled to answer and he won't like it,' Gideon offered dryly, but there was concern in his features as he pulled back from me. 'So, let's hope the fucker isn't possessed – or worse . . . hungry.'

'Hungry?' William squeaked but Emrys continued, letting his pale summoning light imbue the finger as he held it over the remains.

I stood, letting the diary become nothing but a pile of ruined papers in my hands once more.

Emrys spoke over the remains but I didn't understand the terse incantation. Bright magic illuminated his hand. Demon fire. The witch's finger glowing before it shifted into nothing but ash. Sliding off Emrys's palm like dry earth and onto the remains.

A silence followed. Nothing but the whistle of the wind and the irritated rustle of Alma's wings.

'What now?' William whispered. Then the bones choked and appeared to gasp for air. Making William practically leap out of his skin with fright. Much to Thean's amusement.

Alma pecked one of his horns, ruffling his hair. Whether in reprimand or in comfort, I didn't know.

'Here we go.' Gideon stepped closer, blue witch aether in his palms, focus deadly.

'I demand to speak with Lord Turner,' Emrys said, not moving from where he was crouching over those bones. The pale summoning between his fingers not dissipating and small dark veins beginning to appear along the edge of his jaw. As if ready for a challenge.

'A Blackthorn,' the bones croaked, the jaw snapping open and shut as if trying to cough death from its non-existent throat.

Emrys turned his magic over in his hand with relaxed ease as if it was a deadly blade. A different creature than the one I knew. A predatory nature to his movements and a dangerous focus in his dark gaze.

'Maybe your father made good on his promise to disturb my rest after all,' the bones groaned, a weariness in them as a strange mist filled in the gaps, so the remains could sit up. Head hanging oddly like a disused doll.

'Lord Ramsey's diary,' Emrys began with ease as if he spoke to the dead every day. 'He had quite an obsession with the Alder Kings, it seems. What was he after?'

The bones let out a wheezing laugh, rattling with it. 'To replace what was lost. For we know the old mad kings hungered for one thing.'

'A seal,' Gideon answered. 'Lord Ramsey never found one.'

The bones seemed to jump and twist as if reluctant but the croaked words tumbled out ominously all the same. 'He found something greater. The book.'

'Which one?' Emrys demanded, demon fire flaring in his palms in threat, giving the angles of his face a lethal edge.

The bony fingers clawed at the wooden remains of the coffin until they snapped and tumbled across the wood. A futile resistance. 'The only one that matters. The Compendium of Souls.'

The Compendium of Souls. A forsaken tome. A myth. Said to have been touched by the saint himself, hidden away and buried with him. The history of the Verr, the path to all their incantations and the seals that killed them. The history of the old kings.

Emrys didn't show a flicker of either interest or surprise. 'The King was seeking the book.'

In the wars there were stories the mad kings hunted the ancient fey brutally for their knowledge. Because their blood went back to the time of the Verr – back to the magic that those mortal kings sought to awaken once more.

'The King possessed the book,' the bones croaked. 'There was nothing he wished to possess more. No desire more deadly than his for that book.'

That wasn't possible. If the King had the book he would have opened it. All this would have ended long before it began. Montagor wouldn't be seeking the blood to lead him here. To lead him to any clues for it or a way to open it.

Emrys's brow furrowed with doubt as he turned to see Gideon, who looked equally concerned, peering down in disdain at the remains over his brother's shoulder.

If the King had the book, why did none of the lords know of it and why didn't Montagor possess it?

'He didn't use it.' The words slipped free before I could stop them. The skull twisted towards me, the pits of endless darkness that were its eyes staring. Something in the endlessness of it made fear prickle the back of my neck.

There you are. That darkness seemed to whisper in the back of my mind.

A horrid sound rumbled from it, a growl.

'*Don't look at her.*' Emrys dark command wasn't entirely mortal. The skull snapped back to him. Quaking in the remains of the coffin. 'Why didn't he use the book?'

'He didn't have the time,' the bones moaned, twisting as if writhing in agony. William looked peaky and I wondered if Alma being perched on his shoulder was the only thing keeping him upright.

'Why?' Gideon demanded with impatience.

The bones rattled, jaw snapping together, teeth tumbling free as if to keep the answer.

'It vanished the same night the bride did. The bitch that killed the kingdom. The madness that lost him the throne,' the remains mocked with a sing-song tone.

An icy fear bit into my bones, making me move back a step across the uneven ground. Heart slamming into my gut.

Be wary of how far you wander, you'll tread paths you were never meant to take. A horrid warning I should have remembered. Another thing I'd lost. I shook my head, hair loose about my face, but there was no hiding myself. No hiding from this new horrid twist in the tale. Unable to understand why my past kept leading me to this present. How it could all be tangled together so easily.

The weeping bride. The King's betrothed.

Liar, the wind seemed to hiss. An awful feeling moved through me. Slow and cold as if my blood had become congealed. Alma let out a warning caw, her head swivelling sharply towards me, but that ringing had started in my ears. Blocking out everything else.

You never speak my name. Never speak the truth, Tauria. Promise me. The memory of my mother's voice. How clear it seemed, how it gave my magic the compulsion to rise. To incinerate those bones before they could go further. To keep my promise.

'You're lying,' Gideon challenged with exasperation. Only for those bones to creak in answer with what I could only describe as laughter.

'You can ask her yourself.' One remaining skeletal finger raised and pointed right at me. 'She's right there.'

I could've sworn that skull was smiling with its next words.

'Lady Leanna Grey.'

My mother's name.

Chapter Twenty-Five
Kat

Madness comes in many forms. If the fey wished for sympathy, they should not have stolen the King's bride. For what is he to do but be tormented by her defilement. Wondering what cursed corner of the earth they will leave her body to rot once they've had their feast.

Vengeance will be his – and every despicable creature of their line deserves his wrath for their complicity.

Correspondence from Lord Ramsey

How awful that none of the tales even remembered her name. She was nothing but the weeping bride. The girl that broke the King's heart and drove him mad. Her memory bathed in the innocent blood he'd shed in her name.

Liar. The stories the King's sympathisers peddled to ignite their cause in the last war. Of a virtuous beauty stolen by beasts. How long he hunted and killed to save his love. How the blood spilled was nothing but evidence of his devotion.

Only I knew the truth of that tale. I was made of it.

There was a girl who was to be sold to a mad king. A defiant girl consumed with rage and grief. One who wished for nothing but to tear this kingdom down. No matter the cost. Until it cost her everything.

A stillness enveloped Emrys and William as they watched

me. The necromancy spell dissipated as the bones rattled back in the box, back into cursed slumber.

Gideon was still muttering a curse at the grave. 'Bloody stupid lying bastard.'

'Kat.' William's tone was soft, cautious even. 'Why did he call you that name?'

I shook my head, taking another step back, wanting to lie. Feeling its heavy weight on my tongue but as my eyes met Emrys's . . . I couldn't. My lies had led me nowhere but to ruin and I couldn't play with them anymore.

'That's my—' I felt as if I was suddenly underwater. Battling the waves to try to draw one breath deep enough to get the rest of the cursed words out. 'That was my mother's name.'

A name I was forbidden to say.

What people refused to see. Never glancing past the hue in my skin or the vibrancy in my eyes. Never dwelling on any of my other features. How sharply they matched hers. Never caring for the mortal mother who ruined herself with a Kysillian brute.

'No.' The word was breathless through William's lips, the coffin he was supposed to be holding with his magic-coaxed roots dropped back into the hole with a crash and eruption of dirt, sending him stumbling away from the hole.

The snow curled and twisted in the silence.

'Lady Leanna Grey,' Gideon snapped, turning on Emrys as if he was party to my secrets. He pointed a finger in accusation right at me, as if I was her. A ghost stood amongst these graves. 'The weeping fucking bride.'

'I thought—' William stammered, running his hands through his errant curls as Alma cawed and flapped her wings.

'You're telling me *Lady Grey* disappeared and caused the rare fields massacre. Only to run off with a *Kysillian*?' Gideon's aether crackled in the space between his clenched fists.

'Not just any Kysillian, darling,' Thean offered unhelpfully, from where they leant against a wonky gravestone, considering their nails with little care.

Gideon's eyes darted to the hilt where it sat tucked into the belt of my skirt, the gold gleaming in the moonlight as if to taunt him. The fire that silenced that seal, one no lesser Kysillian could have survived.

They want your little pet, Serus. Montagor's mocking words came back to me. Because the dark knew what I'd done. Wielded sacred steel and survived summoning Kyslor.

Knew my magic because it had tasted the fury of my fathers. Tasted the fury of my kin.

'Kayin. King of the North,' Thean concluded, confirming what I knew. They knew of my father.

Gideon seemed to sag with the weight of his rage, turning on his heel but he didn't get half a step before he started to laugh, bitter and self-amused. 'Trust you, *brother*, to drag me back into this. Only to find you infatuated with the only fucking creature that can open a seal. Not to mention the child of the fucking weeping bride!'

Alma gave out an angry caw, swooping to peck at his head.

'Fuck,' he snapped. Batting her off as she flapped her wings in irritation before hopping over to me. Shifting effortlessly back into her shaggy dog form, a growl peeling from her bared teeth.

Murderer. Liar. Coward. A thousand other words I could have called myself in many different tongues. I deserved every one of them.

'My mother didn't have that book. No matter what that thing said.' I knew she didn't. She would have told me. Woven it into her bedtime stories as she did everything else, so I'd understand.

'Are you sure about that?' Gideon challenged. Only for
Emrys to take another step forwards, his magic making the
air even more frigid.

'You'll mind your tone when you speak to her,' he warned.
Unease rippling between himself and his brother, as I heard
Gideon's aether spit in response even though his eyes softened
as they looked at me. Making me wonder if they saw that
grief in me. The burden of it.

'My mother wasn't his bride. She never agreed to any
of it.' My breath caught, my magic rising with fury as if it
remembered too. 'It's all a lie.'

Gideon seemed to chew on that, unable to look at me as
his gaze moved around our strange gathering. 'Does anyone
else have any other family secrets that could make this fucking
day any more abysmal.'

Alma let out a bark, earning herself a glare.

'This is good, isn't it?' William worried his hands, his smile
uneasy on his lips. 'It means Kat could know where it is.'

'I—' Words stuck to my tongue. Because I had nothing,
I knew nothing. Even after everything, I didn't understand
any of this.

'She could have taken it with her when she vanished,'
William offered.

'She wouldn't have brought a book like that to the north.
She wouldn't have wanted it near my father.' Or me. Not
that piece of her past.

'You're sure?' Gideon folded his arms, brow raised.

Emrys came closer to my side. 'I won't warn you again,
brother.'

I shook my head, trying to piece together how she could
have had something that dark. Could have known it and not
told me. 'Any cloaking charm wouldn't have survived.'

'Survived what?' William frowned, lips pursed in confusion.

She was alive when you burnt her, little troll. I shook my head, dispelling that dark voice.

'Me,' I answered, voice unwavering because I'd made a promise not to be afraid of those truths. Not anymore. 'She died holding me. My magic consumed her remains; a command my father had given it.'

Perhaps another reason he'd asked for my forgiveness. I'd lost my voice screaming for it to stop but it wouldn't. Not until she was nothing but ashes in a storm wind. The whole cottage, every piece. It would have destroyed any protective charms, even one strong enough to conceal that book.

I knew there was nothing left. I'd crawled through the ashy remains of my childhood. Held it between my palms. Was haunted by it every night since.

Gideon went so still, as if the pain in my voice saddened him as much as it tore open something in my chest. A wound I'd ignored for too long. 'It destroyed every part of her. As if knowing what horrid things they'd do with even one piece.'

How they'd desecrate the body of a woman who made her own choices. Who loved a Kysillian male and birthed his child. Now it made so much sense. Why my magic would want to protect her even in death, because if she knew where that book was . . .

My eyes moved to the disturbed grave, the loose mound of soil. They'd bring her back somehow. They'd use whatever dark summoning cost them their souls . . . because this madness had no cure.

I looked up into Emrys's dark eyes, blurred with my tears. 'I know it wasn't there. My fire would have undone any charm protecting it.'

'It's all right, Croinn.' He reached for my hand so easily. As if this dark secret between us was nothing at all. As his fingers slipped between my own, tight and forgiving.

'The book wasn't in the King's possession when he died.' Emrys turned his attention back to Gideon, who'd braced his hands on his hips, glaring at the frozen earth as if it held the answers. 'He didn't utilise it during the wars.'

'Which means she stole it just before she ran,' Thean finished, looking unbothered by the entire mystery as if waiting for us to catch up.

'There was nothing in the Ainsworth compendium, William?' Gideon seemed to chew on his irritation.

'The gobrite's residency ruined most of the text. Chewed right through the bloody pages.' William shifted nervously. 'So, the Compendium of Souls could be anywhere.'

It could have been, but in all of my uncertainty, there was one thing I knew more than anything else. I knew my mother. Knew every story she told.

'There is only one place she would have gone.' The only place she would have returned to. If only to say goodbye to the ghosts that lingered there. 'The Greymark estate.'

Where it had all begun for her, and where it had all ended. She spoke fondly of the woodland house. The only place in the world she'd felt safe before my father. Before her monsters arrived to turn it into a nightmare.

'The family sold off their estate decades ago. It was torn down.' Gideon's answering tone had at least softened slightly.

I shook my head. 'No. The northern house. The one bordering the south woods.'

Emrys considered my words for a moment, rubbing his jaw before he shrugged. 'It's a good place to start.'

'And here I was thinking I'd get some fucking rest tonight.'

Gideon pinched the bridge of his nose. Alma barked her annoyance at him.

'Surely it's already been raided to death?' William worried his lip.

'Old houses have tricks of their own,' Emrys offered. 'Especially one left alone that long.'

It was a start. If Montagor was looking into the past – he might not be searching for the Compendium of Souls, might not even believe it existed but if we could find it . . . it would give us an advantage.

'Let's get back in the bloody house. I'm sure it'll be perturbed to be missing out on all the family revelations,' Gideon commanded with a clap of his gloved hands, taking William's shoulder and guiding him down the path towards where the doorway hummed.

Alma gave me one assessing look before trotting off after them. I didn't see Thean leave as I turned to Emrys.

'I should have—' The words felt too heavy on my tongue as I looked down at the horrid remains of the diary in my other hand. How I'd made another mistake so easily. 'I didn't mean for any of this to happen.'

'I know, Croinn.' He gathered me to him so gently, until my unsteady breath brushed against his throat. Needing him even closer. His arms strong bands around me that felt unbreakable. 'It doesn't change anything.'

'Even if I lied? Even if they were right about me all this time?' My voice was so small. So fearful.

Murderer. Liar. Coward, repeated through my mind. All their mocking slights.

That I was some foul thing. Impure. A liar. That panic wouldn't leave me. Even if I didn't regret any of it. That this thing inside of me was smothered for a reason.

294

Yet, the smallest smile came to his lips as his thumb traced my jaw.

'That they should fear you and the chaos you create?' He smiled, so softly as his knuckles traced the edge of my jaw. Then his fingertips finding that sharp point of my ear. 'They should. They deserve every ember of your wrath.'

Then he lent closer, until there was nothing but the faint alluring beasam bark and him. Until his arms were around me and my cheek was pressed against the safety of his chest. 'You burn, I burn, Kat.'

A promise. That no matter where I led us, he'd come with me. Even to that ruin.

'Gideon has a right to be annoyed with me,' I offered, wondering how I'd fix that.

'We'll agree to disagree on that.' Emrys kissed my forehead before he gently untangled us and coaxed me back down the path and into the waiting portal.

Despite my relief to be out of the cold, commotion awaited as we returned to the warmth of the house.

'Don't say another word,' Alma snapped, wearing a robe that was far too big for her. Her clawed nails out and pointed right at Gideon's throat. 'I'm coming with you. If it's there and it's as dark as those creatures, I should be able to sniff it out.'

Because Alma had been one and she never forgot a scent.

Gideon just cast his frustrated gaze to the ceiling. Clearly resigned to his fate of nothing going how he wished before he dropped his focus to where Thean had draped themselves in the closest chair.

'William,' Gideon warned, 'watch Thean.'

The voyav bristled, eyes sharp as they finally paid attention to their surroundings. 'You can't seriously think I'm staying here?'

'I don't want William alone. Not while Montagor has a relic,' Gideon challenged; however, he didn't hide his enjoyment at the voyav's annoyance.

A relic not even the house could defend against.

'Also, the south lands are currently in turmoil with rebel attacks. I'm certain you're not too keen on running into your *friends* right now?'

The voyav showed no reaction. Simply leant further back into the cushions and crossed their legs with a dancer's grace. 'Hurry back then, little witch, I could get up to an awful lot of trouble *unsupervised*.'

'You'll be staying right where I can bloody see you,' William warned like a stern housekeeper.

The voyav grinned wickedly at the boy's attempt at firmness, swirling one of the cushion tassels around their finger. 'We'll see, darling, you might get distracted by the delivery boy again.'

'Thean,' William half whined. His face going beetroot.

'Since it appears we're off to war again – I'll get the gear,' Gideon sighed, resigning himself to the madness of what was about to unfold.

Chapter Twenty-Six
Kat

There was a world before the first star fell, of Old Gods and magic from beneath. There was a realm of princes with darkness in their veins, and truth in their hearts. A world of harmony. Of a deep devotion sung into the dark of night. There was peace before the world burnt and monsters called themselves kings.

The Compendium of Souls – Unknown

I straightened the jacket of my new fighting leathers. The style worn in the wars, from the depictions I'd found in the library. Cut close to the body, the trousers clung to my legs like a second skin – a freedom I'd missed since my days of ransacking the restricted library beneath the Institute in my breeches. Only these leathers were enchanted to resist magic attack, runes pressed into the inside. With the numerous sheaths and pockets it wasn't hard to find somewhere to put my father's hilt.

I was unable to hide it now. What would be the point? The Council were dead and keeping my secrets had done nothing but burden me with guilt. As if sensing my apprehension, the wishing stone thrummed comfortingly against my breastbone as I made my way back to the study, leaving William to get Alma fitted in her own leathers. Despite her reluctance to conform to Gideon's commands. Especially since she tended to end up naked anyway after a change.

Her irritable quips about where Gideon could shove his orders made me smile, distracting me only to stumble to a stop as I entered the study.

Emrys was a formidable dark presence most days. Now he wore his own fighting leathers, all competent thoughts left my head. His jacket was open, showing the thin loose training shirt beneath. The lacings at the collar undone to show the strong line of his throat. How the trousers clung to his muscular thighs. Shadow blades strapped to his belt. An ease to his stature as he braced his palms on the desk, reading something on the papers scattered there.

Maybe it was something in my Kysillian blood. Something about the warrior build of him that made a strange insatiable hunger rise in me so desperately. The thought of him in that fighting pit threatened to consume my thoughts once again, the sheen of sweat on his abdomen. How deadly each movement had been.

Heat flared through me that had nothing to do with magic and was completely inappropriate for such public spaces.

'Watch out, darling, you're drooling,' came wickedly from behind me, making me lurch around to see amber eyes gleaming in delight from where the voyav sat petulantly in the chair by the fire.

'Shouldn't you be busying yourself elsewhere,' I half spluttered.

'Indeed.' Thean rose from their perch, beyond satisfied with my embarrassment. 'However, I wasn't expecting you to have such a cracking arse.'

I half choked, resisting the urge to cover myself with my hand. 'You're supposed to be watching *William. Not my arse.*'

'I agree,' Emrys added. A flush bit at my cheeks at just what part he was agreeing with.

I turned to him, finding his stormy grey eyes on the leathers I wore. Disappointingly not on my arse.

My awkwardness was ridiculous. I'd worn breeches before. Been caught numerous times by the Council in them. But there was something very different about standing before Emrys in them. Having very vivid memories of his hands cupping my thighs with more firmness than the leather I wore now.

'William had to modify this.' I cleared my throat, tugging the hem of the jacket. 'Nothing else fitted me.'

Too tall and too full in certain areas. Magic could do a lot, but it needed something to work with.

'They're mine,' Emrys smiled, small and filled with the faintest shadow of sorrow as his fingers ran over the small repair at the inside seam of the arm. 'My first leathers. Lady Blackthorn put the protection incantations in the stitching herself.'

His thumb and forefinger traced the edge of the sleeve's stitching. 'Emmaline had to repair them for me far too often.'

'I'm sorry you have to see them again on me,' I swallowed, hoping the enchanted tailoring was easy enough to reverse. I didn't want to ruin something so sentimental to him.

'I'm not.' His voice was rough like gravel, as those pitch-black eyes took me in. 'I'm more concerned about just how much I like it.'

There was a simmering in my blood in the hunger that lingered in his eyes. So potent it could have derailed our whole mission – so, like a coward, I moved to the pages he'd been considering.

The remains of the diary were scattered amongst everything else. The curve of dark text and ink smears shaped into demonic form. The pages old and growing older the further I flipped through the pile. Things I didn't know. Had never seen before. So much to understand I felt my shoulders droop. This wasn't healing incantations and fey summonings. It was so far beyond me.

'What is it, Croinn?' he asked, as if seeing the small furrow of my brow and the weight of my thoughts.

'I don't know these things.' I turned another page in the thick ancient script I couldn't understand. All the markings I'd need to learn. The things they could lead to. 'Not as I should.'

No, because I'd read the Councils sterilised records. Listened to their lies and devoured it all like poison.

'You don't need to know everything, Kat,' he offered gently, his hands cupping my elbows in comfort. The softness of those words brushing my neck.

'Then what use am I?' I asked over my shoulder. Knowing had kept me alive. Had kept me safe and it felt strange to venture forward not having that protection.

He turned me to face him, his hands capturing my face with reverence, thumbs gliding across my cheekbones. A small secretive smile on his lips. 'We might need improper storage of a ghoul.'

I huffed in annoyance, aiming my fingers to prod his still healing side but he was quicker. Capturing my hand and laying a kiss against my palm, his quiet laugh brushing against my skin.

'You'll learn everything you need to and before we know it, you'll be telling everyone what to do . . . because, as always, you understand everything better than anyone else could.'

'You might have too much faith in me.' I blew a loose strand of hair from my face.

He caught it, that small smile never abating as he tucked it behind the point of my ear.

'You're the *only* thing I have faith in.'

The depth of those words pierced my doubt so easily. How he hadn't let go of my hand, as our fingers intertwined and I saw the shadow of his magic curl beneath his skin.

Everything had fallen apart, yet we hadn't. This small delicate thing between us.

'What are these then?' I nodded to the papers scattered closest to us. Family trees incomplete and pages from what appeared to be record ledgers.

'The lords' bloodlines and all the bastards that could be used to open those houses' compendiums,' he answered, his free hand running over the lineage lines.

I eyed the list warily. 'There are more than I thought.'

'Most are dead. However, lords tend to produce more of themselves – especially bastards.' Emrys's brow was furrowed as he considered the same thing.

There was something about the pensive stance of him that picked at a loose thread in my mind.

'Do you?' The question slipped free before I could stop the thought. 'Could you? H-have any, I mean?'

Idiot. I scolded myself. Why the bloody hell did that matter?

'I took severan weed when I was seventeen,' he answered, unfaltering. I pulled back slightly, unable to suppress my shock. Severan was dangerous. Yes, it was beyond effective as a contraceptive – however, heirs were prohibited from taking it. It rendered the consumer infertile and was difficult to reverse. Verging on impossible from the books I'd read.

'The withdrawal from severan weed is complex,' I grimaced.

'I wasn't thinking that far ahead.' There was something dismissive in the words and I knew he hadn't believed he'd survive any of it, so why would it have mattered? How he'd never given much thought to his life because he never believed it was his.

I thought he'd say more but instead he reached into his pocket, pulling out two vials that seemed like healing syrup and then a short hilt for a throwing blade. The steel gleaming with a white hue. A shadow blade. Mortal-made to fight the dark. Magic folded into the metal. A summoning that made them more powerful.

'Just in case.' He handed me the vials before slipping the small dagger's handle into the sheath at my hip. Despite my father's blade already resting there. Perhaps he understood my aversion to using it so publicly.

'Also,' his fingers moving the buckles and straps with ease as if he knew every inch of these leathers by heart, 'I do hate to agree with Thean, but you do have a magnificent arse.'

I barked a laugh, watching his eyes darken at the sound as I tipped my head, unable to stop my smile. 'I didn't have you down as a lecher, my lord.'

He moved closer until I was trapped against the desk, his hands coming to rest on the curve of my waist. His warmth seeped easily through the leather.

His smile made my breath unsteady. 'I'm very *particular* in my lecherous tendencies. Mostly for a singular trouble-some Croinn.'

I let my fingers fidget with the buckle on his own jacket.

'You should tell me to stay behind,' I offered quietly, still burdened with all my other mistakes. All the secrets I should have shared sooner.

'I won't tell you what to do, Kat.' He brought our interlaced fingers to his lips. Pressing a kiss to my knuckles. 'Besides, I'm not overly fond of having you out of my sight.'

I was still smiling when he kissed me. Soft and consuming. His fingers slipped beneath the edge of my jacket, finding a strip of warm skin just above my trousers. A low needing sound escaped me as my hands slid into his dark hair. Fingers curling into it at the nape of his neck to keep him closer. Listening to that wild desire coursing through me.

'*Fucking ancestors deliver me,*' came the terse tone of Gideon. The human equivalent of throwing icy water over a flame. Breaking us apart.

'Can we not?' he demanded with a disapproving frown from where he loomed in the doorway. His own leathers making him an imposing figure, his blue eyes almost luminous.

Alma stood at his elbow, hiding her own smile behind her hand. Her petite form looking compact and deadly in her dark leathers she'd borrowed from William.

'Let's get this terrible idea over with so I can have a moment's peace.' Gideon shot Emrys a final warning glance before he moved into the shelves towards the Portium door.

Thankfully my embarrassment of being caught once again with Emrys was short-lived as the Portium door threw us into the middle of an overgrown wood.

There was a little girl who lived in a magical house. With wild roses curling up its side and a stone path that wove like a snake into an enchanted wood.

The story my mother created sang into my memory. How easily I'd forgotten it as I stood on the remains of that winding path.

'I think you're losing your touch, brother,' Gideon muttered, wiping a thick clump of dirt from the side of his boot on a half decayed oak trunk that lay in our path. 'There'd better not be any mud pixies out here. Nasty little bastards.'

'I'm certain you'll be in fine company then,' Alma added, dryly. Earning herself a glare.

'This is the right place on the map,' Emrys replied, looking up at the moon as if the pale disc of it could offer any answers. The ruined doorway we'd emerged from appeared to have once been an outbuilding. Maybe a gamekeeper's cottage.

303

There was nothing but the path before us, and ivy that tangled around my boots. A thick fog curling around the withered trunks.

The Greymarks had sold their ancestral home. The family was rife with debt and their heirs seemed to have a tendency to be drunkards or get themselves killed. The small house hidden in this wood had no value. It'd been left to rot in an old lord's will. A place they used to hide their mistresses in their grander years.

A place they'd dumped my mother to forget about the sin of having a daughter and not a son.

'Alma?' I asked, watching as she turned, chin tipped up as if scenting something on the wind. A shudder moving through her as if resisting the urge to change.

'It's faint.' She frowned, moving forward into the mist. Her hands clenching and relaxing at her side. Unease in the tightness of her shoulders as the wind disturbed the few dark curls that had freed themselves from her bun.

We followed past the gnarled trunks and strange shifting shadows. What alarmed me most was the silence, not even the call of night creatures. I swallowed down my apprehension, kept my focus on Alma's leading pace until the dark sharp outline of the house could be seen through the thicket.

She stopped, glancing over her shoulder, green eyes practically glowing in the darkness like a wolf's on the hunt. Her cheeks marked with a ripple of short feathers as if in warning. 'I think this place is cursed.'

'You know what they say about visiting cursed places.' Gideon released an irritated sigh, stepping gracefully over another scattering of rubble hidden beneath a patch of brambles. 'It's like stepping in shit – you carry it with you.'

The wind gave a sharp howl as if to emphasise his point, making me thankful for the protection charm stitched into the leathers, so the cold couldn't penetrate. Yet, a creaking noise reached my ears. A clatter like a hollow windchime as I took another step. Only to hear a sharper crack beneath my boot. I looked down to see bone instead of a branch. Too large to be from an animal.

'Kat.' Emrys's voice was soft with caution behind me, but it gave no warning as I looked up. To see odd shapes strung from a great oak's branches. Strips of fabric and the clatter of bones in the strong wind.

Traitors of the crown swing. They rot and dance in the wind. A warning made of marrow, a cautious tune as the birds peck at their bones.

All remaining members of the Greymark line had been hanged by the King. I knew that from Council records. Yet seeing it was different. Hanged in punishment for losing his bride. Even the children of distant blood who held that name were guilty. Because a mad king wanted the Greymark name dead.

I didn't know he hanged them here. Didn't know they hung here still. Yellow skin sticking to bleached bones. A warning to all others who let valuable possessions slip from the King's grasp.

'Why would anyone be loyal if that's how they treat their lords?' Alma asked, as fur rippled over the skin of her throat visible above her leathers.

'Lord Grey isn't up there,' Gideon added darkly. 'He was murdered before the rest of his house.'

Alma went still at that, but I kept my expression blank. Even as my magic churned uneasily in my gut. As if it remembered its part in that tale.

My father had killed Lord Grey. Killed him for what he did to my mother.

I could never imagine it. Not when all I knew was the soft patience of my father. A warrior who loved as easily as he laughed. How the same being could have committed such a vicious act. It had been reported in the Council files. The brutality of it, and yet there was no surprise in me. No, because given the chance I knew I'd do the same.

Every fact about my blood and the family I'd been connected to I'd had to learn from dusty tomes filled with lies. The House of Grey was cruel and dark. Its wealth and prestige built on greed. On the abuse of the fey they indentured.

Fey that had raised my mother in servitude. Fey she had loved as her family. So my mother ended this house. She'd cleansed the world of its poison and she'd destroyed herself in the process.

The derelict house before me made the heat of my magic bite ruthlessly into my palms. So small, steeply pitched with a white façade left to crumble and black half-timbering. Alma moved up the stone steps, her clawed hands cutting through the ivy to reveal the door, a chain across it. Thick and rusted. Strung between the chain were saints' charms, left to corrode. Markers that a worshipper had lived here. Had been found unworthy.

'I can fit,' Alma huffed, dusting down her trousers.

'You're not going alone. Not if there's a compendium in there.' Emrys's voice left no room for argument. 'We don't know what such dark magic can summon when left unsupervised.'

I thought she'd bristle at the hint of a command, but the softness of his voice seemed to put her more at ease. One single nod as she considered that thick rusted chain hung with those saints' charms.

'Here,' I offered, moving up the steps. Deciding to let some of my power out, to chase away the tension of containing it. Hoping to soothe its hunger with a small offering. To settle my magic.

I took hold of the chain, allowing the flames to twist between my fingers, catching on the dry ivy clinging to the wood. Those flames raced down the chain and up the side of the door. I poured more and more, until it glowed deep lavender enough to become nothing but molten liquid against my palm, dripping to sizzle on the cold stone ground between my boots.

I pulled back as the flame continued to consume the dried foliage. Illuminating our small gathering as Gideon lifted the heel of his boot, ready to slam it against the door but, before he could, a lock creaked from inside, and it opened as if pushed by the wind.

Only for the rotten wood to break from its rusted hinges, collapsing inward in a cloud of dust that sent myself and Alma a few steps back. Emrys remained where he was, darkness slipping between his fingers as Gideon's aether crackled in his palm.

'If you keep trying to use that leg like a weapon, the incantations on it won't hold up,' Emrys cautioned as he considered the gloom beyond.

'Yes, please inform me what other uses a metal leg has, Emrys?' Gideon hissed back, face weary as the soft blue light of his magic chased the shadows from the door's archway. Making it no less unwelcoming.

'It's in there,' Alma's voice echoed across the cracked tiles of the entryway.

Nothing but dank, stale air greeted us. A bitter coldness that was too familiar. In a blink I was looking at those Fairfax ruins. Where the caymor had dwelled. A creaking sound echoed through the dark, making my heart climb further up my throat. The wishing stone fluttering against my breast as Alma moved into the gloom.

All I could taste on my tongue was decay. All I could hear was the echo of something scuttling. The drip of distant water. So similar to those tunnels beneath Fairfax. I halted for a moment, chest too tight with the panic of it.

I felt Emrys's warmth down my back, how his hands cupped my elbows in comfort. Bringing me back.

'What is it?' he asked, those dark eyes slipping over every inch of my expression as if he could sense the barest change in me.

'Nothing,' I lied. Unable to explain. How strange it was to stand in a place that had caused my mother nothing but pain. Somewhere she never intended me to be – yet we'd been guided here all the same.

Gideon moved down the hall, his aether cutting down the cobwebs from his path as Alma followed. Emrys waited for me, seeming to count my unsteady breath before I allowed myself to enter the house. The wooden beams above sagging with age. Groaning not in welcome but as if another great burst of wind could drag the walls down.

The once-painted ceilings were peeling, large chips of the art cracking under our boots. The irritated rustling from something nesting above as small streams of dust rained down. The main staircase had sunken in on itself. Forcing us down the narrow dark corridor with nothing but Gideon's witch light.

'How fucking depressing. I thought the Greymarks were merchants?' Gideon huffed out a frustrated breath, raising his aether to fully consider the damage.

'They squandered their wealth a long time ago. This was supposed to be a summer residence,' Emrys added, his cautious gaze moving back to me. The remains of the banister had caught my eye. The side of the wood where someone had carved a flower, so small and unsteady as if done by a child's hand. I let my fingers trace the shape of it. Wondering if it had been left by her.

'They left my mother here when she was barely days old.' The words slipped free so easily as I stood somewhere I knew she never wanted me to be. 'Lord Grey had no use for a daughter. So, he abandoned her here with a fey nursemaid to raise her.'

How old and cold this house seemed and how small she must have felt inside of it. Knowing this decay had taken decades, which meant my mother had lived in it in disrepair. How nothing but sadness remained as I moved further down the hallway, how endless and dark it was.

Alma watched me with concern but I reassured her with a small smile as she moved further into the house. Not needing to hear my secrets. She'd heard them all before.

She ducked into a side room, making Gideon swear as he went after her. The remains of furniture lingering inside still covered with sheets. Stained grey and green with mould. The damp leaves that had blown in through the gaps in the boarded-up windows.

The wood-panelled walls were vandalised. White paint flaked where it had been smeared. Marks of impurity from saint worshippers.

'Kat?' Emrys asked, at my side as the sight of it stalled me.

I turned to see him. How carefully he watched me as if trying to understand. 'My mother didn't even know she was a lord's child until he came back when she was eighteen. Surprised to find his unwanted runt a beauty. Out of money and favour in the King's court − he tried to whore her to a wealthy man.'

Such quiet consumed the room for that small moment. How the walls seemed to creak and groan, wary with the tale. One

I knew he'd find familiar. How many of the King's followers had done the same. The horrid things they did for power. Even against their own.

'She refused. So, they used a contortion charm on her.' Shattered the bones in her right arm, so awfully she'd never regained full use of it. How deeply those pale scars had marked her. 'Then they hanged her nursemaid in the town square as punishment. Her name was Katherine.'

Why I held that name. That simple mortal name. Why my mother had given it to me. So Katherine would know, wherever she was, that my mother loved her. Would always love her, the woman she thought of as her mother – no matter how brutally this world had torn them apart.

'What happened to Lord Grey?' Gideon demanded from the shadowed corner of the room.

'My father killed him,' I answered. Unafraid of that truth. How glad I was for it, how my magic flared in my blood. Pleased with its vengeance.

'Good,' Gideon answered, his blue eyes gleaming like his witch aether with his anger. Then came a wooden creak, drawing me to a lopsided sideboard in the corner. My hand moved for my father's blade. Only for my magic to settle inside of me, as if taking a relieved breath. Familiar with this place.

The sideboard creaked again, hinge squeaking as the small cupboard opened slightly, small and weak once again. Too soon to be an accident. I crossed the room and pressed my fingers against the wood, feeling it. The slight irritation of magic, one that lingered deep in the grain of the wood. Weaker than Blackthorn house, but there all the same.

'It's enchanted,' I whispered, wondering how the magic could have survived such destruction. Feeling the sadness pressed into the very dampness of the wood. 'Is that possible?'

Emrys pressed his fingers next to my own, expression pensive. 'It was an old tradition. Most witches were indentured to the house and had no choice.'

It creaked again, persistent and slow like the greeting from an old dog's wary tail. The Grey family wouldn't have cared for it. Not as Emrys or the Blackthorns had cared for theirs. Not as my mother would have. Making me wonder if that was why all her tales included an enchanted house. Yet she'd never spoken of this one.

There was no love left in this house. In this forgotten place that had been a haven for my mother once. Because it would miss her, and I wondered how she had survived the pain of that loss. Of knowing it would be left to ruin without her.

My magic flared. Dragging my focus to the wall next to me, where ivy clung to the remains of the plaster.

Here, a small voice called. My fingers curled into the dry leaves instinctively, and they crumbled beneath my touch. My magic burst from my fingers as the leaves fell charred to the ground. Embers illuminating what was hidden beneath. Where the wood was burnt and bubbled, rough and deep.

I fit my fingers into the gaps and it was like laying my palm into his handprint.

We protect what we love, Tauria. The ghost of my father seemed to linger at my side. The closest I'd been to him in thirteen years. My magic curled like a wounded beast inside of me. He was here. He'd protected her here and so had my magic, because he'd given it to me.

'Kat,' Alma called, breaking the spell of my grief. I followed her voice, finding her in what appeared to be the remains of a library, the shelves scorched as if someone had attempted to set it alight. I avoided the holes in the floor, the boards far too unsteady beneath my boots.

'What is it?' I whispered, feeling an odd sensation move through me. Almost compelling me closer to a set of cupboards on the far wall.

Then her confused green eyes met my own. 'It smells . . . *familiar*.'

Damp remains of burnt books rattled on the shelf making us both jump, leaves tumbling from where they'd rested on top. The cabinet clattered, doors knocking as if something small and feral was trapped inside. I went to grab Alma's arm but she had already slipped easily into another form. Ripping through her leathers easily as a small wrywing appeared. Her spiked tail thumping against the wooden floor, a hiss leaving her maw as she bared deadly, sharp teeth.

The rattling stopped as if cautious of her threat, silence claiming the space before the door burst open. Dust plumed into the room but something else skidded across the ground, to land at the toe of my boot. A small cloth sack tied with fraying string. Alma hissed, circling it warily but I pushed her snout away.

'It's fine, Alma,' I whispered, trying to nudge her meaty form out of the way.

Disgruntled, she leapt up, changing mid-air into a smaller wrywing, no bigger than a bird as she perched on my shoulder. Digging her talons a little deeper than necessary. Warning me against my own foolishness.

I knelt, unknotting the string quickly before reaching inside. Fingers closed around smooth leather and out came an old book. The dark navy of the cover burnt at the corners. The silver decorative border peeled and scratched away with time. The tome bound with worn string despite the rusted blood lock on the side.

A piece of paper pressed carefully into the string. Aged and creased. My magic stirred inside of me, but not in warning. A soft warmth, like a caress from within.

'Kat?' Emrys called, I could feel the brush of his magic up the side of my throat like a comforting caress. Alma growled but I didn't stop. My fingers trembled as I unfolded the paper, the cracking of it too loud in the silence as the book almost slipped from my grasp.

It was in Kysillian.

The curve of her handwriting, the same she'd used to write all my stories. Every tale from my childhood. The uneven spacing of the letters as if she was only just learning. As if this tragic tale was only just beginning, but she knew we'd end at the same place.

Right here.

I had a dream.
I hope you see it.
I hope it's real.

Such raw pain consumed me, my eyes stinging with tears at the sight of the gift she couldn't have known I'd need. The only thing of her now that remained apart from me. Just these words on stained parchment.

Alma whined on my shoulder. Reminding me why we were here. I blew the dust from the cover, showing the carved letters on the front.

Only then did I understand why the house had offered it up so easily. It thought I was her, come back to collect what I left behind.

'Is that—' Gideon choked on the rest of the words.

'The Compendium of Souls.' I stood on unsteady legs, the silver lettering barely glinting as the filagree twisted to depict skulls trapped between thorny brambles.

Gideon stepped forward, eyes moving to Emrys. 'We need to get that book back and—

A horrid pounding echoed into the room. Three strikes. So loud I jumped, stumbling into Emrys, whose arm came around my waist only to move me behind him. The lethal dark of his blade extending in his hand.

'What the fuck is that?' Gideon demanded, aether moving between his fingers, the shadow blade firmly in his grip. Alma leapt from my shoulder, twisting into a larger, more imposing wrywing – sharp claws gouging marks in the damp wooden floor.

The wooden boards beneath my boots began to tremble, thin streams of dust raining down as the abandoned clutter rolled to the shadowed corners of the room as if willing to hide.

'Nothing from this realm,' Emrys replied, eyes full black as the summoning of his magic decorated his skin like dark veins.

Another crash as something slammed the doors down the hall. From the whining of the wood around us, it wasn't the house.

'Did Greymark make a bargain with the darkness?' Gideon snapped out of the side of his mouth, his metal fingers clicking together in irritation, gaze locked on the doorway.

'If he did, I'm certain the demon that came for his soul wasn't happy to find him hanged in a tree.' Emrys slid another blade from the sheath at his thigh.

'He wasn't in the tree,' I reminded them, clutching that book to my front like a shield.

Both brothers turned to me.

The remaining curtain scraps tore free from the windows as if they'd been tugged. Bright moonlight spilling through the spaces between the boards that covered them. Illuminating the room and the rotting wooden floor beneath our feet.

Dark runes burnt into the floor.

I stumbled away from it as Alma recoiled with a chatter of sharp teeth. Coiling for attack as her sharp scales rippled down her spine.

'That's the mark of cruvor,' Gideon said, something distant and cold in his voice.

Cruvor. The dark's manifestation of malice.

Emrys began to scan the corners of the room. As if we were being watched.

'Kat. How did your father kill him?' Gideon moved closer. There was a calmness to his voice but it didn't reach the wild panic in his eyes.

My heart was pounding too strongly in my chest. My magic searing my veins in a strange vicious victory. As if taunting whatever rested here.

Grief and rage could fuel the dark. Could feed things that should never have been made.

I'd brought that magic back here.

'*Saever,*' I whispered, watching Gideon's eyes widen with the ruthlessness of it.

A barbaric sacred punishment in Kysillian law for those deemed worthy of it. Hanging, drawing and quartering with the flame. Relentless in the fact that sometimes they were partially put back together. Forced to take a healing tonic before it began again.

I'd never known if the story was true. Only now I did, as a horrid roar came from the darkness of the hallway.

Chapter Twenty-Seven
Kat

Emrys seized my arm and dragged me back against the wall, an echoing screech tearing through the hallway. Something hunting us. The shadows in the corner of the room rushed for Emrys, gathering beneath his boots like servants awaiting a master's command. His eyes nothing but pools of darkness as that pale demon fire illuminated his fingertips.

The knocking came again. Three sharp blows but further away.

Alma growled in answer, tails thrashing behind her, belly low to the ground ready for her hunt.

'Tell it to fuck off,' Gideon ordered with a quiet hiss from where he'd pressed himself to the other side of the shadowed doorway.

'It's not a *fiend*, Gideon,' Emrys replied. 'It's a manifestation.'

Despite Emrys's command over darkness, I doubted it would stretch to manifestations. Especially one left to corrupt for this long. It would have had nothing to feed off. It would also have become so feral that I doubted the power that formed it remembered anything beyond its own hunger.

The hinges of the door next to us gave a worried squeak. Almost pleading not to be left alone.

'We'll use the portal stones.' Gideon reached into his pocket.

'It'll latch on. We can't let it into the manor,' Emrys protested, more of that darkness spreading up the side of his jaw as if his magic was willing him to become a shadow himself.

'Fuck,' Gideon fired back.

Then came a different sound. A feral screech and the cracking of wood. A horrid laugh. Too much to come from one being. A clattering as if dice were being rolled against the wooden floor.

Gideon darted to the window, looking between the boards before he turned those enraged blue eyes on me. 'It's brought *friends* with it.'

I moved to his side, peering through the gaps only to find those skeletal remains missing. Nothing but rope swinging in the breeze.

Beware the places where cursed bones hang. For they never rest.

They'd been summoned. They weren't just remains; they were *davror*. Cursed bones.

I looked to the book in my arms. What dark power could rest in its pages, what could be drawing it closer. Why such darkness had remained here. It'd been lured by the book kept here all this time.

A hurried clatter across the floor above us. Something moving rapidly. Alma growled. Bringing my attention to her beastly form as she snapped her teeth.

'Alma,' I called. Those annoyed reptilian eyes meeting my own as I grabbed the sack off the floor and pushed the book back inside. Tying it tight before I held it out to her.

Another horrid boom and crack came from down the dark hallway. Closer. Dust rained down from the cracks in the ceiling between the exposed wooden beams above us.

The house whining helplessly.

'It's only going to fuel them.' I offered the sack to her. 'Take it back to the house.'

Cursed items fed the dark. Especially when it was this ravenous.

She growled, tail thrashing with uncertainty before she nudged my thigh in protest. I pushed her snout back, ignoring how she snapped at my hand with irritation.

'Please,' I asked. Those eyes went mortal for a moment, contemplating if she should bite me before her sharp jaws gently took the sack.

She sent an irritated glance Emrys's way. He nodded in some silent agreement before she leapt to climb up the ruined bookcases, curling along the sagging beams and through a hole in the wall. Plaster and wood raining down with the disturbance but as the dust cleared – she was gone.

'At least the bastards can't feed,' Gideon reached into his boot to pull out another shadow blade. His attention on the ceiling above us as another rattle came, almost excited like children rushing about in the midst of a game.

The strange demented nature of it made me pull my father's blade.

'Have you dealt with davror before?' The hilt lengthened against my palm as I pressed myself back against the wall. Slipping into Emrys's shadow.

An ominous groaning came from the walls around us before anyone could answer me.

'They're in the walls,' Gideon warned, barely giving us a moment before the wall between us exploded. Something solid struck my side, taking me down to the damp floor. I skidded into the far cabinet, having enough sense to keep hold of my blade as I rolled to my knees. Seeing the bony shapes of the reanimated remains through the thick clouding of the grime. The sharp blue snap of Gideon's magic and the warning flash of Emrys's demon fire. The wishing stone around my neck fluttering incessantly.

There was nothing but a screeching roar as the remains of the corpse lunged for me. Its bony fingers sharpened to long lethal claws. I swiped with my sword, relieving it of its hands but it didn't stop screaming. Even as I turned again, cutting the creature in half, only for those cursed bones to clatter and scuttle across the floor. Forcing me to kick the snapping skull away with the heel of my boot.

'Bastards!' Gideon snapped, before the bright white of Emrys's summoning cut through the room. Throwing all the creatures back. They flew into the wall, cracking and tumbling into a pile of bone and brittle skin. Only then those bones began to bounce and tumble together. Vanishing into the gaping holes in the floor, dark screeching laughter shaking the boards beneath our feet.

'Gideon!' Emrys snapped, reaching for my hand and pulling me towards him, just as the rotting floor began to implode beneath our feet.

The cold bite of Emrys's magic wrapped around me and then I found myself in a tangle of limbs in the hallway. Gideon cursing somewhere above me from where we'd all been thrown against the wall.

Having the barest moment to draw in a breath before the doorway we'd come through collapsed. The whole room folded in on itself in a cloud of dust. Stinging my eyes as I retched, dirt coating my tongue.

'The fucking house is unmaking itself!' Gideon snapped, as Emrys's hand found mine in the gloom. Pulling me to my feet and further down the hall as I tried to blink the grit from my watering eyes.

Those three knocks grew closer. The rattle and tumble of bone. Quicker and quicker.

Doorways collapsed either side herding us until we stood in another entryway. Further into the dilapidated house.

Another curving staircase of no use, as multiple steps had caved in, the doorways around us either boarded-up or collapsed. Nothing but the endless dark before us. My heart pounded against my ribs.

A horrid demonic screeching laughter echoed from the floors above, banging against the ceiling making the plaster crack, then the walls either side of us.

What the dark hunts it always devours.

Emrys and Gideon turned to watch all the available entrances. Their magic filled the air with a crackling tension.

An inhuman scream echoed down the shadowed corridor to our left. The bright lavender glow from my blade illuminating what leaked from the shadows. What had found us. Gideon's aether burst forward, a blue tinge to the air as he wrapped it around us like a shield.

Something slipped like winter fog through the darkness. Sickeningly pale. Moving slowly and predatorily, taking its time with its prey.

The house whined, the floorboards shaking beneath my boots, the door frames beyond rattling. Then that manifestation brushed up against Gideon's summoning like a tidal wave upon glass. Searching any way through.

Those whisps of smoke became clawed ghostly fingers with sharp tips as they scraped against the summoning. As if the creature would gouge its way through the shield if it needed to.

The manifestation of malice. A sharp elongated face in that strange smoke, mouth drawn open in an eternal scream. Limbs too long and sharp. Its eyes nothing but dark pits. What remained of him. The man who had hurt my mother – and my magic remembered.

Because it was my father's first.

'How the fuck are we getting out of this one, brother?' Gideon snapped, sweat beginning to bead his brow. The dust clinging to it as if his summoning was draining him too quickly. 'You'd better think fast because my protection charms are *not* my greatest asset.'

Emrys's pale summoning flame crackled, the cold of it making our panted breath cloud, his eyes glowing with it. It wove between his fingers and up his arms. The darkness in the hallway seemed to rush for him.

'*Now,*' Emrys commanded in a voice so dark it wasn't his own.

Gideon dropped his summoning. The malice screamed but Emrys's demon fire was waiting. It roared past us, brushing my exposed skin in an icy caress as it cut through the deadly mist of the manifestation.

A boom shook the house on contact like a crack of thunder. The demon screamed, convulsing and twisting in on itself. All claws as it gouged chunks out of the wood that surrounded it. Throwing itself against the walls, shattering wood and plaster.

Floorboards jumped beneath my boots, sending me sidewards against the panelling.

A pounding came against the walls around us in response. Screaming things hiding in there. I moved to wrench myself away before a skeletal hand punched through the plaster. Sharp small fingers curling around my wrist to drag me back.

'Bastard,' I hissed, tugging my arm, but it wouldn't come free, boots slipping on the floorboards. I heated my blade, swinging it downwards to cleave through the bone, rendering the bony fingers wrapped around my wrist to ash.

Cracks formed in the wall, more of those davror trying to break free. I stumbled back towards Emrys and Gideon.

Only then the floor stopped shaking, the beams above us sagged ever so slightly. The whole house seeming to droop. How still and lifeless it was in an instant. The magic gone.

'The house is—' But I didn't finish, pressing my fingers to the panelling next to me. There was nothing.

It was dead.

The manifestation screamed again, throwing itself against the hallway, clawing and snapping its cursed jaws. Twisting into smoke once more. Although, instead of coming towards us, it seeped into the cracks it had made. Vanishing between them. Then there was the retreating scuttle of those cursed bones. Their thrilled little demonic laughter as they left.

'I don't like this,' Gideon whispered, turning in a circle, his aether crackling in his palms. 'Where the fuck—'

'Kat!' Emrys barked the same moment the floor erupted between us. The cursed bones screeching as they shot like daggers through the air. I moved but not fast enough. One slammed into my shoulder. The leathers not letting it penetrate but the force sent me tumbling back, hitting the floor. My blade slipped from my grip as my back made painful contact with the ground.

A flare of Emrys's demon fire filled the hallway. Then as if a great wind had blown through, everything was pulled back towards him. The davror screaming until they rattled and dropped to the floor. Lifeless like discarded dolls. The summoning that had formed them like dark smoke that moved towards Emrys. Gathered between his palms, his eyes burning ethereal white. The dark veins marking every part of his skin. His fingers glowing with that same strange power, and how easily he rendered that summoning to nothing but ash that drifted between his fingers.

Unmaking it in a moment.

A roar seemed to surround us. The manifestation. Watching. The walls cracking and crumbling before us as I got to my feet. The floor trembling as it threatened to cave in. Not welcoming Emrys's challenge.

'Emrys!' Gideon charged, pinning him against the ruined wall and then I saw why. Emrys's gaze was suddenly nothing but darkness, veins spreading up his skin. Head twitching ever so slightly as if he was listening to something.

'Look at me, you bastard,' Gideon commanded, as if trying to call him back from the depths of that summoning. How it danced across his flesh.

Something from one of those cursed tales. He hadn't taken his suppressant. His magic was ruling him because to protect was all he knew.

Then the floor beneath us rumbled, boards jumping as more large fissures ran across the walls. Wood splintering and cracking as if the weight of the house was coming down on us.

Emrys's power rose in answer, the cold of it burning my lungs.

'It's *become* the house.' My words were breathless with my fear. The manifestation had taken over. To bring it down on top of us. We were trapped. Yet before panic could have me, her voice came back. So patient and real:

There was a little girl who lived in a magical house. With wild roses curling up its side and a stone path that wove like a snake into an enchanted wood.

A beautiful woman she called Mera, with small dark horns, forest-green curls and eyes like firelight. Whose voice was as lyrical as song.

How they spotted folk and made potions from the wild shrooms and nettle patches. How they ran barefoot through the wildwood together.

Together. In the home they'd made here. Before this monster stole it all, long before that darkness came for his soul.

Only this was nobody's home. Not anymore. That monster had killed her here. That little girl from those stories. Killed her love for this home, and the woman she called *Mera*.

Mother in the common fey tongue.

She was alive when you burnt her, little troll. No. My mother was dead. My fire wouldn't have hurt her. Couldn't, because it was my father's first.

Just as it could never hurt me.

I'd let them twist my fear with their lies. Let them control me. They'd taken my flame from me first and how easily I'd let them – let monsters like this win.

My father had created this darkness. His rage had formed it. Then I could see so clearly, as if the ancestors wished to fuel my vengeance.

Could see nothing but the memory of the barest pale marks over my mother's flesh. Evidence of where that magic had bit too deeply into her – where her father had tortured her. Tried to break her.

Then the muffled sobs as she woke some nights. My father's voice easing her back to sleep. Or as he'd sit up with her, deep into the darkness until the dawn. How his fingers would run through her hair as it caught the cottage's firelight.

The illusion of happiness for my childhood was chased away, reminding me of the dark ink-blot that had been at its centre. The pain this world had caused my parents.

Fury ignited my veins, the summoning too familiar, my magic moving before I could think of the spell.

So I roared and I let my vengeance free. Just as my father had before me. Let my flame erupt, let it take that stone path in the wood. Let it race up the withered remains of those roses. To the rooms I remembered from her tales. Let it seep into every part of this cursed forgotten place.

'Kat!' Gideon warned over the firestorm. Only there were no warnings left. My hands didn't tremble and my will didn't break.

324

Not anymore. Not as the firestorm grew, as it roared and feasted, circling us in a scorching wind. Devouring with its vicious desire to be free.

Until the manifestation roared, thrashing wildly, becoming white smoke and sharp bone. Slipping through the wooden cracks, slamming itself restlessly into the burning gaps. Trying to get free. Trapped in this house with us. In a cage of its own making. As I poured all my grief and vengeance into these ruins.

The deafening shatter of glass and wood followed, lavender chaos pouring from my palms, rumbling like thunder as it tore through the house. As the taste of smoke and fury lined my tongue. The malice screamed for mercy. Only I didn't stop.

I didn't let go, letting that fire burn and seek. Ravenous as it had been when my father wielded it for the same kill. My flame remembered because I gave it no order and yet it feasted.

I hoped the man that hurt my mother was still in there. If only a fragment. I hoped he felt every moment of it.

My flame twisted around us. A protective circle that foul creature couldn't penetrate.

The house imploded on itself, crumbling into nothing beyond the wall of fire that surrounded us. My flame not easing until there was nothing but dark ash on the breeze. A perfect circle of wood remained beneath our feet, the boundary I'd set.

Fire guttered in my palms, shoulders sagging as my hands fell weakly to my sides. Breaths unsteady as they came panted from my lips. The black charred, mangled remains of the old house. Dead.

The storm had broken above. Raindrops hissing off my hands. Dripping down my face with the ferocity of how it pounded into the earth.

I should have screamed to the heavens. Should have bared my teeth to the ancestors for all my pain. Only then it was understood, they deserved none of me.

Movement came from behind me, turning me. Wild and feral with short breaths, only to see the dark form of Emrys. Those intense eyes scanning over every inch of my face as rain pasted my loose hair to my cheeks. More himself but still consumed by the darker side of his nature. Seeing him considering me for any harm in the middle of my destruction, ash smeared on his leathers and the sharp line of his jaw.

A sharp flickering light began at my wishing stone where it had tumbled from my leathers. Gideon's eyes were on it, then he dug into his pocket, pulling out a crystal wrapped in thin chain. The dark stone covered in ruins. A witch's totem, and the stone was flaring with a pale blue light. A warning.

'Something is coming,' he cursed, pocketing the stone once more. Turning towards the vastness of the wood. We were too far from the Portium door. 'We only have two fucking weak portal stones. They won't carry all of us.'

I looked up at the seared trees. The potency of my magic. How high the smoke from the house had risen even with the storm. An easy target.

'Go,' Emrys commanded his brother as his hand slipped into my own. 'Follow Alma back to the house and we'll meet you there.'

'That stone won't carry you that far.' Gideon's eyes moved between us, worry pressed there like he'd resist. Then the distant horn sounded accompanied by the bark of a hunting hound.

'Now!' Emrys commanded, and we ran.

Chapter Twenty-Eight

Alma

No matter what they take, or how many feathers they pluck. You'll always have your wings, little one.

You can always fly.

I hated the memory of that voice, because it always made me feel nothing but empty. Nothing ever followed it. No name or face. Just a voice. How awful that I wondered if it was simply the echo of my own. So desperate for any comfort, I lied to myself. Even now.

I shook my beastly head, letting the scales ripple and shift down my side to protect me better from the wind. There was freedom in the air. Despite the cold chill of the night as it rushed against my wings. As I stretched them wider and felt the luxurious calm in the tendons. Trying to take my mind off leaving that horrid house. About leaving Kat there.

She was with Emrys and Gideon. I had to be reassured by that, yet my scales still rippled with annoyance. I banked, scenting my way back. A strange primal urge that turned and twisted me through the air without thought. But before I could relish the feeling of being on the right track, a flash came from the dark forest beneath. An orange glow like fire, yet there was nothing below. No small villages this far into the wilderness.

Foolishly, I hesitated, scented the air too long. A sharp pain rushed across my back leg. Molten agony like a claw burying itself into my flesh.

I tried to pull back, sharp teeth bared, but the change was slipping away from me. As rapidly as the air through my wings. A weakness in my jaw making the sack slip free, tumbling though the air below me. I tried to shift to dart and chase it. Become smaller and more agile. Only for my clumsy limbs to struggle. Sending me into a nosedive for the earth. The dark marshy lands beneath looming closer.

Panicked, I twisted into a large bird form, only able to throw my wings wide one more time before they vanished completely, and I tumbled into a short freefall.

I hit the ground, swampy earth breaking my fall but sharp unrelenting stones still dug into my skin. One striking my cheekbone, making light flash across my vision as I tumbled to a halt, skin raw and bones aching.

Pain radiated down my back from where my wings had been, as if they'd been clipped off. I reached behind me, desperate, looking for the wound. There was nothing but the sharp points of my spine as it settled back into mortal form.

My fucking chest was too tight, breaths too short. I tried to summon my beasts but there was nothing. Just silence as I shivered in the mud.

No.

I reached for my leg, feeling cold metal protruding from the flesh that made me wince. A dart, small and gleaming in the moonlight.

With trembling fingers I pulled it free, the metal reeking of a sour, copper smell.

A smell I knew. One that had tormented my nightmares.

A sob clawed up my throat as I threw the dart away from me. Recoiling as I gripped my thigh. Blood seeping between my fingers, but the sickly metallic scent remained.

I rubbed at it hopelessly, no matter how it stung or how much filthy mud brushed the wound.

A magic suppressant. Nulling poison the menagerie used — but that wasn't possible.

They'd been banned. Eradicated. Master Hale had promised that.

A hollowness took root inside of me, like icy claws burying themselves into my flesh. My vision unfocused. Unable to smell anything but wet earth, my heart pounding too wildly.

How quickly my beasts left me. How easily my body betrayed me. Weak and useless against the wet earth. Tremors running through my limbs helplessly.

So distracted by my own pain I didn't hear them approach with my mortal ears. Not the snapping of leaves or the crunch of boots. Not until hands grabbed me, pulling a surprised scream from between my lips.

'What we got here!' The hissed words met my ear, fingers pulling at my hair. I fought. Repulsed by the cool leather of their fingers against my flesh. The bitter scent of saint smoke.

I could barely see the dark uniform of the Council hunter. The gaps in his yellow teeth and the shaggy mess of his hair. The reek of his ale-soaked breath weaker than it should have been in the absence of my senses. I bit and clawed but it was nothing compared to his strength. He struck me across the face, enough to get his meaty arms around me.

'Feral bitch!' he spat as one of my blows landed. Pain exploded in my temple, dark spots in my vision as he tossed me to the ground once more.

My limbs were too sluggish. Thoughts too slow. Then there was the weight of him on top of me, the sour smell of his skin.

'Got something, lads!' he crowed, cruel hands trying to pin me down. In a moment it wasn't him and me against the damp soil.

No. A nightmare filled my reality. Me on a rug in a room reeking of tobacco smoke. Surrounded by cruel laughter, the rattle of a chain and the cry of creatures from rooms beyond.

The menagerie.

A feral scream tore from my lips, jolting me back into now. Through my agony I found something inside me. Some wild strength as my nails painfully lengthened. The barest of claws but it was enough. Tearing through the flesh of his throat like paper, as that warm blood sprayed into my mouth. He screamed, rearing back but I surged forward. Fingers digging into meaty wet flesh as he gargled his own blood.

I screamed and screamed. Uncaring who was coming or the flashes of torches in the distance. Who was listening. I kept tearing at him until there was nothing but mulch between my fingers. Until my limbs weakened. As sound from the woods pierced thought my madness. Forcing me to scramble back. Knowing I needed to run. They were coming. They'd catch me.

I turned. Only to bolt into something hard and alive. I screamed again, trying to buck free but those arms don't let me go. The soft fabric of their clothes, then the familiar rich sent of them penetrating my panic.

'Alma.' So soft. So authoritative. Settling that terror inside of me. Until I could drag in greedy gulps of air. Taunted by that fucking scent. A flash of amber in the darkness.

Thean. The comfort of their presence and the sharp scratch of their fangs against my jaw with how close they held me.

I turned further into that commanding hold, needing to see. Uncaring that I was naked as I knelt in that mud, illuminated by nothing but moonlight. My fingers curling into the fine fabric of their coat. Ruining it with my bloody claws.

Those amber eyes burnt with fury as they dragged over my face. My cheekbone throbbed from either the fall or the hunter, I didn't know. They missed none of it. Dark rage seeping across their expression. Not appearing like any form of Thean I'd seen before.

'I can't change.' The words came panted through my lips.

Then those amber eyes dropped to my thigh where I'd pulled the dart free. Their nose wrinkled as if they could smell it too.

I thought they'd say something. Mock me. Yet this creature before me was too quiet as they pulled their coat from their tall masculine frame and draped it around my shoulders, holding it closed as I slipped my trembling numb arms into the sleeves. Or tried to. My poor attempt at claws snagging on the fabric.

Movement came from the trees. Noises that Thean didn't seem to hear. The close voices of those hunters making me flinch. I'd killed one. I turned to see him slumped in the mud, only for Thean to catch my chin, pulling my focus back to them.

My lip trembled and I hated it. Hated how their eyes caught it. How obvious my fear was. How easily I let myself slip back into the past.

Then there was nothing but the absence of them as they got to their feet, shadow blades appearing in their hands before they vanished. Vanished as if they'd never been there at all.

No. The warmth and scent of their coat told me they were. They'd simply become the creature I should have never forgotten they were.

331

One of the Countess's assassins. A death their mark would never see coming.

Then there was nothing but screaming. Ruthless screaming.

I scrunched my eyes closed but forced myself to listen. They deserved it. All of them. For how they'd turned me into nothing but a shivering lump on the cold earth. I clawed at Thean's coat, trying to drag their scent in. To find any comfort, but that scent was too weak in this mortal form. The smell of wet earth too strong. Like those graves in Daunton Wood. Then I felt that I was drowning merely trying to draw in breath.

A touch brushed my shoulder. I recoiled, kicking and hissing, only to find Thean peering down at me moments later. Shirt streaked with blood, that blade sheathed once again at their thigh. As they reached out to help me, like I was some lame foal.

Then I remembered who I was. My bitterness rising above my fears.

'I don't need your pity,' I snapped.

'I don't have any pity in me, darling,' they sighed and then they pulled me up into their arms so effortlessly. Leaving me no choice but to cling to them for fear of being dropped. For fear of falling once again.

'I was carrying a sack. We need to find—' I barely got the words out before the thing dropped against my middle, forcing me to clutch it despite how thickly it was coated in mud.

Kat had trusted me with it.

'Cursed objects have a tendency to harbour bad luck, sweetheart,' Thean warned, but their voice wasn't as playful as I remembered. Their form too tense as if lost in thought.

Distant torchlight cut through the wood. The echo of voices reaching my ears and making me flinch. A commotion in the darkness from whatever chaos Thean had wrought. Just how many hunters they'd killed, I didn't know. But their pace wasn't urgent. In a blink of an eye the damp of the wood was gone, replaced by the warmth of one of the Blackthorn fires.

Transporting us so effortlessly, as effortlessly as they'd arrived. With me still not understanding how they'd been there or how we were here now as they deposited me gently on the chaise before the fire. The now muddy sack tumbling to land next to my feet.

I recoiled, trying to stand, but a firm hand on my shoulder kept me in place.

'I'll ruin the fabric,' I snapped. Unable to stop shaking. Hating it.

'I don't care,' they answered, with a gentle shove. I had no choice but to mar the cushions with my mud-covered limbs. Then I saw the blood on my hand. Blood I'd now smeared on their shirt.

How instinctive it was to slit that hunter's throat. To be covered in that blood. How familiar it was to me despite how I tried to forget.

'The shock is normal.' Their voice was soft, so soft I hated it. Too calm, almost caring.

'It wasn't my first,' I whispered, deciding the truth was better than wasting time weaving lies. Knowing they saw everything anyway. Saw how pathetic I'd become. How useless all my defences were.

'There is no shame in surviving,' they offered calmly, stoking the fire with one hand braced on the mantle. The dampness of their shirt clinging to the fine muscles of their back. Revealing more of those summoning runes on their flesh. 'No matter how we do it.'

333

'You might think differently if—' My words stuck to the roof of my mouth as the voyav's sharp eyes silenced me with the depth of that strange look that lingered there.

'Trust me, little nightmare. I know it's far easier to judge than it is to understand.' In the hard fury in their eyes, I knew they did. In a way I couldn't explain.

Trust. The thing I could never do. What they'd stolen from me first.

I wasn't like Kat. Soft and forgiving. There was something wrong with me. Something hard and cold caging my heart within my chest. My defences built too well, only a few cracks in the bricks. Enough for Kat's friendship to penetrate but nothing else.

I didn't know what I was guarding. Everything of value had already been stolen from me. Yet, as I looked at the forsaken creature before me, I felt the danger of their attention. How those amber eyes missed nothing, and I was consumed by the fear they'd peek through those cracks and see just how empty I was.

'Bloody saints,' came an exclamation from the doorway. Making me jump, clutching Thean's fine coat closer, resisting the urge to curl my legs to my chest. My fingers ached for claws but none came. No beasts to hide within as my eyes met a shocked William's from across the room, his mouth agape at the state of me. Before he shook himself, grabbed one of the blankets off the chair and pulled it around me. 'Alma, what happened?'

'I'm all right.' I smiled weakly despite the pain in my cheek-bone. By the depth of William's concern, it didn't work, as I trembled so violently.

'She was hit with verium.' Thean's words were curt. Too serious from those usually playful lips.

'Anti-magic?' William paled.

Then he scrambled to one of the desks, rooting through a drawer before dropping a small healing case on the cushions next to me. As a bowl of water with a cloth appeared too.

'First a relic and now forbidden alchemy.' William swallowed, shaking his head. 'Emrys isn't going to like this.'

'If the bastard makes a reappearance,' Thean half sneered.

'The house was—' I began but the voyav simply tugged that blanket more firmly around my shoulders before they crouched before me.

'I don't care.' Their sharp eyes came back to my face, rage so potent their features shifted between male and female. Seeming unable to settle. 'They shouldn't have left you on your own.'

I bristled. 'They didn't know.'

Kat wanted me safe and she knew I'd keep that book safe.

Thean glared at me, a muscle jumping in their jaw almost in warning. Tough. They wouldn't win. Not with me.

'I'll get you some healing tea,' William added awkwardly. His worried brown eyes moving between me and the voyav. Unfortunately, I didn't have use of my beasts, so I'd have to use my mortal wits to deal with the moody creature.

Too annoyed at myself and why the voyav had chosen now to be overbearing, I stared into the fire. Allowing the heat of it to wash over me, but as always it didn't penetrate that coldness deep inside of me.

'Alma.' My name was too soft from their lips. As if it could be an incantation that held too much power. 'Your leg is bleeding, it needs tending. Can I touch you?'

A dry sad laugh left my lips. 'Nobody has ever asked me that before.'

Why would they have? They'd already owned every inch of me. I expected Thean's sly remark flirtatious or dismissive.

Yet, it didn't come. They remained crouched there quietly. Waiting. As if the words from my lips mattered. As if there wasn't already the memory of hundreds of fingerprints upon my skin. Known only by me.

As if my permission could change something.

'Yes,' I answered. A strange honest agreement between us. Something inside of me knowing, even without the curse of all those beasts, that no matter what Thean Page was or what they wanted – they weren't going to hurt me.

Whatever remained of that curse inside me settled before them like a submissive hound, belly low to the ground.

'Inside right pocket,' they instructed, as the warmth of their hand came around my thigh. Easing my leg straight to see the wound. The gentle nature of their touch soothed something in me, made breath slip more easily between my lips, but I doubted they noticed. Head bowed so I could see how the fire played through the auburn strands of their hair, not ceasing their work of picking the thorns from around the wound with tweezers from the healing kit, as if such small things would hurt me.

I did as they asked, reaching into the thick coat, finding a vial inside the pocket. I pulled it free to see it filled with a dark thick liquid. Not needing to open it to know it was blood.

Voyavs were devourers of blood. A weaver of ancient magic that not even the earth wished to keep beneath its confines. Too chaotic for even the Old Gods to master.

Thean then washed the skin of my thigh. Removing the blood and dirt around the wound before they took the vial from me, taking the barest of drops on their tongue before corking it again. A shudder rippled through them before that sharp focus dropped to my thigh once more.

An amber light shimmered against their palm, just as it would a flesh healer's as they pressed it against my wound.

A stinging warmth made me gasp, wanting to pull my leg away out of reflex but there was no mistaking the strength in Thean's grip. Then, as quickly as it arrived, the pain was gone – just as that light flickered out beneath their skin.

Healed. Or almost healed. The skin was still angry and tender beneath my probing fingers that they gently batted away. Then the voyav moved back to the healing kit and pulled out a jar of balm. Their clever, strong fingers working it into my aching muscle with such authority it took everything not to slip into a puddle. Relaxing under their ministrations.

'What's in the left pocket?' I asked to keep hold of some of my sanity. Feeling the weight of the coat I wore, the secrets it could hide. The intoxicating scent of them. I wished I had my magic back for it to be stronger.

'None of your business, little nightmare.' Their grin was small with amusement as they glanced up at me. The sight of them before me, knelt like some repenting worshipper, did strange things to my insides.

Maybe it was nausea from the shock. There was no time to contemplate as they leant closer, their thumb brushing my cheek, just around where it throbbed – cautious of my wince. My fingers curled around their wrist out of instinct. Only to see they were still slightly clawed. A monstrosity.

I tried to wrench my hand back. Shame turning my stomach at the hideousness of it. Of me.

Only they didn't let me go. Didn't let me hide, their fingers slipping easily between mine. They curled my clawed hand around their own. Those amber eyes solely fixed on me in a silent reassurance. It was the kindest act they could have given in that moment. Not the gentle nature of their touch, but that look in their eyes. As if speaking directly to that fear burrowed between my ribs. As if they could understand shame as I did. Knew the horrid weight of it and still – they were here.

They gently slipped two fingers beneath my chin, turning my face to see the aching side. The barest heat from their fingertips, the remnants of that magic they'd stolen from that vial of blood as the ache went away. Healed.

They didn't let me go. Watched me closely, perhaps so I wouldn't hide within the corners of my own mind. They cared, even if they wished they didn't, and I understood *that*, if nothing else. Confused how their presence sent my beasts rolling beneath my skin. Hot and needy. Wishing to perform for the dangerous creature before me more than they'd wanted to perform for anyone else.

The depth of it startled me, too many rushing emotions that I was left alone to face without my defences. The stench of that dank wood clinging to me. That blood. That hunter's blood, the cruelty of his touch still on my skin.

'I need a bath.' I stood, our hands slipping apart as I used the back of the chaise to support my unsteady legs. Not missing how the voyav's hands flexed as if resisting the urge to help.

'I wouldn't soak your wounds until the balm has been given enough time to work.'

'I don't want him on me.' The words were too sharp with my panic. Childish, as I curled my shoulders inwards. Bile rising in my throat at the stickiness between my fingers. The phantom feel of his hands across my flesh.

Thean strode past me, to the door that led to another room. Only to realise it led to my room. Or what had been Kat's room before the house had moved her to Emrys's. They needed no instruction, as if they'd been here before and that thought made me flush. They opened the bathroom door and turned the taps of the bath, bending in to fit the plug. Pulling back to fold their arms and glare down at the water as if watching it would make the tub fill quicker.

'What are you doing?' I frowned, shocked by such mortal movements coming from them.

'You don't want them on you,' Thean replied effortlessly, no annoyance or hesitation in the words.

'The balm—'

'I'll do it again,' they offered softly. But there was an anger in the tension of their jaw. One I thought was aimed at me, but their gaze was looking at my calves. Where they'd cut deeper than everywhere else. Across the curve of my foot, right to my toes.

Nobody who'd seen them before had seemed to care. Not the men my Keeper brought with their wandering hands. Or even Daunton in the end.

I was nothing but something to be used. Used so much I ceased to exist. Every flinch or tear became invisible. For I had been nothing but a thing, and only what they could take had value.

Then I understood Thean's fury – why it was so familiar to me. It was the same feral sharpness I'd seen in Kat's eyes when she looked upon those marks – when she'd seen them the first time in Daunton. Still weeping and scabbed.

Only, if Thean had changed me after I'd become the ravhorn, they would have already seen them. Unless . . .

'You really didn't look,' I whispered, unsure why that truth settled so warmly inside of me. Why it made my eyes sting with tears.

'You didn't give me permission to,' Thean answered.

The simplicity of those words stunned me, shamed me too. What I'd become, to forget my voice and my choices mattered. The space between us seemed too cavernous, filled with this strange game. With secrets and unspoken things – yet, there was something I wanted to say. Wanted to free from the confines of my chest, wanted someone to hear, even if they forgot it eventually.

Even if they forgot me.

'Sometimes they cut away so much I wondered if there would be anything left.' I'd worried how much they could take, worried when they'd find nothing of value left. Wondering what they'd do with me then.

The cruellest part was that even here, safe and warm, it made it worse. What if I'd made it up? What if I was the only one who remembered? What if none of it happened at all and I was simply mad?

'Now it just feels like a dream. Like it never happened at all.' I dug my fingers into their coat around me, painfully. Wishing they were sharper claws so they could bury themselves deeper. To drag the sorrow from my skin. Hating the sting of emotion in my throat.

'It did.' Thean's voice cut through the darkness of those thoughts, like a small lantern swinging in the night wind, guiding me back to sanity.

They came closer, cautiously. Crossing that distance between us, as they slipped into a more feminine form, so effortlessly I didn't think they'd even noticed.

'What's your favourite form?' I asked to distract them – to distract myself, perhaps.

They looked down at their own hand. 'I've never been able to decide.'

'I used to like being a spear finch.' Too small and delicate so my Keeper would be too afraid to handle me. No matter how he spat and cursed to have me back. He wouldn't touch me.

I remembered the small victory of it. How I'd spent hours cleaning those pretty teal feathers. Trying not to think of what would happen when I faltered, and my mortal form came back.

'They're pretty, too.' I shrugged, trying to push away the darkness of the memory. The pain of it.

'Not as pretty as you, little nightmare,' the voyav offered so softly, almost as if the words had slipped free of their lips against their will.

My sharp edges should have cut them for trying to play a game. For the cruelty of pretending those words were true. Only the longer I looked at them, the harder it was to be angry. To find a lie in their soft unguarded expression.

'People pay a fortune for a spear finch,' I reasoned. A price nobody would pay for a nameless girl like me. A monster in human flesh.

'You're not a bird now,' they observed, coming closer still – until there was nothing but the sinful scent of them filling my lungs.

'No.' I'd learnt that the hard way. 'I needed claws more than wings. It took me a shamefully long time to realise that. Too long perhaps.'

Someone stronger might have broken away sooner. Someone cleverer might have found a different way. Then my eyes moved to that blood mark upon Thean's throat. Knowing there were more, there had to be. The more powerful the being, the more blood marks it took to contain them.

Perhaps that was why the Countess liked the strongest creatures – to demonstrate her power. To break even the most monstrous of us.

'You made your vow,' I swallowed. Blood sworn. In service until death. A cruel fate, and even crueller to those who convinced themselves it was better than anything else. That service was better than the danger of freedom.

A dry humourless laugh left their lips. 'I don't remember

that either. Just someone asking a question and being too scared to say no.'

I could never imagine them small or weak. Yet as that wicked amber gaze found my own once more, there were no lies in it. No, just open and lost. Such regret pressed there, making me wonder, if given the choice again, what they'd do.

Say yes, little rat, that voice commanded in my mind. How brutal and cold. Mocking.

Then those eyes went hard, with displeasure as if sensing the rise in emotions within me.

'Pity?' they mocked sharply, flashing fangs, but I could see the sorrow hiding in the dark corners of their amber eyes.

That pain moved me closer, letting me pull in another breath of their cologne. How comforting it was despite how it tightened that strange knot of unease inside of me. Ignoring my beastly urges to want that scent all over my skin. To be claimed by it.

Strangely missing it despite the voyav being right before me.

'Maybe I see imprints of my story within the pages of yours, Thean,' I whispered. Knowing that pain, the sharp and destructive nature of it because of how similar it was to my own. 'And I'm glad you're here, promises or not.'

For a moment their face was so soft and content I could have been fooled into thinking they were mortal.

'That might be the most dangerous thing you've ever said, little love.' There was a soft mirth there but a pain too. Making me want to give them privacy as I moved to the bath, letting my hands sink into the water. Watching it cloud instantly from the dirt caked on my fingers.

'Do you think—' I began, turning, but Thean was gone. The taps groaned as if the house foolishly wished they'd stayed too.

Chapter Twenty-Nine

Kat

A smear of colours rushed past us with the power of the portal stone, making the rain sting my cheeks before the summoning dissipated as quickly as it had arrived. Disorientating me as my boots skidded on wet cobbles, fingers curling into Emrys's leathers as my panted breaths clouded in the bitter winter air. The strength of Emrys's arm around my waist the only grounding thing as reality came back to me.

Murky lantern light revealed the dark street where we'd staggered to a stop. The portal stone flickered out of life against Emrys's palm, casting his face in shadow as the veins of that darkness began to curl and sink back beneath his skin.

A cat yowled, skittering out of the entry we'd stumbled into. Small wooden gates lined the street on either side of us, hanging lopsided on their hinges, and the cobbles covered in moss.

Emrys caught my hand, urging me towards one of the gates, entering a small walled yard with discarded crates, shattered wood piled and discarded. We crossed the space towards a green door of what appeared to be another townhouse. One in a row of many, most of which had been boarded up, but from the flickering of lights through the cracked wood we could see it was still occupied.

We moved up the weed-covered steps. Emrys's other hand illuminated with pale summoning light as he grasped the doorknob and it opened upon his unspoken command. Leading into a short hallway and a rickety set of stairs that went steeply upwards. He shut the door, only to fidget with something next to it in the gloom. A dial. Then the door vanished into nothing but a solid wall covered in peeling patterned wallpaper.

A silence encompassed us, nothing but our breathing disrupting it as our bodies, damp from the rainstorm, were pressed together.

'This way.' He tugged me gently up the stairs, each step groaning in protest. Cobwebs strung across the path. A damp, dead air filling my lungs, the small pictures hanging unevenly on either side showing scantily clad imps with iridescent wings in provocative poses.

It wasn't like all the ruins of the Greymark estate or Fairfax. No sour rot or decay. Just forgotten.

'What is this place?' I whispered as we reached a narrow landing covered in a fraying rug. Doorways either side of us, some bricked up as if this place didn't have the energy to manifest any more rooms.

'Safe house,' he answered, eyes scanning the dim room before us. A welcoming hearth barely sparking. 'What little magic is left here seems to have taken pity on us.'

The room was small and had seen better days. A narrow four-poster bed sat crooked where it was pushed against the wall, one of its legs caved in. A strange relic from a different time. The drapes moth-eaten and stained yellow with age. Before the fire was a scattering of blankets and pillows. As if the room was doing its best to be hospitable despite the ruin that surrounded us. The beams drooped and the decorative paper curled away from the walls.

Rain lashed against the latticed windows; the weak golden lamplight through the storm from the streets below.

My braid sagged with how wet my hair was, so I pulled it free, twisting the water out, examining the space.

Emrys ducked to open a cupboard, pulling out a small chest before he rooted inside. Then in his palm were two portal crystals, one of them like what we'd used to get here. No glow coming off either. Empty of magic. A curse slipped from his lips as he tossed them into the fire.

Natural energy was the only way to charge a crystal. My flame couldn't be trusted not to break the delicate enchanted item, and I supposed Emrys's dark summoning would have the same issue.

'Those stones will need a few hours to charge.' He ran a hand through his damp hair as he tended to the fire, adding the few logs strung with cobwebs that rested next to the hearth.

I bent to pull off my boots, damp and covered in dust.

Not dust. The remains of my mother's house.

I tossed them into the hallway. Not wanting any remnant of it near me.

Not now.

I rubbed my cold fingers. Seeing the residual flare of magic, how they didn't tremble. No, because there was nothing more natural than being as I was always intended to be. I should have felt shame at what I'd done. The viciousness of it. Only there was a strange rightness in my bones. How I felt more myself than I had in weeks.

'Show me your shoulder.' I looked up to see Emrys bathed in the orange light of the fire. Eyes pitch-black as the darkness of his magic rippled beneath his skin. He unbuckled his weapons belt and dropped it next to the hearth where he'd discarded his own jacket. Leaving him in his damp shirt, which clung to the expanse of him.

Something feral rolled through me at the sight. Maybe it was the Kysillian in me that hungered for such a warrior's build. Why I was drawn to power and the strength in it. Or maybe it was just Emrys. Covered in light smears of ash from my summoning.

Like claiming marks.

'I think the leathers worked.' I peeled off my damp jacket, feeling the stiffness from where those davror bones and the debris had struck me. I pulled the lacings at the top of my shirt, letting it slip off my shoulder. Emrys came to a stop before me like a foreboding shadow, the sheer size of him blocking out the fire. His magic touched me before he did. Urgent, as if it couldn't resist.

'It's starting to bruise.' His fingers traced the mark on my flesh, the cool authoritative brush leaving gooseflesh in its wake. 'Does it hurt?'

No, I should have answered, but I was struggling to pull in a settled breath. I definitely felt *something* as his fingers traced my collarbone – and it wasn't pain.

'Kat?' He frowned.

Then I think I surprised both of us as my fingers curled into his shirt. The other sinking into his damp hair as I kissed him. His hands falling to my hips. Dragging me closer on instinct.

The strength of his arms came around me, gathering me closer but I could feel his hesitation. So I slipped my hand beneath his damp shirt, fingers dragging over the hard contours of his chest. Nails biting into the hard plains of his abdomen where the Countess had touched him.

'Croinn.' There was a dangerous edge to that word as his hands captured my face. Despite the softness of his breath as those eyes looked at me, stormy with indecision. A thousand thoughts flicking across his expression.

He remained so still and cautious. 'I'm a curse, Kat.'

Such absolute certainty pressed between those quiet words made my heart ache.

He wasn't a curse. Not to me. And he needed to know that there was nowhere else for me but here with him. No matter what he became or how that darkness called to him.

So I pressed my lips against the scars on his cheek.

'My father created that malice out of devotion to my mother.' I brushed those words against the curve of his jaw, my fingers making quick work of his shirt buttons so I could lay my palm over his mark. 'That vengeance is *nothing* compared to what I'd do for you, Emrys.'

His hand at my hip got fractionally tighter, his gaze heated as that darkness danced beneath his flesh. Yet, he still didn't move.

I was done waiting. Done with not claiming the things I wanted.

'Maybe I should remind you why Kysillians are formidable opponents, my lord.' I understood now. The power I held when it came to him. How restless his magic was in my presence, how curiously it rushed over my skin.

I stepped back the barest inch out of his reach and tugged the shirt over my head. Letting it fall from my fingers to pool at my feet, I bared myself to him completely. Watching how his hands curled into fists at his side. Shadows weaving between his knuckles, wishing to touch me too.

I took his fist in my hand, that darkness wrapping like a caress around my wrist as I eased his palm flat. Running my thumb down his arch. Seeing that magic shift beneath his skin. Alert to my presence. I laid a gentle kiss there. Feeling the cool bite of his summoning against my lips.

I stepped closer until my naked chest barely brushed against his. He was so still I wasn't certain he was breathing as I guided his hand around me to press against the bare skin of my waist. Sliding it right over the scarring at my back.

The pitch-black depths of his gaze awoke something within me. The rage I'd felt tear the Council chamber apart like a dark storm. The ruthlessness of it that had found me beneath Fairfax. Desire coiled tighter in my abdomen at the memory. At the brutality of him, of the things he'd do for me.

I left his hand there, tracing my finger up his chest, pressing a kiss to that mark over his heart.

'*Eria.*' I laid that word there. *My love.* The sacred word he'd given me first.

Then his fingers curled into my damp hair, so he could tip my head back, and his lips brushed my cheek.

'Croinn.' The plea left him darkly, another warning, but I brushed my answering smile against his lips.

'You burn, I burn, Emrys.' I gave that promise back to him. Even if the darkness consumed him as my flame had me. I wouldn't leave him. Even to the monster he believed himself to be.

Then something changed. His hand against my scarred flesh became firmer, pressing me closer as his other cupped my jaw. Thumb tracing the curve of my cheek.

'I could hear them in my head in that pit. In that endless dark. It offered me anything to submit.' His voice was suddenly hoarse as if raw from the pain of that memory. Eyes solemn grey.

I gave the barest shake of my head. 'You didn't.'

'I don't want anything but you, Kat.' The words came in surrender as he ducked his head, his mouth the barest inch from my own. 'I've never wanted anything the way I want you.'

I love you. I wanted to say, but he kissed me. Deep and claiming. I arched myself closer in answer, revelling in my victory. How my hands slid so greedily into his hair. How closely he held me, as if fearful the air itself would come between us. How ravenously my fingers dug into the muscles of his back. Wanting to touch every inch of him. Crazed with the feeling of his skin against my own.

My magic flared and bit where his curled and stroked so teasingly.

His kiss was ruthless and my knees went weak in surrender to it.

'What do you want?' he whispered wickedly against the curve of my throat as I gasped for breath. The same way he had when we'd been tangled like this before.

'You,' I answered, as I always would.

Then I found myself on the scattering of blankets and pillows by the fire. I raised myself on my elbows, breathing unsteadily as I looked down at my body where he suddenly knelt. Right between my legs. My cheeks burnt, my heart racing as he crawled over me. His lips running a torturous trail up my bare stomach.

'Emrys,' I whimpered, but he was clearly done with talking. The only answer to my plea was his wicked smile before his clever fingers pulled at the lacings of my trousers.

I arched my hips in answer as he expertly pulled my leathers away, only to capture my calf and lay a kiss on the inside of my knee, that hungry gaze never leaving my own.

'You're being wicked,' I gasped, flushed at just how exposed I was but unable to find any shame. Not here as the firelight played over his skin.

'It's in my nature, Croinn.' He stroked those words against my thigh before stilling. His thumb dragged over that small raised scar across the delicate skin. Still pink from the forsaken

349

iron from that demonic pit beneath Fairfax. Taking longer to heal.

The wound he'd healed. He went so still at the sight of it I feared he'd withdraw. Only for those dark eyes to meet my own, burning with more emotion than just simply desire.

'I've never prayed for anything. Knowing no blessed ancestors could be watching over a creature like me, but I prayed that night.' His voice filled with such agony. 'I told them I'd give them anything they wanted in return for you.'

My heart dropped within my chest at the weight of his words. Of what it meant. Bargains for life were the most dangerous of all.

'You shouldn't have done that.' I sat up, shaking my head, but he smiled, cupping my face so gently between his palms.

'Then I understood. Perhaps I am the darkness they fear. Because given the choice of this world or you, I'd always choose you, Kat.'

A promise. So steadfast, so certain, that everything suddenly felt safe. A comforting calmness consumed my soul, my magic nestling quietly behind my ribs as his own brushed my skin. Cool enough to raise gooseflesh as it demanded my attention, longing for it as keenly as its master.

He ducked closer, his smile brushing the flushed skin of my cheek as my fingers curled over his broad shoulders. 'Without a thought. I'll always choose you.'

Even if it meant the world.

Verr were devout in their loyalty. Viciously so. That warning whispered through my mind. It should have scared me but I kissed him instead. Deep and demanding. Not caring for anything but him. Not wanting anything but this.

His grip tightened on my waist to drag me closer as his other hand slipped between my thighs. Torturously gentle.

Approval rumbling through his chest at the wetness he found there. At how wildly it undid me. Feeling the teasing desire-filled bite of his magic over my abdomen and breasts, making me arch into the warmth of his skin.

'Say it again,' he commanded against the shell of my ear.

'*Eria*,' I gasped and he rewarded me with a kiss. Slow and torturous. Devouring me as I parted my lips, wanting more, and his tongue claimed everything else, and in that wildness two fingers slipped inside. Curling wickedly as he began those teasing stokes.

My stuttered breath broke the kiss, holding onto the solid firmness of his shoulders as his lips slipped down to my jaw. My head fell back at the ecstasy of his play, as his lips continued their torment down between my breasts.

I fell back against the cushions, arching my hips, wanting more of him as his tongue dragged over my hipbone before his teeth gave a wicked bite. Making me moan, unable to bear it. His fingers curling expertly as his thumb manipulated my sensitive nerves. Too breathless to beg, but I didn't need to. The mere sight of me seemed to shatter the rest of Emrys's control as those teasing kisses moved between my legs.

Then he feasted.

A choked, strangled sound escaped me. Unable to comprehend how good it felt. The memory of it felt like a disservice. Seeing the strong line of his shoulders, the movement of his muscles as he worshipped me. My hands curled helplessly into his damp hair.

Then his fingers continued their torment and all I could do was writhe and gasp. His other hand at my backside, fingers digging commandingly into the flesh to keep me in place. Firmly committed to the task.

Then it came, a soft fluttering that built until my back arched, my toes curling into the blankets beneath me. A delirious tightening in every muscle, making his name escape my lips like some devout prayer. He didn't let me go right away, content to drag it out of me, until I was limp and trembling in the aftermath.

He caressed my thighs, watching my breathlessness with fiendish delight as he made his way up my body, fingertips barely brushing my breast as if to feel the unsteadiness of my breath.

'Fucking beautiful.' He kissed me, all that wickedness on his lips. My hands ran down the hard plains of his chest, nails biting in as they dragged around his waist, wanting him closer. Only for the friction of his leathers across my oversensitive skin to make me pull back.

'You're wearing too many clothes,' I whispered, pushing the shirt from his shoulders before my shaking fingers curled into the waistband of his leathers.

I expected protest, for his darker thoughts to consume him. But he reached between us to undo one button, careful and patient as I undid the last two. Then together we got rid of them. Something so intimate and patient about it. As if nothing else existed but us and the shadows we cast in the firelight. The heavy fall of his boots on the wooden floor, but it was the sight of him that undid me. The curve of his muscles and the line of those scars. The map they made across his body. The imposing form of him.

Mine.

Such a strange primitive thought. I'd seen images of naked men before, in journals or tomes. This was different. I didn't think there was a record of anything as magnificent as Emrys.

I pushed up onto my elbows as he braced his weight on his hands over me, so I could feel the brush of his breath at the curve of my throat.

I ran my fingers from the scars over his ribs, down his side, curving back over his hip and then to the powerful muscle of his thigh. How deep those marks were there, still pink as if they'd been made months ago, not years.

The guttural sound of a breathless curse leaving him as if the barest brush of my touch was enough to undo him. Then I let my hand move to the imposing length of him. Firm and warm in my grasp. Ready.

'Kat.' His hips moved towards my touch, out of instinct. I stroked him once. Exploring him with quiet curiosity.

'Like this?' My voice was the barest whisper, watching how he urged into my touch, wanting more from me. How all the imposing power of him was mine to control for that moment. Then I knew a different hunger. How I wanted him to fall apart too from nothing but my touch. Wanted to relish in making it happen. To hear my name from his lips.

He brought his hand over mine, curling my fingers more tightly, making the movement firmer. A curse leaving his lips, his eyes closing as other darker words tumbled almost incoherently against the curve of my throat.

Verr tongue.

'What are you saying?' I asked, impishly. Intent on driving him to madness.

'It isn't for a lady's ears,' he half cursed, pulling my earlobe between his teeth and I couldn't help but laugh at his helplessness as those black eyes looked down at me darkly. As if my mirth was the most seductive thing of all.

'I'm not a lady,' I corrected. He gave me a secretive glance, eyes crystalline with some private amusement before he ducked to kiss me again. Deeply so I couldn't offer any further protests.

His hand left my own to its work, only for his fingers to curl into the hair at the nape of my neck, gently tugging it so my head fell back and he had full access to my mouth.

My slow steady strokes not stopping – just as he'd shown me, drawing sounds from him that he pressed against my lips. Making him curse and groan.

I could have tormented him all night, but the burning insistence between my thighs was almost a complaint at being ignored. Then I understood. He would have just been content with this. Content with what I wanted. Only I wanted all of him.

'I need you.' Needed him like I needed nothing else. Wanted him like I wanted nothing else. He considered me, as if seeking the lie in my words.

I let him slip from my grasp. Unknowing what to do with my hand as I let it slide across my middle, gently dragging it over my breast as I settled back amongst the cushions, let my legs fall wider. His hungry gaze watching every movement. Making me wonder what would happen if I used that hand on myself while he knelt there to watch.

Such devious thoughts – and I had no Verr blood in me to blame it on.

As if sensing every single desire in me, Emrys bowed his head forward, kissing the valley between my breasts, seeming to drag in my scent. He drank in the sight of me, completely undone by nothing but him.

'*Ala Eria.*' He pressed those words into a kiss over my heart, one hand at my waist to bring me closer as my arms curved over his shoulder.

He positioned himself, the head a firm pressure that slipped in the wetness. Making me curve my hips towards it. Needing more. He gently took hold of my hip, keeping me still. Jaw tense as if that restraint was costing him everything but he'd do it for me.

Yet with each small movement I urged him on. It was a pleasure tinged with the unknown pain. I didn't know what to do. To arch closer or remain still. Too many feelings bubbling insistently beneath my skin. I grabbed his shoulders, breath stuttered with my helplessness.

'Fuck,' he whispered against my neck as he moved another inch deeper. So helplessly I had to laugh. It felt like a strange thing to do. How the motion made me feel every way we were connected.

It was something natural. Unbidden as I slid my knees up to cage either side of him, to let my hips fall wider in invitation. Wanted more of his weight on me, more of that fullness.

'Kat,' he half begged.

He was holding back.

'All of you,' I commanded, despite the strange foreignness of the sensation. Letting my hand drag down to his hip, to his backside. Fingers digging in. Letting my magic bite in warning. Another deeper slide that sent a wave of pleasure through me, made my head fall back on the pillows, made me move helplessly. Unable to keep still, my body knowing what it wanted. Unbidden.

I raised my hips to meet his next gentle, testing thrust. My fingers dancing along his side. Making a shiver run through him. His hand hooked at my knee, bending my leg and bringing it higher so each stroke was commanding and deep.

A new sensation washed over me, stealing all competent thought. Only he was still hesitant, tender as if he'd break me. Too slow. Not deep enough. Making me want to writhe and bite. To trap him like some wild thing in heat.

A feral urge consumed me and I used my Kysillian strength to roll him onto his back. Hands braced on his chest as he

355

landed on the blankets. I gasped at the depth, at the burn of possessing him but it was a madness and I needed more.

'Kat,' he swore, hands digging into my backside, trying to lift me as if to give me some relief, but I didn't want it. I trapped his hips between my thighs, feeling the dig of his fingers into the soft skin of my backside. Looking down at him. At us, how it was a pleasure all its own.

Then I understood what Alma meant about her heats. About the things she'd do in the Institute stables with the delivery boy or in the back cupboards with the maids. She needed it and I'd never understood until now.

That I needed Emrys. Needed to be consumed and undone just like this. As I set a clumsy pace, relishing in the delicious, strange pain of it. My head falling back, wanton sounds, half moaned, escaped me as my teeth bit into my lip. My fingers digging into the hard muscle of his chest, greedy for something I didn't fully understand.

As always, Emrys understood. Understood that fierceness in me and didn't shy from it.

He sat up, making me whimper. His hands curling into my hair as he claimed all those sounds from my lips. As my thighs burnt and I forced myself further into the ecstasy of possessing him. My nails digging into him, biting his lip. Primitively wanting marks on him.

'Fucking beautiful.' His lips ran up the line of my throat, as the roughness of his words brushed my skin, his grip on my backside firmer, commanding in his pace. Whispering his devotion, and I turned my head to claim his words, to drink each one from his lips.

Wanting to taste it as I saw the burning lavender of my eyes reflected in the endless dark of his own. My neck arching back so his lips could find my pulse. To taste the passion of it before he rested his forehead there, so I could feel the harsh labour of his breath brush my breast as more of those dark words fell from his lips in some form of adoration.

'Emrys,' I half begged and, as if knowing every inch of my body, his hand slid between us. Right to where I needed. The cold bite of his magic demanding my pleasure from me.

Everything in me seemed to tense, seizing as my nails dug deep into his shoulder and back. My breath caught as ecstasy rushed through me. My body too tight and tense and loose all at the same time. Emrys felt it. A curse slipping helplessly from his lips was my undoing as he watched every inch of me devour that pleasure he'd given.

Then I was on my back. He didn't stop, drawing it out of me. My fingers digging greedily into the powerful contours of his back.

I was done and yet, I still urged my hips up for him. Still offered myself to more of that pleasure. Wanton, just as the stories said, and I didn't care. Not here.

Such dark and unknown words he whispered against my lips. Yet I knew all of them were nothing but complete devotion as I panted for breath, waves of it still remaining. As he took his fill of me until his own breaths were shuttered against my breastbone with his release. My fingers curling in his damp hair as I struggled to catch my breath.

'You'll be the death of me.' He huffed those words against the curve of my breast.

I smiled deviously at the victory of it despite how spent I was. How breathless. Fingers running across his lips. 'My poor lord.'

'Yours,' he offered darkly, nipping at my fingers, and perhaps it was the Kysillian in me that preened at the battle won.

'Mine,' I answered and he kissed me again.

His finger traced the curve of my ear and the pointed tip as I found myself wrapped in his strong arms, my legs tangled with his own, as the exhausting weight of everything finally caught up with me. As I tucked my face against the curve of his neck and dragged in that forbidden scent of him. Felt the racing of his pulse settle along with my own.

His fingers moved through my hair, so gently. Combing through all the tangles I was certain he'd made.

His lips traced the arc of my shoulder to my throat, right over the scar caused by the galmoth's bite with such soft reverence that emotion clogged in my throat and his knuckles dragged up the curve of my thigh. Over the skin of my backside and to my waist. Right over the scarred skin of my back.

Every inch of me. He wanted every piece. Even marked and forbidden.

I tipped my head to see him. It was different now. In the aftermath of everything.

How his dark hair fell onto his brow, the softness of his satisfied smile, the transparent silver of his eyes as he took me in.

I eyed the red marks on his forearms, the indentation of my teeth and nails in his shoulder. How in disarray he was. Then I realised I didn't fully understand my own strength.

'I didn't mean to hurt you.' My sanity returned as my desire cooled.

His laugh was choked. Something so content in his smile. 'You drove me to madness, Ciuinn, but you didn't hurt me.'

I bit my lip, wondering if he was trying to spare me the embarrassment. I'd pinned him to the floor and had my way with him. The soreness between my legs evidence of it. 'It wasn't very . . . *demure*.'

No. I hadn't lain shyly as the Institute girls whispered that you should. The stories of wanton fey coming to haunt me.

As if sensing that flicker of shame, Emrys caught my chin. The sheer size of him caged over me in a moment, such protective focus, as if he didn't wish for me to miss a single word.

'Watching you demand your pleasure is the most beautiful thing I've ever seen, Kat.' He smiled, so satisfied and boyish it made my heart flip within my chest.

He kissed my hair, his fingers running through it. Spent and relaxed in his arms, my palm still resting over the mark over his heart, as I drifted to sleep. Only two words found me in my slumber.

Serus.

Mine.

Chapter Thirty

Kat

Never take their beliefs as your own, Tauria. Not until you see with your own eyes where it could lead you.

Even Kysillia's stories can be twisted for them to gain power from your ignorance. In that devout blindness, you lose something you can never get back . . . your morality.

Serus? A small strange voice called through my dreams. Icy pinpricks against my flesh chased me from my strange dreams. Waking me to find myself still curled in a collection of pillows, soft dawn light illuminating the specks of dust that danced through the old room.

Confused about where I was.

Then I saw the broad expanse of Emrys's back as he sat up, hands in his hair, a slight tremor making the muscles twitch. The pale slashes of scarring across the taut muscle I hadn't noticed before. How that darkness slipped and danced around them across his flesh.

I gathered the blanket to my front. Yet as I touched him, I could have sworn I heard a small curious voice whisper in the back of my mind. *Serus?*

Almost beckoning.

'Emrys.' Those tremors subsided under my touch but he remained so still.

'He's doing something.' The words were harsh from his lips with an unsteady breath.

Montagor. Dread churned in my stomach as I leant closer, letting my hand rest at the nape of his neck. 'You can hear him?'

His head made the barest twitch as if he wished to shake it. 'It's something else. Like a strange shadow in the corner of my mind. Something waiting.'

I moved closer. Pressing myself against the trembling might of him. 'Has it always been like this?'

'Once,' he swallowed painfully, eyes closing as his dark fingers rubbed at his temple as if it pained him. 'Nine years ago. Something changed. Even the bark couldn't keep it at bay.'

He finally turned to see me, those eyes nothing but darkness. 'Then Montagor came back.'

'Came from where?' I frowned, letting my hand cup his cheek in the small comfort I could offer him.

'He was confined to a saints' house in the south from when he was a boy,' Emrys answered, a dark expression taking hold of his features. 'He killed two governesses as a child and began to demonstrate . . . distressing behaviours. Father said the lords suspected it was a result of the summoning that created him, something . . . wrong with the blood mix.'

My frown deepened. 'What about the wars?'

'Montagor didn't serve in the wars,' he answered, making me jolt with surprise.

'His records are in – *were in* – the Institute halls,' I countered. I'd read them. The glossy stories of victory over the dark, which didn't make sense when compared to the unhinged cruelty of the man. Why he'd ever turn on the King only to emulate him.

Emrys huffed out an unamused laugh, jaw tight with disgust. 'A fabrication to get him a place on the Council. He was crazed. Inhuman. Then nine years ago when I felt something . . . he appeared in the Council chambers soon after with his new title. Unaffected and devout to serve.'

I didn't miss Emrys's slight flinch or the tension in his body. The prickling of his magic against my skin, as if reaching out for comfort. I slid my hand into his own where it had fallen into his lap as if with defeat.

'I thought someone had broken a seal. Only nothing followed. Just this . . .' A strange dark shame burnt in those eyes before he broke my gaze, looking to the dim sunrise through grimy windows. 'Something . . . something felt wrong. Yet, the sensation left as quickly as it arrived.'

There was no hiding his pain, nor how that darkness moved across his knuckles as his grip on my hand became tighter.

Something had changed in Montagor and whatever existed in Emrys had sensed it.

'A summoning?' I frowned. What kind of summoning could ease his madness. Or at least have given it a new direction?

Nine years ago Elysior was at peace, or supposed to be. How would a dark summoning have happened? If Montagor had a relic all this time . . . why wait until now to use it? No. He must have only just found it; only just been given the urge he needed with Fairfax's obsession with that seal.

'You think he felt it too?' I asked. That it drew Montagor back to some semblance of mortal sanity.

Emrys nodded, turning more to see me. 'I think it made Varin take notice. Made him wish to seek power. To return.'

Varin. One of the princes from beneath.

'Do you think there are others?' Other Old Gods given mortal form? Yet if there were, why didn't they seek power and violence as Montagor did? Were they as peaceful as the other Verr Emrys had found? As Emrys himself?

Acarus, Duar, Than and Orus. The Old Gods' names tumbled through my thoughts, then of course Acara, the seer – sister of Serus.

'None from the King after Montagor, Blackthorn made certain of that. I don't know how anyone else could attempt it without me sensing it. Even with the bark.' His words were quiet, shamed. When those eyes lifted to my own they were a solemn grey. 'I wasn't myself. Gideon put up with me for a few years but I don't think either of us were ever the same after the war. We went as brothers with a family to defend and we came back . . . something else.'

He broke my gaze, turning to see where the dawn light seeped through the windows.

'We were rats fighting in a trap. He didn't forgive me for saving him. Didn't forgive himself for not saving Emmaline.'

He ran his palm down his face, trying to pull in a steady breath as his head fell in defeat. 'I wish I wasn't like this.'

'I don't.' I brushed my fingers across his jaw. Watching that magic weakly ripple beneath. Those now dark eyes met my own. 'There is a lie here somewhere, Emrys. This darkness isn't what they said it would be.'

No. There was a feeling in that darkness and in that pit I couldn't shake off. Not evil or consuming. Just desperation. Fear that I'd mistaken for my own.

He shook his head ever so slightly but I saw his hesitation. 'They killed it for a reason.'

'They'd kill me too,' I answered, watching those dark eyes come back to me. The magic rippling across his skin in threat at the mere mention of that truth.

The stories had to be wrong, because how could such evil darkness make something as wonderful as him?

'They can be wrong,' I played with the hair at the nape of his neck, seeing the swirls of silver in his gaze. 'They have to be wrong.'

Had to because there was nothing wrong about the man in my arms. Nothing wicked or strange.

'None of it makes any sense.' Verr couldn't be cursed. Couldn't be so hateful if they remained above. If they were beings just trying to survive, and their presence had done nothing to corrupt those seals. It was mortal men who had. Mortal men who had hungered and sought to awaken the Old Gods. 'I know deep down you believe that too.'

He'd seen. Other Verr. He'd been searching for that very reason.

His forehead pressed against my own as he dragged in a deep breath.

'I'm scared of what I'll become.' Those words were too soft from his lips. Too hopeless.

'I'm not.' I pressed a kiss to his shoulder, his fingers curling into my hair to hold me. I should have felt relief, only the depths of how he cared, of how much I loved him made something else bloom inside of me. Childish, desperate fear. How easily things could be taken away.

A wild, deep sadness suddenly clawed at my ribs.

'My only fear is that they'll take you away,' I whispered into the barest inches between us. The words broke apart, small fragile things I was too scared to hold. 'That they'll take it all away.'

To be left with nothing but the pain of it. To be lost once more. I didn't think I'd survive losing him, not as I'd survived losing everything else.

His lips brushed my brow, gentle in his reassurance before ducking to the shell of my ear. 'There is nowhere I could wander where I wouldn't find my way back to you, Kat. In this life or the next.'

I wrapped my arms around him, perhaps desperately.

'Promise?' I demanded softly, feeling the sheer strength of him as he held me just as tightly as I held him.

He took my hand from around his side, interlocked our fingers and slid it up to that cursed scar over his heart. The crescent moon. The mark of Serus. 'I swear it on my mark, Tauria.'

A dangerous promise tangled with his very being, sealed with my true name.

Unbreakable.

My fears quelled as he fell into the cushions and pulled me to lie on him. As I pressed myself against his chest, feeling the steady beat of his heart against my cheek. The reassuring curl of his magic around my limbs as if it wanted me closer. Knowing how such promises could be broken so easily. Knowing the depth of my parents' devotion to each other, yet seeing how horribly it all ended.

Only that wasn't the point. Emrys gave me his devotion anyway.

Chapter Thirty-One
Alma

Be blessed she sees value in you, little rat.
  For what other use do you have?

None. I tossed and turned with that answer on my lips. A foul taste coating the inside of my mouth. I couldn't sleep with the absence of my beasts. For so long I'd hated them. Hated all the awful things they'd brought into my life. How they'd given me nothing but this pain, yet now I missed them horribly. Felt too vulnerable. Too soft and small in their absence.

Despite the sun only barely threatening to rise, I went downstairs. Needed something to do. Needed to forget. I pulled on a stern navy dress the house produced for me, long having abandoned the maid's attire I'd hidden in for so long. The stiff fabric against my skin gave me some control. How easily I could hide everything behind the tight lacings and pleats.

Nobody could see. And if they couldn't see . . . it never happened.

I rubbed at my fingertips, still wrinkled from the bath. How long I'd hidden in the murky water. Only getting out for the house to make me another. The only mothering I'd allow it to do for me. Anything to chase away the emptiness inside me.

That sensation of falling didn't leave me. The lurching of my stomach unsettling me, how quickly I could be disarmed.

A clatter and grumbled curse came from one of the rooms off the hall as I reached the bottom of the stairs. The entrance hall was made of grand pointed arches, the wood darker and the carpet a deep red underfoot. Reminding me of the blood smeared on my thigh, the splatter of the hunters . . . but mostly how Thean had drunk from a vial of it and how rosy the blood had made their lips.

Another bang and curse reached my ear, pulling me thankfully from stupid thoughts and drawing me into the study to see Gideon at his desk. Shirt rumpled and rolled to his elbows. Hair in disarray where he'd been tugging at it.

'Do you sleep?' I accused. More annoyed perhaps that I'd somehow found company when I wanted to be alone. Or that I'd allowed my thoughts to wander to the voyav once more; they'd left and even the sting of that rejection didn't stir the beasts within.

'I could ask you the same.' Gideon pulled off his spectacles, rubbing the bridge of his nose. 'How are your wounds?'

'Fully healed.' I clutched my forearms, uncomfortable with his concern but Gideon was a healer. It was in his nature to care – even if he apparently loathed it.

He released a sigh, dropping his spectacles onto the pile of papers before him. 'The voyav is being useful again then.'

His features tightened, clearly he didn't appreciate that we'd owe Thean anything.

'You don't trust them.' It wasn't a question. Only Gideon's mistrust of Thean seemed defensive more than anything else. Fearful of their unpredictability perhaps. Especially around those he cared for, I knew the protectiveness of biting first better than anyone else.

'I don't trust the secrets they keep,' he added dryly and I couldn't fault his reasoning as he opened the drawer and held out a small paper packet to me. 'Here. The verium should be almost burnt out of your system but this will get rid of the rest.'

He'd spoken to me about it last night. A gentle knock on my door that I'd answered with bared teeth. I'd made him agree not to tell William, Emrys or Kat. He'd allow the deception on the grounds I took a tonic he produced, accepting my privacy before he left.

I should have rejected his help now. My beasts would come back, they always did. Yet childish fear curled around my ribs. The fear they wouldn't, that I'd be left to face my mistakes alone. I took the packet, opening it to see a pale shimmering powder inside. The stench making me wince even without my more primal instincts.

'It tastes like bad bog weed, so best to get it down in one,' he offered unhelpfully scribbling something down in a notebook.

I tipped the packet to my lips, aiming for the back of my throat. Swallowing it quickly with a wince. 'You're familiar with verium?'

'I've been shot enough times with a dart. Got an awful scar on my arse to prove it.' He rose, making an attempt to tidy the mess before him. 'The last Mage King had an obsession with using them on the battlefield.'

Then I noticed Gideon was still in his leathers. Smeared with dust and dirt from what had happened in the Greymark house. An imposing form, much like his brother – the only thing they shared perhaps. That golden hair catching the light was too perfect. I supposed he was handsome. He was a creature I might have entertained in the Institute stables or storage cupboards when I was bored – anything to pass the time. To quell the darker thoughts in my mind. To feed the restless hunger of my beasts to have a reward.

Only, the healer sparked nothing in me now. Not even for me to try and shame myself as I had before, to destroy something in me just to distract myself from the hollow ache of my own relentless misery.

Something had changed in me and I didn't know how to feel. A tightness to my chest as if I'd outgrown my bones. My agitated focus roamed against my will around the cluttered study, with its decorative arches and endless shelves with carvings of creatures from Elysior. Creatures I was desperate to become again.

I hadn't seen the voyav. Told myself I didn't want to. Didn't want to be reminded of how much I'd needed them. What their care had meant to me. Unable to find what they could have gained from the exchange.

How foolishly vulnerable I'd been. Telling them things I should have kept between my teeth.

They'd left. That was the only thing that mattered.

A croaked growl came from Emrys's desk. Turning me to see the bastard fiend sitting there in its cage. Its head tilting in consideration. Its small wyvern-like form not distracting me from its deadly nature.

It'd tried to kill Kat. The thought made me bare my stupid mortal teeth.

Only then my anger faltered. If she'd never been foolish enough to become entangled with that book . . . we wouldn't have found our way here. Wouldn't have learnt the truth. Wouldn't have seen things as they actually were.

'Why is that thing up here?' I rubbed my temple, wishing to feel the hard press of my scales.

369

I should have made the house take the creature away, only it was clear I'd take anything to escape the hollowness lingering inside of me. I spread my fingers, tensing them, waiting for the flash of scales but it didn't come. As the weak morning light spilled across my too-mortal flesh.

'The house keeps bringing it up.' Gideon came to stand next to me, hands braced on his hips, lips pursed with thought. 'I thought it was just getting amusement out of scaring William.'

'Maybe the house wants it gone,' I offered. Wondering why Emrys had kept the little monstrosity at all. Maybe as some strange trophy.

Gideon seemed to chew over the idea before tugging at his hair again and it was a wonder he had any left. 'The house should be more worried about that cursed bastard book.'

Those words made me turn back to his desk. To the navy tome sat amongst the papers.

My nose twitched, the barest of my instincts coming back. 'It didn't smell like the others. I don't think there is a fiend inside it.'

No, the strange archaic rot had been missing from that tome when Kat had pulled it free. It hadn't made my beasts recoil. Just the faint old ink, dried lavender, clove and a strangely familiar smoky scent I usually only found in Kat's presence.

'What about the pages from the coffin? The diary?' I scraped my teeth over my tongue, suddenly overcome with the horrid taste of decay, remembering rooting through those remains in bird form.

'Nothing but fucking madness about the Alder Kings and seeking something beneath.' He moved back to his desk, the scent of charred wood and apple tea reaching my nose. The scent I had associated with the witch upon first meeting – once the ale and poppy smoke scent had faded. At least my senses were returning.

'Beneath what?' I frowned.

He shook his head, holding out the page to me. I took it, even though I couldn't fully read it. My eyes making the words blur and shift. Then I turned it over, to what I assumed was the last entry in the diary.

Tell him. Beneath. Beneath. They sleep but they can be found. Beneath.

Gideon moved back to his desk, turning over the other scraps of half rotted pages. His scrawled notes next to them where he'd been poring over them most of the night. Muttering to himself as if he could have missed something.

Giving me the opportunity to glance in the direction of where the Portium door was hidden behind the bookcases. Worried how silent it was. How still the house was, too – not up to its usual mischief – as if it was holding its breath.

'I wouldn't worry. Emrys knows the safe house portals better than anyone,' Gideon offered reluctantly, as if the last thing he wished to do was comfort anyone.

I couldn't help the amused huff of breath that left me. Of course, Emrys did. Crafty cursed bastard that he was. However, I thought Gideon needed to reassure himself more than he needed to assure me.

I had to find some positives in all this mess. We might not have the book open, but at least it wasn't in Montagor's hands. We might not know what the monster was after, but at least we'd stopped him gaining this advantage.

Then the study door began to rattle on its hinges, perhaps reminding me too much of that horrid Greymark house. The evil that lurked there. Wondering how such a place could have created anyone who was linked to Kat.

Then I heard the soft voices, the familiar deep tone of Emrys.

I moved around the cluttered mess of the study and into the hall. Seeing it bathed in the weak dawn light, multi-coloured from where rays seeped through the stained glass the house had made the ceiling out of today. Depicting wrywings and griffins in flight.

Kat was in her leathers, her hair unbound, face turned to look up at Emrys. In some deep conversation, their fingers intertwined. Almost unable to let each other go. She was also strangely missing her boots.

'Where have you been?' I asked, slightly appalled at her relaxed ease. Especially after how we'd parted last night. The panic I'd smelt rising from her flesh that I couldn't sense now.

Kat jolted, turning to me. Her strange golden-hued skin flushed pink, making the freckles across the bridge of her nose stand out. Lavender eyes wide as her lips parted, not speaking but somehow telling me everything I didn't necessarily want to know. I suppose I should thank the ancestors I'd lost my sense of smell.

'A safe house. The portal stone ran out somewhere in the west fields,' Emrys replied, saving my dear friend from her own incriminating embarrassment as he pulled her down the hall.

'Bloody saints. Locked in a safe house all night.' William appeared in the hallway, running a hand through his curls as if he'd been summoned by their return too. 'Good job it let you out.'

'Yes, William, I'm certain it was *quite* harrowing for them,' Gideon replied dryly from where he'd come to lounge in the doorway behind me. Unimpressed. 'Now you're back from your *escapades* . . . how do we get this fucking book open?'

I expected the interest from Kat, or her eagerness to get started on the cursed thing. Instead, I felt the gentleness of her touch as she took my arm. That warm bite from her magic as if it was concerned. The deep worry marring her features. So reminiscent of the first night we'd met.

'Are you all right?' She pressed the back of her hand against my forehead.

'I'm fine.' I pulled back, shame wounding deeply inside of me. Of course she saw everything – even the things I wished to hide – because she cared.

I didn't want her to be distracted by me. By how weak I'd become. How useless.

'You look . . . *different*.' Her lavender eyes roamed across my features unable to place what was wrong. I saw her own fear there, as if she could see that pain in me. As she tried to understand it just as she always had.

'That happens when a being gets shot out of the sky,' came the annoyed sharp voice of Thean. Turning me to see the voyav where they had apperated against the wood panelling of the hallway in female form, amber eyes hard with annoyance and focused on me before they moved to Kat.

Of course the bastard would choose now to turn up.

'What?' Kat demanded, her voice hoarse as if she'd been struck by the words.

'It was nothing,' I snapped, wishing there could be a ferocious growl building in my throat but there was nothing. Hating the pain in her eyes, the horror and shadow of her guilt. As if any of it was her fault.

'With a verium dart,' Thean continued, unbothered. Producing the offending item from their jacket pocket with a flourish. The silver dart. I didn't see them pick it up. They must have gone back for it, but why?

Only Thean Page wasn't quite finished ruining my day.

'Not to mention the hunters that caught her. Who knows what would have happened if I hadn't turned up?'

'No.' Kat's voice was nothing but a whisper. Her eyes filled with horrid sorrow as they took me in. 'Alma – I didn't—'

'I told you not to say anything,' Gideon bit out, glaring at the voyav as he snatched the dart from Thean's grip.

'Alma. You didn't say it was *hunters*.' William looked stricken, his freckled skin pale. Blackthorn was considering me with those serious grey eyes where he'd come to stand behind Kat, focusing on the dark circles I knew were beneath my eyes.

Evidence of everything I couldn't hide. Not without the creatures I longed to become.

Too many people watching. Too much concern. Panic and shame coiled inside of me. Twisting into a painful rage. Turning me on Thean with clenched fists. The burning sensation of my claws manifesting. That wildness in my blood unfurling from its slumber.

'Trust me. I'd manage those hunters fine on my own,' I leered. Feeling the sharp point of the barest fang in my mouth, the ghostly pinch of tightening skin at my cheek. The faintest hint of my magic coming back.

'You don't need to prove that to *me*, darling,' they smiled wickedly, those hard amber eyes tracing my features before they softened slightly.

No. I needed to prove it to myself. It was me who had panicked. Me who had let those hunters catch me. A horrid growl rumbled in my chest, slipping easily up through my clenched teeth.

The voyav leant closer, that smile never diminishing. 'There she is.'

It was then I realised I was seeing them through my feline eyes, and that it was claws that bit into my palms. How I'd found my way back to my magic. Incensed the voyav had something to do with it.

Bastard.

'Alma?' Kat asked again, but I stormed past them all and into the study, unable to bear another moment of their proximity. I didn't deserve all of their worry. Thankfully, the house had materialised a tea set on Kat's desk. I busied myself with pouring all the cups. 'Never mind me, we need to work out how to open the book.'

'Why were hunters at the Grey house?' William asked. The question halting the cup halfway to my lips. I turned, seeing Kat the closest. Her confused expression mirroring my own as we both turned to William.

I shook my head. 'They weren't—'

'Alma was over the bordering lands. Weymouth lands,' Thean answered effortlessly from where they lounged in the doorway as if we were all an inconvenience. As if they had turned up for nothing more than to cause trouble. To piss me off.

'Hang on . . .' William held up his palms. 'Did you say Weymouth?'

Although he didn't need an answer as the boy moved to one of the sideboards, ignoring us as he picked up one of the maps and held it open between our gathering. 'Lord Weymouth died in the third uprising three centuries ago. His lands were claimed by the fey and the Council never sought to take them back because of the ancient fey ruins there. The Mouv Settlement was formed shortly after. It's also on the boundary of rebel territory.

Mouv. A fey settlement built on ancient ruins. A place Montagor suddenly had interest in; enough to send his men. Enough to rile up the Countess.

'We need to go,' Kat said, a flare of lavender at her fingertips. She knew what Montagor's men would do. What men like him were capable of in such rural settlements. We both did.

375

'We're not bloody taking everyone,' Gideon snapped, his finger pointed at Emrys before moving it to the rest of us. 'They can stay here.'

'Make me,' I hissed, feeling the sting of my fangs as they slid through my gums. Something writhed inside of me. A wildness that wanted to take flight. To claw and bite.

A horrid whining growl came from the corner of the room, making my ear twitch and unease ripple down my spine as I looked towards the table where the cage sat with the dark fiend curled up at its centre. Glaring at us from where it had wrapped its tail around itself, as if we'd disturbed it from slumber.

'Why is that thing here?' Kat asked.

'It keeps appearing,' William flushed. Making me suspect he was more afraid of the nipping bastard than forgetful of its existence. In answer, the table the thing perched on rattled. The house was clearly not done with the pest to bring it back up here.

Emrys moved closer to it, I saw the rush of that strange darkness beneath his skin. His body tense.

'*Nhair.*' The command seemed to drain all the warmth from the room as it rumbled from Emrys's lips, the morning light fading as if clouds had passed over the house. I felt the chill rush down my spine, hackles rising.

Darkness respects its master.

The beast in the cage began to chortle and growl. Turning itself in circles as if distressed. A horrid retching sound coming from it as it began to convulse.

'Is he choking?' William asked, worry furrowing his brow.

'Good riddance,' I huffed.

'Alma,' William whispered, scandalised. Yet it was Kat who moved, with caution, towards the thing, touching the side of her neck. Right where that bitemark was.

Emrys's dark gaze darted to her instantly.

Thean remained quiet too. Watching the creature with sharp amber eyes, jaw tense as if suspecting something was far worse than the creature simply choking. The voyav reached for that shadow blade at their thigh, taking a step closer to me.

I wish they hadn't. Wished they'd keep their wretched scent to themselves.

The gobrite retched one more time, a clank of metal upon metal before the fiend let out a little uncomfortable whine, its tail curling around itself as if embarrassed. There, at the bottom of the cage, was a small shard. Gleaming like—

'It's a relic,' Kat whispered. 'The fiends from the compendiums are hiding relics.'

Everything crashed together in my brain. The blood. The compendiums. The fiends.

It was why the old lords had protected and hidden them so reverently. Why Montagor was suddenly seeking compendiums. Why he'd been after the Ainsworth one.

And Montagor believed he'd just found another one. That was the only reason why his hunters were in the Weymouth lands – why he would send them to the boundary of rebel territory.

'Fuck,' Gideon cursed – and that was the only warning we got of how much worse this was all about to become.

Chapter Thirty-Two

Kat

The hunters tore through the west and east. Nothing but cruel men given permission to do cruel things. Their loyalty driven by hatred. Driven by the poisonous greed that this land was theirs, that it hadn't existed before their saint had deemed it so. That their king's dogma was true, and they were destined for a greatness that would never come.

Reaver records of the east – papers of the second purge

Weak men hunt the innocent. For cruelty and hatred are the only pleasures they'll ever know. My father had taught me that. Words never truer as I watched the hunters move through the cobbled streets and the quiet distress of fey echoed back through the narrow village.

Images of the purges, the cruelty of the kings before, flickered through my mind like pages turning in a book. The hot fury of my magic bit into my bones, making my veins glow with a lavender hue. My father's blade in my hand and vengeance singing in my blood.

Fuelled by the cold bite of Emrys where he crouched at my side, so still and watching in the shadows, those dark veins across his jaw, down his throat and twisting between his gloved fingers. Nothing but focus in his pitch-black eyes. A predator on the hunt.

Of course, he'd woken the morning knowing this threat was coming. Those instincts in him correct. Varin was moving, only I didn't think he was here now.

We'd barely had time to prepare. I'd managed to find some new boots as William put on his own leathers. Demanding to come despite Gideon's grumbled reluctance. But up against hunters who hungered for something – and with verium in their arsenal – we needed all the help we could get.

'Thean, you should be hiding,' William whispered sharply behind me.

'I'd rather die than scuttle about in the mud, darling,' was the voyav's dry reply from where they leant against an old woodshed, partially concealed in a strip of shadow.

Gideon sent the voyav an irritated glance from where the rest of us were all crouched in the mud. All except the voyav, who appeared completely bored by the danger just around a few corners. Of course, I imagined Thean's usual order of business was to kill first and wonder later. Or perhaps never wonder at all.

'Here she comes,' William hissed, thankfully saving us all from another spat between Gideon and Thean.

I don't know when William practised the art of holding a cloak out like a magician to catch Alma's bird form and knowing when to drop the bundle as she shifted. So it fell to the ground to cover a crouched Alma, as her head poked out. Her eyes gleaming with anger and the impression of feathers still against her flushed cheeks. Her flight and landing weren't as smooth as I'd seen, her recovery still ongoing, but she'd refused to be told what to do and I wasn't going to make decisions for her.

'They're digging,' she panted, sweat from the flurry of her flight making her dark curls stick to her brow.

'Digging?' William repeated, voice far too high in pitch to be calm.

'In the ruins in the woods. Twelve hunters. Four dogs.' She nodded. 'They have fey locked in the main hall and some in caged wagons.'

'They've found something,' Gideon cursed. 'The lords of old buried their treasures.'

'Why?' William's fingers were buried in the soil between his knees as if seeking some comfort from the earth.

'In case a Kysillian came by with a firestorm.' Gideon's eyes met my own. 'We all know how well those flames suppress Verr summonings.'

Of course. It was why the King wanted Kysillians gone before all others. Kysillian flame was the only thing that could compete with such destructive dark summoning. Why the Countess held those blades like a trophy. Protection from the dark magic she played with.

'We need to summon Priscilla,' Gideon added irritably, tugging at his hair in frustration as he peered around the cottage again.

'Her Reavers won't enter territory so close to the lines held by the rebels,' Emrys warned, his eyes not leaving the hunters that moved distantly down the narrow streets, tone flat with rage.

We were on our own.

'We need a distraction,' I offered. Distraction to get those fey to safety, somehow. To pull the hunters' focus away. Knowing we were running out of time. There weren't enough hunters here and if Montagor was interested in what could rest here, he wouldn't be far behind. He never was.

'Can we just have a moment to—' Gideon didn't have a chance to finish before Alma shifted again. The cloak dropping to the cobbles before her crow form took off into the skies, before she shifted into her wrywing form with a loud roar. Silver scales gleaming in the low winter sun.

'Bollocks,' Gideon snapped, pulling his blade from his belt and glaring at Emrys. 'This is like the fucking east hills all over again.'

'How would you know, you were busy crossing swords with two guards in the armoury,' Thean snorted, picking at their nails with their dagger. Only their eyes tracked the form of Alma as she swooped behind a tree line.

'I was getting *information*,' Gideon bristled, ignoring the panicked shout of hunters.

'*Vigorously* from what I heard, little witch,' Thean added unhelpfully with a sly smirk.

Emrys – thankfully – ignored their bickering as he dug a hand into his jacket pocket. 'William. Get the fey out and open the wagons.'

He pulled out a portal stone and a rune marker, handing them to William. Everything the boy would need to make a usable portal for a short period of time.

'Where are they going?' William nodded, face serious and determined.

'The eastern fields,' Emrys replied. 'Stay out of trouble.'

'I'm sure Priscilla will fucking love you dropping them on her doorstep,' Gideon griped as William darted around the side of the cottage and into one of the other alleyways. Emrys's jaw was tight with worry, those dark eyes watching him go.

'I'll help William with the portal stone,' I offered. Worried about leaving him on his own, and knowing Emrys's focus needed to be on the hunters and what they were doing. Not on the boy he cared for like his own son.

Without another word I followed William down the other side of the alley. Silently jumping over scattered market baskets where someone had dropped their wares. The hunters arriving too swiftly. Then I turned another corner and saw William's fiery head crouched in the bushes.

'William,' I whispered, still managing to startle him as I stopped to join him in his hiding place. Considering the town square ahead of us. Quaint, surrounded by small cottages with smoking chimneys and narrow cobbled streets. The kind of village my mother would illustrate in her stories for me.

Two guards stood watch of a caged wagon, fey men inside. Beyond them, the main hall doors rattled slightly. Voices crying and shouting to be let out, before one of the guards kicked the doors to silence them.

A few kelsh fey men knelt at the side of the wagon. They had patches of a scaled texture on their arms and face. Earth summoners, mostly land workers now. Small black horns protruded from their brows. From the bulk of them, it was apparent why they all had bleeding wounds. They'd been hit with verium. Their hands behind their heads, faces bloody as if they'd put up resistance. One I was certain they'd pay for the moment the hunters got what they wanted. They wouldn't leave witnesses. Not to this.

A boom shook the earth and made me grip William's shoulder as smoke rose over the small cottages from the direction we'd come. At the same time a large flock of birds rose from the surrounding wood. Followed by the roar of Alma's wrywing form in the distance.

I suppose that was the sign we were waiting for. The guards watching the wagons turned, distracted.

'I'll knock them out.' William buried his hands in the dirt beneath the bushes. His fingers giving off a faint green glow, eyes shut tight with concentration.

Then the ground quaked for a different reason. William sucked in a breath through clenched teeth, his shoulders bunched with the might of his summoning. His roots exploded from the earth across the yard. Screams filled the air from startled fey. The hunters flew into the air, only to land with a sickening crunch against the cobbled road, necks no longer at the right angle.

William looked stricken before he shook his head, steely determination filling his flushed face. 'Serves the bastards right.'

'Ready?' I asked as Alma roared overhead again and I heard a boom. Either from Gideon or Emrys's summoning. The cries of hunters in the distance grew louder.

William nodded, sweat beading his brow as we lurched forwards at the same moment, crossing the space.

'Oi!' a hunter cried, coming from around the wagon. Hand on his sword. I let my father's blade twist in my palm, small and swift. I threw it. It sailed through the air with a streak of fire. Burying itself home in the bastard's chest. He fell backwards with the force just as Alma roared overhead. Dropping two screaming hunters she'd picked up from somewhere – who weren't screaming any more as they hit the cobbles with a horrid wet crunch.

'Use the storehouse doorway.' I grabbed William's shoulder where he'd paused with worry. Turning him towards the large carriage house doors hanging open from the raid. 'I'll open the wagons and the hall.'

William's boots skidded as he turned direction, jumping over the hunters' bodies and sprinting to the carriage house. Pulling the rune marker and portal stone from his pocket.

I pulled my blade from the hunter's chest, his wide red-rimmed eyes filled with nothing but death before I moved to the wagon.

I let my blade lengthen again, slashing through the chain threaded through the kelsh men's bindings. They recoiled in an instant, stumbling to their feet. Pulling those short, strange darts from their flesh. Their vibrant green eyes sizing me up for a threat.

'*Get them out,*' I commanded in Mican, not wasting a moment as I climbed the wagon step to find the lock.

'Rebels,' one of the women hissed inside as she clutched a crying swaddled child to her chest. A duok with pale markings up the side of her face – an earth healer.

'*No. We're here to help,*' I answered in Mican, startling her before I grabbed the lock, heating it until it warped easily against my palm. I leapt back, the door swinging free.

'*Get to the portal,*' I commanded, pointing them in William's direction, where he waved frantically, the Portium light glowing behind him.

Then I moved to the next lock, getting that one open too as one of the villagers took an axe to the lock on the main hall doors and fey came rushing out. The crowd pushed and moved towards William. Children crying as the elderly hobbled with the help of the young. Some hesitated at the dark shadow of Alma roaring from above.

'*Move!*' I barked.

A scream came from behind me, turning me to find a girl clutching a straw doll as her mother pulled her away.

There was a horrid crack of bone as the corpses Alma had dropped started to undulate in their own puddles of blood on the road.

'Bollocks,' I hissed. The hunters had sworn themselves. They were becoming fiends.

'Fuck,' William exclaimed, eyes wide with panic through the crowd as he realised at the same time.

'Keep going, William!' I ordered, stepping into the street. I let my flame sing in my veins, let it race across the cobbles and form a barrier. Keeping the fey and William on the other side, as the dead rose before me, if pulled on strings by a master.

The corpses undulated. Eyes full black. Teeth snapping. It should have reminded me of the thing Master Hale had become. Should have consumed me with that childish fear.

Murderer. A dark voice hissed in my ear. Only it didn't strike as it once had before.

No. Because I was a murderer and I'd do it again. The fiends screeched and charged. I'd fought a fiend before. Two couldn't be much harder. I just hoped no more turned up.

A roar pealed from my lips as I let flame race from my palm. Forced it forwards, engulfing them in its deadly jaws, becoming nothing but ash.

I should have remembered how many Alma had dropped. A force hit my side. Sending me slamming into a wooden hut. Hay and dust exploded around me, filling my mouth with grime as I tumbled across the wreckage, my blade sliding from my grip. I kicked debris off myself, seeing the shadowed shape of the fiends moving through the dusty air.

'Bastard,' I hissed, surging to my feet and rolling flame between my palms before thrusting it towards the creatures. They screamed and thrashed as my summoning devoured them.

I lunged for my sword that had fallen next to me beneath the debris, getting my hand around the hilt before a clawed hand seized my jacket, wrenching me backwards.

I threw my elbow back, catching the creature's jaw enough to get free. Turning and letting my flame consume its skull. It screeched, clawing at its own eyes. Scrambling backwards. Only for something else to catch my jacket, throwing me into the brick chimney.

I bared my teeth, about to turn on the fiend, only to feel the sting of a blade at my throat.

'What do we have here?' a strange voice asked. The cool metal at my throat biting deep. Stealing my breath, my heart hammering into my ribs. The wishing stone flickering wildly just as my magic flared in my veins.

Then the stone guttered out. Darkness filled my vision. A chaotic, vicious air, a pained cry and then a sickening crash of bone against stone. The blade against my flesh.

It only took a blink for the darkness to abate, for Emrys's strong hands to suddenly be there. Hauling me behind him. Those dark-tipped fingers curling into my jacket, as if to comfort himself I was all there. His deadly gaze fixed on my throat, making my trembling fingers move to it, but there was no blood. No cut.

'A Blackthorn making a mess. I can't say I'm surprised,' came a smug voice. I was unable to see anything but Emrys's broad chest, blocking my view of the speaker.

I pushed up on my toes, glancing over his shoulder to find ourselves surrounded.

More guards and, standing in front of them, was a water nymph. An imposing, striking creature. All sharp angles and deadly handsomeness. That impossible inky blue hair, dark eyes and iridescent skin designed to drag foolish maidens to the depths.

Then I saw the emblem pin at the lapel of his own tight-fitting black fighting leathers. The fist and dagger.

The rebellion.

Chapter Thirty-Three

Alma

What a vicious little beast.

That voice. So lyrical and soft. How those blood-stained nails bit into my skin. So cold. A strange deadness to those crimson eyes.

No. I shook the memory away.

My claws dug into the bark of the tree before me. Wishing it was flesh. My chest too tight, no matter how deeply I tried to suck in breath. Greedy for it. My lungs were too small and tight, but as I opened my eyes – I hadn't shifted.

Crouched in the wood, perfectly concealed in a strip of shadow the trees offered. Yet, I felt so small. So strange and weak.

That insignia. The rebellion was here. The shock of it had made me pause, made me shift and tumble to the earth. Barely having a moment to catch myself before I landed in the dirt.

The aches and scratches didn't matter.

The rebellion. They were here and Kat was down there. Yet I couldn't move. Could only bury my claws deeper into the tree, cold sweat sliding down my back.

Move. Help. Do something, little rat.

Only I remained still. Stuck within my fear. It churned wildly in my gut until I vomited between my bare feet once more.

'Fuck,' I hissed. Dragging my hand across my mouth, a repulsed shudder moving through me at the vile taste left behind. The bloody chunks in the leaves before me.

I didn't mean to bite them, but the bastards wouldn't stay still. Eating in one of my forms never ended well, especially not something so . . . fresh. In my anger I forgot myself. Listening to the cries of those fey. Smelling fear.

It fuelled a part of me I wished never to remember. A twisting form of nothing but darkness and claws. Endless. Uncaring who it consumed.

I shuddered again, trying to pant through the next wave of nausea. Flying always took too much energy. Especially in a form so big. The rage of my beasts had taken over, pushing my limits too soon after the verium.

Now they were so quiet, faltering with my fear. I should have raced down the hill, should have helped Kat. Yet, I hid – vomiting up all my guilt.

I just needed a moment. Needed to focus, and then I could think. The brambles dug into my bare feet, making me growl as another shiver moved down my spine. Fur rippling across my forearms to try and stave away the chill. Breath clouding before me from the winter air.

'Little nightmare,' came the soft taunt on the wind. Turning me so fast I almost fell amongst the soggy leaves. Only for this whole episode to get worse as my gaze met the troublesome amber of the voyav, where they leant against a door frame – a cottage – just beyond the trees I'd chosen as my hiding place. The residents were clearly gone. Warm light painting a path through the thicket.

There was something distracting in the sharpness of Thean Page's gaze, in that amber as the light from the doorway made it glow. That cloak slung over their arm as they waited. Waiting for me.

I should have hissed. Changed and fled. Only my panic didn't dissipate. Nor the ghostly taunt of the voice I wished to forget. *What a vicious little beast.*

I didn't feel vicious. I was tired, sad and scared. Reminding me too much of the girl I'd never be again.

I rose against my better judgement. Unable to wallow any longer. Repulsed by the stench of my own fear. Unbothered by my nakedness before them, knowing they wouldn't look.

'Why are the rebellion here?' I demanded, irritated I needed any help at all as I kept my arm across my breasts.

I wanted to bare my teeth but no fangs would manifest. If my beasts were silent, then I'd deal with the bastard voyav in mortal form.

'Probably the same reason we are,' they offered as I snatched the cloak off them, holding it across my front.

'Stop helping me,' I grumbled, another shiver coursing up my back, leaving sharp bumps in its wake.

They glowered down at me. 'Stop getting caught.'

I bared my useless mortal teeth. I wasn't caught. That was the problem. If I was caught, I'd have no choice but to choose fury over fear.

I moved inside the cottage. Needing to collect myself, to get the flesh from between my teeth. Wash the rancid taste from my mouth. To think.

'You need to get down there to—' Only as I stepped into the cottage, it wasn't a cottage at all. There was a rush of magic against my skin, pinching and old.

The familiar bookcases and desks of the Blackthorn study. The fire roaring, the doors across from me creaking open and shut like a waving hand glad to have us back.

We were back in Blackthorn Manor. Impossibly. My head spun. I turned back to the doorway. Only to find bookcases behind me. The house covering up where it had pulled me through the portal door. Away from that village. Away from Kat.

No.

Thean was fixing the cuffs on their jacket, short auburn hair disturbed by the wind. Completely unbothered by the ease of their deception.

'You bastard!' I seethed, turning to go back, finding nothing there but the space between the bookshelves, and the voyav standing with folded arms. Jaw tense as if the sight of the bramble scratches on my calves personally offended them.

'Get out of my way!' I shrieked, the cloak forgotten, tangling around my feet as I lashed out with my claws. Intent on going for their throat.

I was quick. Always had been, but the voyav was quicker. Catching my wrists so gently, as if I was nothing but a petulant child.

Forcing me back against the shelves.

'Not likely, darling,' the loathsome creature grinned, yet there was a wildness in their eyes. Maybe fear, but it flared into amusement too quickly for me to be certain.

A growl rumbled in my throat. Fuck them. I let my scales ripple, starting to change. My beasts not complying as I wished, cowed by the mere presence of this being, and I hated it.

Thean's hand took my shoulder, pinning me in the blink of an eye. The cupboards rattling with the house's input. Somehow complicit in this madness.

My breath was too panted. Too wild. I'd abandoned my friends to my fear. Left Kat there. William too.

'Let me go,' I sneered.

Thean leant closer until that rich fucking scent chased away the stench of cursed blood and my own fear. 'You're the one holding on, sweetheart.'

My claws curled into their shirt, almost desperately. Even now.

'You wouldn't have been hiding if you wanted rebels sniffing you out.' Their words were terse with warning and soft with seduction all at once as they stirred the loose hair next to my ear. That bastard warm clove smell filling my lungs.

I bared my fangs, ignoring the warmth of their skin against my collarbone. Only, just like the heat of their proximity, those words settled my rage. The rebellion. The strange threat in Thean's knowing. They'd seen things I never wished anyone to. The power of my beasts, how valuable I was.

Fear gnashed at my heart.

'Just as I thought.' Those amber eyes dropped to where my pulse fluttered in my throat.

'You don't know anything about me,' I spat, pushing them away. They went easily. Which I hated most. That they knew I was all bark and no bite. That I wouldn't leave. Couldn't.

'Strange . . . your Kysillian said the same thing. Perhaps that's why you huddle so closely, finding commonality in the secrets you keep,' they taunted, hands slipping so easily into their pockets. But there was nothing relaxed in their stance, eyes too dark with the hunt.

Only their words struck their intended mark. How similar me and Kat were. With all the things she didn't know. That she was far more dangerous than she seemed. So was I. How long had I been running from that truth? Changing into anything to avoid it?

How the voyav mocked me with it now. I was sick of them. Sick of how they wished to play me like a fool.

'Loyal pets don't stray this far from their leash. You're hiding right here with me, Thean,' I spat. Hating how easily their name slid between my fangs. 'Lies and games. Don't you ever tire of it?'

I couldn't help the humourless laugh that slipped from my lips. The exhaustion that bit into my bones. The games I also played, irritated every time I fought with them. It unsettled me how much it felt like fighting myself.

'It's kept me alive and you enjoy the challenge too much.' They studied me too closely. So many emotions hidden in the depths of those otherwordly eyes. That gaze never straying lower than my face, because as they said – I didn't give them permission to look. Despite standing naked before them, covered in nothing but mud and my own fearful sweat.

'You incense me,' I snapped. Yet no other forms came, no growls or sharp scales. My beasts were not in agreement with me. Fuck them. Fools to be seduced so easily. I'd fucked strangers I trusted more than this creature.

Thean leant closer. Their smile slow and wicked. 'If only you didn't want it so much, little love.'

Those eyes dipped down to my fangs. It was too hard to catch my breath. Their thumb and finger caught my chin as if they wished to examine them more closely. I should have hissed or pulled away, but I was a fool. I always had been, wanting too much to see what they'd do next.

'Did you think of me when you made those little fangs?' The words were soft, cautious. A question they knew they shouldn't want.

'Only how viciously I'd bite you.' My voice didn't sound steady. Not with them holding me like that. Not with how focused they were on my lips.

'Don't tease.' They were too wicked with their amusement, making my anger curdle inside of me. At myself. At all my secrets and lies.

'I'd be an interesting pet for your master.' I let my lips curl into my own vicious smile. Watching amusement gutter out of their eyes. 'But you already know that, don't you?'

What a vicious little beast. Those words came back to me from that fucking awful witch's lips. Only she wasn't wrong. Was she?

How valuable. Valuable enough that I'd be seen as a prize and if Thean handed me over, how she'd reward her voyav. Let them back in so easily no matter how far they'd wandered or for how long.

'Yet. Here we are,' I taunted. Home. '*Safe.*'

Something moved across the voyav's expression, their features shifting in the blink of an eye. Unsettled between female and male as if I'd unnerved them. 'Foolish to think you're safe with me, little nightmare.'

My thigh burnt from the memory of their touch last night. My beasts letting scales tickle the corner of my jaw they'd touched as if relishing in the memory of it. My tongue darting out across my lip as if to taste even the fucking perfume of them in the air between us.

How they tormented me. So I'd give this madness back to them. I stepped closer, seeing them tense, how their pupils got impossibly darker. Verr. That's what they were, a predator. Only I was a predator too, and perhaps I'd forgotten that in this mortal skin.

I was right. The voyav wasn't as loyal as they seemed. A necromancer was a creature the Countess would cherish, yet she didn't have one. Couldn't, because if she did, the Council would never have stood a chance against the death summoning the Countess would command.

Thean hadn't given that necromancer over. They hadn't said a word about Kat's blade, nor her true line. They'd kept quiet, because they wished to stay here. Far away from that master.

'Who is the liar now?' I whispered against the curve of their neck. Letting my tongue drag across their perfumed

393

throat. Feeling the unsteady beat of their pulse, the killer in me relishing it. Letting my fangs give the smallest nip.

My smile sly as I pulled back, finding victory in the stillness of them. Only I should have known better. Their retaliation was quicker.

Their fingers curled into a fist in my wild dark curls, pulling my head back to claim my eyes. Rough and gentle all at once. A strange mewing sound slipping from between my lips. Betraying me as desire sparked warmly in my core.

'If you want to play . . . all you have to do is ask.' Those ancient eyes traced every inch of my face. Breaths unsteady as if trying to find their patience. 'You can use those scales to cover yourself.'

The words came reluctantly, as if the thought to help me had squeezed through their lips against their will.

Shock flashed thought me. I'd never thought of it. Always seen myself and those beasts as two sides. That they couldn't meet, not even as I felt soft scales ripple and twist across my skin, covering my nakedness at their suggestion. Listening to them.

I snapped my teeth. 'Repulsed?'

At the mess of me. The uneven flesh and the creatures that prowled beneath. I didn't care if they were. Maybe I'd prefer it.

'Beautiful little nightmare.' They smiled, the knuckles on their other hand dragging the barest ghostly path so gently down my breastbone, yet those eyes stayed on my own. 'You haven't been paying attention.'

The taunt spurred something feral inside of me as my claws dug into their jacket. Thean came closer, until I could feel their breath caress my throat, until I couldn't smell the remains of my fear or the mud. Until all I could scent was them.

I wanted the madness of it. Only Thean Page had no mercy in them.

Those fangs dragged over my throat, almost in promise. A delicate scratch that made a wanton needing ache between my thighs. How delicately they touched me, the brush of their fingers teasing. Knowing they didn't need to be gluttonous, to grip and demand my flesh. No, it was as if I was a feast to be savoured.

Delicate.

You're not real, little rat. How the Keeper would spit those words as I cried. As I lay broken before them. No matter the pain or the blood. No matter how raw my voice became with my begging.

His words never changed.

I'd never been real. Their use of me shouldn't sting as it did. I was just some simple strange thing pulled into existence against its will. Fleeting and easy to break. Like a feral fucking dust-sprite.

That wasn't how I felt with Thean's lips on my pulse. I felt real. I felt every breath, every hair on my flesh, painfully. I became real between their palms and I recoiled from the agony of it.

I retreated. Shifted and changed so small they couldn't see me. Then I fled just like the coward I was. Ignoring the whimper of the beasts within.

Chapter Thirty-Four

Kat

No Kysillian bares a mark. For no being can best the Queen's blood. Only the unworthy accept defeat and the unworthy shall never summon her flame.

The Rule of Kysillia – Unknown

I felt instantly uneasy and not just from the armed rebels in the ruins of the room, or the deadly sharpness of Emrys's magic surrounding me. I hadn't interacted with many fey, especially not those of ancient blood. Being locked in the Institute had stolen more from me than I'd first anticipated. Had made me fear my own kind just as those mortals did.

The fury rippling from Emrys was little comfort, as the rage of my own magic from my small battle churned inside of me and made my palms sweat. That horrid cloying fear consuming me that the nymph had seen my Kysillian blade or witnessed me summon.

As if scenting the unease I was certain seeped from my pores, the nymph's grin didn't falter. Like a cat considering a lame mouse between its paws.

'Aster,' Emrys greeted with no warmth.

The slender nymph's skin shifted between blue and green like oil catching sunlight. The pattern of scales faintly visible, dark blue hair braided severely back from his face, the plaits decorated with small silver beads. Sharp pointed ears – larger than my own – pierced with varying small rings.

'You've injured my men,' the nymph chided. 'However, I am feeling generous enough to give you a merciful minute to explain yourselves.'

His companions shifted behind him as if to remind us we were surrounded. One with a bloody broken nose thanks to my fist.

Emrys would have a portal stone on him, but I doubted he could reach it, and one wouldn't carry us far. Also, the rebels were too close. We might accidently port some of them with us.

'I'll explain myself to Callen,' Emrys's voice didn't sound entirely his own.

The nymph straightened and so did I. My gaze darting to Emrys before I could think better of it.

Callen? Why would the Kysillian be here and why would Emrys know it? The nymph let out an unamused sound before sheathing his short blade.

'Very well.' The nymph's smile was sly, those eyes moving to me as he stepped back with a mocking bow. 'It's your funeral, Blackthorn.'

Two rebels moved forward only for the bitter chill of Emrys's magic to snap like a wyvern's tail. Sending them stumbling back into the crumbling remains of the walls around us, their own summonings crackling in their palms in retaliation. Aster simply held up his hand to stop their retaliation.

'Careful, Blackthorn,' the nymph warned, the air suddenly damp with the threat of his own power. 'Your pet wood imp and bastard brother are waiting.'

William and Gideon.

'Lead the way,' Emrys offered. Seeming to make some attempt at being civilised.

The nymph turned sharply to lead the way out of the ruined house. The guards tugged at their jackets, muttering their displeasure before they moved outside. The streets strangely quiet in the aftermath of the Hunters attack. Or maybe it was just the ringing in my head dulling everything from hitting the wall.

The village's roads were thin and winding, like that of a rabbit's warren. A foreboding quiet had permeated the air in the absence of the chaos only moments before. Smoke curled and danced like thick fog before us.

Gideon and William did appear, guided by another small gang of rebels through the narrow cobbled street. Smoke curling in the air from where my fire had caught on the thatched roof.

William had his hands raised as if he was being taken on a death march, looking sickly pale. Gideon grabbed his wrist and yanked the boy's hand down. Making William flush scarlet. Clearly this wasn't Gideon's first time being captured and he wasn't about to be embarrassed while doing it.

Gideon gave Emrys a sharp warning look before he fell into step with us.

'You all right, Kat?' William asked out of the side of his mouth.

'I'm fine,' I answered trying to brush some of the hay dust off my leathers. How long I'd be fine for was yet to be seen. My eyes tracked over the rooftops and then the forest that bordered the village. Turning to assess the space around us. Looking for a familiar pair of green eyes. A flutter of wings or flash of scales. My panic rising, flame churning in my gut.

Alma.

'Safe,' Emrys's answer came as soft as breath as it brushed my ear. I hadn't even realised I'd spoken. I turned to see him, only for his deadly focus to be on the road ahead. On the rebels who were spread out across the streets, searching the remains of the village as if any hunters could remain.

The echoing thump of our footsteps matched the wild beating of my heart. Until we were led into a small court-yard. Hunters or the fiends they'd become lay sprawled on the ground. Eyes glassy with death. Entrails scattered across the cobbles thanks to Alma, and the stench of burnt flesh from what limited damage I'd been able to do filled the air.

Sheet-covered bodies lay there too – fey. Cut down so pointlessly. The brutality of my magic turned within me, forcing my hands into fists.

We weren't quick enough. Would we ever be?

The hunters these rebels had managed to catch knelt against a remaining charred stone wall. Hands bound behind their backs, faces bloody. Eyes red from the venom they'd drunk. Half mad with it. Crazed enough to follow any order. One's lips moving in quick succession, eyes rolling back in their skull in devotion to their saint. Others snapped their teeth, frothing at the mouth as if they'd taken poison.

Evidence of the madness that had torn this world apart too many times in human form. Hatred.

Our guard slowed as a striking figure observed the same carnage before us. My magic flared with curiosity, recognizing such flame in another.

Callen. The Countess's Kysillian. Those sharp lavender eyes met my own as he turned from his consideration of the hunters. He was still wearing the same leathers as he wore in Lady Ramsey's fighting pit, his cheeks flushed from battle and splattered with horrid dark blood. Dark hair tied back from his face as he glowered down at us all.

'You're in the middle of my rebellion, Blackthorn,' Callen greeted, folding his arms, making his leathers creak. 'Catching too much attention once again.'

'Last I heard, it was the Countess's rebellion,' Gideon countered, hand resting on his weapons belt with ease. 'You're also beyond your bounds.'

I saw the slight flex of Emrys's fingers as darkness rippled across his knuckles. Close to summoning.

'Montagor is moving his hunters too quickly for us to dawdle in the north,' the Kysillian countered, exhaustion clinging to his stoic features.

'You followed them,' I spoke before I could think. How else would they have known to be here?

Unless they'd spotted the same pattern that William had in what was catching Montagor's attention.

'They've decimated two fey settlements further south.' Callen chewed over the words with displeasure.

'Survivors?' Emrys asked.

'Those who survived fled east.' Callen rubbed his jaw, his eyes moving over Aster. As if assessing he was all in one piece, before those piercing lavender eyes returned to us. 'I suspect that's where your little imp sent the villagers. Your Reaver loyalties are showing, Blackthorn.'

'It'll be interesting to know how long you've had a wrywing in your arsenal?' Aster added, his smile sly.

Dread curled in my gut. The rebels couldn't know anything about Alma. That was a danger that had chased us for long enough.

The nymph's focus dropped oddly to Emrys's hand. 'I also didn't know you were taken, Blackthorn.'

Then I saw exactly where my father's hilt had gone. A gold ring glinted on Emrys's ring finger. Standing out so prominently against that dark summoning staining his skin. Like a mortal wedding band. My cheeks flushed at the insinuation.

My eyes shot to Callen's, watching a stillness come over him. Wondering if he knew. If he could sense what it was.

'I suppose your master doesn't know you're both free of your leash,' Gideon huffed, folding his arms with ease, thankfully offering another distraction and ignoring how William's knees practically knocked together next to him.

'From the stories you're supposed to be dead, Gideon. Or fucking your way west,' Aster's reply was terse.

'Interested?' Gideon raised a brow in challenge.

Callen, to my surprise, laughed. A sudden ease in his bulky form that hadn't been present in Lady Ramsey's fighting den. No, this creature seemed so different to the one held so tightly on the cruel blood-witch's leash.

'*Ancestors guard you*,' he greeted me in Kysillian, inclining his head. Some great distant pain moved through my chest hearing the warm greeting I last heard come from my father's lips.

'*And guard you*,' I replied, struggling to keep my voice steady.

The nymph shifted with irritation, a sharpness to their eyes on my lips, understanding. Making me wonder how they could know Kysillian.

'Why would Montagor care about settlements south of here?' Gideon interjected.

'They're after fey ruins. The bastard remains in hiding, sending his rats out to forage,' Aster answered, but from his curled lip I could tell he didn't wish to offer us anything. 'The real question is what are *you* after, Blackthorn? I don't suppose it's good luck that has drawn you across our path. Maybe the work of the dark fates. To seek a position of power in this coming war?'

'The Reavers wish to get the fey to safety. I offered my assistance in their plight. As I always have,' Emrys replied, unbothered by how his words might incriminate him in the rebellion's eyes.

'She doesn't like excuses,' Aster countered, dampness in the air intensifying with the nymph's power.

'She doesn't like the truth either,' Gideon retorted.

Where I expected feral brutal loyalty at such an insult, Callen and Aster remained quiet, almost solemn in the face of such a truth.

'Be careful, Blackthorn, you have no idea the lengths she will go to win this. The bargains she'll make with monsters themselves.' Callen's eyes gleamed with warning, but there was no anger. Not even a threat in the flare of his magic. Nothing but a strange desperation, as if conveying a message with no words at all.

'Montagor is ravaging these lands because he wishes to control dark artifacts. The more he acquires the further his reach will grow. It's only a matter of time until it leads him to a seal,' Gideon answered, uncaring for the threat.

'How can you be certain of that?' Callen frowned, only those eyes sharpened with concern at the darkness laced within the words. The threat of what Montagor could be up to.

'A children's tale,' Aster scoffed, yet Callen's lavender gaze grew hard with worry.

'Is that why your Countess hunted it too for a time?' Gideon countered. A smooth rhythm between them that told me they'd all met before.

My hackles rose at Gideon's slight. What use would the Countess have for artifacts? Especially of the Old Gods?

I felt Emrys's power bite but I kept my gaze on Callen. On the blood we shared, on the barest hint that he was not where the ancestors willed him to be. Just as Thean wasn't.

'*This won't be a war if Montagor possesses anymore relics,*' I spoke in Kysillian again. Wondering if they too found it strange to see another of us in the wilderness of the world. *'He's going for the seals. He'll need Kysillian blood to finish this.'*

Callen stayed silent, but there was no hard edge to his gaze or those words.

A heart seal was bigger than all the others if the tales were to be believed. It had taken seven kings to seal it, therefore it only stood to reason that it would take seven Kysillian lives to open it. Powerful bloodlines.

Fear bit deep into my bones, the scar at my neck almost burning in warning at that truth. How fey had already been taken so senselessly beneath Fairfax. All that pain and blood . . . for nothing. It was a drop in the ocean of what was to come.

'They tried to take mine,' I offered, pulling the collar of my leathers aside to show the marked skin at my neck. The paleness of a scar only a demon could leave.

Callen had gone very still. Either sensing the ferocity of it and the truth in my words or repulsed by the weakness in me to allow my Kysillian flesh to be marked in such a way. So visibly.

I'd been bested. Time and time again. Yet I stood here still and I refused to be ashamed. Because as I looked at that blood mark on Callen, he'd been bested too – and there was no shame in it. Not here with me. Not if it had let them survive.

'Fairfax was using ancient blood. An experiment Montagor seemed interested in,' I continued in mortal tongue, unafraid of what that revealed. 'Surely you've heard that *tale.*'

The rebellion would have known. They knew everything. The cruelty they allowed because beaten fey were a weapon they could wield to their advantage. Desperate fey would pay any price for protection, a price their Countess liked to reap.

Callen gave no answer. Couldn't because I'd seen that ring on her finger. The artifact she used to hone her power. How ruthlessly she kept these beings like pets. Wore our sacred blades as jewellery. I knew that pain and I knew the shame of it.

'Callen,' the Nymph reprimanded, as if knowing every thought in the Kysillian's head. A worry formed at Aster's brow, one that spoke of something deeper than simple camaraderie between the two.

'You shouldn't have wandered across my path, Blackthorn,' the Kysillian warned, a slight panic filling those lavender eyes. 'She wants your attention too much.'

Fear coiled tightly in my chest at that warning. The Countess wanted Emrys. Of course she did with her interest in the seals and Verr relics.

Yet Callen turned back to me. '*A free Kysillian is a gift these days. It seems the ancestors watch over you. So, who am I to make you stray from your path, Nuva?*'

Nuva. Sister. A form of respect I'd never heard before. One between warriors.

To keep this secret and lie to his master? I didn't need to wonder why. I knew.

The scared Kysillian blades in the Countess's grasp chafed against the loyalty in his blood as much as it chafed against mine.

'*You'll let us go?*' I demanded, still not trusting him. Not believing that something as simple as my blood could sway him.

'*With a warning.*' His lavender eyes gleamed with it. '*Pray those monsters in the north stay away. Or they'll kill you slowly as penance for what he is.*'

He nodded his head in Emrys's direction, yet the caution in his stare pinned me in place. No disgust or disdain. Almost pity.

What the elders would have done to my mother to punish my father for his disloyalty to his blood. For wasting sacred magic on half-breeds.

Then I watched Aster shift uncomfortably and avert their gaze. Saw why perhaps Callen would feel the need to warn me – when he himself was in the same danger.

'*I'm not theirs,*' I challenged.

'*We all are. Even if they don't want us.*' Callen's smile was small with sadness. '*They care for honour too much.*'

They cared about their honour so much they'd rather destroy this world and the truth to keep their power.

Even Kysillia's stories can be twisted for them to gain power from your ignorance. A truth my father had given me long ago. How corrupt our own elders had become for nothing but pride.

'We cannot stay much longer.' Aster warned softly, noticing the rebels struggling to keep the captured hunters under control.

Callen ran a hand down his tired face, nodding before looking at me one last time.

'*Take heed. A milvok lies on the path ahead,*' he offered. An old strange tale. A milvok was an invisible creature, a trickster with a poisonous bite.

Some say it never existed at all. That it was a warning for something else, almost in code. Yet as he gave it I saw the discomfort on his features, as if the words felt like glass tearing from his throat.

Of course. He was sworn to the Countess, and when she demanded secrecy he had no choice but to give it. Not about the plans she had or who they involved.

Pain flickered across his expression before he turned, shouting a command to withdraw to the rebels that lingered close by. Spurring them into motion. A tiredness apparent in the fall of his shoulders. Aster watched him cautiously. Concerned.

Reminding me that Callen has been offered as payment to the Countess. A horrid feeling that it'd happened against his will. This strange entrapment, by elders we were supposed to respect. Who were supposed to guard us.

'*May they guard you, Nuor,*' I called in parting, watching his back tense. He didn't turn back to me, as if to dismiss that ancient word between us, as if he wasn't worthy of hearing it.

Nuor. Brother. What the warriors would have called each other before battles.

'Move them!' a rebel shouted to another who was moving two hunters, their hands bound. A group of rebels dragging those remaining hunters away from the wall – to whatever grizzly fate the Countess had planned for them.

I couldn't look away. Seeing how the hatred burning in their eyes met my own. No different from those corpses that had risen again.

Then in a moment all I could see was those small bones glinting in the pit. There was enough fury in my blood to incinerate this village. To turn the very stone to nothing but ash. I knew it and yet I remained still. Allowed it to coil viciously inside of me.

'Kat.' Emrys took a gentle hold of my arm to guide me away, as if he could feel it stirring within me.

I needed to leave. My anger would fix nothing here. No. We'd been too late.

One hunter lurched forward from the rebel's hold, screaming and snapping their teeth against their restraints. Forcing more rebels to try and drag them back.

'Get them gone!' Callen commanded. Only then did I see the momentary distraction. How one of the other captured hunters was so still in the chaos. How their bound hands reached for their belt. The gleam of green. The crazed toothy smile in the mass of bodies. Lost in the chaos.

Something was in his bound hands. A dark metal sphere, a green sheen to the markings on it. The runes I couldn't mistake.

A vorg.

Dark storms came across the battlefields of the west.

Blood and screams. Tearing through the innocent and leaving nothing but terror in their wake.

Wild fiends locked in weapons. Bringers of nothing but death.

'Emrys!' Gideon cried a moment too late as the static of his aether hummed in the air. That vorg flared a blinding bright green. It imploded with a scream from the rebels closest to it.

The force tore me from Emrys's grip. My back hit stone, debris striking my skin. A cry burst from my lips. There was no demon fire, nothing but the looming demonic storm freed from its trap.

Pale grey smoke and sulphuric dark flames. Sharp flashes of teeth and claws. Too many tumbled together, screeching and making the ground quake. Undulating and twisting with a deadly ferocity.

A demonic storm. One that stole my breath. Smothered my air before I could summon. Whipping all around me. Sparks flaring and guttering in my palms. Screams filled the air, chaotic shouts but I couldn't see what was happening.

The terrified shriek of William.

Someone screaming my name.

Then there was nothing. Only darkness and pain as I drowned in the pressure in my lungs.

I tried to summon my magic, but no flames would catch. The icy bite of fear stung my heart. Then that dark storm brushed my exposed flesh. Like a hundred icy blades piercing at once. A searing pain coming from the scar at my neck as if the galmoth's fangs had dug in once more. I bucked wildly as agony tore through me, screaming until my throat was raw with it.

Please, I pleaded helplessly in the back of my mind. Then bright white demon fire stung my eyes, air rushed down my throat. Clean and sharp. Filled with nothing but the scent of beasam bark.

The ground cracked beneath me. Deep fissures as the fine dirt began to bounce with the ferocity of the quaking. A boom made my ears ring as if thunder had broken above. The darkness abated in an instant, suddenly swirling across the courtyard from my panting form like a storm cloud.

The village came back into focus, cobbles and dirt splattered with blood. Lifeless eyes looking at me. As the cloud of forsaken smoke continued to undulate and scream. Being pulled by some invisible wind as flashes of bright ethereal light came from within it. Whisp-like claws attacking itself, as it was pulled in and in on itself.

Smaller and smaller. That pale demon fire at its centre growing brighter. Until a dark figure could be seen in the middle of it. That pale summoning like bright white fire all around him.

Emrys. Burning the creature from within. Until with one final demonic scream, that storm fractured in a deadly boom. The force of it almost sending me back to the ground. The fiend becoming nothing but thick ashy clumps that rained down on my prone form like snow. I panted, palms braced on the cobbles beneath me. Looking up at the imposing bulk of Emrys.

His hands were still outstretched, that blinding light between his fingers where he'd unmade it. Darkness rippled and danced across his pale flesh. Making his features sharper, deadlier. Something else was in there looking back at me.

Nothing but darkness in male form.

Serus.

The wishing stone practically trembling against my breast-bone, as if even the power contained there wished to be free and return.

The distant moans of the rebels caught my ear as they regained their feet.

'Emrys?' I stumbled to my knees and then my feet, ignoring Gideon's call of warning. The stillness in Emrys felt like a threat. I reached for his hand. His skin was ice cold, almost making me pull back, my magic flaring in answer.

Only for his dark shadows to strike out, wrapping twice around my arm to keep me in place.

He looked down at where my touch curled over his own wrist. Blankly as if he didn't recognise me.

The breeze didn't stir his hair. He didn't even breathe. So still and strange.

The Old Gods know no mortal vices. They know no pleasure or pain. Only power. Horror clawed at my heart at that ancient hymn.

'Emrys?' I called again, only he didn't move. Didn't look at me. So still and so lost. Until movement came from behind. Those deadly jet-black eyes focusing on something over my shoulder. A strange sound rumbling in his chest in threat. I turned to find Gideon there, William tucked safely behind him.

A warning crackle of magic was building around us as the rebels took stock of what stood before them. A rumbling like a storm rolling overhead as the sky darkened.

'It's us, Emrys,' Gideon warned, but I saw the flash of panic in his blue eyes. The movement from the rebels rising around us made the ground shake again, made that darkness in Emrys lash out and bite. Curling around my wrist almost painfully.

Those demonic eyes darted over every perceived threat, his lips pulled back in a feral display. A crack as the earth beneath his boots split, strange ethereal runes glowing up from the quaking earth.

Beneath. It comes from beneath.

'Emrys,' I barely breathed, heart breaking to see him so confused. So unlike himself. The version he never wished to be.

So predatory. That darkness moving beneath as if it was a living thing, curling around his limbs with such authority I felt the primitive side of my magic bite in response. Wishing to challenge what it was trying to take from me.

His head twitched, those eyes closing. The cold sting of his magic biting deep like claws. Painfully so. Something was speaking to him.

I stepped closer, until the icy sharpness of his magic sank into my exposed flesh.

'*Eria*, we need to go home,' I called, needing him to listen. Hoping I hadn't lost him so easily.

That strange twitching stopped as if the voices had been held at bay. The grip of his magic eased ever so slightly on my flesh as his eyes opened.

Endless darkness stared back at me.

Before it rose from his skin like smoke.

Gideon gave a cry of warning but it was too late as the ground moved beneath our feet, sending us tumbling into nothingness.

Chapter Thirty-Five

Kat

The dark ones hold no form. Cannot be contained nor chained.

Those golden beasts didn't believe our tales. So they made their own.

Poisoned that darkness with their own might, then brought the world crashing down on the innocents who had no choice in their blood.

The blessed saviours who watched it burn and concealed the blood of their own crimes in rivers of gold.

Compendium of the Lost, 1536

Serus? A strange small voice called as the world was torn apart and put back together in a smear of colour and wisps of darkness until reality lurched back towards me. A maze of bookshelves with tall ladders leaning against the intricately carved shelves, showing depictions of a forest and the woodland beasts that dwelled there. Every piece of furniture in the room was piled with texts, the hearth roaring, the comforting scent of books and old magic dragged into my lungs with every short panicked breath.

Blackthorn Manor.

Home. We were home.

'Emrys,' I panted, spinning in a circle. Trying to right my unsteady legs as I stumbled into my own desk, as if I was on a ship in a storm. Gideon was across from me doing the same as he clung to the door frame. I could only see William's boots from between the bookshelves, a retching sound reaching my ears.

We'd been thrown too quickly from one place to the next.

Whisps of darkness remained in the air as white dots marred my vision.

Emrys had ported us. With nothing but his magic. A power I couldn't even comprehend. Void creatures were rare, none having been seen in centuries. Yet an Old God would have that power – or a child of their blood. The house released a weary groan, the doorway Gideon clung to sagging and beginning to quake.

Then I saw where the darkness curled in the centre of the room. How shadowed and cold it grew in an instant. How the dark form of Emrys braced his hands on the floor, head bowed, his fingers digging into the wood as if it was nothing but paper. How easily it splintered between his touch. His head twitched, limbs tensing as shudders rolled through him. That dark summoning beneath his skin twisting and pressing against his flesh, forming strange runes like those that had appeared by the cracked earth.

To summon such darkness is to be consumed by its hunger.

'Emrys,' I whispered.

He shook his head as if trying to get free of something, curling forwards as he pulled at his hair Almost convulsing as the shadows deepened. Then, in a moment, he was gone, in a flare of dark smoke. The hearth flickered, light coming back to the room the same moment a crash came from above us, reminding me of those cursed bones in the Greymark house.

'What on earth is—' Alma called, rushing into the room with her robe around her, wet hair stuck to her cheeks as she dripped water onto the floor. She was here. She was safe. Only there wasn't a moment for that relief to soothe me. Not as another crash came from above.

'Emrys,' I moved for the doorway, stumbling sideways. My knees still unstable from the shock of the magnitude of the magic I didn't understand. The house creaking in distress as all the cupboards and drawers rattled.

Magic had a price and I was fearful of what it would make Emrys pay.

'Kat!' Gideon grabbed my arm, turning me towards him as we both panted wildly on the stairs, holding onto the banister for dear life.

'He's dangerous like this, Kat,' he warned, a wild panic in those words that made dread claw at my insides.

'I'm not leaving him like that.' Not as something he didn't wish to be.

I'm wrong, Kat. The gutting desperation in his voice as I remembered those words from Emrys's lips.

He'd done this to protect us and I hated that most of all. Gideon grabbed my hand, hesitation flashing in his features, his jaw set as if he was going to protest again as another crash came from above. 'I don't think—'

'Help me, Gideon.' I begged. To find something. I knew Emrys would listen to me. No matter what consumed him. He'd told me that.

'Why is William vomiting?!' Alma half shrieked from the study. Only to go quiet as another boom followed, the house practically whining.

'Fuck's sake,' Gideon snapped, grabbing my arm and half dragging me up the stairs after him, following the ominous noises and the distress of the house. The clatter of doors and the rattle of the windows.

The hallway above was plunged into darkness, our breath misting before us.

'Emrys?' Gideon called into the abyss. Moving forwards with no hesitation. Towards the faintest glow of light coming from the end of the hall.

The doorway creaking as we entered Emrys's bedroom. He stood by the fireplace, illuminated by the dying embers. His hands were braced against the wall, head bowed, his fingers digging into the plaster. A hole gaped in the brick as if he'd struck it. Over and over.

His leathers were gone, dark summoning rippling from his skin, leeching free to tangle around his legs and waist as if he was half consumed by shadow. His muscles twitched, tensing as shudders rolled through him. There was a slight shake to his head again. Something was in there. Speaking to him.

Some nights I can hear them. He'd told me that. I'd seen it with my own eyes.

I stepped towards him only for Gideon to pull me back, words sharp and instant.

'Get the remains of that fiend off you. It'll make him worse.'

I looked down, realising I had strange grey dust all over my leathers – I'd been the closest to that fiend. He pushed me towards the bathroom. I went numbly.

I undressed quickly. Grabbing a towel, I scrubbed at my face and shook out my hair. Another bang and horrid creaks echoed from the room beyond. The calm tones of Gideon's voice.

I took my nightgown from the back of the door and pulled it on. I should have been worried about the indecency. The thin cotton did nothing to combat the icy chill consuming the space, breath clouding before me as gooseflesh covered my legs.

'Emrys?' Gideon called, aether glowing between his fingers to illuminate the space. Emrys didn't respond, continued to shake and convulse in agony. Gideon let out a frustrated sound before he moved to the desk, ransacking the drawers. 'Where did you put it, you hoarding little bastard?'

I ignored Gideon's rummaging, my focus solely on Emrys as I let my magic flare, warming me ever so slightly. Taking the barest step closer to him.

His dark form stilled, his head turning predatorily, considering me over the bulk of his shoulder. He felt it. Felt the barest flare of my flame.

I heard you too. He'd given me that. Reminded me of the power I'd given him. To call to me just as I called to him. Then I saw the gold glinting on the darkness of his hand.

Where my father's hilt remained wrapped around his finger.

To wield a Kysillian blade was to be bound to its master, to be trusted the same. My blade trusted him. My magic trusted him – and so did my heart. Even in this strange form.

I didn't hesitate in my approach, calm and gentle as I pressed my lips to his shoulder blade. Right over those dark marks. Let my hands rest on his ribs. Felt him shudder. Heard the unsteady nature to his breath. That darkness curling beneath his skin. His magic sharper than I'd ever felt it. Almost feral as it streaked across his pale scarred flesh towards my touch.

'Emrys,' I breathed against his skin.

His dark-tipped fingers grasped my hand desperately. Painfully, as if it was a tether. Pressing more harshly against his skin. I let my nails bite, and my magic too. Anything for him to focus on me. To focus on my voice.

The house trembled as that darkness seeped like smoke from his skin. His breath was laboured, the darkness becoming more lethal in its dance. Another tremor took him as a strange, pained noise rumbled up his throat.

Did you think you could keep him, Tauria? The darkness in my mind seemed to mock.

He recoiled from me as if he heard it too, forcing me away. Gideon was suddenly there to steady me. Emrys stumbled slightly, shaking his head as he fell to his knees, fingers curling into his hair, bending forwards with a silent scream on his lips. The house was groaning around us, cabinets and drawers rattling with worry.

'He needs to stay still.' Gideon said, his voice breaking as if he couldn't bare it.

'Emrys.' I dropped to the rug before him until our knees touched. Pressing my hands against his bare thighs. Only for his skin to become nothing but black smoke beneath my touch. Warping and changing, slipping between my fingers as if desperate to hold on.

My breath was tight with panic as I clutched uselessly at him. The bite of his magic was frantic. I could feel him flinch and tremble. His head shook again as if refusing to listen to the voice in his head.

A voice I'd heard too.

The fury of my fire bit into my bones, straightening my spine and hardening my will.

Yes, I could keep him . . . because he was mine. He'd given me that vow.

Gideon moved around to his back, resting an arm across his shoulder, almost holding him up. Not caring for any of the darkness consuming him, nor how it bit and twisted. 'Don't listen to them, Emrys. You're home.'

Emrys began to shake, his fingers like claws digging into his own temples.

'Keep him still, Kat,' Gideon ordered.

416

I cupped his face so gently between my palms, thumbs running over his cheekbones, over that scar that pulled painfully, as his skin became shadows and strange demon fire between my hands, but I didn't let him go. Couldn't.

I'd promised him I wouldn't.

'Serus,' I called softly, startling Gideon. His eyes burnt bright blue with witch fire and warning.

Emry went still beneath my touch, eyes opening. Nothing but darkness answered. No recognition, just that strange stillness.

This was his Verr form. A child of the Old Gods. Yet he wasn't a myth or a story. He wasn't a fear or a nightmare. Not as I drew in the barest scent of beasam bark. The rich scent of his summoning and him. The gleam of my blade that hadn't left him in this form.

He was mine.

Bright blue embers of Gideon's aether flared in the hearth. Emrys seemed to recoil from the heat but Gideon tossed something into it. Whatever he'd been searching for.

Thick white smoke suddenly curled from the hearth, smelling of healing herb, lavender and beasam bark. The mixture surrounding us in a strange fog.

Emrys flinched, tried to pry himself from Gideon's hold almost desperately. Only Gideon was unmovable, that metal arm a band across his chest, forcing him to drag the mixture into his lungs. One breath and then two, deeper as his tension dissipated ever so slightly.

I ran my trembling hands up his throat to ease him. Feeling the frantic beat of his pulse against my palm. '*Eria*.'

That word he'd given me. All the promises too. The house quieted in a moment. Gideon's breath was unsteady, as if holding it with hope that something as simple as those words could work.

417

Then there was the barest flicker of life in those dark eyes as he came back to me. As that gaze ran over my features. He became real beneath my touch. Smoke dancing and slipping back into his skin, content.

I kept touching him, trying to soothe his tremors.

'You burn, I burn,' I whispered. Even if it all fell apart, we'd fall apart together. Even as that darkness burnt through him, just as my flame burnt through me.

'*You're mine, Serus,*' I commanded in the old tongue, feeling magic flare in my palms, a lavender hue and I knew he felt that warmth bite into his skin. Just as the ferocity of his own summoning could bite into mine.

'Tauria,' a hollow voice answered, filled with nothing but darkness. Guttural with pain.

Gideon jerked in surprise.

'Yes,' I smiled, brushing the damp hair back from his fore-head. Then those dark hands moved, confused and sluggish to rest over Gideon's arms around him. His head turning to see his brother.

He blinked once, as if struggling to recognise him.

'Gideon?' he asked. Gideon's smile was small but I saw the wetness gleaming in his eyes.

'I'm here,' he reassured him, loosening his hold but only to press his fingers into Emrys's hair and lay a kiss at his temple. 'You're home, Emrys.'

Home.

Emrys seemed to sag with exhaustion. A calm settling as we held him between us, as light slowly seeped back into the room. The hearth warmed with orange flames, chasing away the icy chill. Yet, Emrys shivered, muscles still twitching with whatever had haunted him, his eyelids drooping with fatigue. Gideon released him gently, moving to the bed and pulling a blanket free to drape over his brother's prone form.

Crouching there to assess every one of his now steady breaths before those concerned eyes met my own where I still knelt. Then his eyes darted to the doorway. Of course. William wasn't well.

'I've got him,' I smiled, letting the magic flare in my palms to try and warm Emrys where they pressed against his skin beneath that blanket.

'I know you have.' The words were soft from the healer's lips before he ran his hand through his hair and let a long breath escape him. 'Call me if you need me.'

He hesitated a moment longer, as if the last thing he wanted to do was leave. Until his shoulders slumped in defeat and he left Emrys in my care. I brought the blanket further over his shoulders, pushing the dark hair from his brow.

Then tentatively his hands moved over me – curious, as if trying to remember every part. To make certain I was real. My thighs, my waist, my arms and up to my hands where I held him.

Those dark-tipped fingers traced the edge of my jaw and the arch of my ear, his head ducking ever so slightly to the curve of my throat. Right over that scar made by the galmoth, a dark sound rumbling from him as if in displeasure at the sight of it.

A sudden stillness consuming him. Making me worry he was overrun again by that darkness. Only his touch was still soft, his breath even where it brushed the side of my throat.

'*You smell like you're mine,*' he spoke in that dark tongue. The words difficult to understand as his lips grazed the side of my throat. It was such a strange, delicate and primal thing.

'*I am.*' I answered without hesitation. Verr were territorial beings. Lustful and primitive in their hunger.

Loyalty came first and Emrys had already given me his loyalty. I knew that in my bones. Just as I knew he'd crawl across that cursed earth to make certain I wasn't alone. Even if it destroyed him.

Perhaps then I understood the Kysillians' hatred for Verr. Kysillians valued their honour, their blood and their pride. They were loyal to only the ancestors that had come before – to keeping the purity of their name.

I knew in my heart, Emrys would forsake everything for me. For those he loved. No matter that I was marked, no matter the danger in my blood or how it would ruin us both. Even if all those Old Gods awakened and commanded him not to.

He'd told me as much.

'Kat.' He brushed my name against the curve of my cheek and emotion burnt in my throat, stopping any answer as I caught his beautiful face between my hands, pressing my lips against his, quick and chaste. He'd come back to me. Just as he promised. Tears dampened my cheeks, and he caught every one. In all this darkness, loving Emrys was the easiest thing. The only part that made sense. So essential to me, like my own breath or the company of my flame in my blood.

Home. One I'd been searching for where all the grief and hurt slipped away. His fingers curled into my hair, his magic still sharp and dragging down the arch of my back. Making me move further into his arms, almost onto his lap, as the chill of him brushed against the inferno in me.

Only for his breath to catch, for the muscles of his chest to tense beneath my palm.

'Let's get you into bed,' I offered, pressing those words to the underside of his jaw, laying my palm flat over his mark beneath that blanket. Before gently untangling myself to get to my feet, hoping he'd follow or ready to help him if he couldn't. To stand before him. Just like one of those offerings in the tales of old. Of foolish girls and Old Gods.

That wildness still too close to the surface in him. His eyes flashing that brilliant ethereal white before retreating to jet-black once more. 'This is a darkness said to devour this world.'

My smile didn't falter. Nor did my affection for him. 'Then you can devour me first.'

He wasn't the monster those stories and nightmares forced him to believe and I wouldn't make him feel that he was. Even if he was consumed. Even if it ended that way. He'd ruined me too, and I wished for no other fate.

A strange dark rumble came from his chest. Almost a growl of disapproval with the distance between us. His hands took a teasing trail around the back of my bare calves where he still knelt. Those eyes didn't leave mine as his lips pressed so devoutly against the inside of my knee.

'I could have hurt you.' His magic bit playfully as if it wished to form claws. To claim me in the ancient way our ancestors would have. In a way I wanted him to mark me now, so he could always see that devotion on my flesh.

I ran my fingers through his hair. 'You think I would have let you?'

No. Because we were equals in the forbidden nature of our power. He'd taught me that. There was no fear here. Not between us.

He stood slowly at that challenge, reminding me how much larger he was than me. The light grey shift in his eyes, the mortal quality returning to his features. Yet those shadows remained, two pieces of his crafted so beautifully. The strange makings curving around the muscled contours of him fading but not fully dispersed.

My hand found his own, the metal of my father's hilt still at his finger. The ring so warm against his skin. Content.

421

'Come on.' I pushed up onto my toes to lay a kiss against his lips and then I coaxed him into the bed as another tremor moved through him.

There was such a weighted exhaustion in all his movements. So unlike himself, as if the change had taken something. Reminding me why the Old Gods didn't take mortal form.

Such power shouldn't be contained by flesh and bone. Why Kysillian power rendered their own Kysillian kings to ash in the end – chaos had limits for a reason. In all its forms it would seem.

The house let the fire flare. Then manifested towels and a steaming bowl of water. A pot of tea and an elaborate tray of biscuits as if frantically trying to find any way to help. Amongst all the items now littered on Emrys's bedside table was a glass filled with what looked like brandy.

'What is that?' I reached for it, expecting the strong smell of liquor. Wondering why on earth the house would think brandy would help. Only to find it smelt like burnt sugar, a strange herbal perfume coming from the amber liquid.

'Harborne extract mixed with other things. Gideon made it years ago.' Emrys signed, reaching for the glass. 'It takes the edge off.'

I gave it to him, watching the strong line of his throat as he downed it in one. Harborne was a toxic herb, any potion brewed with it highly volatile. Yet it seemed to settle him just as he said, breath slipping a little more easily through his lips. Those shadows slipping deeper beneath his skin.

'I thought you were drinking,' I admitted, remembering him with the same glass that day in the library.

His eyes were closed as his head rested against the dark wood of the headboard, yet a small devious smile pulled at his lips. 'Drink doesn't effect Verr, Croinn.'

My cheeks flushed, remembering the last time I'd accused him of being drunk. When he'd kissed me that first time.

Sensing where my thoughts had gone, one eye opened. Such a beautiful light grey as he reached for me, pulling me down to rest against his chest.

'A lecherous drunkard.' He pressed his lips to the side of my head. 'What a type you have, Miss Woodrow.'

I couldn't help but laugh, settling against him. My thumb tracing the edge of his jaw, feeling the steady beat of his heart against my cheek. Realising just how tired I was in the absence of all my panic.

'Speak, Croinn,' he asked softly, sleepily as the hearth dimmed.

'I don't know what to say,' I had too many words smothered inside of me. Too much hope and too many fears. Unable to understand how everything was unravelling, all the loose ends I hadn't yet been able to catch.

'Anything. Everything is better when I can hear your voice.' His magic made a soothing pass over my arm, raising goose-flesh in its wake.

'*Amartis*. Do you – do you know what that means?' I asked, tracing those dark marks on his skin across his chest. Following the scars that led to that mark right over his heart.

He didn't answer but his hand caught my own, pressing it against his skin more firmly. That ring glinting in a flare of orange light from the hearth.

I pushed up slightly, tipping my head to see his beautiful soft grey eyes watching me, waiting.

'Call me back to you. Wherever. In whichever life,' I smiled. A Kysillian devotion I knew the stories told. That he'd know that promise in its simplest form, know it from the tales that had survived. 'I'm yours.'

He went still, so many thoughts moving across his shadowed features. As if trying to sense a lie.

'You knew what I was then,' his words were rough, almost with warning. The doubt he expected to see. That I'd want him so completely, even knowing it would never end well.

'I was already yours.' I didn't let my smile falter, let him see the depth of just how much I meant it. Watched the lavender of my own gaze reflected in the depths of his. 'Even if it was never meant to be. Even if it ended in that pit, even if it led to nothing but my ruin. I was yours, Emrys.'

Even if it was wrong and never destined to be. I'd still want this right here. Cursed or not.

'Kat.' My name was so quiet and so broken from his lips as he curled me closer into his arms.

'You're stuck with me,' I taunted softly, wrapping my arms around him. Relishing in the weight of him on top of me.

'Careful.' He pressed a kiss lightly at my throat before the scratch of his stubble came at my jaw and his lips found my own. 'Verr take vows very seriously, Croinn.'

'*Amartis*,' I repeated between his kiss. Offered my soul. My heart. Everything. Watching a tremor move through him at the pleasure of it.

'Thank you for staying with me.' The words were so soft as his head rested on the pillow next to my own.

'Where else would I be?' I asked, but he was already asleep.

I lay there with the comfort of Emrys's magic around me, but I couldn't rest.

The house as always, seemed to sense my unease – a sliver of golden light crept across the room, the bedroom door opening ever so slightly. From the rustle of papers I heard beyond, I knew it didn't lead into the hallway.

Then I realised, Gideon had taken care of Emrys. He'd left to see to William and I knew without a doubt he'd probably assessed Alma too – even at the risk of getting bitten.

Yet, who had checked on him?

Careful not to disturb Emrys, I slid from the bed and pulled on my robe.

I made my way to the door to find the study beyond bathed in nothing but firelight, playing over the small form of Alma curled up on the chaise before it. So tightly I wondered if she still thought she was in cat form, her dark curls poking out in disarray from beneath the blanket concealing her.

Gideon sat at his desk, a glass of amber liquid in his hand.

'Gideon?' I asked, watching him turn with one raised brow as if anticipating my interruption. Looking just as tired as I felt. Only I understood his reluctance to rest.

'Before you lecture me . . . it's fucking apple tea,' he sighed, taking another sip from the glass before he sat forward so his elbows rested on his knees and rubbed his neck with those metal fingers, wincing as though they pinched the skin. 'How is he?'

'Sleeping.'

'Thank you.' He looked up at me but defeat still sat heavy on his shoulders as he turned his attention to Alma. 'I told her to go to bed. Unsurprisingly, she told me to sod off.'

A quiet laugh left me. How I missed her when she was right there. How our quiet moments alone seemed so seldom.

'What of William?' I asked.

'Chucking his guts up. He never was good with portal stones – never mind whatever in the dark gods' name that was,' Gideon sighed. 'I gave him a tonic and put him to bed. Had to move about fifty fucking brambles off his bed.'

He held up his hand as evidence, showing the small red scratches across his non-metal palm that made me smile.

I was unsure of what to say after the strange intimacy of the last few hours. My eyes fell to the papers scattered on Emrys's desk between us, searching for anything to talk about. Seeing uneven letters, wobbly as if made by a child's hand, the corners covered in small drawings.

'These are children's notes. Are they William's?' I frowned, turning another page. Seeing the detailed words of Verr history. Line after line, so neat.

'They're Emrys's,' his answer was reluctant, almost guarded. 'Father took him to the ruins. Made him write down their secrets. From as young as he could understand. I think that's why he's always been committed to understanding it. Even now.'

Of course. He'd understand Verr even if he'd never heard it.

Grief clawed at my heart for the boy he'd been. Made to feel that he was a curse. A danger.

'He was only a child,' I whispered. I hated it. Hated how long he'd feared this and it had come to pass. 'He isn't like Montagor.'

Emrys wasn't cruel and he wasn't mad. He didn't seek to destroy this world or the fey that occupied it. He didn't crave power. Not like the stories claimed he should. He'd lost control in that village because he was trying to protect something. Not mindlessly tear it apart.

Gideon rubbed at his temple, wary with his own theories. 'I don't think Emrys and Montagor were made the same way.'

The pages slipped from my grasp. 'What do you mean?'

He sat back in his chair, the metal of his finger whirring as they drummed on his knee. 'The Old Gods were said to be tricksters and bargain makers. The demon princes weren't really born, as such – they pass on their entire essence into anything they create. I believe Emrys was born, why the control of his magic is so similar to fey. That Serus indeed *willed* him to be created.'

'Why would Serus will that?' Why would the Old God wish to wake? And if the Old God did . . . why wouldn't he do something more destructive with his power?

Gideon moved to Emrys's desk, turning the pages littered there until he pulled out a depiction of a dark figure, the crescent moon and an ancient sword sketched close by.

'Serus was said to be the guardian of his people. It was why he took a cursed blade to the heart rather than sacrifice them. There also aren't any records from the old ruins of him harming the fey. Nor his sister, the twin moon, Acara.'

Acara. The seer. Queen of the Damned. I knew only fragments of her. Daughter of the Old Gods. The only daughter. Yet, if Serus's goal wasn't to harm the fey, why would his tales be so tangled with that of the darkness beneath?

Gideon turned over another page, showing the other depictions of the Old God in question, the lamb standing beneath the crescent moon. 'The siblings acted as guardians, the two united could tame the deadly night and keep the other more troublesome gods at bay.'

Yet the sealing of the earth would have torn them apart. Forced them beneath and rendered that protection useless.

'There are stories of dark madness. Where the Old Gods or the princes possess a being for a short period of time. However, their sanity and their life soon run out. The darkness of the summoning burns though their lifeforce. My father believed Emrys would be consumed sooner rather than later. It was why he was adamant for him to never summon that side of his nature.'

He believed it would kill him or drive him mad. Neither had happened, which meant Serus wasn't possessing Emrys. They were one and the same.

'You think Montagor was made wrong?' I asked.

'I think Varin is trapped in Montagor's head and will do anything to get out. However, if Varin consumes another vessel of the Old Gods' power he'll become more powerful than Emrys. So either he's opening that seal to summon . . . or he's hoping someone will turn up to stop him.'

Varin — one of the princes beneath, a creature of wrath. One that spilled fey blood across the lands and demanded worship. Varin wished to do battle with Serus. Just like in the tales. Only this time, no other princes or Old Gods were awake to pick sides.

'Emrys should be as far from this shit as he can get and so should you.' His warning was gentle — concerned, even. Reminding me that Callen was right about those elders.

Of what the Kysillian's would do if they knew Verr existed. If they knew what lay between me and Emrys.

I didn't wish to think on that. To think of the elders who slumbered far in the north, ignoring all this pain. Just like those ancient beasts in their tales. I turned my attention back to the table, something dark glinting in a flare of firelight. Sitting amongst those papers was the hilt of a blade. Tarnished silver with black gems decorating the hilt.

The blade of the Old Gods. The echo of Lady Ramsey's voice penetrated my thoughts.

That darkness crafts blades with demon fire. They gleam and shatter seals. How cold they burn and decimate the fragility of fey magic. Too powerful to exist, even to their own kind.

A chill stung my skin, my magic surging to make the veins in my hands glow faintly with my power. 'What is that?'

'The Old Gods' blade,' Gideon answered without hesitation. Despite how unsteady I suddenly felt in such an ancient relic's presence.

Lady Ramsey had known. Of course she had.

'It's been here all along?'

Gideon nodded as he tugged at his golden hair. 'My father found it. It's how he met my mother. Both of their masters were seeking it. How strange they'd find it long before Emrys was even born, as if something has been guiding us along this path all along.'

Lady Blackthorn was in service to the rebellion. Lord Blackthorn in service to the mad king.

'The Countess wanted it?' I demanded. Lady Ramsey had given us that warning and Gideon had dismissed it so easily. Yet now his jaw was tense as he nodded. The Countess was seeking an Old God's blade.

'The relic she possesses calls to it. Or the madness does.' He took something from his desk – the shard from the gobrite's cage – and placed it on Emrys's. It slid across the papers to be closer to the blade. Seeming to have a mind of its own, practically vibrating with its need to be connected. Just like my father's sword when it wished to demonstrate its will.

Only as I faced such strange truths, a different sadness pierced my chest at what that blade meant. 'Emrys has been like that before. What would Blackthorn do if he didn't come back?'

Gideon's brow furrowed with a deeper emotion. 'It's said the only way to kill an old god is with their own blade. It's why they battle between themselves for power and rank. There is no threat greater than their own blood. Kysillians might have buried them and removed their mortal form, but they didn't destroy that power.'

He swallowed painfully, almost resistant to tell me the rest. 'I fear my father kept the blade as a last resort.'

My heart sank. For the little boy who never had a chance, never had a moment to falter before they'd labelled him a monster. Emrys would have known by looking at it exactly why his father had it. He'd have known it was because no matter what he did . . . he'd never escape how they feared him.

'Why is it out now?' I demanded softly, feeling my skin heat. My fingers curling in anticipation of summoning.

Gideon considered me, watching that fury flicker in my eyes. A small smile coming to his lips. 'You think I'd hurt him?'

No. I didn't think he would but the presence of that blade and the threat it posed to Emrys made my magic feral. Especially with the vow I'd just given him so new between us. Seared into my very bones to protect him.

That smile didn't falter on Gideon's lips, but hurt sank into his eyes. 'We were born the same night. Under the crescent moon. A bad omen for a witch, but my mother made certain I was born first. That makes Emrys my little brother.'

He picked up that shard again, such deep pain cutting across his expression. 'He was mine to take care of and I didn't protect him. I let my father hurt him. Let him torment him and I let him call it love.'

He tossed that forsaken shard back onto the desk, its clatter so loud in the silence between us.

'I'd rather commit myself to the fucking saints before I laid a finger on him. Even if he was the darkness promised to ruin this world.' Gideon sank back into his chair, resting his head in his hands. 'I should have told him that from the start.'

Weighted with such pain.

Because he loved him. The house let out a small sad groan in answer to those words.

I crossed the space between us and laid my hand gently on his shoulder. 'You were a child too, Gideon.'

'You sound like Emmaline,' he snorted but didn't shrug off my touch.

'Then maybe we're both right,' I smiled, wishing she was still here for both of them. How painfully that wound still gaped.

'He thinks I left because I'm ashamed of what he is.' He rubbed at his jaw, his eyes shone with unshed tears. 'I'm ashamed of myself. Ashamed of the times I should have chosen him over my father's schemes.'

'You *did* choose him Gideon. You're here.' He'd come back. Emrys had listened to me but he'd listened to Gideon too. He'd needed him. 'I don't think the crescent moon was a curse at all. I think he was blessed before he was born to have a brother like you.'

Such agony cut across Gideon's expression, yet he didn't fight those words. Not as he turned his attention to the fire. It was strange to see such depth of emotion from a man I knew was reserved and sharp.

But living with Alma, calling her my friend, I understood Gideon. He felt too deeply and wished not to.

'You'd better get back to him. He'll know you're missing.' His voice was the barest rasp, as if struggling to swallow down his feelings. 'And I'm certain we should be anticipating a right bollocking off Lady Ramsey any time soon.'

Not a dismissal. A request for privacy I understood as I smiled again and moved to bid him goodnight.

'Kat,' he called, making me pause at the door. 'Thank you for caring for him. Even now.'

Even knowing the truth of it all.

'I'm glad he found you. Even if you are both massive fucking pains in my arse.'

I couldn't help the small laugh that burst from my lips. How true those words were. 'Get some rest, Gideon. Please?'

He nodded in small surrender just as the house manifested another apple tea for him and a small tray of tarts. I also noted the small handkerchief on the edge of the plate.

I went back into the calm darkness of the bedroom. Emrys was still as I'd left him. I curled into his side. Slipping back into the bed, sliding back into his arms and pressing my palm against that mark over his heart, watching the darkness slowly moving beneath his skin. As if recognising my presence.

'Shh,' I chided. Unwilling to disturb him. Burdened with the sadness of everything that had come before. But knowing, no matter what came next . . . he was mine, and this world would know it. I'd make certain of it.

Chapter Thirty-Six

Kat

There was a sorceress formed of moonlight who danced between the shadows of the wood alone. Too powerful for her kin . . . too wild for the world to catch. Until a demon prince sang to her untamed heart. A storm of silver and endless night. A love pressed between the shadows. A courting of nightmares that danced into the everlasting night.

Song of the Eternal Night – Unknown

I woke to the barest brush of something against my temple. I was curled around Emrys's pillow on his side of the bed. A bed Emrys wasn't in.

I forced myself onto my elbows, taking in the room bathed in morning light. A rustle came from the pillow, catching my attention. A small paper bird perched there, its head tilted expectantly.

A note. I pushed the unruly hair from my face.

'You have something for me?' I held out my palm for it to hop into. The paper unfurling immediately.

Croinn.

You were too beautiful to wake.

Lady Ramsey sent summons. I assume she wasn't best pleased by our delivery yesterday. I promise not to fight with any mirocs.

Yours, always.
Emrys

Of course. Gideon had said as much. We'd dropped those fey at the eastern border with no warning. I pressed the note to my chest, tumbling back to the pillows and staring up at the canopy above the bed. I should be relieved he felt better – that he'd gone back to working on all the things we still needed to do. Yet unease remained, prodding incessantly against my ribs as if I had missed something.

I pulled myself from the bed, and moved to where I'd left my leathers, pulling out my mother's note where I'd tucked it into the pocket. I pressed it to my nose again, seeking her scent that had long faded.

Leaving nothing but dust and the bitterness of ink behind.

'I miss you.' I ran my thumb over the parchment. Over the familiar curve of her writing. My only wish was that they found each other. That all the stories were real and something existed beyond this. I'd face whatever the ancestors sent my way, as long as they could be together again.

I tucked the last fragment of her safely away in Emrys's desk, grabbing my robe and making my way downstairs.

I didn't get far before the bustling presence of Alma greeted me. Seemingly her usual self. Her dark curls pinned beautifully away from her face, a simple blue cotton dress making her green eyes appear sharper than ever.

'The dead awaken at last,' she teased.

'How are you?' I demanded. Pulling her into a tight embrace. Surprised that she let me. Wondering where she'd gone and how she'd missed the rebellion. Thanking the ancestors silently that she had. Also for how quickly she seemed to now be recovering from her changes.

'Remind me never to take a bite of a hunter again,' she mumbled against my shoulder before pulling back, and there was something about the avoidance in her gaze – I couldn't help feel that she was hiding. Every inch of her covered.

'I'm certain you already know Lady Ramsey summoned them before dawn. As you can guess, Gideon was thrilled.' She rolled her eyes before doing her own inventory of me, as if she needed to check every freckle across my nose. There was a strange intensity in her stare – unsettled, perhaps.

'I should have been with you.' Wondered if she was angry with me – even distantly. Her small smile didn't falter, but the sharpness in her gaze softened.

'You can't save me all the time, Kat. The hunters and the verium wasn't your fault.' She hooked her finger around one of my own.

I'd promised her safety and I'd failed her. Failed to find any purpose to all this chaos.

A rattling turned our attention to the doorway where William stood grinning, cheeks flushed as he hopped on the balls of his feet as if unable to contain his excitement.

'Good, you're both here,' he began. 'We have something . . . *wonderful* to show you!'

'Who is *we*?' Alma demanded, her hands falling to her hips. A dangerous pose – I'd learnt the hard way.

'You have to promise not to get mad.' The boy held his hands up in surrender, but he barely got a moment to finish before the dark head of a hound poked between his legs.

A hound formed of dark matter and smoke. Like a . . .

'What the bloody fuck is that?!' Alma seethed, grabbing my arm as if to wrench me behind her. Her hands twisting into claws in an instant.

'Look!' William smiled, dropping to one knee to scratch behind the fiend's ear. 'Isn't he *delightful*?'

435

'Please tell me that's not the gobrite,' I half stuttered, unable to put it all together.

Did we lock the cage again after Gideon had removed the shard? I couldn't remember.

'I want to call him Orin,' William announced, ignoring me. 'It means dark ghost. He does his business outside and everything.'

'It should be in its *cage*,' Alma warned as she bared her teeth at the creature. The fiend's ears went flat, head bowed as if scared.

'He looked sad.' William's face fell.

'I'm sure it'll cheer up when it's ripping out our throats in our sleep,' she snapped.

'I already have you to worry about for that, darling,' Thean interjected as they suddenly appeared at the bottom of the stairs.

They were in a feminine form, billowing shirt, tight riding trousers and corset, a multitude of weapons at their belt as if they'd been on patrol. Hair braided and twisted around their head like a crown, dangerous amber eyes gleaming with irritation.

'I think whatever you did to trap it made it lose its power, Kat,' William reasoned, petting the fiend's head again. The bastard creature had the audacity to tilt its head in enjoyment. 'It's quite tame.'

Then I saw the delight in the boy's eyes, an almost shy pleading. Asking something with no words.

'I am *not* talking Emrys into letting you keep that thing,' I protested. Aghast he'd even think it was an option.

The boy's face fell. The fiend whined. Sulking.

Bollocks. How was I going to convince Emrys to let William keep a *fiend* as a pet?

Thean sighed, pushing their hands into their pockets as they glared at the creature, which instantly cowered, lowering itself to the ground. Simpering. 'The beast is completely null. I assume Emrys's performance last night has rendered most dark summonings contained in this house quite *impotent.*'

The dark respects its master. What was more masterful than the power of Serus given mortal form?

'The relic must have been powering it. Or corrupting it. Maybe they're all like this really,' William offered weakly, which didn't reassure me one bit. 'Didn't you say skelmor were peaceful creatures?'

Then the thoughts began to click within my mind, turning like cogs. I'd used Kysillian flame to conceal the gobrite. The old texts talked of Kysillia's flame cleansing the dark – only maybe it didn't mean destroying it. The dark summoning of the gobrite had been changed by my flame. Brought into submission.

'If we knew how to get the other books open, that might give us a clue as to why the relics affect them so much,' William sighed.

Because the Compendium of Souls would hopefully explain this ancient magic better than any other tome. My magic sparked in my fingertips, stinging my thumb and forefinger where I had held my mother's note.

A note she'd left, on the paper from that text.

'It was open,' I whispered.

The Compendium of Souls had been open. My mother had written a note from its page.

Lady Leanna Grey. A lord's daughter.

There were no powerful compendiums in the Greymark line or mages. So why did the Mage King suddenly want her? Why would he want a consort of inferior blood? Why would he care when he was bedding and sacrificing fey to try to reawaken the Old Gods?

I moved to the desk in the study, looking to the overlong family lines. Finding the Greymark one. How it twisted and weaved through all the others. Picking up the scraps at the end of every branch, as if they were always the last option.

A reluctant bargain.

They mixed with every line. Whored their daughters to keep favour in the courts. The fate my mother was destined to face.

Lord Turner said the King wanted the seals more than anything. More than any desire.

I turned to Alma. 'In the Greymark house – you said the scent was familiar.'

She frowned. 'Because it smelt like . . . you.'

Why would a king want an unknown girl for a queen? The question mocked in the back of my mind. Blood. The Greymark blood had mixed with every line. My blood.

Never speak my name. It was a promise my mother made me keep. Not out of fear for herself – out of fear they would know I was hers.

I turned, grabbing one of Thean's blades and I pressed it to the heel of my palm. The barest bead of blood appeared. I dragged the Compendium of Souls closer and let a drop hit the cover.

No. It couldn't be that simple. The answers couldn't have been with me all this time.

The lock clicked, the book flicking its pages open of its own accord. Forcing me to move back as if a fiend could burst free at any moment.

Only nothing followed, just the answer sitting silently before us.

'He wanted her to open the books,' I whispered. All that pain for nothing but this. He would have broken my mother apart for nothing but this. For curses that should have been left to rot.

Blood from every line. I saw then how deadly she was, what my Kysillian side had concealed. Why my mother held her secrets so close to her heart.

The words lining those stained pages were a dark scrawl, strange and unknown to me. The wishing stone at my neck fluttered. Emrys's magic concealed within it – an Old God's magic. Magic that this darkness feared.

I pulled the stone over my head, letting it touch the page. Watching that bright white light illuminate the text.

'Show me.' The dark language was sloppy from my lips. Only it didn't seem to matter as the ink began to ripple and curl, twisting and forming new shapes. Shapes I recognised as the coast of Elysior. A map.

The runes for the Old Gods were spread across the land, as if they had . . .

Places of worship.

Conquerors write the history of their conquest. Gideon's words came back to mock me.

'Montagor was seeking something in fey ruins.' William's words penetrated my slowly building panic.

That was what Callen had said. What if mortals had learnt something from fey after all? A way to hide the past. A way to bury what they didn't wish their followers to see.

Why the Councils and the mad kings of old had buried their predecessors' failures.

I moved the papers aside, flicking through them like a madwoman until the map of Elysior fell open next to the page in the book.

Every fey settlement with its sacred ruins was exactly where the Old Gods' runes were written in the book.

The fey had hidden them – or maybe the Kysillians themselves. Because what was the best way to defeat an enemy? By taking away the power of their story. By making them little more than a myth. It was why the fey settlements had always been affected first by breaches.

That darkness wasn't seeking them out. The fey were just the first beings to cross their path.

I turned to the fiend. *Orin.* Now rubbing itself against an unbothered Thean's leg.

'We need to find the other pieces,' I demanded. The relics that would lead Montagor to the same conclusion.

The gobrite turned as if understanding me, barking as if in agreement.

I remembered so vividly the fear in that darkness, as if it knew it didn't stand a chance. It was sentient. Wild and cruel, but that was what it had been forced to be.

The gobrite had been forced into that book. Forced into it for a reason. Corrupted against its will.

I looked at the creature now, how it had manipulated itself to appear as something we would accept.

'Dark magic can find its way home,' I barely whispered. A fiend that houses part of a relic could find others. Just as Alma had been able to track the scent of that blood seeker she'd become.

'You cannot seriously be considering trusting that thing?' Alma hissed, slipping around the desk, her hands curling into fists, resisting the urge to shake some sense into me.

'I think she's beyond merely considering it, love,' Thean added unhelpfully.

'You stay out of this,' Alma sneered with a flash of fangs

at the voyav, sharp enough to make William wince before her annoyed serpent-like gaze met my own. 'Have you lost your mind? It tried to kill you last time.'

'I'm sure Orin didn't mean it,' William offered.

'Stop giving it a name,' Alma snapped with frustration before turning her irritation on Thean with a sharp pointed finger. '*You*. Talk some sense into the pair of them.'

'I thought you wanted me to stay out of it?' The voyav smirked.

'Thean!' Their name came between her lips in a growl and I ignored how they seemed to luxuriate in the sound of it.

'Worry not, darling, the little beast is terrified of Emrys and considering our foolish Kysillian is covered in his *scent* . . . I guarantee the little creature will be on its best behaviour,' Thean continued in a teasing tone. Clearly ignoring my mortification at the statement.

'*Barlov*,' Thean commanded. The gobrite's hound head twitched. Then it jumped up against the table to where the maps rested, tugging them down to the floor before it rooted through the mess with its snout.

Alma came closer, her curiosity clearly getting the better of her as she leant over my shoulder to see the map. The gobrite's shadowy paw pressed against one spot.

'It could be leading us into a trap,' Alma hissed quietly, as if cautious the creature could hear her.

'Dark magic does have a better respect for being bested,' Thean observed. 'That's how most ancient dark creatures amass such power.'

'Why Montagor is so set on taking Emrys off the board.' William swallowed loudly, seeming very pale at the thought.

An Old God can only be slain with their blade. That

was why Montagor was after one. *Of course.* It was why the Kysillians had seen Verr as nothing but brutes. They didn't share the power of their blood.

Thean shooed the creature off the paper with a flick of his bejewelled fingers.

'It's our lucky day.' The voyav shrugged, yet their face remained pensive. 'It's in a brothel.'

'What?! Why on earth would it be in there?' Alma recoiled.

'Not in. Under,' Thean continued their explanation, hands braced on their hips. 'Lord Barton decimated the fey ruins on his land three centuries ago to build his house.'

'The Barton lands are lawless. Like the bone markets.' They continued. 'The patrons got bored of paying the lord's prices so strung him up in the street and continued their frivolities.'

'You seem to know a lot about this *establishment*,' Alma added a tad too sharply, making a sly smile slip across the voyav's lips.

'There was a story about how Lord Barton went mad after he trapped an ancient creature within the walls of his house. Or so the tales say.'

Thean turned their attention to the other mark on the map, set in the middle of a smaller village. 'It's *very* occupied and they won't take kindly to intruders.'

I glanced at the window. 'It's barely morning.'

Thean just gave me a bored pointed look that made me flush. Of course. People did have sex in daylight.

'Hang on, if something is beneath that house—' William ran his fingers through his curls. 'Why is it just sitting there?'

'It will have a very strong spell on it. One created around the same time as the compendiums. One by the same bloodlines,' Thean offered, folding their arms. Just as old as the book.

A book I could open. I looked down at my bloody palm, so maybe I could break that concealing enchantment too.

'Then we'll find out,' Alma answered, startling me with her sudden determination and change of heart. I noticed she startled Thean too. 'If we've figured this out, Montagor won't be far behind. He already has a relic and is crazed enough to attack rebel territory. It won't be long until it guides him here.'

William looked as if he might be sick. So I focused on the voyav instead, who hadn't offered any objection to the plan.

'I doubt the clientele are used to Kysillians. Especially one as wanted as our darling Kat.' Thean's voice sounded hard with displeasure.

'I'll wear a glamour. It should last long enough,' I shrugged. It wouldn't be that hard. Nobody would look too closely at a female in a brothel. Or be sober enough to care.

'I'm sure your dark prince will love this,' the voyav warned.

'Surely we should run this by Emrys? Let me get Gideon's speaking crystal!' William darted for the drawer of Gideon's desk. Orin barked as if to hurry him as he rummaged like a desperate thief.

Producing a black speaking crystal wrapped in enchanted parchment and tied with salt-soaked string. The boy frantic-ally tapped the large crystal on the desk's edge. 'Come on. Come on.'

But it remained dim, the runes carved into the stone not glowing. Silent.

They couldn't answer and we couldn't waste time waiting.

William looked stricken. 'I think we need to reconsider this plan. I doubt we need Emrys's wrath chasing us through the streets because Thean made Kat get her breasts out.'

'My breasts will *not* be out,' I countered sharply.

'Don't speak too soon, darling.' Thean's grin became almost feline. The dark fiend hound barked excitedly at his side and I couldn't help wonder if the bastard was, in fact, leading us to our demise.

Chapter Thirty-Seven
Kat

Varin was made from the Old Gods' anger. Others from their hunger, gluttony and lust. For the Alder Kings were many. Only Serus and Acara were made from their devotion to the creatures they created. They knew no greed or hunger for power. Only protection of that endless night and all who dwelled within it.

Serus to guard and Acara to see the path ahead.

However, in the end, even the great queen beneath lost her way in that darkness.

Compendium of the Lost, 1536

'Are sure you did it right? She looks the same to me,' Alma frowned, her skin gleaming from the oil she'd rubbed into it. A jangle coming from the bracelets William had put around her wrists to cover her scars.

'It's working,' Thean added irritably in the alcove where we all hid. A thin curtain dividing us from the ruckus beyond.

I noted Thean in their masculine form had simply unbuttoned their shirt. The only part of them exposed being a strip of their lean muscular chest. Lucky for some.

I tried not to touch any of the walls, considering the lack of fabric covering me. The smell of pleasure smoke in the air tangling with the odour of sweat and ale.

A brothel. What a wondrous idea.

A sweetness clung to my lips from the smoke in the air. My skin was flushed, a heat seeming to simmer close to the surface that had nothing to do with my magic.

'I didn't know pleasure smoke was this sickeningly sweet.' I rubbed my arms. Finding myself unable to stand still.

Alma turned, her sharp gaze missing not a moment of my discomfort before she looked at the voyav. 'Didn't you weave a protection into the glamour?'

Thean seemed genuinely confused by the idea. 'Now why on earth would I do that?'

Alma pulled back, appalled. *'To be helpful?'*

Thean had the audacity to laugh softly, which only made her lips peel back, green eyes practically glowing in the dim light as another peel of drunken laughter moved past our hiding place.

'I'll be fine,' I lied. Pulling at the measly fabric that was supposed to cover my breasts. 'What will you two do?'

Thean slapped my hand away with irritation. 'Stop fidgeting. You're supposed to want the thing off. I'm certain our beautiful Alma can scent anything valuable that may be up here while we wait.'

That led to the problem at hand. Thean might be able to find something Verr but they couldn't open it. The same for Alma, and nothing would look more suspicious than all three of us wandering through a brothel.

But the thought of leaving Alma up here alone to deal with any consequences didn't sit well with me.

'It'll be dangerous,' I said, chewing on my lip, my flame churning in annoyance inside of me. Clearly not liking my current predicament.

She rolled her eyes, her own poor excuse for a lace slip not bothering her in the least. 'You're the last person that should be lecturing anyone on *danger*.'

'Fine,' I huffed out. Knowing she was right. 'I didn't antici- pate it being so *busy*.'

Why were so many people here?

'You can unbuckle someone's trousers any time of day, darling,' Thean taunted. 'Who knew you were such a prude. Poor Emrys.'

That slight earned the voyav an elbow in the ribs from Alma.

'Go,' she commanded me softly. 'Leave me to deal with this miscreant.'

I suddenly felt ill. This was a wretched and foolish idea. My most idiotic to date. I wrung my hands, hoping Gideon had picked up his bloody communication stone. If not, I was certain William had suffered heart failure from the stress of our departure.

I sucked in another breath of the sweet smoke, that worry in my chest only tightening before I forced myself beyond the thin dingy curtain—

Only to almost be trampled by three drunk men staggering past. Two topless girls with rouge smeared all over their breasts from kisses laughed as they followed, green bottles of ale in their hands splashing onto the carpet.

The grimy corridor was made no better by the flickering of the lamps on the dark green walls. The carpet was stained beneath my feet, making me grateful I'd won the battle with Thean to keep my shoes.

A room opened up before me, circular and filled with too many people. Black paint smeared across the arched windows. Dark and dingy, as if every patron had an allergy to light.

The chant from the summoners seated at jewel-decorated tables with their misty orbs filled with trapped souls made a shudder roll through me. Dark summoning for entertainment, speaking to souls – or being distracted by them to have your pockets picked. Unfortunately, the glamour wouldn't hide my revulsion. It also felt like painful pinching against my skin, as if it was too tight.

The brothel was in the centre of the Barton lands. The small town still thriving from what I glimpsed out of the filthy window before Thean had pinched me and forced me to pay attention.

A town with veins of canals running through it, long narrow boats moored on the murky waters. The streets were bustling with night markets, so many beings unaware of what lingered here. What *could* linger beneath this building, and if it did . . . I didn't want to think of what we would find.

I passed booths with worn curtains closed, devious laughter within. I made sure to keep my eyes on the plush blood-red carpet, avoiding the wet patches. Half-naked women and men lounged on chaises with pipes, blowing thick smoke into the already cloying air.

The madness of it all made me move more quickly down another dark panelled hallway, ignoring the drunken mirth and piano music as I passed another archway that led into what appeared to be a card room, keeping close to the long empty bookcases, holding nothing but discarded drinks now. Nothing caught my attention. The wishing stone around my neck silent.

I couldn't see any passageways, or any way down to where a door to any lower chamber could be located. Mostly I couldn't see through the smoke that curled like fog before me.

It was the bastard voyav's fault for not warning me. Or perhaps it was my own for my impatience to try to solve everything myself once again.

448

Too many people, too much noise. Laughter and music. Naked bodies mixed with partially dressed or fully clothed spectators. A strange sordid mix of formality and depravity.

Fumes clung to my lips, an aphrodisiac to heighten pleasure. Something to make the working girls' and boys' jobs easier. Considering most mortals could barely last when dosed with the stuff. How they reclined in low chairs in a daze, pockets probably empty.

I ran my hands nervously over my skirts, or tried to. The thin silk did little but remind me of how much of me was on display, how sheer the fabric was in the barest light. Another deep breath threatened to pop the tiny pearl buttons stopping my breasts from being exposed.

I felt clumsy and ridiculous. Yet as I pulled in another lungful of that smoke, delicious pleasure rippled though me. But not for anything in this room.

Fucking beautiful. The dark tone of Emrys's words seemed to brush against my oversensitive skin. Making me turn like a madwoman, anticipating him standing behind me.

He wasn't.

Ancestors above. Maybe I'd breathed in too much. Then all I could think about was Emrys's hands, the rough tightness of them on my hips. How they'd dragged up my thighs. The brush of his lips up the column of my throat.

I pressed my hand to my breastbone, the need to see him, to touch him, almost painful.

'Fuck,' I hissed, irritated with my own frustration and the wanton nature of my thoughts. I didn't need to be distracted right now. I needed to find the bastard relic, or door – or *anything*.

The wishing stone flickered, almost mocking me.

449

With a frustrated groan, I made my way back into the hallway. I had to be missing something. I was so distracted I collided into something, making me stumble into the filthy wall.

A man stood in my path. His thinning hair in disarray like he'd already used the services and hadn't even bothered to button his trousers back up. Any haze of mad lust for Emrys dissipated like a cold slap.

'Pretty girl like you shouldn't be alone,' he leered, flashing me a grin to show blackened teeth as sour breath met my nose. I had nothing but pity for the poor creature who'd had to service this filthy bastard.

'I have someone waiting,' I smiled tightly, remembering I was supposed to be polite. Despite how the flames in the lamp just above his greasy head seemed to taunt me into singeing the bastard.

'How much?' He stepped more into my path, despite the weedy nature of his appearance and how badly I wanted to knock him back.

'Too much,' I bristled. Then those grabbing hands curled into the thin lace that concealed me.

Quick and sharp, with only a quarter of my Kysillian strength, I punched him in his lower abdomen. He folded with a wheeze, as if he was made of nothing but paper.

That's when two other stumbling idiots entered the passage. Bollocks.

'Trouble?' one of them asked. I parted my lips, trying to work out a lie, when I felt a familiar cold brush at my back. That flutter of desire came back. My magic almost preening through me, making my breath catch. The wishing stone hot where it hung between my breasts.

The men went rigid, as if they were nothing but puppets whose strings had gone taught.

A familiar strong hand looped around my middle, the same moment the scent of beasam bark touched my nose and I was pulled back into a hard chest.

'I think you'll find she's mine.' A dominance laced those words that matched the threatening pressure in the room.

Then all three men dropped to the ground in an instant.

I spun round to face an angry pair of midnight eyes.

Emrys.

Bollocks.

Chapter Thirty-Eight

Kat

I wasn't completely certain I wasn't hallucinating. Worried that maybe there was more in the air than simply pleasure smoke. This version of Emrys in his leathers, as if he'd come straight from meeting Lady Ramsey. Not looking like a brothel patron at all.

Then again . . . I didn't know what Emrys would wear to a brothel.

Why was Emrys in a brothel?

'Can I help you?' I demanded, suddenly angry enough to feel my flame stinging my fingertips as I untangled myself from his hold. Why was he talking to whatever version of me he saw? And what was he doing declaring that whoever she was . . . was *his*.

His dark eyes narrowed for a moment, before a huff of breath left him.

'I know it's you, Croinn.' His fingers curled around my wrist, before he tugged me into one of the dark alcoves. Out of the path of another passing group of patrons. Crowing with amusement as they found the three men sprawled in the hallway.

What? My thoughts felt as clouded as the air before us.

'How?' I demanded, looking down at his hand. At the gold band still on his finger. At how my father's blade had stayed with him all this time.

'Glamour doesn't work on Verr.' His dark brow raised, pulling on that scar at the side of his face.

Of course. I knew that. Well, not exactly, but the myths did say some summoning didn't affect Verr as they would fey or even ancient fey.

'Of all the dangerous and reckless things I could anticipate you doing . . . *this* has won. *By far.* I was absent for a few hours and you've turned to . . . *espionage.*' That exasperated crease at his brow didn't cease, making a delicious shiver run down my spine. 'And you're dreadful at it.'

'You said I was remarkable at everything,' I countered, suddenly unable to stop playing with the buttons of his shirt.

He ducked his head so those pitch-black eyes met my own. 'Croinn, sneaking about isn't your strongest suit.'

I should have been aghast at his observation, however he *had* found me here with little difficulty. I continued to let my fingers play over the buttons, all the way down until I reached the waistband of his trousers.

'Kat.' He caught my curious hand.

I felt like a ghostly caress was brushing over my overheated skin. My magic practically fluttering in my abdomen at his presence, making it impossible to stand still.

'I think something is wrong with me.' I blinked, thankful he was holding my hand because I was fearful I was about to rip his clothes off. Or put it between my thighs.

He caught my chin, examining my eyes. 'It's the smoke.'

'You seem fine,' I accused, tongue darting out to taste that sweetness on my lips. Noting how he tracked my every movement.

'*That* doesn't affect Verr either.' He released my chin, making my lips pucker, but he slid his fingers between my own, trapping my hand from any further wandering. 'Let's go.'

'No.' I stood my ground, pressing myself against his firmness

453

for nothing more than my own pleasure. 'There is a relic here. The gobrite said so.'

'Gobrite?' His brow furrowed, his fingers pressing against my forehead as if I was ill.

'Orin,' I answered absently. Only then I shook my head, realising Emrys wouldn't know William had given the creature a name yet. Maybe I should tell him.

But my thoughts halted as Emrys caught my face between his rough palms.

'Croinn, have you taken something?' His frown deepened, as I felt the pinch of his magic with concern or anger.

'The gobrite turned into a hound and William wants to keep it. He's called it Orin.' I shook my head and ran my hand over the strong line of his throat, up his jaw to trace his lips. 'The Compendium of Souls was open. My mother opened it. The Greymark line mixed with all the Lord's lines . . . so I can open the compendiums too.'

I showed him the cut on my palm, only he didn't seem too pleased about that, so I hid it behind my back. 'Anyway, in the book there was a map of the Verr temples, exactly where the fey ruins are now. I think the fey hid them.'

'This house was built on desecrated fey ruins,' he answered, but my gaze fell back to the golden band on his finger.

'Why are you still wearing that?' I ignored the thrill that went through me and how my stomach swooped. That desire only coiling tighter there, painfully so.

His lips twitched, his eyes suddenly molten despite his annoyance. 'It won't come off.'

'It must like you,' I smiled, only then I had to bite my lip. That incessant need brewing inside me refusing to be ignored. 'You've caused a problem.'

He closed his eyes as if pained before he shrugged out of

his jacket. My breath caught with wanton excitement, only to earn myself a sharp reprimanding look as he held it out to me. 'Put it on, Kat.'

'You don't like it?' I looked down at the slip William had found for me. It was revealing but it wasn't hideous. Not as bad as some of the ideas Thean came up with.

'You're cold, Croinn,' Emrys replied, his tone darker as he glanced over his shoulder, as if hearing something.

Then I noticed my skin was covered in gooseflesh. How had I forgotten I was cold?

'Nobody can see me,' I muttered but obediently put it on, glad to be covered even if it did brush my oversensitive skin. Being enveloped in Emrys's scent wasn't helping my focus.

Only then I noticed how still he was, how his head was tilted, listening. Only I knew it wasn't to the ruckus of the brothel around is.

Darkness calls all dark things back.

'Can you sense it?' I whispered, worried instantly. Remembering the agony it had caused him last night. Hating that I'd brought him closer to something so old.

He nodded. 'It's here.'

He slipped his hand into my own. The barest touch did the strangest things to my body.

I pressed up onto my toes to whisper in his ear. 'When we get home, you'll need to bribe the house to leave us be for a long while.'

An amused – or frustrated – huff of breath slipped from his lips.

'When you're sober, my love, I'll give you anything you want.' He pressed a kiss behind my ear as if to seal the promise.

'I could ask for a book,' I challenged. Maybe to see what lay in those cellars beneath the house I still hadn't been able to look though yet.

455

'No book is as interesting as what I'm going to do to you, Kat.' He kissed the heel of my palm, right over the healing cut before pulling me from the dark. As if knowing I needed the distraction of movement.

'We should get Alma and Thean,' I worried.

'Gideon is on it,' he answered, moving with predatory ease down the corridor.

'I'm sure he's thrilled with that responsibility,' I muttered, suddenly very distracted by how his trousers hugged his backside. Had it always looked like that? And if so, how had I not noticed sooner?

'Croinn,' Emrys half-growled. Making me wonder if he could in fact read minds. The wishing stone gave a flutter against my skin in strange contentment.

Nobody looked at us as we made our way through the halls. They were all too busy doing . . . other things. I kept my gaze firmly on Emrys's broad shoulders, where his shirt clung to the strong contours of him.

Thankful I was behind him. I didn't need any further ideas. Emrys ducked into one of the passages, moving as if pulled by a soundless command – where we found an old arched wooden door hidden between two large cabinets.

It was locked. Emrys's dark-tipped fingers curled around the padlock and with one sharp twist he snapped the metal. It hit the stone with a clang. Making me wonder just when he'd started being able to do that.

The door opened to narrow stone steps that curled around and around as they led downwards. Strings of dust webs rippling in the slight breeze.

We moved down the stairs, where the air grew close with damp. Unease prickled my skin at the darkness before us, at Thean's warnings of what could be lingering down here.

When we reached the bottom I let flame consume my hand, the lavender illuminating nothing but damp stone and a small circular space where someone had dumped crates and old candlesticks a long time ago, judging from the dust coating them.

'It's a dead end,' I whispered.

Emrys's gaze swung to me, brows knitting together. 'You can't see it?'

His eyes returned to the shadows before us, fixed on a point ahead. What seemed to be nothing but crumbling stone.

Glamour didn't work on Verr. The doorway was hidden. It was why nobody had found it, and even if Verr could, they couldn't open it without the right blood. Just like those compendiums.

'Croinn,' Emrys ordered softly, his jaw tense with disapproval as if knowing my next movement. I extinguished my flame and slid my father's blade easily from his finger. It hummed with energy, displeased with being used against its own blood but turning into a small sharp blade.

I pressed it into the just healing wound, ignoring the painful pinch.

'Show me.' I held my palm out to Emrys. He wasn't pleased to see the blood pool in my palm, but he turned and pressed it gently against the stone.

A moment of silence, then it began to quake and rumble. The large stone blocks shaking, mortar cracking and spilling down the wall. My hand dropped as the glamour faded. The bricks moving to reveal a narrow passage strung with thick webs.

Emrys didn't pay it any attention, ducking to the bottom of my flimsy slip and tearing a strip of fabric free. Then he made quick work of bandaging my wound.

I felt the blade in my other hand curl itself back into a ring. Clearly having a new preference for how it wished to be concealed. One far too big for my hand.

I couldn't blame it. Emrys wouldn't lose it like I had a tendency to.

I slid it back onto his finger for safekeeping, then his hand captured my own once more.

'Ready?' he asked and my mouth suddenly felt dry. A strange wariness consuming me as I looked at the darkness beyond.

Everything seemed to have come together too easily. Thean's warning about what could be in there.

I couldn't speak, too much of a coward, so I nodded – and let Emrys pull me through.

Chapter Thirty-Nine

Beware of the places the world forgets. For the memories that remain there are creatures all their own. Feral with their despair and looking to share misery with their bite.

Myths of the Damned, 1645

We were greeted by total darkness until the wishing stone around my neck flared bright like a guiding light, chasing most of the shadows away but leaving us with an overwhelming stench of earth rot, covered with incense and the bitterness of old dead magic that hung in the air. Endless stone corridors branched off in different directions. Some alcoves filled with shelves that were piled with nothing but dust as if all records had rotted in place.

A terrible sadness lurked in the dead air – the kind that came with all forgotten places. Made only more unsettling by the distant echo of noise from high above. Where the streets were alive and trading. Where life was existing, but not down here. A trickling of water echoing through the gloom, reminding me of the canals that snaked through the town above us.

I turned to see the doorway we'd come through was suddenly nothing but a stone wall. Emrys didn't move, didn't look behind him, just tightened his hold on my hand as if to ease me.

My pleasure smoke-addled mind suddenly completely clear.

'A thieves' trap,' he whispered, not sounding as concerned. Despite the fact my heart felt like it was pounding in my throat.

A thieves' trap, designed to keep unwanted guests trapped until the master returned. Only this house's master was long dead.

'Thean said there might be a collection of forsaken things down here.' I shivered as my breath clouded before me.

'Nice and vague,' Emrys grumbled, moving forward with ease. As if a thieves' trap wasn't an impossible maze to get out of. He seemed to have a sense of direction. Following that instinct that would draw him to the artifact we needed.

'You've never seen a thieves' trap before?'

'A few. Never this old.'

There was silence for a long moment, so quiet it felt like we were wandering through the past. Coming to nothing but a labyrinth of shelves piled with trinkets – old scrolls with frayed ribbons and orbs with smoke shifting inside of them. Just like the ones summoners used above.

Curiosity made me want to reach out and touch them, only for a distant sound to meet my ears. A quiet, strange mewing.

'Can you hear that?' I whispered, stepping closer to Emrys, my fingers stinging with the flare of heat from my magic. He nodded, moving us further into the maze until the shelves opened up, bright moonlight spilling down in a single beam from a crack in the stone high above.

Candle wax formed puddles on the cobbled floor, a trail leading to a circular space with what appeared to be a pile of moth-eaten cloth at the centre. Rusted chains snaked around the strange small chamber. Only for that pile of cloth to move, revealing a dusty, haggard face. Thin white hair clinging to an almost skeletal head. Lips missing, permanently peeled back to reveal large yellow teeth.

I should have felt fear or shock. Yet the stone around my neck didn't even flutter. Instead that sound came back to me, the desperation in it.

'Can you see that?' I could feel its sorrow, like an icy chill biting into my skin. Unnerved by how still Emrys had gone. How close that ancient text was to the skin across his knuckles. As if that darkness inside of him was close to rising once more.

'Our dark prince can see me well enough, fair Tauria.' The creature's voice was a creaking sound, like an old hinge, disused. Dust tumbled from its dry, parchment-like skin Milky white eyes staring back at me.

'It's a fate.' Emrys's voice was terse as he moved in front of me. A shadow blade forming against his palm even though we both knew it would be of little use.

There were little records of fates for a reason. For few survived their wrath.

Some fey were better left forgotten. Too deadly to exist even in memory. I'd read that warning once and never understood it. Not until I felt how my magic thrashed and knotted inside of me.

Fates weren't gods even if some worshipped them as such. Powerful creatures of ancient magic. Formed long before the world itself, or at least as we knew it.

'It was told a prince from beneath would set me free. I am glad it's you, Serus. For you mean me no harm.' The creature inclined its head, curious. Almost childlike. The chains that held it scraping against stone. No. Those chains were rune bound. Aged magic. Older than any of the records. 'You come seeking truth, little prince?'

Tension rippled off Emrys, shadows weaving restlessly between his fingers. Knowing that in a moment he could unmake the creature with the brutality of his magic. Because Verr came first. Even Kysillian flame feared them.

As the fate moved, dust slipped from its shoulders like pale ash. Tipping its head. Contemplating us with those sightless eyes. 'You seek something in the dark.'

'Tell us and we can help you,' I offered, knowing bargains were foolish, but I couldn't think of any other way out of a thieves' trap.

'Lies I've heard before,' it laughed hoarsely, dragging those long black nails across the filthy stones between us as if wishing to write something. 'Only, you do not lie, do you . . . Serus?'

'I do not.' There was a darkness in Emrys's voice that made it sound not wholly his own. As if that name drew something out of him.

The creature's head jerked to one side as if to see us better, like a string-puppet. Thinking. Slowly the chains scraped against the stone as it raised its thin hands, skin crinkled like old paper with age.

Emrys's face remained stoic as he looked down at the endless length of chain curled around the chamber.

'Can you heat the metal?' he asked out of the corner of his mouth. If he was set on letting this thing free, I couldn't argue with him. Not when we didn't appear to have any other options.

I moved closer to the bolt on the wall strung between the decrepit shelves, unfortunately closer to the creature. Finding it to smell of nothing but earth and old books.

'Let's hope my flame doesn't wake anything else up in here,' I sighed, knowing what the potency of my power could do as I let them twist around my fingers, hoping whatever was in the metal would respond to my touch.

The creature moved too quickly, those thin bony fingers so long they wrapped around my wrist twice like a shackle. Smothering my flames.

'Release her,' Emrys's anger turned the air glacial between us. The room plunging into almost full darkness, except for the stone around my throat, casting the fate's face in pale light.

The creature clicked its teeth in dismissal. The dry ancient voice attempted to soothe as it peered up at me with those milky unseeing eyes. 'Fear not, I mean Little Lady Greymark no harm.'

The creature released me, humming to itself as it sank back to the stone floor. Then I noticed it had a smear of my blood on its pale long fingers that vanished inside its moth-eaten robe. Emrys's hand curled around my arm, forcing me back behind him as the fate stopped its rummaging, before shaking its curled fist then opening its hand and releasing a scattering of small white stones to tumble across the stone floor.

Not stones. Bones.

'I offer truths, for a debt unpaid, Little Lady Greymark. Your grandmother was a vain and insolent child, married to a cruel and greedy man. A barren wife has no value to an old house. So she made a bargain with a creature she believed to be a healing witch.'

The creature held up a single bony finger almost in warning. 'One child. To bring power. To bring a new legacy to the House of Grey.'

I shook my head. Unable to bare the story no matter how closely it matched what little my mother had said about her past. About the people who had made her.

'The witch obliged.' The fate nodded. 'Only, the witch had been wronged by the Greymark house, so she planted her revenge right in your grandmother's womb.'

Where witches meddle, only anarchy follows. That story hissed through my mind, spiking my dread. I found my hands curving around Emrys's forearm, feeling his muscles tense beneath my touch. I needed something to tether me. To make this madness real.

The fate bared its large yellow teeth. 'A weaver was born. To unpick the threads of that house. A daughter destined for a king. To birth chaos entire.'

A weaver.

A weaver was an ancient witch, one beyond simple fey. One that could command their own fate. A deadly gift. Why none survived beyond stories. A myth better forgotten. A living curse.

The fate was taking about my mother.

'She wasn't a weaver.' I shook my head. She would have told me that. I would have known. She was mortal, the most magic she possessed being to create enchanted bags or small summonings.

I had a dream.
I hope you see it.
I hope it's real.

Only for the memory of those words to echo back to me.

Live, Tauria. That command lingering even now. Had she seen this?

'Did she not weave her own destiny?' the fate continued, ruthlessly. 'Your mother chose her king, she chose her chaos and she chose her death.'

My head stuttered in my chest. A cold dread seeping into my veins. The fate leant forwards to collect their bones and examine each one as if they were priceless gems. 'Only, weaving destiny bears a heavy price. One I fear you can't afford to pay, Tauria.'

464

'I'm not a weaver.' The words scratched my throat on the way out. I didn't possess that magic. Couldn't. Yet it sounded like a lie as the words sat in the dead air between us.

'Are you not?' The fate smiled, showing all their teeth. They held up their hand, curling three of their six fingers against their palm. 'By my count you've weaved *thrice* in surviving your flame.'

My heart pounded, unsure if the ground had truly shifted beneath my feet as everything snapped into a painful reality.

Kysillians burn. I'd spoken that truth. Knowing that was my death and yet I'd survived it. All the things that were never meant to be. I'd called chaos three times. When my mother died. When I'd killed Daunton. And beneath Fairfax in that pit when I'd sealed the dark with nothing but a mere command. I'd refused to die. Refused to allow my magic to die. I'd found my way here, right where my mother wished me to be.

Live. That word mocked me once more. A command I could never ignore, not if my mother had woven it into my destiny. She'd made certain it was her final word. To protect me from the chaos inside of me. A command that my father's magic would never disobey.

'What a deadly creature your parents made. The fire that eats the world with no consequences to her fury,' the fate added. Kysillian fire was given limits for a reason. For all the danger it could cause.

I should have died yet here I was. I'd orchestrated every step of my own destiny, just as my mother had done hers. I realised Thean had been right all along. I didn't know myself at all.

'That's enough,' Emrys commanded and the creature slunk back, head bowed recognising a threat greater than itself.

Before it laughed dryly. 'How well you guard those of your heart, Serus. Just like your mother.'

He froze. So still I wasn't certain he was breathing. 'Keep your cursed words behind your teeth.'

Shadows leaked from the corners of the room. How those dark runes seeped across the side of his neck and jaw. His face nothing but a mask of hardened rage.

Only his anger didn't stop the fate. Not as they pointed a gnarled finger right at his heart, where his mark rested.

'How easily you erase her, little prince. Just as Blackthorn intended. For imagine what you'd become with the truth?'

Emrys's body tensed, his eyes pitch-black in an instant. 'For how powerful would you become, if you knew how tightly she wove herself around your life threads. Streams of moonlight through the darkness within.'

'I'm certain she wished for none of it.' Emrys's response was near guttural, such raw pain pressed between the words at the horror of how he'd been created.

'You think the mighty mad king simply took her?' the fate laughed darkly. '*She?* A creature able to make bargains with the darkness beneath? A sorceress divine? A consort of the Old Gods?'

The fate shook their head, limp strands of hair clinging to their wrinkled forehead as the motion released another plume of dust.

'Your mother was a zalec. A sorceress of the night.' Ancient forgotten magic. Just like this fate. Nothing but a children's rhyme not to go too deep into the forest. Of dark witches who sang to the moon and had death in their veins. 'A child of the night who was too powerful for her kind. A wanderer, a creature without bounds. A raven-haired beauty who found a demon king in the darkness of the wood. Hiding in the

466

shadows of the world who had slipped free of his bonds from beneath.'

Emrys's breath stuttered as if he'd been struck. His eyes moving rapidly as they fought to sense the lie that wasn't there.

'Serus. Prince of the crescent moon. Son of the Old Gods.' The fate nodded, amused with their tale. 'She loved that darkness dearly and he loved her with the deadliest of devotion. Then a greedy mortal king trapped Serus with a curse and tried to twist that darkness to conquer this world.'

The fate flicked its long fingers in warning. 'Your mother wouldn't allow it. For her love to be defiled. For Serus to be used against her, nor her child. So she summoned and she tricked. She stole her beloved's power back from that monstrous king – right in his bed, and wove it into her unborn son.'

My heart pounded against my ribs.

Why Emrys was different. He was born different, just as Gideon said. Serus had willed it so.

The fate's head tilted as if with sympathy. 'Madness cannot pierce your heart as it has all the others for there is nothing mortal in you, little prince. Nothing of that king's seed, for that is not how you were made.'

Emrys wasn't the King's child. No. He was born of the Old God himself. Why he was nothing like Montagor.

'What a fanciful tale you weave.' The voice that left Emrys's lips was not of this world, a coldness licking up my spine as I saw the darkness spread beneath his skin. Shadows curling in the corners of the room, a strange trembling in the stone beneath our feet.

'She didn't die pathetically on some birthing bed with neither name nor will,' the fate scoffed, as if disgusted by the idea. 'That King was dead long before you cut off his head on a battlefield, *boy*. She made certain of it before she followed her lover to where they could be together once more.'

The fate clicked their long fingers before they dragged them across the dusty stone, making strange rune shapes in the dust. 'A bargain was made. One born of her love for the darkness beneath. For her dark prince and for the world that would not accept her.'

Then I understood the marks the fate made. From the dark sorceress's text, of promises and bargains with death.

Savera Nor. An ancient bargain. A deadly devotion. His mother had given her life for his. For Emrys – a being that shouldn't exist – because the children of the Old Gods couldn't take mortal form while the earth was sealed. She'd willed it by sacrificing herself, her magic. Paying every price to save what she loved.

Emrys's magic silenced in an instant as the weight of the fate's words seemed to sink in. As he read those symbols so clearly. Understood them in an instant.

Blackthorn had lied to him. Lied so awfully and Emrys had never seen it. No. Because he was Verr, he was loyal to his core.

'You wear her name well, *Emeri*.' The fate's haggard face softened as they pulled their gnarled hands back into their moth-eaten robes, those clouded eyes focusing on nothing but him.

Emeri. The name of a fey sorceress from long ago. Beautiful and wise who trapped demons in a lake and used their power to save her people. A blessed name from ancient times.

His mother's name.

There was a tragic beauty to it. As I looked at Emrys's face, all I saw was pain in those dark eyes. Blackthorn had known and not told him. Emrys had carried his mother with him all this time.

I moved closer, touching his face. Needing to help him with this pain but being unable to take it from him.

'The Prince from beneath and his Starlight Queen,' the dark creature mused, baring their teeth in some form of demented smile. 'Be careful, little prince. Varin hunts viciously with that madness devouring his soul. He can hear another on the wind. Only he cannot see her as he sees you.'

'Another?' Emrys demanded but the fate clicked their teeth.

'Can you not feel that she waits? That she calls?' they reprimanded weakly before they flicked those long fingers in a dismissive gesture. 'My bargain is made.'

The maze of shelves around us slipped away, revealing a passage. A way out, or a way to what we needed to find, I didn't know.

Didn't care. I wanted to get away from this. Only, the fate had made a bargain. Freedom for something we needed.

I stepped forward, gathering the length of that ancient chain as those sightless eyes took me in.

'You're free,' I whispered as I let fire consume the chain, as I allowed the power of Kysillian flame to corrupt the enchantment wrapped around this being. To break the spell. As their bindings shattered and slipped from their form.

The fate's head twitched just like I'd seen Emrys's do when the darkness spoke to him.

Then I felt a sharp scrape against my mind. As if claws were trying to gain access, a magic I'd never felt before. My breath caught as I realised they didn't wish to come in. They just wished to leave a message.

How powerful are your promises, Tauria? came the whisper of that strange voice. A warning almost. *I'm sorry there wasn't more I could do.*

Icy dread churned inside of me. Those sightless eyes looked down at the wishing stone hanging between us as it suddenly began to burn. That horrid pain consuming the side of my neck, right over the bite as a cry almost left my lips.

In the blink of an eye, the creature was gone. The chains in my palms rendered to nothing but dust as they slid between my fingers.

'Kat!' The temperature dropped as something rolled through Emrys, his magic rising with such intensity my temples ached and the stone beneath my feet cracked.

Something was wrong.

A horrid whizzing cut through the air, turning me towards the darkness that surrounded us beyond that maze of shelves.

'Emrys,' I reached for him, but suddenly he was pushing me back, the might of him wrapped around me. The suddenness of it sent me stumbling into the shelves, ancient priceless tomes tumbling to the ground releasing a cloud of dust as I caught myself on the edge.

Too late.

Emrys was in front of me. Blocking something's path. His breath so laboured, clouding in the little space between us.

'Emrys?' I reached for his face but he was so still, so tense.

Then I looked down.

Blood seeped into his white shirt, too much blood.

A dark gleam from something at the centre.

Right through his heart.

Only a sacred blade can kill an Old God.

Then I was screaming.

Chapter Forty
Alma

'Careful, little nightmare. The blush will give you away,' came the silky taunt from my side. My plan of moving into the reek of the overcrowded rooms to dissipate the allure of the voyav's scent hadn't worked.

'It's the powder,' I snapped, averting my gaze back to the table. Hoping it was just the pink powder William had assaulted my face with. Seeming far too cheery when presented with the task of dressing us up. Ignoring every protest I'd made as if he'd been given a doll to dress with firm instructions from the voyav.

Only this time this whole thing was both mine and Kat's stupid idea. At least she'd had the mercy to be glamoured.

I wasn't so lucky. I'd been forced into a silk monstrosity. It clung to my hips and waist. The bodice was low enough to reveal the swell of my breasts and disturb the old withered men at their gambling table. Despite the young women draped around them. Some missing most of their clothes altogether.

Thankfully the lanterns and pipe smoke in the den were enough to cover the rest. Though I doubted anyone in here was sober enough to care.

I'd heard of places like this. My Keeper had used them as a threat. Unsavoury and sinful places. Ones that had made me beg and whimper at the mere thought. Thinking my Keeper's treatment a blessing in comparison.

Most were underground. Set up in old sewer tunnels, ruins of king's keeps or travelling markets. This one occupied the old lord's house. Walls painted garish red and silks hung from the ceiling, threatening to catch on to the plethora of candles occupying the cramped main hall.

'I was a maid, not a nun,' I sighed, keeping that ridiculous pleased smile I'd seen on the other women's lips, as if they were nothing but dolls to be paraded by children.

'You had a lover?' Thean inclined their head, their curiosity sharp. I didn't know what surprised me more. That we were onto this subject, or the voyav's apparent genuine interest in those amber eyes as they focused solely on me.

'No,' I snorted. A quick rutting in the back storeroom with a carriage doorman or delivery boy couldn't be described as anything other than seeing to a need. 'Quick and unmemorable.'

Never the same twice. Never allowing them to leave their claim.

I'd refused to be ashamed by it. The things my body wanted. The relief it sought.

'My beasts have urges.' Why most shapeshifters had found themselves in the trap of being owned. Having their bodies used. Their relaxed ease with sexuality weaponised against them.

I'd never discussed it with Kat. Didn't need to. She always knew everything anyway. Instead, I'd found tonic tucked in my skirt pockets and a warm tub of water afterwards. She'd always find somewhere else to be, even if it was to be berated by a master or one of the librarians. As if knowing I'd want time alone. To put myself back together.

Thean's lips pursed and I couldn't determine if they were displeased by the revelation or unbothered.

'You've had a lover?' I hated the strange bite of interest in my voice. Unable to let this small thread go. Distracting me momentarily from my hunt. Not fully understanding why I'd want to know. Why something vicious curled in my gut that felt abominably like jealousy.

A short laugh left Thean's lips, their smile tight as if pained by it. 'Nobody is foolish enough to love *me*, darling.'

Emmaline did. Only I didn't say the words. Understanding that the voyav was bound to the Blackthorn house out of loyalty. A loyalty I understood without confirmation.

They'd loved Emmaline in their own way. Loved her enough to keep their promises. Blood oath or not. Just as I loved Kat, even if my secrets would be dangerous to her.

'She wouldn't let them.' Thean let the words slip out so softly they were almost lost in another screech of laughter from a passing group of patrons.

I couldn't miss the pain burrowed in those words. The small dismissiveness of them. Knowing they didn't intend me to hear, or simply that they were too used to nobody listening.

My nose stung, strange emotion clogging my throat, confessions wanting to spill from my lips, but that was the little fool I had once been. The one who took her punishments too easily.

'You should have helped, Kat,' I admonished softly as I turned my attention back to the wretched room.

'I thought it was clear by now, little nightmare.' They brushed those words with the barest whisper of breath up the side of my throat. 'I'm only interested in helping you.'

'How lucky for me,' I turned to look at them, how close they were. The warmth of them brushing down the length of my back. How desperately my beasts wished to arch back into it. To demand more.

Yet I knew where such a foolish hunger would lead.

Instead I focused on that horrid burning stench in my nose, so similar to the claw I'd cast into the kitchen fire. So similar as I slipped my hand into the voyav's, pulling them along. Following that urge, hoping I could find something before we'd need to help Kat. Hoping she hadn't got into any bother. The quicker we found something, the quicker we could leave.

The faint scent guided me until I reached a nondescript door, going for the knob only for it to remain stiff in my hand. Locked.

'It's here,' I hissed, turning to find Thean contemplating the door. Reaching out to drag a finger along the frame. Something working in those sharp amber eyes. 'How can two things be here at the same time?'

Was Kat on a wild goose chase? Had we found it first or was this something else?

'The old mad bastard was a hoarder,' they offered. 'It's warded against spells.'

'I can change.' It would be easy enough, but then those strange eyes darted to my own.

Thean's eyes flashed, their grip tightening on my hand. 'You're not going in there naked.'

While I seethed at being told what to do, I also did not like the idea of being found naked in a room with no idea of what – or who – was in it . . . I relented.

'Fine. You can,' I offered sharply, resting my hands on my hips in frustration. 'You can use my blood.'

Thean seemed to go tense at the suggestion but it was their own bastard fault for giving me commands.

A chatter of voices echoed down the dark hallway, coming towards us.

474

I grabbed their arm, pulling them with me into the alcove that led to a small office some fool had left open. It appeared there was nothing to steal but some tobacco and papers. I shut the door, turning the rusty lock. A large dusty window let moonlight fill the space.

Then I had a moment of panic, biting my lip as I looked down at my bracelet-covered wrists. Knowing the marks that lay beneath. The skin too damaged, and then there was my throat. Only that could be seen too.

'Little nightmare,' the voyav asked as if concerned I'd lost my mind. Maybe I had.

I pressed myself back against the desk and reached for my thin silk skirt, pulling it up. I'd drawn enough blood to know where was best as I revealed the smooth skin of my inner thigh.

'Here,' I commanded.

'Alma—' They almost seemed to choke on the word. Their eyes the most unguarded I'd ever seen them. As if I'd shocked them.

'Now,' I snapped, voice too unsteady with an anticipation that set my heart fluttering in my chest. As soon as we found something we could get out of here, and I could get Kat away from this mess.

My heart began to riot in my chest, as if one of my smaller winged beasts was trapped within my ribcage. We didn't have long. I didn't have long until I found my sanity again and realised the recklessness of what I was doing.

The voyav seemed to see that, and where I thought they'd mock or tease, a different flash of emotion crossed their features.

A madness consumed me as they sank to their knees before me. As those amber eyes didn't leave my own. Awaiting some refusal from me or further permission. I didn't know, could do nothing but give the barest nod as I felt the warmth of their fingers run up the delicate skin of my leg. Curling around my thighs as if they were something beautifully delicate. My breath caught, their touch like kindling to a fire in me I knew never led to anything good. The torment of the whisper of their breath against my flesh, unsteady as if this was also too much for them to bear.

Then their tongue ran across my flesh in a sensuous caress, my fingers tangling mindlessly in their hair. They hesitated. Head tilting for the barest of moments as if to relish in that touch.

Then their teeth bit down and feral pleasure tore through me, my fingers holding them closer. Wishing those lips were inches higher. I urged my hips closer, a sound clawing up my throat that thankfully wasn't unfamiliar in a place like this.

Thean's fingers dug into my thigh, greedily. Taking another pull of that blood even though I knew they didn't need it. Gentle and reassuring, as their fingertips brushed my skin in the softest caress. As if testing a limit. Their nose dragging over my flesh with their retreat. A hesitation in them. Unable to let go. They rose, my hands still limply resting on their shoulders as I tried to catch my breath. Feeling the warm trickle of blood, how it reminded me of that warmth between my thighs. Unhinged desire at their mere touch.

Their eyes were jet-black with nothing but an amber ring. Like some starved beast. Then I saw the blood on their lips, painting their sharp masculine mouth red and I'd never felt hunger like it.

I pushed myself closer, pressing my lips against their own, tongue dragging over their lip. Needing to taste it. Any part of me on them. The copper tang of my blood. Surprise flashed in their eyes, so surprised they shifted back into female form and I kissed them again. Deeper and harder.

The hunger not abating. No matter the form they took.

Thean's hands fisted into my hair, tipping my head back to demand more of my mouth.

I gave it. Anything they wanted. With wild abandon I wanted their scent all over me. To hoard secretly like a dragon. Even if they'd never know.

I wanted it between my legs, soaked into my pores to ease my restless beasts – and my heart. My fingers curled greedily into their ridiculous silk shirt.

That place on my thigh stung with the absence of them, I gasped for breath as their kiss moved to my throat, taking mercy on me. Those fangs dragging over my throat, almost in warning. I pressed myself closer, feeling the ache of the fangs that had appeared in my mouth.

They hoisted me up, turning so my backside rested on the side table. Knocking over an inkpot and creasing the papers so they could have better access to my mouth.

I knew myself well enough to know what my body wanted. What it wanted from them.

'Touch me,' I begged.

'Which form, little love?' their voice trembled quietly with the anticipation of it. The pause. The hesitation.

'All of you,' I could barely gasp.

Wanting them. However they wished to be.

Thean froze at that. Making me fearful I'd ruined it. Those dark amber-ringed eyes stuck on mine. As if wishing to see every moment of my stuttered breath.

Their knuckles dragged over the soft skin of my inner thigh but I grabbed their hand, forcing it between my legs.

A gasping whimper leaving me with the ferocity of how I needed to be claimed.

Skirts crumpled between us as I watched their thumb tease me exactly where I needed.

I should have been embarrassed, shamed by that wildness. Only as Thean watched that pleasure shift in my expression, I saw the hunger in it but also the reverence. As if I'd given them a precious gift, just letting them please me.

Scales flushed the tips of my cheeks and the curve of my shoulder as if performing for them. Thean kissed every rough one. Leaving me to whimper as they slid two fingers inside. The cursed hiss slipping from between their lips at how greedy I was for their touch as I pulled them closer. Making them stroke deeper as I ran my tongue over the sharp angle of their jaw. Tasting salt, the perfume of them. A purr rumbled up my throat. I lapped at their pulse. Wilder than I'd ever allowed myself to be. A whining desperate sound escaping me.

Thean didn't stop, ruthless with their strokes, their thumb mastering that bundle of nerves. As the scent of them drove me to insanity. One palm pressed against my spread thigh, keeping it open as it trembled. So they could watch every moment of what they did to me.

The dominance of it sent me quickly over the edge, consumed by the madness of that pleasure.

Then I bit down at the curve of their throat, right over the blood mark. Something feral in me wanting to destroy it. Blood filling my mouth. Delicious and just as rich as their scent. Making my hips move closer to their hand, moaning as it crashed through me.

My tongue dragged over the mark, wishing to soothe it. Their hand curled into my hair, pulling my head back, then they kissed me with a brutal claiming. Their hand still between my legs, as if relishing in the aftershock of that pleasure around their fingers. Cupping me with dominance that made a shiver run up my spine.

Devouring me, nipping at my lips before those kisses brushed my cheek and jaw.

Their nose running up the curve of my throat as if they could smell the pleasure rising from my skin. Scenting me. So gently, keeping me in place as they took their time, as if wishing to remember each moment.

They pressed the softest kiss against my pulse. Down across the curve of my breasts with reverence that spoke of nothing but worship.

My eyes fell to the mark I'd made on their throat. How it cut through that blood mark. There was some strange rightness about it. As if I'd broken a bar on their cage. A strange soft smile coming to my lips. A warm peace I hadn't experienced like this. As if I was one of my creatures, burrowed somewhere safe.

A horrid boom shook all the trinkets in the room. The window's glass cracking as a strange orange glow enveloped us. Then the screaming started.

I was untangled from Thean and across the room in an instant, pressed against that glass, seeing the streets filled with fire. With a strange dark cloud on the horizon, twisting between the thatched houses that made up the town below.

A dark storm.

Montagor.

'No.' Fear gripped my heart. I spun for the door, hands becoming claws.

'Alma!' Thean grabbed me, harsher than they ever had before. Forcing me back against the panelling. Winding me with the force of it.

479

'Leave.' The command was given through clenched teeth, fingers digging ruthlessly into my flesh.

Another boom shook the room, pictures falling from the walls, screams coming from beyond the door. Something was happening. Something I didn't understand.

The beasts in my blood were whining. Scared.

'Thean?' I didn't understand. I needed to find Kat. We needed to leave. Only their grip tightened, pushing me further into the room. Towards the window.

Away from the door.

'Leave!' they barked. Their eyes fully black, something strange moving through them. Something I hadn't seen in them before.

Desperation.

A horrid memory surfaced in my mind. Of a bloody Kat knelt before me.

Fly away. Be a bird and fly away.

Please, Alma.

The last time I'd seen desperation like that.

Something stirred in my beasts within, a flick of an ear or the flare of nostrils. Sensing something I shouldn't have missed.

Then Thean's entire demeanour changed in a moment. They didn't look the same. The form they shifted into one I hadn't seen before. Too broad and masculine. A warrior's build. Stern and bulky. So unlike them.

Confusion furrowed my brow. There was such a strange broken look in their eyes as they watched me. As they realised I wouldn't do it. Wouldn't follow their command.

'I told you to leave, little fool,' they breathed. Such sadness sticking to their plea.

They were mad. They were mad and I had no time for it.

I twisted, changed into my mouse form. Vanishing before them. Quick and fast. Not giving them a chance to stop me.

Too lost in my fear to notice they weren't trying to stop me.

Kat. I needed to find Kat.

Only, as I slipped beneath the door and shifted into feline form to dart down the hallway, filthy carpet beneath my paws, my fur rippled. Body too tense. Something wrong.

'No, Valeska,' came the soft, quiet command, startling me. Amused. She was always so cruelly amused.

I went still in a moment, but my residual momentum sent me slamming into the filthy wood panelled wall. My beasts abandoned me in the blink of an eye. Leaving me lying on that stained carpet, naked.

My fingers curled into it desperately. The chill of the air licking its way up my naked spine.

No.

'Stay,' came another command. Freezing me in place. So exposed, listening to nothing but those screams in the distance, as the ground beneath me shook again, dust lining my throat.

No.

No.

No.

This was nothing but a dream. A nightmare of the past. The screaming and rush of beings. The distant smell of smoke. A horrid keening sound sliding from between my lips.

You can always fly away, little love. No. It was a lie. Not when she owned my wings. Owned every part of me.

All I could see was the ground as the rough carpet dug into my cheek, as boots passed me. Thean's. Foolishly I wanted to grab them, dig my claws through them but I couldn't move. Couldn't feel rage, not when fear clogged my throat and made it impossible to draw breath.

There were beings in the hall. So still. Waiting. Watching.

'You let her mark you,' that soft feminine voice taunted.

'When this is done . . . you'll show me just how much you missed me and I'll decide how useful you still are, Thean Page.'

Thean.

The trap. It had been a trap.

My heart cracked inside my chest. A horrid wailing cry consuming my ears that was mine – only it wouldn't escape my lips.

'Kneel, Valeska,' came the next command and there was no choice. My limbs moved like a puppet on her string. Kneeling there. So exposed. Tears blurring my vision, spilling pathetically down my cheeks, dripping onto my bare thighs.

Then all my nightmares became real. Those blood red eyes, how useless and weak I was, just as she'd met me the first time. That strange form of Thean stood at her side, not looking at me, neither did the other rebels further down the hall. Watching their master.

'Did you forget, little rat?' Her voice mocking as her head tipped to one side, dark hair spilling over her shoulder as a malicious smile came to her lips. 'There is no outrunning a blood oath, Valeska. Your Keeper should have taught you better.'

That name I'd done everything to forget. The mistake I couldn't outrun. All my hopeless prayers, and they'd just led me back to her.

'The hunters are close, Countess,' a voice called from down the hall but she didn't stop her observation of me. The victory shining in hideous eyes.

Then she turned back to the rebels in the hallway. Awaiting her command like pets.

The Hunters were here. Montagor.

Kat.

Fear curled ruthlessly inside of me, beasts clawing at my ribs until I could taste blood at the back of my throat.

'Blow it up. Bury it.' She clicked her bloodstained fingers, and suddenly there were hands on me, dragging me to my feet.

The command was ruthless, uncaring about what was here. That Kat was here.

No! I screamed, only my lips didn't part. No sound escaped. It couldn't because all of me was hers.

Chapter Forty-One

Kat

There was an endless roaring in my head. A horrid wailing. A banshee screeching for a feast. Only to realise it was coming from me.

The only way to kill an Old God is with their own blade.

Blood slipped too easily between Emrys's fingers. His back arched, lips parted in a silent scream of pain as he fell to his knees.

'Emrys!' I cried out, lurching for him, only for something sharp and ice cold to strike my thigh. Sending me down to the dusty ground with a cry of agony. A metal dart protruding from my skin, my blood or Emrys's staining my slip.

No. My limbs suddenly too heavy and tight. I grasped at my thigh as agony poured through my limbs, fingers meeting cold metal. Sticking out of my flesh, blood rushing between my fingers.

No.

I tried to summon my flame. It spluttered uselessly. A chasm opening in my chest with distress. My magic severed from me as only coldness slipped into my blood and I panted for breath.

They'd taken my flame.

Emrys. I needed to help Emrys.

Hands grabbed me, my arms twisted and pulled behind my back. That pain in my thigh intensifying. I kicked and fought. A scream tearing from my lips, shouting Emrys's name but my strength was gone.

Wild red-rimmed eyes of hunters, skittered laughter and the horrid screech of fiends. Darkness swirling around the outskirts of the room, a dark summoning awaiting command. Prickling my skin. Endlessly cold without my flame.

My arms held too easily, legs useless as fingers gripped my hair, wrenching my head back.

An inhuman roar came from Emrys's direction. The scuffle of feet before the horrid sound of a fist meeting flesh. The bitter bite of Emrys's magic trying to reach me but it was the barest brush against my skin. Too far away. As if that shard was like having a dart buried in his own skin.

The shard of an Old God's blade.

'Emrys!' I kicked at my captors, anything to cross that distance between us.

'I wouldn't,' came the calm and careful voice that made terror take a vice-like grip on my heart. That stone fluttering wildly against my breast. Illuminating Montagor from the gathering of shadows that clung to the corners of the vast chamber we'd found ourselves in.

No.

Something cruel was carved in the severity of his features, too angular to be found handsome.

'Such a wild and savage thing,' Montagor taunted as he crossed the distance between us. His eyes full black, veins spreading from their corners as if a dark fiend took up residence under his skin. Eyes sunken as if he'd devoured nothing but dark magic and hate. A calmness to him as he straightened his gloves before crouching before me.

One captor released their grip on my hair, but my head fell forwards weakly. I couldn't move. Couldn't summon.

'The ancient blade has debilitating effects, I'm told,' he continued, either oblivious to my fear or relishing in it. 'You should thank your pet, Emrys, for giving me the idea. Those golden beasts needed some way to bind our kin after all. Before they sent them beneath.'

Montagor peered down his straight nose at me, those gloved fingers taking hold of my chin brutally. 'They used our own power against us.'

'I'm going to kill you.' Emrys surged against the two hunters who held him, teeth bared, a feral sound ripping up his throat. He almost broke free despite the wound in his chest, more blood seeping down his front. A wildness in his dark eyes that he didn't care. Cared about nothing but the distance between us.

'I wouldn't move too much,' Montagor cautioned dismissively over his shoulder, his predatory focus coming back to me as he reached for the curve of my cheek with his finger. I wrenched back, despite the pain and the absence of my flame. It wasn't far enough.

He grabbed my loose hair, twisting it around his fist. Using it to tug my head brutally to one side. I bit back my cry. Breath panted through my teeth.

'If you lay another finger on her, that darkness won't recognise you when I'm finished with your bones.' The voice that came from between Emrys's clenched teeth wasn't of the mortal realm, his magic like midnight smeared across his skin. The blade kept his magic trapped within, but barely. I could see the dark corners of it, swirling in warning.

Montagor ignored the viciousness of Emrys's resistance, bringing the fistful of hair to his nose.

Holding it for too long. Dragging too much in as revulsion crawled up my throat. Then he drew his blade from a sheath at his side, pressing it against my throat. Hard enough that I felt the warm trickle of blood down my skin. He dragged that blade against my flesh, up to the tip of my ear.

'Say please and I might let you keep them, troll.' He almost brushed those words against my lips with his closeness.

He wanted to hear me beg. Only, I was done begging.

I spat in his face. Rewarded with his choked surprise before a blow came across my face that sent me down to my side.

Light danced before my vision. The tang of blood in my mouth.

An animalistic roar erupted from the darkness. Emrys. The bitter vengeance of his magic lashing through the room but unable to strike. The stone beneath cracked deeper, a quaking as the shelves began to crumble around us.

Hands were on me, twisting my arms behind me as they dragged me back to my knees.

'I've been seeking such sacred things for so long. Listening to those whisperings in my dreams, Emrys.' Montagor straightened his coat and smoothed down his hair as if surprised by his own lack of control. 'I followed where others wouldn't dare.'

He turned to where Emrys was sneering, dark veins covering every inch of face. Four hunters had hold of him, struggling by the shadow of fear in their crazed eyes.

'Where should it lead me but right back to you, brother.' He smiled. 'I know you have the Old God's blade. Now the question is . . . how long will your pet have to suffer until you give it up?'

The blade. It had driven Montagor to Emrys. Driven him here.

The only way Montagor could win. If he took down Serus's power – and with that blade in his chest, Emrys wouldn't be able to fight it.

Shadows wove themselves between Montagor's fingers. He moved them the barest inch and the shard twisted in Emrys's chest. Making him roar again. Making blood spill and spread across the stone.

'Stop!' I screamed.

'Listen to your pet, brother,' Montagor mocked, his attention coming back to me. 'Are you so righteous and loyal to Blackthorn's commands you'll let your Kysillian whore die for you?'

'I need my hands to summon it,' Emrys sneered in response. Not looking at me, at the horrid sob that left my lips. As I slipped in my own blood, trying to move.

'I know,' Montagor nodded. 'You can suffer first for all the time you've cost me.'

He turned to see me, watched every painful pant of breath from my lips with cruel satisfaction.

'I will say . . . after your performance in the Council chamber, you've given me the most alluring idea, troll.'

He grinned. Something about the hideous enjoyment of it was so familiar to me. Suddenly I was so small under that gaze. So weak and cold.

Then a dark summoning filled his hands as he spoke. A summoning I knew. One I could recount in my worst nightmares. Knew what was coming as the hunters released me. As horrid laughter filled the cavernous chamber.

Curse casting. Torture through summoning. A horrid roar came out of Emrys and that was the only sound before my own screams consumed every one of my senses as Montagor pushed that darkness towards me.

How easily it slipped into my flesh like a knife.

Agony tore through my limbs. As if my bones were twisting within my skin. Sharp brutal claws grating against my tendons.

The horrid pain of my magic trying to rise but trapped too tightly within my flesh. The taste of copper on my tongue from my blood where I'd bitten down in the torment of it. Agony erupted in every part of my body, the wildest sounds escaping my lips until my voice broke.

Then it abated as if it had never been. Leaving me hollow with the barest brush of that pain rushing through me.

I panted, too shallow and sharp. Bloody spittle dripping from my lips. The air as thick as water in my lungs. Drowning. I was drowning in panic.

'*Valin!*' Emrys roared, almost desperately, but it wasn't enough. He was weakened and so was his command.

'Begging,' Montagor laughed, his voice distorted with that darkness. 'How unlike you, brother.'

'Take it,' Emrys commanded. Voice too hard. Words too sharp.

Take his power. Take everything if it gave me a chance.

Then those dark eyes met my own and for a moment they were so pale and clear. There was nothing but Emrys looking at me.

'*Aest'rea.*' His voice broke saying it but I wouldn't have missed a word.

I love you.

In every life.

Mortals had no equivalent but he'd learnt it for me. A Kysillian devotion. A binding promise for life.

He loved me and he was saying goodbye. Because we were never meant to be.

No. I wanted to scream the word but there was too much blood in my mouth.

'You've been bested, Serus, remind our masters of it when you return,' Montagor mocked. A dark summoning rose in his palm again. The blade turned further in Emrys's chest. He'd kill him.

Only Emrys's gaze remained on my own. As if I was the last thing he wished to see.

No. I gasped, desperately reaching within but my flame was silent. Chest too tight. The taste of blood too acrid on my lips.

Araya, my father's voice called in the back of my mind. I shook my head. I didn't need ghosts. I needed my power. Needed my flame.

I cried and thrashed. Those hunters tightening their grip, my magic useless. So cold. So weak.

You're named after a warrior who never summoned a flame. Never held that blade and yet she was more powerful than any elder. Those words pierced my panic. Stilling my heart for a moment. Words my father had given me all those years ago.

I wasn't just a Kysillian. A danger to this world or its chaos. I was his daughter and I needed no flame to prove that.

Show me, Tauria, his ghost whispered into my ear and I could see that warm smile that never faltered in my memory.

Mine. Emrys was mine, and I wouldn't lose. Not like this.

The fury in my blood made my breath steady, made the pain abate for the barest moment.

A horrid destructive boom came from above, shaking the chamber. Dust raining down as cracks spread across the stone. Chunks of brick fell from the supports above, the hunters crying out. Then water followed.

Something was wrong. Something above. Making Montagor pause for the barest moment. A mercy from the ancestors or from the fate I had no idea.

'*Kinsfyre!*' I roared, the command pulling on my aching muscles and bruised skin.

Montagor turned, those dark and deadly eyes meeting my own. Not understanding the true danger before him.

Kinsfyre was the name of my father's blade. Kysillia's heart.

Not my father's blade. Not anymore. It was mine, to protect what was mine.

Emrys lurched. The blade leaving where it had wrapped around his finger. Soaring towards me. I threw out my hand to claim it. Fingers curving around the hilt as it materialised. All the fire the sacred blade had stored roared free. Enveloping me and the hunters closest to me. They screamed, recoiling, but that fire didn't let them go.

Not as it roared across the chamber. Catching on the shelves and the scrolls there. Heating the glass until they exploded – summoning smoke streaking through the darkness – awakening the other slumbering magic here forcing all the hunters and fiends Montagor had brought back. Consuming them.

Fire consumed me, melted the dart in my thigh until it ran down my flesh like molten blood. Rendering the hunters closest to me to ash that caught on my lips.

Then the fire guttered out, steam and the stench of burning flesh remained. I felt the deadly sting of Montagor's brewing summoning, whatever defence he'd thrown up to save himself.

I lurched forwards through the smoke. Letting the blade lengthen despite the pain in every limb.

Montagor recoiled, teeth bared. He raised his summoning arm, lips parted to command the shard from Emrys's chest.

To kill him.

I threw myself forwards just as fast as my father taught me. Despite the agony – I'd faced worse than this monster. I turned and brought the blade down. Severing through Montagor's summoning arm.

He screamed, stumbling back, blood gushing from the stump to splatter the stone. I screamed too, baring my teeth as I pulled the blade up to slice across his face, making him tumble back against the stone floor.

The fiends screeched as they battled the remains of my flames – the crash and boom of feral magic feasting. Stored down here too long. The surviving hunters barked their commands. The room shook again with another horrific boom from somewhere above, water spilling down the walls as stone crashed around us. Dust filling the air, the flames my blade had left making smoke curl and catch in my throat.

BOOM!

I fell to my knees with the might of it. Trying to shield my head from the falling chips of stone. Only for blue aether to fill the room. A crackling storm of witch power. Making those fiends and hunters scramble in the darkness.

I sobbed with relief. Gideon.

'What the bloody fuck have you done now?' came the enraged voice of Gideon from between the bookcases. In disarray, as if he'd run the whole way here. Sodden and covered in dust. His blonde hair dark and stuck to his face.

I ignored him, ignored the roaring of Montagor and his hunters as the aether made the magic in the room erupt. Booms made my ears ring as the stone beneath quaked. Too unstable.

'Emrys,' I panted, crawling. Slipping in my own blood until I was beside him. Pressing my hand against the wound desperately.

'Emrys,' Gideon snapped, but I heard his voice break. Saw the panic as he dropped to the other side of Emrys, saw the tremble of his hands as he tried to help me stop the blood.

How he froze when he realised what it was. The strange sheen to the forsaken metal buried there.

'Tauria,' Emrys panted so weakly. His fingers curling into my hair to hold me closer. An unfocused nature to the darkness in his eyes.

492

Too weak. His breaths too laboured. Too much blood spilled on the stone between us.

He wouldn't leave me. Not like this. I looked around desperately, expecting Thean and Alma as the room shook again. Distant screams from above, as if the house was collapsing. That couldn't be us.

It had to be something else.

It was coming down on top of us.

We had to move. We had to leave.

I couldn't breathe. Couldn't think.

Alma. Where was Alma?

'Kat. You need to cauterize the wound.' Gideon tore off his jacket, bundling it and forcing it against the wound around the blade shard still buried there.

'I-I can't.' The words broke between my lips. 'He took my flame.'

The agony in my thigh. How cold my blade was in my grasp. All the flame spent.

When those blue eyes met mine, there was nothing but desolate hopeless pain. Too much of Emrys's blood coating my hands.

Breath too heavy in my lungs.

No.

In an instant my mother turned to ash in my memories. The echo of my screaming filling my ears. The cold, bloody and bruised flesh of Alma beneath my small hands. Slipping from me.

No. Not Emrys. He promised.

He promised.

Did you think you could keep him, Tauria? That voice mocked once again.

The ground trembled, runes appearing to slip between the stone. Illuminating a circle around us.

'Emrys! Stop!' Gideon demanded.

Only the dark summoning of those runes didn't feel familiar. The wishing stone around my throat was so still. Too quiet. The same runes Emrys had summoned in that village when he'd lost control.

'It isn't him,' I whispered. No, the runes were too dark. Too unbearably cold. Too strong for how weak and limp Emrys was in my arms.

This was something else.

Serus? A little voice called into my mind. Curious and distant. *Come.*

The light grew blinding, a screeching buzz filling my ears as the rush of water started and the room's supports faltered. I barely had a moment to understand what was happening before the stone vanished from beneath us as we were torn through a portal.

Chapter Forty-Two

Kat

Thick green blades of grass tangled around my knees. The wind was warm and fragrant with the wildflowers that covered the meadow before us. It was spring.

It couldn't be spring.

The long grass was covered in blood. Only my hands remained tangled in Emrys's hair, feeling the desperate breath from his lips brush my cheek.

'Emrys.' My fingers curled into his damp hair. My palm kept pressing against the wound. His blood slipping too easily through my fingers.

A shadow cut across us, making me bare my teeth. My blade ready for battle as I hunched my body over Emrys's. No matter how darkness bit into the corner of my vision.

I looked up to see a man.

No. Not a man – a skeleton wearing a farmer's hat, with a wheelbarrow in its bony fingers. Fingers held together with wire. Its head tilting in contemplation of us.

I'd lost my mind.

'Back to work, Fergus,' a feminine voice called. Heavily accented. Then she appeared behind the skeleton, her gloved hand curling over its bony shoulder before she pushed it away in dismissal.

The skeleton went obediently, abandoning its wheelbarrow.

Dirt clung to the woman's breeches, a rag tied in her white hair to keep it off her face. White hair despite the youth in her features. A warning in the old language. A being touched by death held a mark like that. Her eyes were dark and ringed with silver, possessing a reflective quality like a cat.

'You'd better have a good reason for ruining my vegetable patch,' she enquired, pulling off her muddy gloves to reveal pale tattooed fingers marked with black runes.

It was then I noticed a spatter of scarring under her left eye. Like pink tear drops that spilled onto the side of her face, burnt skin long healed. A vicious web that disappeared down the collar of her shirt.

'Who the fuck are you?' Gideon sneered, aether crackling in his palms where he crouched on Emrys's other side as if ready for attack.

'Where is Thean Page?' she demanded. A distant concern burning in those strange silver eyes as she took us in.

This woman knew Thean. Her white hair catching the breeze. Reminding me of the mark of a death on her.

Necromancer. Thean's necromancer.

'Necromancer,' Gideon spat, his aether snapping in the air between us. The necromancer in question just crossed her arms.

'Clever little witch,' she goaded.

Then a clatter of commotion came from behind her. A crunching as if someone was running up a gravel path. Emrys let out a groan, twisting slightly, his hand curling around my wrist in a soundless warning.

'Emrys,' I begged, more of his blood seeping between my trembling fingers.

A girl came to a skidding halt next to the necromancer. Her blonde hair braided neatly back from her face, a white ribbon tied at its end. Skin sun-kissed and eyes a strange swirling of grey as they went wide with surprise. Her hands running down her pale cotton dress, as if self-conscious it was creased.

She couldn't be any older than eight, maybe nine.

'Isabella,' the necromancer cautioned, but the child was focused on the prone form of Emrys on the ground.

'You're here.' There was a shyness to her grin but an expectation as if she knew we'd arrive, unfazed. Something shifted inside of me. That sense clawing at my skin. Not in warning . . . but recognition.

Then I saw it, the barest shadow of darkness beneath the little girl's skin as she beamed down at Emrys.

There is a demon that knows all the twists of time. That sees all the moments never lived and commands the fates to meddle. That childish rhyme sang into my mind. Something from my memory mocking me as Emrys groaned. Darkness curling between his fingers.

'Stop,' I warned. Panicked at what trap we'd tumbled into. How defenceless I was against it.

The girl's wide eyes met my own, now full black with the loveliest smile on her lips. 'Please don't cry, Tauria.'

I heard talk of another in the wind. That croaking misty voice of that fate came back to me. Mocking me with all the things I'd forgotten. *Can you not hear her, Serus?*

The last.

'Hello, brother,' the little girl smiled down shyly at the prone form of Emrys between myself and Gideon. 'I've been waiting for you.'

I know there is another. Montagor's words bit sharply into my mind. The madness in them. The blood he'd spilt to make those words true.

Emrys said he'd sensed something. An awakening . . . nine years go.

There were two princes of the Old Gods who fought into the night. Serus and Varin. I knew that story. Yet Serus was the only one to have loyalty in the realm of darkness.

A twin moon. A sister that shared the demon's might.

This was what Emrys had felt. A threat that could have made Varin rise in Montagor to do battle as they had before.

Because Varin was outnumbered.

Another child of the Old God had awakened.

She was here. Waiting for us.

Acara.

The seer.

Queen of the Damned.

Acknowledgements

There were points when this book felt beyond impossible. How do you even begin to write book two when book one still feels like a strange dream? Alas, I did it! But, it wouldn't have been possible without some amazing fiends on my side.

My amazing agent Suzannah Ball, who believed in me even when I'd lost all belief in myself. *TALES* and her emo sibling *TOADD* would be nothing without you. Thank you for cheering for her like you were on this journey from day one. You're a superstar and I could never have dreamt up an agent as amazing as you. Thank you for making me excited to tell stories again.

Esmie. Where would I be without Esmie! My champion. Thank you for inspiring me every day and for fuelling the fire to create. For being yourself. For answering the phone and supporting me even when I wanted to give up – I'd be beyond lost without you.

The beautiful Áine. For telling me straight when Kat is moaning a bit too much. For being an endlessly supportive gothic loving queen and a wonderful friend. My dearest Erin McBurnie for listening and being there when I needed a friend the most. For reading *TOADD* and saving me from my own madness.

499

Scarlett St Clair for celebrating every win with me as if it was her own. Sarah Hawley for constantly building me up even in my moments of chaos and for giving the best advice which is . . . 'You have magic – make things happen.'

Jen Sugden for being the biggest *TALES* champion and making sure everyone knew she existed! Thank you for only being a message away in this isolating profession. Kate for supporting me, for stepping up whenever I need someone in a blazer – and for simply being a wonderful friend along this entire journey. Laura for the endless support and listening, Lexi for fangirl DMs – I could only have dreamt of someone loving Emrys as much as you do.

None of this would have ever begun without my mum and dad. Thank you for all your sacrifices, hard work and endless love. To Christa, Tyler, Casey and Trudy for loving me even if you must live under my tyranny.

The hardworking team at Gollancz! Bethan, Zakirah, Jenna, Lucy and Sarah. Thank you for all you've done.

Tales of a Monstrous Heart and *Tales of a Deadly Devotion* would be nothing without my wonderful, amazing readers. Thank you for finding me and for loving these characters as much as I do. You've made me nothing but excited for all the stories left to tell and all the adventures yet to go on.

Credits

Jennifer Delaney and Gollancz would like to thank everyone at Orion who worked on the publication of *Tales of a Deadly Devotion*.

Agent
Suzannah Ball

Editor
Bethan Morgan

Copy-editor
Andy Ryan

Proofreader
Gabriella Nemeth

Editorial Management
Sarah Fortune
Zakirah Alam
Jane Hughes
Charlie Panayiotou

Lucy Bilton
Patrice Nelson

Audio
Paul Stark
Louise Richardson
Georgina Cutler-Ross

Contracts
Rachel Monte
Ellie Bowker
Tabitha Gresty

Design
Rachael Lancaster
Nick Shah

Deborah Francois
Helen Ewing

Photo Shoots & Image Research
Natalie Dawkins

Finance
Nick Gibson
Jasdip Nandra
Sue Baker
Tom Costello

Inventory
Jo Jacobs
Dan Stevens

Production
Paul Hussey
Katie Horrocks

Marketing
Lucy Cameron

Publicity
Jenna Petts

Sales
Dave Murphy
Victoria Laws
Sammy Luton
Group Sales teams across Digital, Field, International and Non-Trade

Operations
Group Sales Operations team

Rights
Rebecca Folland
Tara Hiatt
Ben Fowler
Maddie Stephenson
Ruth Blakemore
Marie Henckel